Praise for *Cracked Up to Be*

"Summers creates a gritty world of teenagers living on the edge, complete with explosive interactions and rocky relationships, without getting mired in angst . . . this compelling read is taut with tension."
—*School Library Journal*

"The voice is incredible, similar to that of *Speak* by Laurie Halse Anderson . . . no matter how many hints Ms. Summers drops, you'll never be able to guess Parker's terrible secret. This debut author is just that good."
—*Teens Read Too*

"Summers is one to watch." —*RT Book Reviews*

"Told in beautifully rendered, spare, haunting prose . . . Courtney Summers has written a remarkable debut. I thought about this one long after I'd reached the end." —Alyson Noël, author of *Saving Zoë*

"*Cracked Up to Be* gives you Parker, her world, her friends, straight up, no chaser. You won't forget her." —Kathe Koja, author of *Kissing the Bee*

Praise for *Some Girls Are*

"Frightening and effective. Regina's every emotion is palpable, and it's impossible not to feel every punch—physical or emotional."
—*Publishers Weekly* (starred review)

"This story takes an unflinching look at the intricacies of high school relationships and how easily someone's existence can change. Fans of the film *Mean Girls* will enjoy this tale of redemption and forgiveness."
—*School Library Journal* (starred review)

"Powerful and compelling." —*Kirkus Reviews* (starred review)

Also by Courtney Summers

Cracked Up to Be
Some Girls Are
Fall for Anything
This Is Not a Test

what goes around

two books in one

cracked up to be & some girls are

courtney summers

 St. Martin's Griffin 🐾 New York

WHAT GOES AROUND: CRACKED UP TO BE copyright © 2008 by Courtney Summers and SOME GIRLS ARE copyright © 2010 by Courtney Summers. All rights reserved. Printed in the United States of America. For information, address St. Martin's Press, 175 Fifth Avenue, New York, N.Y. 10010.

www.stmartins.com

Library of Congress Cataloging-in-Publication Data

Summers, Courtney.
  What goes around : two books in one : Cracked up to be & Some girls are / Courtney Summers.—1st ed.
    p. cm.
ISBN 978-1-250-03844-9 (trade paperback)
ISBN 978-1-250-03845-6 (e-book)
1. Emotional problems—Fiction. 2. High schools—Fiction. 3. Schools—Fiction.
4. Popularity—Fiction. I. Summers, Courtney. Cracked up to be. II. Summers, Courtney.
Some girls are. III. Title.
  PZ7.S95397 Wh 2013
  [Fic]—dc23

                                                                        2013015011

St. Martin's Griffin books may be purchased for educational, business, or promotional use. For information on bulk purchases, please contact Macmillan Corporate and Premium Sales Department at 1-800-221-7945 extension 5442 or write specialmarkets@macmillan.com.

First Edition: September 2013

10 9 8 7 6 5 4 3 2 1

cracked up to be

To Lori Thibert,
for inspiring me as a reader,
writer and a person (TG4E),
and to my family, for everything
(and then some)

acknowledgments

This book would not be off of my computer and on shelves without: Amy Tipton, my agent, and Sara Goodman, my editor. Amy works tirelessly on my behalf—never failing to be awesome while she does it—and her passion and savvy makes me glad she's in my corner. Sara's keen insights helped me shape this novel into the best it could be, and her thoughtfulness and sense of humor made writing it a very cool experience to boot. Amy's and Sara's enthusiasm for and belief in this novel made all the difference. To those fantastic folks at St. Martin's Press who worked hard to turn these words into something that could actually be held, thank you.

This book would not have been written in the first place without: Susan and David, Megan and Jarrad—thanks for the title, Meg—Marion and Ken, and Lucy and Bob. My family. Words fail to adequately express the ways they inspire me and how much their love, support and encouragement has meant. These wonderful people heard it all: Josie B, Whitney C, Ashlee C, Ursula D, Mehmet E, Lynn E, Kristen F, Tiffany G, Fiona H, Tristan H, Kim H, Marcia J, Carina J, Veronique M, Shaina M, Carly P, Alicia R, Jessica S, Lori T, Kelvin T and Briony W. Thanks for yer friendship, bbs. Thanks to Brad Sucks for the use of his music. Finally, special thanks to: my seventh-grade teacher, Mr. Kelly, my blogging buddies and the Blueboards.

one

Imagine four years.

Four years, two suicides, one death, one rape, two pregnancies (one abortion), three overdoses, countless drunken antics, pantsings, spilled food, theft, fights, broken limbs, turf wars—every day, a turf war—six months until graduation and no one gets a medal when they get out. But everything you do here counts.

High school.

"No, seriously, Jules, just feel around in there and tell me if you have one—"

"Fuck off, Chris—"

"And tell me where it is, the *exact* location."

"You're disgusting!"

"Hey, Parker!"

He reaches out and grabs me by the shoulder. I shrug, shrug, shrug him off.

"Fuck off, Chris."

He's been on about the G-spot for, like, a week.

"Don't fail me now, Parker. Where is it?"

"*Cosmo,* December '94. The Sex Issue. Came with a map and everything."

"Hell yes! I knew I could count on you." He points at me, grinning, and then the grin falters and he says, "Wait. You bullshitting me?"

I make him wait for the answer because I'm bullshitting him.

"Chris, I respect you too much to do that."

"That's so sweet. You look good today, Parker."

"You bullshitting me?"

"I respect *you* too much to do that."

I look like shit today for a variety of reasons, but let's start with the muddy running shoes on my feet. Running shoes are expressly forbidden to wear with the school uniform, but damned if I know where my dress shoes disappeared to between now and yesterday. And then there's my uniform skirt, which has a mustard stain on the front because I can't do something simple like make a sandwich for lunch without screwing it up. I plucked my rumpled polo shirt from my bedroom floor and I guess I could've brushed my hair if I'd wanted to forgo the bus ride and walk all ten miles to school, but supposedly if I miss any more classes I could maybe not graduate, and if I have to spend another year in this concrete block—

"Shoes, Parker!"

Principal Henley's got her arms crossed and her eyebrows up. I bring my hands together like I'm appealing to God. I might as well be.

"One day only, Mrs. Henley. See, I got up really late and I couldn't find my dress shoes and I was *so* worried about getting here on time—"

"And the hair—"

"Can be brushed," I say, smoothing my hand over the tangles.

"You're due at the guidance office in five minutes."

"Oh, joy," I say. Her eyes flash and I smile. "No, really."

Her eyebrows go down. It's good, but not as good as when I

got away with everything. I elbow my way through a mass of people to get to my locker because there's something immensely satisfying about the toughest part of my arm connecting with the softest part of everyone else. A shapely embodiment of a female Satan appears on the horizon, flipping her long blond hair over her shoulder as she commands the attention of her many underlings. My former underlings.

Becky Halprin.

"—I just bluffed my way through it," she's saying as I pass. "Hey, Parker?"

I half turn. "What?"

"Did you get that essay finished for Lerner?"

Shit.

"That was due today?"

Becky stares at me.

"You only had the whole weekend."

I open my locker. "Why do you sound surprised?"

"Bet you fifty bucks you're fucked."

"You're on," I say. "I can do a lot with fifty bucks."

She laughs and heads wherever she's heading. Cheerleading practice, maybe. No. It's too early, and anyway, I don't care.

Lerner's essay.

I grab my English binder and flip through it until I find the page with FRIDAY and HOMEWORK scrawled messily at the top but nothing underneath. Great. The bell rings. Guidance office.

Shit.

I grab my brush, slam my locker shut and race against the flow of students heading to their respective homerooms. I reach the office while the bell's still ringing. I take a minute to catch my breath, stalling, because Ms. Grey would cream herself if she thought I actually made the effort to be on time and I don't like giving people false hope. I count to ten and run a brush through my hair. One. Two. Three. Ten. Again. A few minutes go by. A few more.

When I finally decide to enter the office, I'm still brushing my hair.

It's not meant to be insolent—it's *not* insolent—but the thing is, I can't stop. My hair looks fine, but I just stand there brushing it in front of Grey, who sits at her desk looking all devastated, like I'm mocking her somehow.

Sorry, I can't stop, I want to say, but I don't. I don't think I'm really sorry about it, either, but she should know this isn't some kind of slam at her for making my life a little more inconvenient than it already is. If it was, I'd be a lot more creative about it.

I sit down across from her and run the brush through my hair a few more times.

"You're late," she finally manages.

My hand relaxes. I lower the brush and rest it in my lap. Grey looks like a bird, a dead-eyed sparrow, and if I had her job, I'd want to kill myself. It's not like well-adjusted people ever come into the guidance office. You get either the crazy underachievers or the crazy overachievers and both come with their own depressing set of problems.

I don't know. I'd just want to kill myself if I was her, that's all.

"Yeah," I say. "So we'd better get on with it, huh?"

"Right." She clasps her hands together. "You already know this, but I think it bears repeating: no cutting, no missed days, no exceptions. You *will* complete your homework and you *will* hand it in when it's due. Off-campus lunch privileges are suspended until you can prove to us that you're trustworthy again and—"

"But what if I wake up one morning and I can't stop vomiting or I'm hemorrhaging or something? Do I still have to go to school?"

She blinks. "What?"

"What if I'm really sick? What do I do then?"

"A parent would have to call in for you. Otherwise you'll receive a warning—"

"Right." I nod and start chewing my thumbnail. "Okay."

She clears her throat.

"On Friday, you'll meet me here and we'll talk about any troubles you might have had throughout the week, the progress you've made both in and out of school, and—"

"But what if I miss some assignments, though? I've gone so long just not doing them, I think it's kind of unfair to expect me to get back on the ball right away. You know what I think, Ms. Grey? I think I should get a grace period."

She leans across the desk, her dead eyes showing a rare sign of life. It freaks me out so much I have to look away.

"This *is* your grace period, Parker."

Then I have to run all the way to homeroom. Mr. Bradley makes a point to glare at me when he marks down my attendance because they all must have gotten the Tough Love memo over the weekend. I pause at Chris's desk and tap my fingers along the wood until he looks up from the math homework he's scrambling to finish.

"Becky knows where it is."

He laughs. "Becky? You're talking to her now?"

"Yeah. About G-spots. At length. She's an expert."

"Okay." His pale blue eyes twinkle. "Send her up."

I wink at him and head to the desk at the back of the room, where Becky's alternately painting her nails and the cover of her binder with sparkly red polish. A nail here, a red heart there. I slide into the seat next to hers and I don't waste time.

"Chris wants you."

Her head whips up.

"Chris wants *me*?"

"Yeah. Go see."

She looks from me to him to me again, to him, to me, and she grins. Chris is popular, cute, all dimples. He wears his uniform shirt a size too small because it makes his muscles look bigger than they actually are and he's never wanted Becky before.

"Thanks," she whispers, standing.

She squares her shoulders and walks up the aisle as sexily she can, which is not very sexy at all. As soon as her back is to me, I grab her binder and flip through it, carefully avoiding the drying polish decorating the front. It's so beautifully organized, I find Lerner's essay before Becky even gets to Chris.

We were supposed to write about patriarchy and *Beowulf*. I had no idea we even read *Beowulf*, but I'm resigned to the fact I can't bullshit my way through this essay as effortlessly as Becky probably has, and since I'm pretty confident she can do it just as effortlessly again, I rip it from her binder.

It's my essay now.

"He's disgusting," Becky says when she comes back.

The funny thing is, she won't even notice the essay's missing until Lerner's class and even then she won't suspect me, because I may have done a lot of stupid things in the last year, but that doesn't mean I'm an *essay thief*. People are kind of stupid like that when they think you're tragic. You get away with a lot even after you're caught.

"You obviously like disgusting," I tell her.

She smiles this big blond smile.

"He asked me out, but I wanted to make sure it's okay with you first."

Right.

"Screw him, Becky. I don't care."

"Parker—"

"Becky, really. I don't want to hear it. You're dull."

She rolls her eyes. "For five seconds you almost seemed human."

"Five whole seconds, huh? That's an improvement. Tell Grey; she'll love that."

The bell rings and Becky lunges out of her seat. Chris waits for no one.

"Becky," I call after her. She turns. "I hope you have that fifty on you. I'll need it for after school."

I copy her essay during history, unnecessarily exerting myself with a little creative rewriting so it sounds authentically Parker.

After history, I run into the new kid.

The bell has rung, the halls are filtering out and when I spot him, this new kid, he's doing that confused stumble around the halls that makes it painfully obvious he has no idea where he is. He's got brown hair that sort of hangs into his brown eyes and I stare at him when I pass, because new kids generally can't handle eye contact and I find that amusing. He looks about eighteen and I bet his parents are assholes to do whatever it is they did that he had to transfer in the middle of senior year.

"Hey . . . hey, you—girl!"

I turn slowly, debating. Do I make this easy on him or do I make it hard?

A good person would make it easy.

I decide to start with mocking and work my way up.

"Hey . . . hey, you—New Kid!"

He takes it well.

"Uh, yeah. Hi," he says. "Maybe you could help me?"

"I'm late for class."

"That makes two of us." He smiles. "Of course, you have an advantage in that you probably know where class is. Could you tell me where Mr. Norton's room is?"

"Sorry, New Kid. Can't. I'm late."

"Oh, come on. You have time—"

"No. I have no time."

Pause, pause, pause. We stare at each other for a good minute.

"You're just standing there," he finally splutters. "How can you have time for *that* but not enough time to tell me how to get to Mr. Norton's room?"

I give him my most winning smile, shrug and resume the walk to *my* next class.

Art.

"Are they all like you around here?"

I wave over my shoulder, but I don't stop.

Norton says he's going to tell on me for being late. Henley and Grey will get the notice and I'll have to discuss it on Friday. *Why were you late, Parker? What did you think that would accomplish, Parker?* And then the tough question. *What destructive behaviors were you engaging in for the five minutes you weren't in class, Parker?*

I'm going to tell them I'm on the rag.

Anyway, I have two classes with Chris and this is one of them. We sit next to each other because his last name starts with *E* and mine starts with *F.* Ellory and Fadley, Winter Ball King and Queen three years running.

I can't stand being around him, but I fake it pretty well.

"You're late," Chris says. We're working with charcoal today. He passes me a pencil and a sheet of paper. "Where were you?"

"If I told you, I'd only disappoint you."

"Jesus, Parker."

I start working on a charcoal blob. Abstract charcoal. Whatever. The black flakes off the pencil tip, making a nice mess of my fingers pretty quickly. Then I smudge until my masterpiece is ruined. I bet Norton will report that, too, like I didn't *try,* even though it's art, where no one should be able to tell if you're trying or not.

The stupid thing is, I like art. I mean, it's okay.

"Oh, Jesus yourself and take a joke," I tell him. "There's a new kid. He asked me directions. It took a couple minutes."

"Oh." He sounds relieved. "Hey, your hair looks nice all brushed like that."

"Took you long enough to notice. It was brushed in homeroom."

"I've got a date with Becky for Friday."

"Chris and Becky," I say thoughtfully. I try it again in Movie Announcer Voice: "Chris and Becky. *Presenting Chris and Becky . . .* "

He stares. "What?"

"It doesn't sound right," I declare. "There's no ring to it."

"Yeah, well, you broke up with me."

"I know; I was there. And that has nothing to do with how stupid your names sound together." I try it again: "Chris, Becky, Becky, Chris . . ."

He stares some more.

"Seriously, there's a new kid? You're not drunk?"

"No, I'm on the rag."

Enter New Kid. The door swings open and he's flushed and out of breath like he ran all the way here. Everyone gets quiet—fresh meat—and Norton *harrumphs.*

"Better late than never. Gardner, I presume?"

"Yes, sir," Gardner mumbles. "I got lost."

"Late slip?"

Gardner looks like he can't believe it. "I'm *new.*"

"Thank you for that, Gardner. Take a seat over there, help yourself to some charcoal and paper and get to work." Norton's such a hard-ass. He reminds me of George C. Scott sometimes. "I expect you to be on time tomorrow."

"That's not the guy you gave directions to, is it?" Chris asks.

"I didn't say I *gave* him directions; I said he asked me for them."

"Christ, Parker, you're a real bitch sometimes."

Gardner skulks over to the table next to ours, sets up and starts drawing. I stare at him until he feels it and looks my way. His eyes widen and he points his charcoal pencil at me accusingly.

"You," he says. "You're in this class?"

I smile. "Hi. I'm Parker Fadley."

Chris reaches past me, extending his hand.

"Ignore her. I'm Chris Ellory. Welcome to St. Peter's."

"Thanks," Gardner says, looking relieved that they're not all like me around here. He and Chris shake hands. "Jake Gardner. Nice to meet you."

Now that I've heard his name, I'm doomed to remember it. Just more useless information taking up brain space that could be better served for more important things like . . . stuff. Jake and Chris talk through art and discover they have so much in common it's amazing. Like, They Could Be Boyfriends If They Didn't Like Vaginas So Much Amazing.

By the time the period is over, my charcoal blob has eaten all the white space but for one solitary speck to the lower left side of my paper. When Norton does his rounds, he leans over my shoulder and, in his best George C. Scott, says, "I like it." Then he glances at Chris's halfhearted elm and goes, "It's always trees with you! How many times do I have to tell you to *think outside the tree,* Ellory?" And I laugh so hard I cry a little.

Then the bell goes off again. The bell goes off too much.

We eke our way out of the room and Chris turns to Jake and says, "We're gonna check out the fast-food strip for lunch. Wanna come?"

"Sure," Jake says.

"How about it, Parker?" Chris asks me. Then he brings his

hands to his mouth in mock horror. "Oops, forgot. You're not allowed off grounds for lunch anymore! Oh, snap."

I roll my eyes. "That wasn't a snap."

He says something else, but I don't hear it because I'm gone. I drop my things at my locker and search out a spot in school that isn't around people, but there are none and that's when I notice that the halls are way too crowded.

There are bodies everywhere.

At first I do okay. I hover by the drinking fountain and try to look like I've got somewhere to be. Then I start hearing this sound, like this sighing, no—not sighing. *Breathing.* Everyone breathing. I can hear the people around me sucking up all the fresh air, leaving nothing for me.

My chest tightens and I can't breathe.

"I can't breathe."

I scare the hell out of the school nurse. He darts up from his chair and makes a big fuss while I try to explain the problem.

"I can't breathe. The air in here is too stale. . . . No, my chest feels fine. Yes, I can feel my left arm. . . . Make them open some windows; they're using up all the air. . . ."

He doesn't get it, but he directs me to a cot at the back of the room anyway. No one else is sick today, so I get a little peace and quiet. I lie on my back and scan the shelves across the room for a bottle of ipecac, but no such luck.

I close my eyes.

When I open them again, it's last period and I'm in English and Becky is freaking out and flipping through her binder while Lerner looks on. I don't know what she's so worried about; she's golden. She never misses an essay and Lerner likes her. He's even saying, "No worries, Halprin, just get it to me by the end of the week—"

"But you don't understand, sir; I *did* the essay! I *had* it! It was *here!*"

"I'm sure it will turn up," he tells her soothingly. "Just make sure you hand it in by Friday. . . ."

Becky looks like she's going to cry. Lerner moves on to me.

"I don't even have to ask, do I, Fadley?"

Lerner likes me, too. Not as much as he used to. What I like best about Lerner is he's been teaching so long, he doesn't waste time. He readjusted his expectations of me immediately after the first time I got wasted and fell out of my chair in class.

"I think you should," I say, smiling. "Go on, ask."

His mustache twitches. "Well, I'm afraid to now."

Becky's mouth drops open as I make a show out of taking the essay from my binder and handing it to Lerner. He stares at it, and then me, and for a second I wonder if he knows it's Becky's. But then he tucks it away with the other papers he's collected and it's good. Only I hope he doesn't do any expectation readjusting after this because then I'll have to disappoint him.

Becky gapes at me, still teary eyed.

"When the fuck did you do that essay?"

"History, lunch. I'll take my fifty dollars now, please."

"I was joking, Parker. The bet was a *joke*."

But I won't let it be a joke, so when the last bell, finally, mercifully, *rings,* I chase after her down the hall, screaming her name.

"Becky! Hey, Becky! *Becky Halprin!*"

She pauses, stuck. At one end of the hall, her posse—my old posse—and at the other end, me. She thinks about it for a minute, sighs and heads in my direction.

"What?"

"What time's your date with Chris on Friday?"

She blushes.

"He's picking me up at six."

"Do you still have that pink sweater? The one that's supertight

across the chest? You should wear that, he'd like it." She looks all
disgusted because she's too stupid to realize I'm helping her out.

"Uh." She blinks. "Okay. Thanks. I think."

"No problem." I pause. "Hey, if *you'd* won the bet, would it still
have been a joke?"

"Becky, come *on,*" someone whines behind us. I glance down
the hall. Sandra Morrison is tapping her foot impatiently and giving me a look of utter disdain, which is pretty amazing considering
she wouldn't have dared to do it when *I* was the one leading her
around by the nose. Becky sighs and briefly closes her eyes before
reaching into her book bag, finding her wallet and pulling out a
few crisp bills.

"Thanks," I tell her as she hands them to me. "I hope your essay turns up."

She looks touched, like I mean it.

"I do, too. You know, Tori quit the squad. There's a position
available."

I snort. "Like I'd ever let you captain me."

Her mouth drops open, but I don't give her the chance to say
anything back. I walk away, get my things out of my locker and
head home. I'm tired of being around people my age, so I skip the
bus, make the short walk to the city's main street and hail a cab.

I can afford it now.

two

"V-I-C-T-O-R-Y!

"HIT 'EM LOW AND HIT 'EM HIGH!

"V-I-C-T-O-R-Y!

"LET'S GO, JACKALS! WIN OR DIE!

"V-I-C-T-O-R-Y!"

Grey says I'm not allowed to spend lunch period in the nurse's office anymore because no one will take me seriously should the time ever come that I actually *can't* breathe, so I go to the gym and sit in on cheerleading practice instead. It's a pretty low-key affair. The squad takes up the far side of the court and Chris, his buddies and his new puppy, Jake, play a game of twenty-one on the opposite end.

It's sort of like old times except I'm not on top of the pyramid anymore. It was a relief for everyone the day I quit the squad. Jessie had been gone for a while. On a number of occasions I'd miscalculated how many shots of vodka you could down without going to class completely wasted, and anyway, I hadn't been showing up for practice for ages, and seeing as I was captain and everything . . .

Becky made herself cry so it looked like she actually cared about my well-being, like she was only taking over captaining duties *super*reluctantly, but because her mascara wasn't waterproof she wound up looking so ridiculous I laughed in her face in front of the whole squad. What was supposed to be a superficially touching moment for the girls and me didn't end very well.

In fact, they hate me now.

I broke up with Chris pretty shortly after that.

"V-I-C-T-O-R-Y!"

Chris emerges champion of twenty-one and the boys start an impromptu mini-game, except for Jake, who doesn't know I know he's been watching me every chance he gets, these "subtle" glances out the corners of his eyes. He casually removes himself from the game and makes his way up the bleachers. Our impending encounter has already left me exhausted, but at least I look better today than I did Monday. Dress shoes on feet (they were under the bed), clean skirt and shirt. My hair's brushed and in a tight ponytail at the back of my head. I slept well last night.

He sits down beside me. "We got off on the wrong foot."

"Did we?" I inhale. "Ew. I hope you're going to shower before class."

"Or maybe there is no right foot with you."

Silence. Jake shifts, laughs nervously and runs a hand through his hair. People always get uncomfortable when I decide to shut up. You'd think it'd be the opposite, but no.

After a couple of minutes, he bravely soldiers on:

"Chris told me I had better things to do than talk to you, but I kind of wanted to do it anyway."

Oh, Chris. I owe him a thousand apologies, but I don't have the time and he doesn't want to hear them. Also, I'm not sorry.

"He said that because he's not over me," I explain.

"Oh." Jake nods. After a beat, his eyes get comically wide. *"Oh."*

"Yeah."

I stand and stretch and he does the same, shifting some more. I focus my attention on the cheerleaders. Becky is in her element now that she's captain. She wants to coach professionally some-day and the reality is she could do far worse and not much better. She shouts the girls into a ragged formation. We're not going to win any awards this year. I'm gone, Tori's gone and Jessie won't be back for who knows how long.

"Anyway," Jake says. I turn back to him. "I just wanted to start over on a good note, that's all."

I have to put this poor guy out of his misery.

"Look, Jake, I'm not in the market for—" I almost say *a boyfriend*, which is true, but this is even truer: "People."

"The-that's presumptuous of you," he stutters because he hears the *boyfriend* of it anyway, like I knew he would. "I . . . I'm not—"

"Aren't you?" I study him. I'm really not that presumptuous, but I need to kill this conversation. "Why else would you want to talk to me?"

"I was giving you a chance to redeem yourself for being such a bitch on Monday," he says, turning red all over. What a saint. "I thought I'd be nice to you—"

"And get into my pants in the process, right?"

"HIT 'EM LOW AND HIT 'EM HIGH!"

He's completely gobsmacked. Maybe they don't talk so for-ward wherever he came from. And I've no doubt he's probably a nice guy who poses no immediate threat to my hymen—if I still had one—but I meant what I said. I'm not in the market for people.

I want to be alone.

So I leave Jake on the bleachers.

After math, I'm due at the guidance office for my first of many sessions where I talk about my adventures on the straight and narrow and how I *feel* about it. Grey's in a cheerful mood when I sit across from her. Cheerful for Grey, anyway.

"I'm glad you showed up," she says. "Principal Henley and I

had a bet on whether or not you'd skip and now I'm twenty dollars richer."

"She underestimates how much I want to graduate," I say.

"Well, I didn't." Grey smiles. "Let's get started. I want you to be open with me, Parker."

I take a deep breath. It smells suspiciously like bullshit in here.

"Open?" I repeat.

"Open. This is your space. Feel free to say anything. You have my word it won't leave the room. I want you to trust me. In learning to trust me, I learn to trust you, and from that trust we go forward. You get your life back and you graduate a person everyone can be proud of."

She looks over a piece of paper in front of her. I'm betting it's some kind of Parker Tally Sheet.

"You did well this week, mostly," she says.

It's funny—I think I'd actually rather be learning right now.

"I guess."

"You've done most of your homework. Good. Next week try for all of it, okay? Mrs. Jones informed me she's willing to be lenient about math since you've managed to get behind an entire unit, but that's not indefinite. I thought that was generous of her."

"Oh yes." I nod. "Very."

We get quiet. Grey's office is such a pit. There are no windows in here and some dumb ass thought fluorescent lights would be a great way to compensate. If anyone comes in here ready to die, they probably leave feeling that way, too.

"What are you thinking about, Parker?"

I'm thinking about Becky and Chris and how they've been making eyes at each other all day, and how in third period I realized by this time tomorrow both of us will have kissed him and how if they fall for each other, that means I'm replaceable. If I'm replaceable, if I step back and put something in the space where I was, I can probably get to be alone faster than I already am. Like, Becky and Chris get together and some new girl joins the squad and they forget about me. Next, I find someone who fucked up worse than I did, like some student prostitute who cuts herself, and that takes care of Henley and Grey and then—maybe I can convince my parents they need a puppy.

"I'm not thinking about anything."

"Fine." She purses her lips. "Let's get back to the week. There were a few glitches. The nurse's office. I don't know what that was about. And you were late for Mr. Norton's class on Monday. Mind telling me why?"

"I ran into the new kid. Jake something. He needed directions."

"Oh." She seems relieved. "So you weren't—"

"Don't worry, Ms. Grey. I wasn't drinking, smoking, toking or snorting in school. I keep the recreational drug use at home where it belongs."

"Parker," she warns.

I lean back and stare at the ceiling. The first time I was in this office was the last time I was drunk at school. I was slumped over in the very chair I'm sitting in now and Henley and Grey discussed my "situation" right in front of me, like there was no way I could follow what they were saying or remember any of it in the morning, but I did.

This is sad; this is so sad. . . .

"So," she says.

"So."

"So . . . ?"

She's superineffectual. I don't see the point of being a guidance counselor in high school if you can't have a gun. If you want a teenager to be open and *especially* if you want them to be honest, a gun to their head's probably the best bet. It doesn't matter, anyway. I decide to mess with her.

"Actually, I kind of liked getting back into the swing of things. Becky even offered me a position on the squad and that was *so* nice. Handing in my homework, talking to that Jake guy—it almost felt . . ." I insert a carefully calculated pause here. "Never mind; it's stupid."

"No, no." She leans forward eagerly. "You can trust me, Parker."

I stare at my hands.

"It almost felt like . . . *before*."

Grey loves it. She almost falls out of her chair; that's how convincing I am.

That's great, Parker; that's wonderful! See? We'll get you back yet! And then I clam up. *No, it's stupid. You're wrong. It's stupid. Never mind.* Because there's no qualifying exam to be a high school guidance counselor. All you have to do is watch a bunch of cheesy movies about troubled teens and take notes. This is how Grey expects the meeting to go down and I'm giving it to her because it might get me out of here faster or, at the very least, end this discussion.

"No, it's stupid," I repeat robotically.

"No, it isn't. It's not stupid. *Never* think it is."

I offer a cautious smile. "Thanks."

She creams herself.

The bell rings. I make a beeline for the door.

"Parker?"

I don't turn, just wait.

"That was really good," she says. "You know, I think there's a lot more hope for you than *you* think there is."

I roll my eyes.

"Thanks, Ms. G."

Becky accosts me as soon as I step into the hall, waving a sheet of paper in my face.

"Here," she says, as I take it. "I copied down homework for you. Lerner had a headache so he told us to read 'The Yellow Wallpaper' again—"

"We read it before?"

"Yeah, in ninth grade. Anyway, he wants us to write a thousand words on how we relate to the story now, as seniors, compared to how we related to it as freshmen. It's pretty half-assed, but like I said, he had a headache."

" 'The Yellow Wallpaper' is the one where the chick goes insane and starts humping the wall at the end, right?"

She stares. "You might wanna reread it again to be safe."

Pfft. "We'll see. Ready for your date tonight?"

"Yeah, got my pink sweater dry-cleaned and everything," she says, and then she puts on her fake-interested face. "How'd your meeting with Grey go?"

"It's six o'clock, right? The date?" I ask. She nods. "Look, I've got to go. I don't want to miss the bus."

On the ride home, I pass the time imagining their date. Chris will take Becky somewhere predictable and nice, even though he could take her Dumpster diving and she'd be happy because she's wanted him so long, and he'll spend the whole time trying desperately hard not to stare at her breasts, because that G-spot stuff is all bravado, but by the end of the night he'll be feeling her up, telling her she's pretty, *the prettiest,* and she'll blush and say, *Oh, Chris,* and they'll make another date and they'll fall in love and she'll be a cheerleading coach and he'll be an heir and they'll have two-point-five kids and, and, and . . .

"I think we should get a dog."

It's one of my better entrances. Dad lowers the paper and Mom drops the potato she's peeling over the sink and they look at me like I'm certifiable, but I'd rather be certifiable than perpetually boring, which is my parents in a nutshell. If I had to own up to resembling either one of them, it'd be my dad. We both have brown hair and sharp features. Mom's less sharp, more Pillsbury.

"A dog?" Mom says, retrieving the potato. "You think we should get a dog?"

"That's what I said."

Dad returns to the paper. "I've always wanted a dog."

"Well, a puppy actually," I say

"I've always wanted a puppy," he amends. "They turn into dogs."

"What?" Mom demands, turning to him. "What's that supposed to mean? We're getting a puppy, just like that?"

"No, not just like *that*. We'd have to talk about it more. Figure out the logistics." He glances at Mom. "It wouldn't be so terrible, would it? Having a dog?"

She turns to me.

"Where did this come from, Parker? You don't want a dog."

"Yes, I do! Ms. Grey said it would be good for me to—to . . ." I chew my lip and start making faces that obviously indicate I'm in the process of lying, but my parents hate believing I do that. Lie. "She said it would be a good learning experience for me. By learning to nurture a puppy into a healthy dog I could . . . in turn . . . learn to nurture myself again! *And* I did all my homework this week, so I'd say I've earned it."

"You couldn't start out with a goldfish?"

"Goldfish die at the drop of a hat, Mom. It could die of completely natural causes after two weeks and I might think it was something *I* did and I wouldn't be able to live with myself. Puppies are harder to kill and more challenging to take care of and I'm pretty sure that's the point."

Mom and Dad exchange a lo-ng look.

"We'll have to talk about it," Dad says, which means we're getting a dog.

"Great. You two do that and call me when dinner's ready. I'll be in my room."

"But don't you want to tell us about the rest of your—"

I'm a bad daughter. I don't go to my room at first; I hang back in the hall and listen. Mom and Dad are quiet for a little bit and then Mom goes, "Did you find that as oddly encouraging as I did?"

And Dad goes, "Yeah. She hasn't really talked to us in a long time."

"You think her guidance counselor really thinks she should get a dog?"

"It could be a lie."

"And if it is?"

"We can check. But look, if she *is* lying it's because she wants a dog. It's not like she's lying about where she's been and who she's been with. . . ."

My dad, the softie.

"And that makes it okay?"

"No, but maybe a dog could foster some kind of . . . sense of responsibility and . . . discourage her recklessness. . . ."

"So we should get a dog? That's what you're saying?"

"Who knows? But she talked to us, Lara. She asked us for something we can give her."

"It would be nice to feel like we were doing something." Quiet. Mom clears her throat. "Now come over here and taste this and tell me if it's awful. . . ."

I check out at dinnertime. I mean, I'm there and I'm eating, but I spend the meal staring into space, nodding my head every time it's clear my parents are talking to me and sometimes when it isn't. When our plates are empty and we fall into that awkward silence that happens between digesting and clearing the table, I come back to myself.

"May I please go for a walk?"

It's a big question because I have a curfew now, but my parents' spines are so pliable I don't think it'll be a problem. Mom and Dad exchange a nervous glance and have a telepathic conversation about it. I hear every word.

Do we let her out? It's past curfew.

True, but look at that   at least she asked!

I know! I can hardly believe it!

She could have just sneaked out, but she asked!

I know! We're good parents!

"What time will you be back?" Dad asks.

"What time is it now?"

"It's seven."

"Within the hour, I guess."

"Where are you going?"

"It's just a walk." I make sure to look them both in the eyes. "That's it."

"Sure . . . ," Mom says slowly, staring at Dad, who nods slightly. "That would be fine. Thank you for asking, Parker."

I'm out of the house quick in case they change their minds. It's dark out, but I have a Mini Maglite attached to my key ring, so I'm not worried. It feels nice having the streets to myself. Every so often I hear the sound of cars in the distance navigating some faraway road.

Chris lives two blocks from me, in the nicest house on the nicest piece of property in all of Corby, Connecticut, and I'm sure he's still out with Becky and no doubt his parents are at the country club. When his house comes into view, I walk up the gravel driveway casually, so if any of the neighbors happen to look out their windows I'm only here for a visit. Nothing unusual.

I bypass the front door and edge my way around the house, maneuvering past shriveled flower beds and tacky lawn ornaments until I find myself in the backyard, facing the woods behind the house. These woods never change. The pine trees stand tall and separate, illuminated by the light of some far-off source. When I come here, it always takes me a while to get my bearings, but I can't afford to do that tonight because I promised my parents I'd be home within the hour and I'm not wearing a watch.

I trudge into the trees and pull out my Mini Maglite. One step, two steps, ten steps, twenty, twenty-five steps. I turn the flashlight on. A feeble, yellow light reveals a small strip of ground laden with pine needles.

It was around here . . .

And then, without fail, I hear the music from that night, like I always do when I come out here. A heavy bass line and an ear-splitting drumbeat winds its way into the woods from Chris's open bedroom window, where he likes to mount the speakers of his sound system for optimal noise blaring into the neighborhood. And then there's splashing sounds coming from the pool and everyone's laughing and talking and shrieking and having a good time.

His parties are the best.

I stick the flashlight in my mouth, get down on my hands and knees and start pushing aside pine needles. Five minutes later, my throat hitches. I rip the flashlight from my mouth, scramble backward and throw up.

Fuck.

I wipe my mouth, force myself to my feet, move past the puddle of vomit and get back to work. I don't know what I think I'll find out here, but I stay on the ground for a while anyway, searching, until I know the hour's gone and I'm late and I'd better go. I don't want Chris to come back and see me here and ask me what I'm doing.

Finding the bracelet that time was just a fluke, Parker, you idiot.

three

Jake's a rather tenacious young man. Monday starts with him waiting for me by my locker, and I'm really not in the mood for it because I might have a hangover.

Okay, that's not true. I'm kind of in the mood for it because it *is* vaguely intriguing. I have clearly charmed the guy out of his mind.

"You're in my way." I nudge him aside. I think Grey knows I'm hungover. She gave me this extralong look when we passed in the hall earlier, and that's never good. I grab my history books and slam my locker shut, which makes the bad headache I'm nursing worse. Like that, my vague state of intrigue fades. "What do you want, Jake?"

"In your pants." He turns red and cringes. "I mean, I don't want into your pants. And I didn't. I'm not interested in you."

"Okay." I bite the inside of my cheek to keep from laughing. "Thanks for that."

I head for homeroom, but Jake expects more apparently, because he follows after me.

"That's it? That's all you're going to say?"

"You don't want in my pants. Duly noted."

A couple passing freshmen give us startled looks.

"Look, I was just trying to be nice to you and—"

"Give me the chance to redeem myself; I know," I say. "When you were obsessing over our conversation this weekend, did you take a moment to appreciate what a jerk kind of thing that is to say?"

"I offended *you*?"

"Not likely. I just thought you'd want to know how it made you sound. You're obviously one of those people who really care about what other people think of you."

"*What?*"

I stop; he stops.

"I didn't really think you wanted in my pants, Jake, but if you spent the whole weekend waiting for today just so you could clear that up, you have some issues."

"*I* have issues?"

"There. Admitting you have a problem is half the battle."

"You know, you're not half as clever as you think you are."

"This still makes me a lot cleverer than you."

We arrive at homeroom. Perfect timing. I get to leave Jake sputtering in the doorway. It's almost worth being early for that alone.

The room is only half-full and Becky is nowhere to be found, but Chris is seated in the middle row, working on his homework. He's almost as bad as I am, if not for the fact that he usually gets it done.

"Uh-oh," he says, looking up as I approach. "I know that face."

"Do you ever do your homework at home?"

"About half." He finishes up some English and I sit down beside him for the hell of it. He closes his book. "You're hungover."

"I have a hungover face?"

"It's subtle, but it's there." It's stuff like this that makes me glad we broke up. He pauses. "You want to talk about it?"

"I think my face says it all. How was your date with Becky?"

He forces a smile. The right corner of his mouth starts twitching.

"Good," he says, in a voice that belies the word "It was good."

"Uh-oh, I know *that* face."

He groans and leans back in his seat. "Becky's a great girl—"

I clutch my heart. "There's not going to be a second date!"

"Did I say that?"

"Yeah, when you called her a *great girl.*" This poses a problem. Becky's supposed to be my replacement, or at the very least they could distract each other from me for a while. I'll have to lie, but it's for a worthwhile cause. "She *is* a great girl. You'd be an idiot if you let her go."

"Parker, you hate Becky. And you're taking an unusual interest in my date with her. Jealous?" I laugh and he gives me this look. "No, really. Why do you care? And why are you hungover?"

I put on my most Obnoxious Teacher Talking to a Really, Really Stupid Student voice.

"Well, Chris, sometimes when someone overindulges—"

"You do know that Becky and I are supposed to report any kind of behavior like this to Grey and Henley?"

"That's funny. Tell me another."

"It's not a joke."

"It was because she's not me, isn't it? That's why it didn't work out, huh? Becky's a *great girl,* but she's no Parker Fadley. It's okay. I understand. I *am* pretty awesome."

"Fuck you."

"Fuck you, too. And if you tell Henley or Grey, I'll kick your ass."

He snorts. "Oh, really?"

"Yeah, and I'll probably get away with it, because I'm a girl. Make sure you hit me back. That'll only improve my odds."

He shakes his head. "You have to take it that one step too far, don't you?"

"Always." I won't do it. I won't. I will not. "Sorry."

Goddammit.

"Forget it," he mutters, waving a hand. "I won't tell on you."

"That's not why I said it." *Goddammit.* "Look, just give Becky another chance—"

"Only if you ease off on Jake Gardner."

"Ease off? I've only talked to him, like, three times."

"Yeah, and every one of those times you've been a bitch—"

"What is this? Have you taken a *shine* to the boy?"

He rolls his eyes. "Yeah, Parker. That's exactly it."

"Well, why didn't you say so? I'll lighten up on him then."

"Really?"

"No. God, do you know who you're talking to?"

"Unfortunately," Chris says. The bell explodes in my head or rings, whatever. I wince and rub my temples. "And consider this a favor. If you come to school hungover again, I'll go straight to Grey."

"*Thanks,* Chris."

"You're *welcome,* Parker."

Becky makes a mad dash into the room a minute after the Pledge of Allegiance starts over the PA and I wonder if she's avoiding Chris, like if their date went that bad. After we recite the Apostles' Creed, I move back to where she's sitting despite Chris's best efforts to convince me not to.

"How'd the date go?" I ask.

She smiles. "Okay. Chris is a great guy."

It's enough to make a girl depressed. When Chris says Becky's a *great girl* it means she's boring, but when Becky says Chris is a *great guy* it means she's probably started a scrapbook of the time they've spent together.

"Details, details," I sing. "Where did you go and what did you do and do you have a Tylenol on you? I've got a killer headache."

She unzips her pencil case and retrieves a Baggie of white pills and I can't help but laugh at how suspect it looks. I help myself to two and swallow them dry.

"We went for a ride around and we stopped at that diner out on Route Seven. It was mostly just talking, you know. He talked about you a lot. Like, the whole night was mostly about Parker, actually. It was lovely."

I pretend she didn't say it.

"Did you make plans for a second date?"

"No," she says. "I don't think there'll be one."

"What? Come on! You said he's a great guy!"

"I also said he talked about you for the whole date."

She says it with a voice that totally hates me, even though I can't be held responsible for Chris being such a fuck. We stare at each other. It's way easier to not be Becky's friend than it is to not be Chris's girlfriend.

"He liked the sweater though," she adds. "A lot."

My head buzzes through history while I wait for the Tylenol to kick in. By the time art rolls around I feel less hungover and more charitable. We're working with paint today and I pick the easel next to Jake's. It thrills him.

"What do *you* want?"

"I want to apologize if you're offended by the way I am," I tell him. "But that's the way I am with everyone. I was just trying to make you feel welcome."

"That's the crappiest apology I've ever heard."

"Well, that's because I'm not really sorry."

He rolls his eyes. "Right."

We get to painting. I wish I could have art forever. Senior art, anyway. Norton's a hard-ass, but a lazy one. At our age, he figures, we've learned everything about art that can be learned in high school, and now we spend the entire period trying to create things that he might not have seen in the last twenty-five years. Every forty minutes is another opportunity to surprise him. The bigger the surprise, the better the mark.

"So, where do you come from and how come you moved here?"

Jake reaches for the red paint. "West Coast. My dad wanted a new scene."

"He couldn't have waited until the end of the year?"

Jake snorts. "Nope."

"And how are you finding St. Peter's? Do you like it here so far?"

He gives me a look. "Generally."

What can I say? I stare at the paper in front of me and try to figure out what to create. I glance across the room, at Chris's easel. Sure enough, he's painting a tree. I grin, reach for the black and get to work on a stick person.

A stick person with its head on fire.

"So, what's your deal?"

It takes a minute before I realize Jake's talking to me. There's something very enthralling about painting a stick person with its head aflame.

You just forget the rest of the world.

"What do you mean?"

"I heard you used to be captain of the cheerleading squad."

"Now where did you hear a crazy thing like that?"

"Chris mentioned it."

"Then it must be true."

"He said you used to be popular."

"Mentioned that, too, did he?"

"I asked, but if you were head cheerleader, I guess I didn't need to. I was surprised. Not many people give up those kinds of perks."

"Hmm."

I think I'll turn this stick person into Chris. All I have to do is put an orange jersey with the number 22 on it and he'll know it's him.

"So, what's your deal?" Jake asks again.

"Jake, I barely know you."

I spend lunch in the gym again, watching the boys scrimmage and the girls eating carrot sticks before they get ready to cheer. This kind of routine could get monotonous fast, and not in a good way.

I stretch out on the bleachers, shoving aside the lunch Mom packed for me. My headache is gone, but I don't think I can handle food. I shouldn't have finished off the bottle of vodka in my room last night. It was left over from before, hidden in the back of my closet, and I drank until I fell asleep. That's the only reason to do it now and I don't do it very often, contrary to what everyone else thinks. Back then, I drank to be caught. It was the start of my great campaign to distance myself from everyone. I even had a checklist and everything. First item: indulge in alienating, self-destructive behavior.

It worked beautifully at the start, but I hadn't counted on my family and former friends conspiring against me. The problem with alienating, self-destructive behavior is people get it into their heads it's a cry for help. It wasn't. It was just a really poorly executed plan to get everyone off my back. So now I'm halfway between where I started (not alone) and where I want to end up (alone) and I just have to roll with it if I want to graduate or else I'll never be alone. It's stupid. And not just because of the homework thing. Oh shit.

Lerner's essay.

Shit.

I tear out of the gym with such zeal the boys stop playing and the girls stop cheering to watch me go. I rip my English binder and pencil case from my locker and find the page Becky gave me with the assignment on it.

Write a thousand-word essay comparing how you relate to "The Yellow Wallpaper" as a senior to how you related to the story as a freshman.

My headache flares up. I press my palms against my eyes and try to wish, wish, wish myself out of this situation.

A thousand words?

I sit down, my back against my locker, and glare at the opposite wall, right into the eyes of Jessica Wellington. Jessie. Her photograph, anyway. I forgot. Four years, two suicides, one death, one rape, two pregnancies (one abortion), three overdoses and one missing person. Jessica Wellington. Since late junior year. Just up and ran away.

I'd give anything to be her right now.

So it's one missed essay. What's the worst they could do? Maybe I'll cry in front of Lerner. He *hates* that. He grants extensions at the drop of a hat if girly tears are involved. It's what he's famous for.

"Parker?"

Chris. He sits beside me, arm close enough to touch mine. I resist the urge to flee. I can't stand being around him in class, but it's easier than being around him alone.

"Didn't you get enough of me in homeroom?" I ask.

"Are you okay? Your exit from the gym was . . . startling."

"I forgot to do an essay for Lerner over the weekend, which wouldn't be that big of a deal if it wasn't a point against me graduating with the rest of you at the end of the year."

"Bet you wish you hadn't gotten drunk on Sunday now."

I bat my eyelashes at him. "Chris, I believe you don't feel sorry for me."

"I think you do it to yourself."

"Of course I do." I should at least be trying for a thousand words, but I don't. I just sit there while he stares at me. "What?"

"You were right."

"I'm right about lots of things. Be more specific."

"Becky's not you and that's why I don't want to date her again."

I laugh.

"Many girls aren't me. You'd better get used to it."

"Can't."

"Why? I did awful things to you and I'd do them all over again."

He winces. "I don't think you meant them."

"I meant them."

"You know, that '94 issue of *Cosmopolitan* didn't have anything in it about G-spots," he says. "But I should've figured you were lying."

"Yeah, you should've."

"But Becky *does* know where it is." My mouth drops open. I try to recover, but it's too late; Chris saw it. I don't know why I expected Becky to tell me something like that. He smiles. "Doesn't bother you, does it?"

"No." I swallow. "Okay, so *why* exactly can't you go out on a second date? If it doesn't bother you that she's not me when you fuck her, I don't see why you can't—"

He holds up his hand. "We didn't fuck."

"Oh, I see. Congratulations."

"Where do you think she is?"

"What are you talking about?"

He nods at the poster of Jessica. "Where do you think she is?"

"Dead," I say. "Either that or working as a prostitute. But probably dead."

"Nice. I can't believe you just said that." He blows a strand of hair out of his eyes. "You didn't used to be this cold."

"You know, if I do my homework and I don't come to school hungover anymore, it's still going to be like this. It's not a phase, Chris. This is who I am."

"Do you ever hear yourself?" he asks. "You're so full of shit."

"No, I'm *not* anymore. That's the point."

He grabs my arm and leans forward, unbearably close. His lips graze my neck and get close to my mouth. I shiver.

"Fuck off, Chris."

He lets me go and stands.

"Good luck with your essay."

He heads back in the direction of the gym. I reopen my binder and poise my pen above the blue lines. I should at least try.

Write a thousand-word essay comparing how you relate to "The Yellow Wallpaper" as a senior to how you related to the story as a freshman.

I didn't even reread the stupid story and the only memory I have of it isn't entirely accurate, if I'm to believe Becky, which in this case I do. Still, I'm a fantastic liar in all other aspects of my life, so writing a thousand-word lie should be easy.

I can do it. I can do this.

As a freshman, I found "The Yellow Wallpaper" to be—

Fuck it, I'll just cry.

four

I'm a fantastic crier. Everyone is on suicide watch.

Plus: I don't have to do the essay.

Minus: it landed me in Grey's office and she called my parents.

Plus: we're getting a dog this Saturday!

On Tuesday, Norton surprises everyone by giving us an honest-to-God project that will take up a huge chunk of our time and account for a huge chunk of our grade and I don't like him so much anymore.

"Two sides of the same landscape," he announces, standing before us like Patton. "That's what this project is about. You'll pair up—"

Norton's momentarily interrupted by the sound of screeching chairs as best friends skirt close, claiming one another. You don't want to wind up with someone like me for a partner. He frowns.

"On second thought, *I'll* put you into pairs—" Everyone groans. "Quiet."

Chris glances at me. Bet he was going to ask.

"Two sides of the same landscape," Norton repeats in his gravelly voice. "Here's what you're going to do: You're going to arrange a time to meet with your partner to scout the local landscape and take a picture of it. You'll bring that picture to class. Are you all with me so far?"

I'm bored already.

"You will, as partners, proceed to paint the left and right side of the landscape, respectively, using the photo as a reference for the *base*. I want you to reimagine the landscape itself. The colors, the season—turn a paradise into wasteland! There is one caveat: you and your partner must reimagine each side of your landscape independently and figure out a way to bring it together to form a whole. I want unity and disparity here, people! Surely with everything I've taught you, you can manage *that*."

I've never seen Norton so excited. He's dancing on the balls of his feet and I imagine him lying awake in bed late last night, the idea coming to him like a flash of lightning. He bolts upright and shouts, *Eureka! A new way to torture my second-period senior class!* Or something.

Chris raises his hand.

"I don't get it, sir."

Norton surveys the room. "Does everyone else here get it?"

No one says anything. Silence is always consent.

"Looks like it's just you, Ellory, but at least you'll be partnered with someone who does and has the time to explain it to you slowly and repeatedly until you understand."

I can't help it; I laugh. Chris glares at me and Norton starts pairing us up. Every set of names called is met with either groans of derision or happy little shrieks of joy from all sides of the room. I hold my breath, expecting Chris because it would just be my life to have to fend his lips off my neck while we scout the area and take pictures, but it's not Chris; it's Jake.

Which seems so much more obvious in hindsight.

"Fadley and Gardner."

"Shit," Jake mutters. I waggle my eyebrows at him.

He rests his head on the table all *kill me now.*

After the bell rings, he approaches me very, very cautiously. It makes me feel very, very intimidating. I like that.

"Let's make this as painless as possible," he says. "When do you want to start scouting out locations? Tomorrow?"

"Whoa, slow down. We have to get the cameras and every-thing—"

"I have a digital camera. We can use that; it's no problem."

"Fine, but tomorrow's still too soon."

"It's a huge project," he says. "It's probably not soon enough."

I pull out my ponytail and retie it, thinking. It would've been easier if he'd volunteered to take the pictures himself, and from what he already knows about me I don't know why he didn't. A couple minutes pass.

Jake clears his throat. "Oh, sure, feel free to take your time. It's not like I want to eat lunch or hang in the gym or anything."

So I let a couple more minutes pass.

"How about Friday after school?" I finally suggest. "I have a meeting at the guidance office last period. You can meet me there when class lets out. Bring your digital camera and get a note so you can come on my bus—"

"I already go on your bus. Our bus, actually."

I blink. "You do not."

"Yeah, I do," Jake says in a *duh* voice. "Bus four-twenty-six is my bus, too. I've been on it every day since I started here and I've seen you on it. You sit at the front."

"This is fascinating. I never even noticed you."

I try to recall the seating arrangement, but I can't. The bus is worse than school. At least at school there are a couple of places I can hide, but there's nowhere on the bus. I usually sit at the front, close my eyes and open them at my stop.

"Do you sit at the back?"

"Near the middle," he says. "Anyway, Friday's fine. See you then."

Nothing happens Wednesday and almost nothing happens Thursday until I accidentally overhear Becky and Chris schedule their second date for Saturday. I make a mental note to find out the time they're taking off so I can sneak into his backyard again.

"You said you felt overwhelmed on Monday," Grey says. "Let's talk about that."

"What else do you want me to say? I was overwhelmed."

"Actually, I was thinking 'hysterical' would be a more apt description. . . ."

The thing about crying in Lerner's was once I started, I couldn't stop. I didn't even mean it or really feel it, but I couldn't stop. I could waste time analyzing that, but I won't. It got me out of the essay and it's getting me a dog. That's all that matters.

"The moment got away from me, I guess," I say.

But Grey wants more than that, like last time, and even though I'm kind of bored, like last time, I don't want to overextend myself. I need that energy to take pictures with Jake after the bell.

Fridays are turning out to be a major pain in the ass.

I shrug. "Maybe it was because it felt too much like . . . before?"

"You mentioned that last Friday, things feeling like before," Grey says. She opens her Parker notebook. "It seemed to be a good thing then. What's changed?"

I stare at the inspirational poster tacked to the wall behind her head. Something about not giving up. Lame.

"I had a lot of responsibilities," I say. "I was thinking about it. I was captain of the cheerleading squad, I was a straight A-plus student and, let's be honest, I was popular. All of that takes *a lot* of work. I did some stupid things and lost it all, but that also meant I

got rid of all those responsibilities and you know what? I liked life
a lot better. Before, I was suffocating. So, lately, I've been trying for
the homework thing, because I want to graduate, but that essay . . .
every time I sat down to write it, I just *couldn't because—*"

"You felt suffocated," Grey finishes.

She's so smart. I mean, *I'm* so smart. She's so predictable.

"Yeah."

"Well, I sympathize, Parker, but we can't make many more al-
lowances for you. As it stands, we've—"

"I wasn't asking," I say, laughing a little. "I mean, it's not like I
cried in Lerner's on *purpose.*"

Shit. It comes out of my mouth wrong, like I *did* cry on purpose, which I did, but Grey's obviously not supposed to know
that. And of course she catches it.

Her face darkens.

"Ms. *Grey!*" I bring my hand to my mouth and try to sound
scandalized, to diffuse the situation. "You don't think I did it on
purpose, do you?"

But *that* comes out of my mouth wrong, too.

"You just don't learn, do you, Parker?" She closes her notebook and glares at me. "You run everyone around in circles—"

"I run everyone around in circles?"

"You do."

"I do?"

"Stop that." She takes off her glasses and rubs her eyes. "You
want everyone to think your problem is what happened over the
summer—"

"No, that's what everyone *wants* to think—"

"But it *is* your problem!" She puts her glasses back on. "You
manipulate. You make it your excuse and that's exactly how you
push it away."

The party starts at eight, but I show up early so Chris and I can have

sex. Another year at St. Peter's is almost behind us and we've already
slept together eight times. This will be the ninth and there's going to be
a lot more sex in our future.

We go to his bedroom. The speakers are mounted against his win-
dow and he turns on some sweet-sounding music really low and he
kisses me and I kiss him back and then, I don't know, I kind of seize up.

"What's wrong?"

"That doesn't even make any sense," I tell Grey.

It's the last thing I tell her. We sit in silence until the bell
rings. I feel like I should be furious with her, and I might be, but
more than that, I'm annoyed. I have to remind myself she wasn't
there and she doesn't know a damn thing so I can't really blame
her for making half-assed assertions once a week. I just wish she
wouldn't.

When I get out, Jake's waiting for me at the door.

"I've got the camera," he says.

"Great."

We head outside.

I can't believe he goes on my stupid bus and I didn't even notice.

"You can sit where you normally sit," I tell him.

"Don't worry; I was going to," he replies. "So do you have any
idea—"

"Yeah, I have an idea: please stop talking."

We climb on the bus. I take my usual seat at the front and he
heads for the middle. I rest my head against the window and close
my eyes. I don't mean to, but I fall asleep, and fifteen minutes later
Jake's shaking my shoulder and looking pretty irritated. All
through art he pestered me, "Where are we going? What are we
taking pictures of. . . ."

"I *think* this is your stop," he says sarcastically.

I rub my eyes. "Yeah."

We inch up the aisle and step onto the street. I can see my house from here, but I don't want to go through the hassle of introducing Jake to my parents because they'd interpret it all wrong and it'd give them false hope and, like I said before, I don't do that.

"We'll go this way." I point in the opposite direction. "If we go down this street, turn left and walk through the park there's this kind of wooded area. Beyond that, there's a ravine. We could probably get some really good pictures there."

"We're not going to your house first?"

"I don't want you to know where I live."

He laughs. "Like I give a damn. But sure, let's go to the ravine."

We walk. I don't know if I should be nice to him or if this technically makes him my guest because we're near where I live and he has no idea where we are.

"So you and Chris really hit it off, huh?"

I keep my voice light and conversational, but Jake still seems to weigh every word like he's trying to figure out which one of them is poisoned.

"He's cool," he says after a while. "I mean, he didn't treat me like a new kid, you know? We hang."

"He and Becky are going out—you know Becky, right? Becky Halprin? She's captain of the cheerleading squad. Anyway, they had a date last Friday and they're having another one this weekend, I think."

"Yeah, Saturday," Jake says. "It's not really a date, though. A couple of us are going to go shoot some pool at Finn's, wherever that is."

"Finn Walters?"

"Yeah, you know him?"

"Yeah. He's on the chess team. He's, like, this superintellectual and yet still cool." It could be all the blow he deals in the boys' washrooms. "So it's a night thing, right? When are you going? Around eight?"

"Chris says he'll pick me up at—" He stops. "Why? Are you fishing for an invite or something? Because you're not going to get one from me."

"I've got better things to do with a Saturday night, but thanks."

"Like what?"

"Like not hanging out with you?"

"Walked right into that one, didn't I?"

"Yeah, you did."

We laugh. And then we realize we're laughing together and then we stop and then it gets awkward. I don't do awkward well, at least mutual awkwardness, so I snap my fingers to make the feeling go away.

And then I can't stop.

Even after Jake points it out.

"That's really annoying," he says.

So I kick it up a notch just to bug him and I keep it up until my fingers start to hurt.

We trek through the park and enter the woods beyond it. They're not like the woods by Chris's house. They're a little denser, a little easier to get lost in, but I'm not worried. I like them. Nothing bad happened here and it makes the air less polluted, somehow. It doesn't make me want to throw up.

"It's really great out here," I say without thinking. "There's nothing—"

I shut my mouth.

"What?" Jake asks.

"Nothing. We'll get good pictures out here, that's all."

He reaches into his book bag and pulls out his digital camera.

"But not here—it's a little farther in. Give me that." I hold out my hand and he steps back, clutching the camera to his chest.

"Oh, come on, Jake. I'm not going to steal or break it. I may not respect people, but I do respect their property."

He groans and hands it to me.

"I must be crazy."

"You're right; you are."

I take it and run and the look on his face is *so great.*

"Parker!"

He has no choice but to chase after me, and I have a hell of a lead. I can hear my pulse pounding in my ears and the air is cold and sharp in my lungs and I like that. I get to the ravine ages before him, scale the nearest tree—which is also the biggest and the oldest—and wriggle my way along the thickest branch out.

The one that hovers directly above the thirty-foot drop.

When Jake finally catches up to me, I'm dangling from a pretty precarious angle, nearly upside down, and it probably looks terrifying from where he's standing.

But it will be so worth this shot.

"Are you trying to kill yourself?" he yells, panting.

I keep my leg muscles tight around the branch so I don't, you know, die.

"If I was trying to kill myself, I'd make sure you weren't here."

"Parker, get down from there. You're making me nervous—"

"Pansy."

"Fuck off."

A little more . . .

The branch makes a few disconcerting creaking noises, but I'm going to pretend it's not giving out under my weight. I hold the camera up to my eye, the view through the lens making me slightly dizzy, and get a good focus on the ravine. The edges of either side of it creep up the corners of the frame.

Jake's either holding his breath or wetting himself.

Got it.

I right myself, snake backward and hold the camera out.

"Catch!"

"Parker, no—"

I let it go. It seems to fall in slow motion. Jake catches it like I knew he would and he starts swearing at me like I knew he would. When he's finished, he turns the camera on and checks out the shot.

"Decent," he mutters. "But you're lucky I caught my camera."

The branch I'm on protests a little more. I stand very, very carefully and maneuver my way to a branch on the opposite side. It's tricky.

"You're good at that," Jake says, as I settle on my new branch.

"I've lived in trees my whole life."

"Do you have some kind of retort for everything?"

"I'm the straightest talker you've ever met."

"Oh, really? I think most of what comes out of your mouth is—"

And that's when the goddamn branch gives out.

five

The fall takes no time and forever.

I land on my feet for a split second and then my legs crumple and I'm flat on my back and I don't know whether to laugh or cry or swear because I can't believe the *other* branch broke, so I just lay there not moving instead.

"Jesus—Parker?" Dead leaves crunch under Jake's feet as he hurries over. I should say something. He kneels down. "Parker? Are you okay?"

"I can't feel my legs."

He turns white. "Are you serious?"

"No."

"Not funny," he snaps. "You're okay?"

"I'm fine."

I prop myself up on my elbow and ignore the insistent, toothachelike pain going on in my right ankle. Jake doesn't need to know about that.

"Nice catch," I say.

He laughs and stands, brushing the dirt from his knees.

"Like I was gonna catch *you*. Come on, let's get out of here; it's getting dark."

I extend my hands. Jake looks surprised, but he grabs me by

the wrists and hoists me up. I stumble into him. Busted. He gives me a look.

"You hurt yourself, didn't you?"

"Nothing's broken."

"But you hurt yourself, didn't you?"

"I've had worse injuries on the cheerleading squad."

"Parker," Jake says impatiently. "What hurts?"

"Ankle."

"There, that wasn't so hard, was it?" He pauses and looks awkward. "Uh . . . do you need to lean on me or—"

"*No,*" I say emphatically. "I'm good for limping, thanks."

"I have this crazy feeling you'd say that even if you weren't."

We make our way back through the woods. I take a sharp breath in for every step forward, but I don't think it's anything serious. I'll get the compress out when I get home and I'll be good for Monday or I could run up and down the stairs until it's so inflamed I couldn't possibly make it to school.

But I'll give Jake credit. He slows his pace to accommodate my stupid injury and he doesn't go tearing off into the woods like I might've done to him.

I kind of wish he would, though, as he feels the need to pass the time by talking.

"So what'd you do that you have to see Ms. Grey once a week?"

"Run-of-the-mill-delinquent stuff," I say. "It's none of your business."

"Okay."

Limp, limp, limp.

"I got drunk at school. A lot. Earlier this year."

I only admit it because it's something he probably already knows. People talk. I can't be the first person he's asked about me.

He shoves his hands in his pockets. "Do you have, like . . . a problem?"

"Yeah, and that was my solution." He looks all uncomfortable and I laugh. "Lighten up. If I say I don't, you wouldn't believe that, right? Anyone who says they don't have a drinking problem usually does."

"Do they?" he asks. I take a hard step on my ankle and gasp. He pauses, but I wave him off before he can ask if I'm okay. We keep moving and he starts talking again. God, I wish he'd shut up. "So why did you drink?"

"I—" Limp, limp, limp. "What does Chris tell you about me?"

"He said the pressures of being popular made your brain snap."

"Seriously?"

"Yeah."

I'm so touched; he lied for me. Might as well go along with it. "It was something like that, yeah."

"I'm sorry it was so hard for you," Jake says. He *means* it. And then he gets quiet, but now *I* want to talk.

"Do you feel you know me a little better now?" I ask.

He gives me an appraising look.

"You're not that bad."

"It's the sprained ankle. It ups my likability because I can't kick your ass with a broken foot. You probably have a thing for girls when they're vulnerable because they make you feel like that much more of a man—"

"I take it back; you *are* that bad. You're—" He shakes his head. "Never mind; just shut up."

"You totally softened after I fell out of the tree. I'm just saying."

"Yeah, well, I think any decent human being would."

He picks up the pace. My ankle gives me no choice but to fall behind.

"*I* wouldn't," I say to his back.

We split up at the corner to my house after I give him directions to Chris's and it's tense and awkward and unhappy, but that's the way I like it. Jake should know—well, everyone should know—there's no such thing as a decent human being. It's just an illusion.

And when it's gone, it's really gone.

six

"WIN OR LOSE!

"IT'S ALL THE SAME!

"WE DO OUR BEST!

"WE'VE GOT GAME! . . ."

"Stop!" I shout. I don't even want to hear the rest of it.

The girls stare at me, frozen in a ludicrous pose, arms up and out. They remind me of Barbie dolls wearing orange and yellow. This is a new cheer. Becky tabled it. I didn't want to do it, but she begged for months. "You have to let us try it, Parker! The girls will be great!"

But they're not great. They suck and the cheer sucks.

"No," I tell them. "Absolutely not. It's a cheer about being okay with losing—how can you think that's appropriate on any level, Becky? Do you want us to look like fools when we play against St. Mary's?"

"It's not about being okay with losing," Becky snorts. "It's about good sportsmanship!"

I ignore her. "Line up! We'll do the Victory chant for now and I'll figure out something else later, but forget this 'do our best' piece of shit. We're not doing it. And you were all terrible."

Becky's mouth drops open.

"I'm sure she doesn't totally mean it like that, guys," Jessie says, staring at me.

Mom bursts into my room and opens the blinds. I pull the blankets over my head and groan. There's something about the early morning rays of sunshine beating down on my face that makes me want to puke.

"Today's a big day!" she announces. "How does your foot feel?"

"I don't know; I haven't stepped on it yet. Oh my *God,* Mom, would you close the blinds—"

"You should be excited! Today's the day we're bringing Bailey home!"

Bailey. The dog. We passed the interview process, filled out the adoption forms, and I chose the dog next in line to be put down, even though he's not a puppy, because I'm thoughtful like that. Bailey's a ten-year-old harrier with a happy disposition and I think he'll make a great daughter, for a dog.

Mom leaves. I swing my legs over the bed, touch my foot to the floor and stand. It feels better, but I doubt I'll be walking Bailey this week. Falling out of a tree was good for something; Mom or Dad can bond with the dog during the first few integral days and then they can forget he was ever supposed to be for me.

"Oh, Bailey, look, Bailey! Say hello to your new mommy and daddy and sister! Oh, that's a good boy!"

The shelter volunteer is this huge woman who slobbers nearly as much, if not more than, the many dogs surrounding us. Most of them are barking like crazy and there's something about the sound that goes straight to my stomach. The shelter is too small for the number of animals here and it's hot. I snap my fingers to make the feeling go away and glance at Bailey, who stares at me with these big golden-brown eyes. For a second, it's weird. I feel like I'm doing something good, but not just for me.

"Now, Bailey, you be *good,* you hear me?" The woman kneels and gives Bailey such a long hug I think he'll suffocate and die. "We'll miss you. . . ."

Oh my God, I think she's crying.

Sure enough, when she stands, her eyes are bright and her cheeks are damp. Lame, especially considering they were gearing Bailey up to die in a couple of days anyway. The woman passes the leash to Dad, stifles another sob and wishes us well. Bailey's strangely calm about the whole thing. Even the car ride home. Maybe he'll be such a good dog we won't even know we have him.

When we get home, he explores each room at his leisure, sniffing at anything and everything, every nook and cranny. He does it with a practiced disinterest and I wonder what his deal is. His last owner was abusive.

Bailey edges up to the door of my room.

"Bailey." He turns and looks at me. "No."

I block his path and close the door so he can't get in. And then I say it again:

"No. That's *my* room. You're not allowed in there."

He just looks at me and wags his tail. I hold my hand out and he sniffs it.

"So what did you do that no one wanted you, huh?"

I crouch down and scratch him under the chin, behind the ears. I think he likes it; I don't know. We've never had a pet before.

"One of you should take him for a walk soon," I call down the hall to my parents. "I would, but I can't on this foot."

Mom and Dad decide to make it a family outing and walk him together.

It's already working.

I have to sneak out later that night. I lock my bedroom door and crawl out the window. The trip to Chris's takes longer with a sore ankle and sneaking around his house becomes less graceful, but I wind up in the woods all the same, on my hands and knees, digging while the ghost music thrums in the background. I don't throw up this time, but there's a feeling in the pit of my gut that tells me I could.

After a while, I stop looking. There's nothing here. I know that. I *know* that.

But there was something here.

I rub my wrist and let my fingers drift over the bracelet. This was here. Delicate, thin and gold. It should've been impossible for me to find, but I found it. Weeks and weeks after the fact. I did a terrible thing and I get to wear it on my wrist. And I guess I sort of hope there will be more of these kinds of things here, waiting for me to find them even though I know, logically, there won't be. Still, I have to come out and look because the feeling that there *might* be won't go away until I do.

And then it goes away.

Until it comes again.

Monday, my foot feels fine. I stave off zoning out on the bus just so I can see Jake get on. Our eyes meet when he climbs aboard. He shrugs his book bag over his shoulder and it kind of seems like he's going to say something, but he doesn't. He finds his spot in the middle.

"Got a dog, huh?"

I pause and look down at Chris. He looks up at me. His math homework is open on his desk, half done. He pulls out the chair beside him.

"I saw your parents walking it. Sit."

I raise an eyebrow. *"Sit?"*

"Would you please sit down?"

I toss my books on the desk and do as I'm told.

"I'm so behind in math," I say, staring at his book. "A full unit behind, almost two. I haven't even bothered trying to catch up. Maybe I'll just drop out. It'd save me the trouble of working this hard to graduate."

"That's always one option," Chris says. "Heard you fell out of a tree last Friday."

"Heard you were at Finn's. High times?"

"Not all visits to Finn's end in drug use. There were a lot of us there. Just shot the shit, introduced Jake to some people. Good party, I guess."

"You used to throw good parties."

"Didn't I, though." He looks away. "I could get used to Becky. I was thinking about it. Wouldn't be so bad. Just for senior year."

"Lucky Becky."

"Like I said, I'm thinking about it. It's ill-befitting someone of my popularity to go as long as I have single, which is your fault."

"You think you can make me feel guilty?"

"I'm trying."

Just like that, I'm tired of this conversation. I grab my books and stand even though it's not like I have somewhere else to go. The bell will ring in ten minutes.

But in ten minutes I could be far away.

"Sit," he says again. I sit and reach for his pencil. Twirl it between my fingers.

"You can't make me feel guilty," I tell him. "About any of it."

And now it's not just about Becky anymore.

He opens his mouth and closes it. Opens it. Closes it again.

"Or sorry," I add. "You can't make me sorry about any of it either."

"Okay," Chris says, "but whether or not you're sorry or guilty doesn't change the fact that I forgive you anyway. And I don't blame you."

"Yes, you do."

"I don't."

"You do. You're just saying that because you want to—"

"I *don't* blame you, Parker. You weren't thinking clearly—"

"Why are we talking about this?"

I have no patience for this kind of bullshit. It's like now that I'm seeing Grey everyone's all, *Oh, she must have her head on straight, so I can move in again,* which is what I was afraid of, but no one gets to move in ever again because it's better for everyone this way. People are so stupid. They don't even know when you're helping them.

"You brought it up," he says, and then he smiles. "You know, we could work something out. You be my girlfriend again, I give you my math homework . . ."

"Right."

"Okay, skip the girlfriend thing and let's make it sexual favors."

I can't tell if he's serious or not.

"Do I look that cheap to you?" I ask.

When Becky enters the room, he moves to the back to sit beside her.

"WIN OR LOSE!
IT'S ALL THE SAME!
WE DO OUR BEST!
WE'VE GOT GAME!"

I'm dreaming again. I pinch myself. Ouch. Not dreaming. It's lunchtime in the gym and Becky is actually leading the cheerleading squad in that stupid cheer.

"—Unity and disparity. I've been thinking about this a lot and I'm totally confused—"

"Did you hear that?"

Jake looks up from his spot beside me on the bleachers. "What?"

"The cheer about losing. Did you hear it?"

"Uh, not really," he says, annoyed. "See, I was talking about our *art project*—"

"Shut up; they're doing it again. Listen. It's really awful."

The girls resume triangle formation, Becky at the point of it.

"One, two, three!"

The cheer starts up again. Jake and I watch, transfixed. The beat is painfully off, the dance steps contrived and awkward. Cardboard cutouts of cheerleaders operated by arthritic monkeys would move more fluidly.

They finish and Jake—bless his heart—says, "Yeah, that was pretty bad."

"You suck, Becky!" I shout.

The cheerleaders twitter. Becky places her hands on her hips and turns to me. I've heard around the halls there's nothing more terrifying than being glared at by St. Peter's High's cheerleading captain, but that was when *I* was the captain.

When Becky glares, it's just funny.

"There was a reason I wouldn't let us do that cheer, you know," I say.

She frowns.

"You're not captain anymore. You don't get a say in it."

"Yeah, and you might not be captain for much longer. They'll oust you from the squad if you perform that at the next game."

The girls twitter some more, but I can't tell if it's agreeable twittering. They should know from past experience I'm always right about stuff like this.

Becky orders them to take a break and storms up the bleachers to me.

"Uh-oh . . . ," Jake says under his breath.

"Fuck off, Parker," Becky says when she reaches me. "That's my squad out there. *My* squad. Not yours, *mine*. How *dare* you humiliate me in front of the girls—"

I burst out laughing.

"It's an awful cheer and you know it. You think you'll prove me wrong by performing it? You think I actually care? Because I don't—"

"Then why did you feel the need to mouth off while we were practicing it? You wouldn't have tolerated that from anyone, and if I remember correctly, you *didn't*—"

"Jessie would've vetoed that in a second if she was here, and she *did* the last time you tried to get us to do it. Remember?"

"Jessie's not here, you bitch."

She storms back down the bleachers.

"Becky, I lied!" I yell. She doesn't turn around. "I do care. The squad will look like total douche bags if they perform that cheer."

She returns to the girls. I rest my chin in my hands.

"Are you ready to talk about our project now?"

"No," I say.

"Okay, good," Jake says exasperatedly. "So basically, Norton is fucked. Unity and disparity is . . . ridiculous. But I was thinking we should do one side really, really, really dark and the other side really, really, really light—"

"But how do you connect that? It has to connect in the middle."

"Right. Damn it." He groans and stares longingly at the game of basketball Chris & Co. are having on the court.

"Let's make it subtle," I say. "Maybe one side can be spring and the middle can be summer and the other side can be fall. . . ."

Jake nods eagerly. "I like that!"

"Oh, really? I thought you wouldn't. We can't do that. That's what Mindy Andrews and Cory Hall are doing. I overheard them."

He rolls his eyes and checks out the cheerleaders.

"Do you miss it?" he asks.

"No."

It's not true. I kind of miss cheerleading sometimes. The squad. Just for something to do, to distract myself with. I know they don't miss me. I was a nightmare captain and they had to be perfect. But I was like that about everything. My grades, my relationship with Chris, my friends. Everything perfect.

The bell rings.

"You didn't get to play," I say.

Jake sighs. "Yeah."

"You should try out for the team."

"Can't. My knee's all fucked up. I hurt it during the most important game of the season at my old school. Little games at lunch are about all I can stand. I miss it a lot." He sounds wistful. "I love basketball."

Great. Just more useless information I won't be able to forget.

seven

By Wednesday, word around the halls is Chris and Becky are a couple. By Thursday, it's confirmed. They've got the Public Displays of Affection thing down pat and I have to hand it to them, they look pretty happy for two people who have absolutely nothing to be happy about. He's with her because he can't be with me and she's got to suffer every kiss knowing that, and boy, does she know that.

By Thursday night, Bailey knows how to fetch Dad's slippers.

"Look at this!" Dad says, after he calls Mom and me into the living room. He's stretched out in his recliner and Bailey's sprawled out on the floor at his feet. Dad snaps his fingers. "Bailey!"

Bailey raises his head.

"Fetch, Bailey; fetch me my slippers, boy!"

It's terribly exciting. Bailey rises slowly, totters out of the room and totters back in with Dad's slippers in his mouth. Mom squeals a little and claps her hands.

This dog is mad talented.

"Good dog!" she gushes, patting Bailey on the head. He looks pretty satisfied with himself, for a dog. He nestles back into his spot at Dad's feet and Mom rushes into the kitchen to get him a treat.

"Good job, Bailey," I say.

But I'm not talking about the slippers.

The party starts at eight, but I show up early so Chris and I can have sex. Another year at St. Peter's is almost behind us and we've already slept together eight times. This will be the ninth and there's going to be a lot more sex in our future.

We go to his bedroom. The speakers are mounted against his window and he turns on some sweet sounding music really low and kisses me and I kiss him back and then, I don't know, I kind of seize up.

"What's wrong?" he asks. He's breathing heavy.

We separate and I wipe my mouth.

"What have you been eating?"

"What does it matter?"

"Were you eating something with garlic in it? I told you not to eat garlic before you kiss me anymore. It's gross."

He sighs. "What's wrong, Parker?"

"You know I hate garlic breath and you eat it anyway, that's what's wrong."

"That's not what I mean."

I untie my ponytail and retie it. I think every so often, Chris should have to work for sex by listening to me.

"Jessie thinks I'm coming down on the other girls too hard."

"We stopped making out for that?"

He leans in for another kiss and I push him away.

"Fuck off, Chris. I'm serious."

"You're always serious."

"You say that like it's a bad thing."

"It can be." He flops back on his bed. "You should loosen the fuck up every once in a while; the world wouldn't stop. No one would die."

He's such a bastard. I loosen up, sometimes. And even if I didn't, it's not like there's something wrong with being focused. Some people are focused.

That's what they do.

"She says I'm coming down on the girls too hard," I repeat.

"Is she right?" he asks. "I bet she's right."

"I may have let them know how much they suck lately." The memory of their total suckiness gets me pissed off about it all over again. "But I want us to be good, you know? Is that too much to ask? I work my ass off thinking up cheers and dance moves and if they can't get them right, what, I'm supposed to congratulate them for it?"

Chris stares.

"It's just cheerleading."

"Oh, really? And if I said that about one of your basketball games—"

"That's different." He sits up and wraps an arm around me. "I've seen you captain. You're anal. You're anal about everything, though."

"I like things a certain way."

"You're a perfectionist. You like them perfect. There's no margin for error or you go crazy."

"If I can do things right, I don't see why everyone else can't." I untie my ponytail again and do it back up. "She called me a Cheerleading Nazi in front of the entire squad. We got into a screaming match in front of everyone—"

"That's so cute," Chris says, laughing. I glare at him and he stops. "Look, you'll see her in a couple of hours when the party's in full swing. Get her after she's had a couple shots and she's mellow. You can make up, no biggie. You're best friends. That's what you're supposed to do."

He kisses my neck.

"God, you're tense," he murmurs. "Maybe you should quit the squad, take a break or something. You're, like, this close to the edge—"

"That's funny, Chris," I interrupt.

"I'm not kidding. Loosen the fuck up." He kisses me again and slides his hand up my shirt. "Forget it. We'll talk about it later—"

"No," I say. "We won't."

My hand is wet. I open my eyes, hold it out in front of me and stare. Wet. *Tap, tap, tap.* Rain against the window. It's raining out and my hand is wet.

I sit up in bed, groggy. Is there a leak?

A loud clap of thunder startles me and there's a whimper at the side of my bed. I turn on the light. Bailey. It's three in the morning and he's been cowering on the floor, licking my hand. The thunder sounds again and he cries.

"Bailey, you're not allowed in my room." I climb out of bed and grab him by the collar. "Come on. Out."

He resists. I give his collar a sharp tug and he whimpers, anticipating the next round of thunder, but he can anticipate it in Mom and Dad's room for all I care. I lead him down the hall. Their door is closed, of course.

I let go of his collar.

"Stay," I say firmly.

He stays. I head back to my room and crawl back into bed. The storm picks up. Every so often I hear Bailey whimpering and pawing at Mom and Dad's door and pretty soon I accept the fact I'm never getting to sleep again, so I get out of bed and find Bailey curled up in a terrified ball at the end of the hall. I slip my finger under his collar and we head downstairs to the living room.

A flash of lightning reveals Dad's armchair. I let Bailey go, grab an afghan and wrap myself in it. The dog sits beside me, frightened out of his mind. I reach out and run my hand over his head. I might scratch him behind the ears if I'm feeling particularly inspired. The thunder goes again and again and he shakes and cries.

"It's fine, Bailey," I say. "Don't be such a wimp. It's only a storm."

I wake up to Mom and Dad hovering over me. Bailey's asleep at my feet and—

Mom's holding the camera.

"You didn't," I say.

"That's one for the photo albums!" Dad winks at me. "You'd better hurry, Parker. You'll be late for school."

I hate my parents.

Chris and Becky enter homeroom joined at the hip and I make a gagging noise when they sit behind me, just because I can. Becky's still sore at me about cheerleading practice, so she calls me a bitch and excuses herself for the washrooms to confer about it with whatever minion she's got stationed there.

I turn to Chris as soon as she's gone.

"I've been thinking about the offer you made," I say. "About math."

He straightens. "Yeah?"

"I'm game if you are."

He looks around the room to make sure no one's overheard.

"Becky can't ever know," he says, an odd gravity to his voice.

"We'll see."

"*Parker.*"

"Becky can't ever know." I hold up my hand. Scout's Honor. "Got it."

He frowns. "Meet me in the guys' change room at lunch."

"That soon, huh?"

"Just in case you change your mind."

Becky comes back five minutes later and Chris wraps his arms around her and they start sucking face. I know he's trying to make a statement, but I have no idea what that statement is. Bradley breaks them up when the Pledge of Allegiance starts, and we all stand, hands to hearts, hands to hearts—hands always to our hearts.

"If I tell you something about me, will you tell me something about you?"

Jake and I are sitting close, trying to sketch out the landscape in pencil before we start working with paint. Norton advises us to plan everything down to the most painstakingly minute details. It should be days turning into *weeks* before we get to the actual painting, he says. I think he doesn't want us to finish anytime soon, lest he be forced to think up new ways to occupy a class full of eighteen-year-olds. Either that or this is one of his cruel tricks where he waits until we're good and relaxed and tells us, whoops, his mistake, the project is actually due tomorrow and still counts for half our grades. That's the kind of teacher Norton is.

"No."

I've been tracing the same rocks for the last thirty minutes.

"Come on," Jake says. "I'm going to make you tolerate me if it kills me. Or you. Preferably you. But we should get to know each other on some level or else it will be impossible to work on this together."

"I don't know; it's working okay so far. And besides, what about you could I possibly want to know?"

"Try me. I will hold nothing back."

I decide to shock him into silence.

"Which do you prefer: top or bottom?"

His mouth drops open a little and I go back to my rocks. Mission accomplished.

"Up," he says unexpectedly. "Against the wall."

I laugh, my pencil hovering above the paper. "Right."

"Top."

I glance at him. "Really?"

"With my last girlfriend," he says. "More often than not."

"Sure. She still in the picture, this last girlfriend?"

"Dumped me when I told her I was moving."

"Ouch."

"Eh." Jake shrugs and works on the base of a tree stump. "We were together too long. How long were you and Chris together?"

"Why would I tell you that?"

"Because we agreed—"

"No, we didn't."

His eyebrows come together as he replays the conversation in his head and realizes I'm right, but I decide to go ahead and share because what I've chosen to share might make him realize I'm not a person worth getting to know. Get him off my back.

"Actually, Chris and I were together since the ninth grade. We broke up after I stole about three hundred dollars from his savings account. Let that be a lesson to you, Jake: never give your high school sweetheart your PIN number, no matter how many times you've had sex or been Winter Ball King and Queen."

And that's not even the worst thing I've done. Jake studies me.

"Wow," he finally says. "Why'd you do that?"

"Gambling addiction," I say without missing a beat. "I spent all my money and some of his betting on horses and racked up a little debt. After a while Chris goes, 'Look, Parker, I'm not giving you any more money!' So I stole it from him."

"Actually, she ran away from home."

I plaster a bright smile on my face before turning around.

"Chris!" I say, all exaggerated cheer when I do. "And just how long have you been standing there?"

"Obviously long enough!" he says with a similarly exaggeratedly cheerful voice. He pushes past me, for Jake. "Anyway, Jake, I'm not going to be in the gym at lunch, so take center. Tell the guys I said you could. Aaron will want it, but I want to make Aaron cry like a little bitch for being such an asshole last Thursday."

Jake nods. "Center. Got it. Where will you be?"

"Nowhere special."

"Nowhere special" is a pretty apt description of the boys' changing room. Its rows of orange-painted lockers and square windows that filter weak rays of real light into the room—real light that's promptly swallowed by the fluorescent lights overhead.

And it smells bad.

Chris is sitting on the bench closest to the door when I sneak in. There's a binder resting beside him—math homework. At least it better be.

"What if someone comes in?" My voice echoes around the room.

Chris stands, drags the bench to the tiny alcove where the door is and wedges it in such a way that no one should be able to get in. There was definitely a time when he wouldn't have cared if anyone caught us in here—and we'd been caught a few times—but now he's with Becky and those days are dead.

"So." I clear my throat. "How many pages of math will this be worth?"

He nods to the bench. I sit. He sits beside me.

This is the skankiest thing I've ever done.

I try to ignore how it starts with his hands carefully coming up past my cheeks and around my neck until his fingers are in my hair. He doesn't kiss me then, but he brings his face close, forehead against mine, and breathes me in because he wants me to feel guilty, I think. I think maybe it's working.

I haven't thought about the money in a long time.

His lips get excruciatingly close to mine and he pauses.

"Do you even miss me?"

"No," I say.

He finally kisses me, presses his lips lightly against mine. I know what he's doing. He's teasing me and I won't have it. I make him *really* kiss me, full on the mouth, and force his lips apart with my own.

And then he stops.

"What about everything you felt about me? Where does that go?" He leans in again and stops before anything can happen. "I would've stuck it out. You wouldn't let me help you."

"I didn't need your help."

"Yes, you did. You do. Everyone got through it together but you. You're so perfect, you just couldn't handle it—"

"You're as bad as Jake," I say. "You talk too much. Shut up and forget it because it's not worth your homework for me to sit here and listen to you nitpick the past."

That kills it. After a second, he presses his binder into my hands.

"Take it," he says, before I can ask. "Have it back to me by tomorrow morning."

"Oh, come on. Afraid you won't respect yourself afterward?" I study him. His cheeks are pink. "I'm not going to tell Becky."

"I just wanted to kiss you again."

"Stop it."

"You could've said no," he says, standing. He pulls the bench out. "You know I'm not over you. You could've said no and done the homework yourself, but you didn't."

"You're right," I say. "You know what? You're absolutely right. Call it a momentary lapse of sanity."

He opens the door.

"Or maybe you just wanted to kiss me again, too."

I roll my eyes.

eight

Bailey's developed this weird attachment to me. He follows me from room to room, lays at my feet under the dinner table and stands guard in the living room for the two hours it takes me to copy Chris's math homework. My parents can't shut up about how *cute* it is, so three guesses for how I feel about it, and the first two don't count.

"Maybe you could take him for a walk, now that your foot is better."

Mom says it in a voice that tells me it's less of a suggestion and more of a command. I go along with it because I want out. I throw my coat on, attach Bailey to the leash—his tail wags back and forth excitedly—and escape.

"Hey, Parker!"

I've been walking a good forty minutes when I hear my name. Somehow I took a turn that landed me on Victoria Street, where the traffic is kind of heavy and I cross the paths of more people than I normally like to do. I cock my head to the side. Nothing. Maybe I didn't hear it after all. I keep walking.

"Parker!"

Damn. I turn in the direction of the voice and spot Jake emerging from the video store, holding a plastic DVD case in his hand. He jogs over.

"Didn't figure I'd see you before tomorrow," he says.

"That makes two of us."

"Who's this?"

Jake crouches down and gives Bailey a vigorous head petting. He scratches Bailey behind his ears, under his chin, the works.

"This is Bailey. Bailey, this is Jake Gardner."

"Hi, Bailey," Jake says, patting his nose. Bailey loves the attention. His eyes half close and his tongue hangs out, but his tongue always does that. I realize it's been thirty seconds and I haven't said anything mean to Jake.

Jake smiles at me. "I think Bailey likes me."

"Bailey doesn't have very discriminating taste," I warn him. "He adored his last owner and his last owner used to beat him, so it doesn't really say much about you."

Still got it.

Jake gives Bailey one last pat on the head and stands.

"So why did you run away from home?"

"How many minutes a day do you spend thinking about me?" I ask. "Like, do you have anything else to live for?"

"It's your own fault," he replies. "The less you want me to know about you, the more I want to find out. Especially if it bothers you."

"Nice. What gives you the right?"

"You kind of set the precedent when we met, didn't you?"

"Bailey, attack!"

I give his leash a sharp tug. He only stares at us happily.

Jake laughs. "So cute."

"Yeah, well, I don't know about you, but I'm walking now."

"Wow, that's practically an invitation coming from you."

So we walk.

"Got any more ideas for our project?" he asks.

"I'm supposed to be thinking of ideas?" I ask back. "I wonder if Norton knows how dumb this assignment is. Do you think he does? Think he's just fucking with us?"

"I don't know, maybe. So why did you run away from home?"

"Okay, Jake?" I stop; he stops. "I'm going to tell you something and I want you to listen carefully and then every time you want to ask me a personal question, you can just refer back to this answer. Are you ready?"

He nods and his hair falls into his eyes. He brushes it away.

"I'm really fucked up," I tell him. "And I don't like people."

"Got it," he says. "But why?"

"It doesn't matter why. I don't give the people I *know* valuable insight into my psyche. You're the new kid. You have no chance."

"I'm going try to have a conversation with you anyway. Are you ready?"

I think if I roll my eyes any more this year, they might get stuck in my head, so I refrain. But not rolling my eyes leaves me with an anxious feeling, so I hand Jake Bailey's leash and start snapping my fingers.

"So, Parker," he begins. "How are you?"

"Oh my God." I give in to the eye roll. "I'm fine, Jake. How are you?"

"I'm good. Getting used to St. Peter's and stuff."

"Why bother? You'll just be leaving soon anyway."

"I believe in making the most of my time," he says. We head farther down the street. "It hasn't been easy. I used to go to a public school and now I'm stuck in your stupid uniforms. And the praying drives me crazy."

"You and everyone else." I stop snapping my fingers and cross my arms. It's chilly out. "Do you know how much harder it is to become popular when you have to wear a uniform? You can't rely on being fashionable to help you climb the social ladder. Becky and Jessie and I had a hell of a time working our way up in those uniforms."

"Tragedy," Jake says.

"Definitely," I agree. "Were you popular at your old school?"

"Would you like me less depending on my answer?"

"Jake, I don't think I could like you any less," I assure him. "Besides, I know you were. Popular people give off pheromones only other popular people can pick up on. Chris really took a liking to you, so I put two and two together."

"My best friend was the most popular guy in my old school," Jake admits. "His name was Adam Jenkins."

I don't say anything.

"I didn't necessarily want it," he adds, like that'll make me think more of him. "Why did you want to be popular?"

"Who says I wanted to be popular?"

"Please. You just said you worked your way to the top. Why?"

"Why does it matter?"

"I'm curious."

"You should really do something about that." I take Bailey's leash back. "I thought it would be easier."

Jake nods like he understands, but popularity is always different for guys—way less maintenance involved. It really is easier for them. And besides, I'm totally lying anyway. I didn't want to be popular because it was easier; I wanted to be popular because in high school that's the best thing you can be: perfect. Everything else is shit.

We keep walking and I wish he'd leave. Being on this street feels wrong. All these people, the cars flying back and forth—it's like a scene out of a movie and I belong to it with Jake and the dog. It probably looks perfect to someone watching from the outside, but it really freaks me out, so I keep glancing up and down the street, hoping for an opportunity to ditch him. And that's when I spot this familiar face outside Al's Convenience Store and everything stops. Like time. Everything.

He looks terrible, gaunt. A male anorexic. Even from across the road, I can see the hollows of his cheekbones, and he's slouched over and pale and his hair's longer than he'd ever let it grow last year, like really long, like hanging in-his-eyes long, and I don't understand why he's back. Why is he back and how soon before he leaves again?

"What are you staring at?" Jake asks, following my gaze.

"Becky."

I grab her by the arm and pull her away from her group of parasite-girls, the ones that live to bask in her reflected popularity because they haven't got a hope in hell of being popular themselves. It's funny because that's who Becky used to be.

"What the fuck, Parker?" She wrenches her arm from my grip and takes one look at my face. "This better not be about Chris or that stupid cheer, I'm warning you. You'll be thrilled to know we're not doing it—"

"Becky, shut up. Is Evan back?"

"Evan?"

"Yeah. Is he back?"

She stares at me.

"Goddammit, Becky, did you forget to turn your brain on today?"

"Don't talk to me like that!" At least she knows when she's being insulted. Chris sidles up and snakes his arm around her waist. "I don't know if he's back or not."

She's so useless. I press Chris's math binder into his free hand.

"Thanks," I tell him. "Hey, do you know if Evan's back or not?"

courtney summers

"What was that?" Becky asks Chris. "Why did Parker have your binder?"

"It's just math homework, Becky," he says vaguely. "Is who back?"

"Ev-an," I say slowly, and Chris gets this surprised look on his face—his eyebrow goes up and everything. He didn't know.

"*Evan?* Haven't seen him. Have you seen him?"

The lightbulb goes on over Becky's head.

"You let her copy your math homework?!"

She totally screeches it. I've always had the worst urge to tell her about how we used to make fun of her at the squad sleepovers she couldn't make. We'd up our voices nine octaves and say the most inanely stupid things because that's Becky for you. She was the most expendable member of the squad and now she's, like, Parker Lite.

She owes her magical senior year to me and she knows it.

"We're not supposed to be enabling Parker like this!" Becky says. What an ingrate. "That's what Grey and Henley called it—enabling! She uses you and you get nothing in return—"

"Oh, he got something," I assure her.

"Parker, shut up—" Chris turns bright red and since he's one of those people who like to make sure they do everything to the best of their abilities, especially the stupid stuff, he blows it: "You weren't supposed to say anything!"

Becky does a quadruple take and figures out what that means to the best of *her* abilities. She's probably decided we've had sex. Close enough.

"Fuck both of you," she spits, and storms off.

Jeez. Chris closes his eyes and brings a hand to his temple.

"So anyway," I say, "I was just walking down Victoria Street yesterday and I think I saw Evan outside of the—"

"Shut up, Parker," Chris says, strained. "Just shut up."

He chases after Becky.

We come downstairs looking like two people who've spent the last thirty minutes having sex. Chris insists on it because the basketball team has to know he's getting laid, so his hair is sticking up all over the place and the buttons on my shirt are strategically undone. Like any of the wasters on the team will notice, never mind the fact it's going to be the first thing he tells them.

The house is filling up with people from school. I spot a few girls from the squad, but they won't look at me because of what happened at practice earlier.

Chris grabs some of his buddies and gets to work on the tunes. In the minutes before the sounds of the latest popular white rapper start playing, I wind my way through the house and spot Evan in the kitchen, already working on some shots with Jenny Morse, who is not his girlfriend. This wouldn't matter if they were just doing shots, but after he passes a slice of lime to her they start kissing.

I clear my throat and they part fast.

"Parker," Evan says nervously. He runs a hand over his prickly black hair and holds out a bottle of vodka and a shot glass. "Uh— shot?"

"All students will proceed to the auditorium for a special assembly." Henley's voice crackles over the PA. "All students to the auditorium for a special assembly."

"Hi," Jake says, sitting beside me. For a second, I'm reminded of Bailey. "This is about the missing girl, isn't it?"

"What was your first clue, the mounted picture onstage?"

We are, in fact, skipping art for an assembly about the missing girl. There's a mounted picture of her onstage next to the podium, which is waiting for Henley. Rows of hard plastic chairs have been halfheartedly arranged in the center of the room and I've chosen a seat near the back and Jake has chosen the seat next to it.

This is the second assembly we've had for Jessica Wellington

since she disappeared. First we pray to Jesus and ask him for her
safe return, next Henley says a bunch of nothing platitudes, then
Jessica's friends take the mic and share their favorite memories of
her and then we pray again and then we're dismissed. Student
Council hands out white ribbons in Jessica's honor at the door, so
we never forget.

I look around the room. The auditorium is filling quickly.
Everyone's talking in quiet voices on their way to their seats.
Something about it makes me feel queasy.

Too many people.

"Chris is really pissed at you," Jake says. "He won't say why.
What'd you do?"

"Nothing."

I inhale. How can the auditorium be only half full and have all
the air gone from it like that? I'm not getting any air. As students
continue to mill into the auditorium, it gets smaller and smaller
and my heart beats this insane rhythm in my chest. I rub my
palms on my skirt. They're sweaty. I really can't breathe. No, I can.

I just think I can't.

Everyone's in. The teachers line up on either side of the walls,
ready to shush us should the need arise. The lights overhead dim,
but the stage remains bathed in an eerie golden glow. I take a few
short breaths in and bring my hand to my chest because I'm afraid
my heart is going to pop out of it. The tips of my fingers are tingling.

I close my eyes.

"Are you okay?"

I ignore Jake and exhale. Breathe in. Breathe out. That's how
you take care of these things, isn't it? In. Out. Again. Slowly. I've
read it. Deep breaths. But what do you do when there's no air?
When you're sucking in everyone else's stale breaths?

What if I really *can't* breathe?

"Wait, this is a test, isn't it? And if I ask if you're okay, it's because I have a thing for girls who are all vulnerable because they make me feel like a macho man, right?"

I stand up so fast the back of my chair flies into the knees of the person behind me. They throw whispered insults my way and Jake stares at me, surprised. Henley strides across the stage and I stumble past Jake and down the row of teachers, some mangled explanation about having to go to the bathroom falling off my lips. And then I finally, *finally* burst through the doors to the hall and when I take that first breath in all I can think is *air* because I'm dying for it, gasping for it, and I can't stop.

Henley's voice floats into the hall.

"I've called this assembly today to pray for Jessica Wellington's safe return home. As more time passes, I know—as you all know—the outcome seems grim. But there is something else I know: If we put our hands together and appeal to God, we have a chance. *She* has a chance."

I end up on the floor, resting my head on my knees and trying to block out Henley's voice while I wait out my spastic heartbeat.

I focus on taking even breaths in and out.

"Wow. You're actually not okay."

"Would you quit stalking me? It's creepy."

I force myself up and brush off my skirt. In. Out. In. Out. My heart is starting to feel more normal, which means it's going away. Good.

"Sit down if you need to," Jake says. "I won't hold it against you. And I'm not stalking you. Grey told me to see if you were all right. It wasn't one of the most subtle exits ever."

"I'm fine," I mutter. "It's like some kind of claustrophobia. When I'm in a room with a bunch of stupid people like you, I get a little overwhelmed—"

"How were you *ever* popular?"

"I don't know."

"Do you want me to get Ms. Grey or a teacher or something?" he asks, awkward. "Or walk you to the nurse's? What do you usually do when you have a panic attack?"

"That's not what it was," I say quickly, but he's skeptical. "Just forget it. I'm going to skip out on the assembly. Tell Grey I have really bad cramps, okay?"

Jake makes a face. "Gross! I'm not telling her about your feminine problems—"

"Don't be such a sissy!" I snap. "Just do it and your chances of getting into my pants increase tenfold."

I turn my back to him and start down the hall.

"Hey, wait! It'll be lunch soon! Am I gonna see you in the gym?"

I think of Becky and Chris glaring at me from opposite ends of the court and I don't have the energy to deal with that right now.

"No."

Later that night I find myself at Chris's again, except this time, on my way to the woods, I somehow manage to knock the top off this cement bird fountain and the sound it makes when it hits the driveway is awful. I dart out onto the street and I never look back, but I swear I hear Mr. Ellory open the front door and shout, "Who's there?"

nine

Chris and Becky are still furious with me. They won't look at or speak to me and, I won't lie, I feel pretty accomplished about it. Somebody give me a gold star.

Word around the halls is they're not totally broken up yet, just on a break. And I suspect word around the halls is I had something to do with it, because nothing else explains the dirty looks I'm getting from the cheerleading squad and the basketball team.

I guess that means I've almost arrived.

"So I was looking at the Honor Roll plaques," Jake is saying. Art again. He's making amazing progress on our landscape, and wouldn't you know it, he's actually kind of gifted at this drawing thing. I'm still tracing the same rocks. "And you know what name kept showing up? At least for the last three years?"

"Hmm." I pretend to think about it. "Parker Fadley?"

"Not only that, you were on the Honor Roll *with distinction*. What does that mean? I've never been on the Honor Roll before."

"It means I was better than perfect."

"And modest. Must've worked pretty hard to get there, huh?"

"I worked my ass off."

He nods and goes back to filling in the ravine with his pencil. A couple of minutes pass and I wonder what he's getting at.

"That's it?" I ask. "Aren't you going to ask me what happened or how I went from top to bottom in such a devastatingly short amount of time?"

"Were you really making out with Chris in the change room? And that's why he and Becky are on a break?"

"Maybe," I say. "Hey, that wouldn't be why Chris isn't in art today, would it? He's not off somewhere crying about it, is he?"

Before Jake can answer, a burst of static and white noise fills the room. Everyone quiets and the secretary's voice explodes over the PA.

"Mr. Norton, would you please send Parker Fadley down to the guidance office?"

"You heard that, Fadley," Norton says. He gives me this look like I've done something wrong, but that's okay, since it *is* the only reason I ever get called down to the office anymore. "Get down there."

I grab my books and make my way out of the room, Jake's eyes on me as I go.

"It's not Friday—"

I stop talking as soon as I enter the office. This is unexpected: Grey and Henley are sharing space behind Grey's desk and both of them look superformidable.

But even more unexpected than that is Chris.

He's sitting in a chair in the corner looking so guilty I know I'll have to kill him when this is over.

I force a winning smile at all three of them.

"What's the occasion?" I ask.

"Sit down, Parker."

Henley and Grey say it in unison, but judging by the looks on their faces, they don't mean to. I shoot myself in the foot and laugh. They both frown at me and I sit. Chris stares at his shoes. I

ignore the knot in my stomach. I'm a great improviser, but I generally prefer having an idea of what I'm getting into.

Grey starts us off: "Parker, do you have any idea why you're
here?"

It comes to me like that: the math homework.

"No, ma'am." Pause. "Ma'ams."

Henley stands. She never wastes time, ever. She may have told
my parents she was wholly committed to getting me back on the
right track, but she has a school to run. I can trick Grey into chasing her tail, but Henley I can't trick into doing anything.

"Mr. Ellory has informed us you copied his last unit's worth of
math homework—homework you were supposed to have com-
pleted on your own." She rests her hands on the desk and leans
forward, nearly elbowing Grey in the face. I have the sense not
to laugh this time. "Homework Mrs. Jones was generous enough
to grant you an extension on to complete. *On your own.* What do
you have to say for yourself, Fadley?"

I concentrate on not blinking. I hear that's a sign of weakness.

"Well, what's Chris's punishment?"

His head snaps up. "*My* punishment?"

"I just did what everyone expected me to do," I tell him.
"You're the one who's not supposed to enable me."

He starts spluttering.

"Now, just a minute here," Grey breaks in with that watery
voice of hers. "What Parker means is—"

"Enough." Henley's voice is as hard as her face. "Fadley's right,
Ellory. You're not supposed to be enabling her and I speak for Ms.
Grey and myself when I say we're disappointed in you. However,
given the nature of your relationship with Fadley and her pen-
chant for manipulating people, the fault does not entirely rest
with you."

Chris exhales. That's when Henley focuses on me.

"Parker, everyone in this room is on your side. You're a smart girl; you know that. Did you really think you'd get away with this?"

I can't believe someone as smart as Henley would be stupid enough to ask that question.

"Obviously, I did," I say.

"Don't get smart with me—"

"But I am smart; you just said it yourself." I'd better quit while I'm ahead. "Look, I wouldn't have done it if Chris hadn't offered. It's all his fault for giving me the option."

Chris sits up. "If I hadn't, you would've found someone else—"

"Oh, really? Like who, Chris? I find it pretty fucking amazing—"

"*Language,* Fadley!"

"That you're sitting here acting like a victim of my calculating mind considering what I had to do to *get* that math homework—"

"She came to school hungover!" Chris blurts out before I can tell everyone he used his homework to get my goods. This is so great.

Grey and Henley stare at me.

"When was this?" Henley asks.

"He *thinks* I came to school hungover," I say.

I will kill him.

Grey looks all disappointed. "Oh, Parker. Did you?"

"He *thinks* I came to school hungover," I repeat. "And besides, what I do in the privacy of my home is my business. You can't penalize me or take away my diploma for anything I do on my own time, in my own house, outside of—"

"But if you're caught drinking at school again, you *will* be expelled and you won't graduate. You know that," Henley says sharply.

Yes, yes, yes. I know that. I know that. *I know that.* I bite my cheek and nod, my chest tightening. I want to snap my fingers, but I won't do that in front of them.

I won't.

"Which brings us back to the issue at hand. copying Chris's math homework." Like I said, Henley doesn't waste time. She paces in the narrow space behind Grey's desk. "I only have one question, Parker. Why?"

"Well, it's not like I didn't try to get caught up."

It's not a total lie. There were a few nights where I stared at the homework and considered doing it. That should count for something.

"It's like every day I get further behind, no matter how hard I try to catch up, and it's all I can think about because I actually *do* want to graduate, but when I sat down and tried to do that stupid math unit it seemed so impossible, it made me want to kill myself."

It figures the last thing I should say is the first thing out of my mouth. The room gets so quiet I can hear the faint sounds of the chemistry teacher shouting formulas all the way down the hall through two closed doors. Henley stops pacing and glances at Grey, and Chris looks like I've slapped him across the face.

"Ellory," Henley says. "You're excused."

He forces himself out of the chair and looks all sad because of what I've said. I'd feel bad about it, but it's technically his fault I said it in the first place. As soon as he's gone, I put on my best *sorry* face, because this has the potential to get way out of hand.

"I didn't mean that," I say. "You don't need to call my parents."

"We have to call your parents now," Grey says.

"You said anything I say in this room is totally confidential, so we can trust each other! Don't you want me to trust you?"

"You'll never trust me, Parker."

I guess Grey's not as stupid as I thought or she looks.

But I can't let her do this.

"You *can't* tell my parents."

"*Enough,*" Henley says again. The bell rings. "Ms. Grey, call her parents; arrange a meeting. In the meantime, I'll be discussing what to do about this math situation with Mrs. Jones. Go eat lunch, Parker. You're excused."

Chris is waiting for me at the end of the hall when I come out. I maneuver my way around students on their way to the caf to get to him.

"I can't believe you told them even after I made myself *kiss* you!"

"I can't believe you said you wanted to *kill* yourself!"

"I wouldn't have said it if you hadn't *told!*"

"I *didn't* tell!" Chris yells. People stare at us. He grabs me by the elbow, drags me down the hall and pulls me into an empty classroom. As soon as the door is shut, he turns to me. "Becky told."

I cross my arms and wait. He looks nervous.

"Because she was mad at you, because of what we did—"

"How come she wasn't in the office with us?"

He shifts.

"*Chris.*"

I have perfected the way to say his name when I want information he doesn't want to give. I hit exactly the right tone, frequency, whatever, and it never fails: he caves.

"She told Henley and Grey she was afraid of you because you're so . . . volatile, and then she cried until they let her go. But you can't blame them for believing her and—hey! Where are you going?"

I hate her. I hate her. *I hate her.*

My feet walk me to the gym at top speed while a terrified Chris follows ten paces behind and I keep thinking about my parents. *My parents.* I don't even want to guess what I'll have to sit through when I get home.

I am going to *end* Becky Halprin.

3

I push through the gym doors so hard they *whack* against the wall. The basketball players—Jake among them—stop playing and the cheerleaders' heads snap up from their carrot sticks and water.

"Becky!"

I storm across the court. Becky drops her carrot stick and stands, all white-faced and wide-eyed. She smooths her skirt and moves to meet me halfway. When I'm close enough and she's close enough, I reach out and shove her.

Hard.

"Holy shit," one of the basketball players says behind me.

The other members of the squad flank Becky instantly, but it doesn't matter. I only needed to shove her once, put the fear of God into her, that sort of thing.

And like I'd rob myself of the opportunity.

"Parker, don't," Chris says. I ignore him.

"I just realized it must really suck to be you," I say. "And it's all my fault."

She raises her chin defiantly. "What are you talking about?"

"I was a better cheerleader; I was a better cheerleading captain; I was a better student; Jessie liked me better; Chris liked me better; hell, Chris *likes* me better. How must that feel? How does it feel to know that even at my worst, you're still not enough?"

"Fuck you." She turns this hideous shade of red and her hands start shaking because the truth hurts. "Parker, I could make your life seriously miserable from where I'm standing."

"Becky, you're only standing there because I decided I didn't want to."

"Holy *shit*," the same basketball player repeats behind me. *I clear my throat.*

"Parker," Evan says nervously. He runs a hand over his prickly black hair and holds out a bottle of vodka and a shot glass. "Uh—shot?"

Jenny Morse flees from the room. I take the bottle and the glass.

"Wow," I say. "This is so interesting."

I move to the kitchen counter, pour my first shot and knock it back. It burns going down and I have to make a concentrated effort not to choke. Chris says it's pathetic that after three years of high school I haven't mastered the taste of alcohol.

Chris says I should loosen up.

"You and Jessie made it up yet? Because she feels terrible about what happened at practice and she wants to make it up with you."

The words tumble out of Evan's mouth and I can't tell if he's lying. I pour my second shot, which is really stupid because it's not even dark out yet and it's the kind of thing I wouldn't let Chris get away with.

Evan watches. Hesitates.

"You're not going to tell her, are you?"

I shrug. He takes the vodka from me and pours himself a shot. Knocks it back. Then another. And another.

"I can't believe you," I say, reclaiming the bottle. I don't even bother to pour a shot this time, just drink it straight. It's gross, but Chris says I should loosen the fuck up. "I thought you loved her."

"Oh my God, I do," he says desperately. "Seriously, look, Jenny doesn't mean anything to me; she's just—"

"She's just a lay, right?" He doesn't say anything. "I knew it. I totally knew it. I had a feeling and I was right. I'm always right."

He's sweating now. "You're not going to tell her, are you?"

"I haven't decided yet."

I leave him there. When I step into the foyer more and more people are arriving and Chris has the music going proper, really loud. It's in my feet, up my legs, in my lungs, my heart.

The party has begun.

"Do you want to go to the mall with me?"

Jake glances over his shoulder. "Are you talking to me?"

He's such a dork.

"Yes, Jake, I'm talking to you."

"Me? Go to the mall with you?" He frowns. "Why?"

I don't have the patience for this.

"Because it's fun! I don't know, why do people go to the mall? I just thought since I was going to the mall after school and you're practically stalking me all the time, you'd probably wonder why I didn't get on the bus and spend all night obsessing over it, and I don't want to be responsible if *you* don't get a good night's sleep."

"You're having a rough day, aren't you?" he asks. "Everyone's talking about what happened at lunch."

I inhale slowly through my teeth.

"Look, do you want to go to the mall with me after school or not?"

"Uh, yeah!" Finally. He forces a smile. "Sure."

"Meet me outside after the bell."

There.

I've decided to kill as many hours as I can at the mall because I don't want to go home and face my devastated parents right away and I know the phone call from Grey will devastate them. Maybe they'll send me to an actual therapist or something; I don't know. I just don't want to go home until I absolutely have to, even if it does make everything worse, and I figure toying with Jake will be a good distraction from that eventuality, because I need that, too. A distraction.

"So why'd you ask me to come with you?"

The outside light and fresh air is immediately swallowed behind us as we step through the doors of the Corby Shopping Center. It's crowded, but I can stand being around this many people. It's not like school, where everyone knows me.

"Why not ask you?" I shrug. "Where do you want to go first?"

"I don't know. This is my first time at your local mall. Give me the grand tour."

"Well, we simply must start with the food court. Does international cuisine interest you? The first slice of pizza is on me."

"Just a sec." Jake reaches out and feels my forehead. "Temperature's normal. Invasion of the body snatchers, maybe? Have you been possessed? Remember, like, two days ago when you told me I didn't have a chance with you?"

I brush his hand away. "First slice of pizza is on you."

We don't have pizza, we have Chinese food and Coke on Jake at my insistence, but I think he's the type of guy who would pay anyway. The food court is really packed, so we have to eat at the fountain. We sit on the edge of the pale pink tiles while water gushes out of the mouth of the large metal fish behind us. Loose change scattered over the bottom of the fountain catches the weak light overhead and glints at us. Annoying elevator Muzak is piped in from God knows where, but hey, it's a mall.

We're quiet at first and then I start thinking about my parents again, which I don't want to do, so I try for a conversation. A nice one.

"Tell me about you," I say.

Jake takes a sip of his Coke and stares at the shoppers passing by.

"What do you want to know?"

"Anything. Tell me about your family and life at your old school and—I don't know—what's the worst thing you've ever done?"

He laughs at that last bit.

"Uh, my dad is Earl, my stepmom is Wanda and my stepsister is Carrie. Carrie's in her first year of college, so she's not around." He thinks about it. "My dad works in tech support and Wanda does voice-overs for commercials. Pretty neat, huh? She's good, too. My mom's a zoologist. She lives way on the other side of the country."

"How come you don't live with her?"

He shrugs. "I had to choose. I don't have a problem with my mom; I just have more in common with my dad. No big deal."

That probably means it's a big deal.

I take a bite of a chicken ball. It tastes like paste.

"So what's the worst thing you've ever done?"

"I don't know."

"That must mean you're a good person."

"Define 'worst.' Are we talking academically, socially? I cheated on every single history test I had in the ninth grade. Socially—being popular is pretty bad, isn't it?" He cracks a smile. "I let my friends get away with things I couldn't live with if I'd been the one that did them. Or maybe I shouldn't be able to live with the fact I let them get away with that stuff, who knows?"

"What kind of things?"

"I don't know. What's with this question, anyway? What's the worst thing *you've* ever done? That's why you asked me, isn't it? So I'd ask you. I'm getting a handle on you, Parker."

"Why do you like me? I know you like me or you wouldn't put up with me or bother me as much as you do."

That shuts him up. But not for long.

"If I knew exactly why, I'm pretty sure I'd talk myself out of it." He clears his throat and looks away. "I don't know if you know this, but you're not the most personable . . . person."

"And you like me."

"Is this going to end with you telling me I'm never getting into your pants?"

"Even after what you saw in the gym today?"

He forces himself to look at me and he's totally embarrassed. I can tell this is really hard for him and I feel sorry for him because it's really complicated and stupid when you can't even figure out why you like a person—especially a person like me—but everything inside you is telling you that you do. It's not like I ever gave him a reason.

I just wouldn't want to be him right now.

"Maybe you like trying to figure me out," I suggest. "So maybe I should tell you what my deal is. Get it out of your system."

"Maybe I like trying to figure you out because I like you against my better judgment." He pauses. "Or maybe if I figured you out, I'd like you more."

"I don't think so."

We stare at each other. I sense the kiss coming before he actually leans in, and because I'm anticipating it, I get all anxious and I start pulling at the tips of my fingers because I don't know what else to do. His face gets closer and closer and then I lose grip of my index finger and my elbow rams into his Coke and spills all over the floor. The kiss never happens. I scramble for napkins and sop up the golden-brown liquid even though a janitor will clean it up.

"Were you raped?"

I stare at him. "*What?* Is that some kind of come-on?"

He's *really* uncomfortable now. "I've been trying to figure out why you're as fucked up as you claim you are. Is that what it is?"

"No." I bend down and grab the empty cup. "No, I wasn't raped."

The city bus drops me off two blocks from home. It's dark and cold out and I make it a slow walk, even though I'm tired and want to sleep. When I pass Chris's house, I notice a small sign on the lawn that wasn't there before. It's planted in front of the walk and has an air of authority despite its size. I crouch down and read it.

PROTECTED BY LETHAM'S HOME
SURVELLIANCE AND ALARM SYSTEMS

I feel like I'm going to throw up. I can't see the cameras from here or the little strips of laser light that sound the alarm as soon as you trip over them, but I know they're there and just like that, I can't go into the woods anymore

I force myself up. Close my eyes. Open them. I'm outside my house, at my front door, and I'm trying to figure out how to open it because this is the moment I've been dreading and my fingers aren't working right.

After a second I get it.

I'm not inside two seconds when Bailey runs at me, barking happily. I pat him on the head. The dog who's decided to love me no matter what I do.

"Where have you been?"

Mom and Dad pussyfoot into the hall from the kitchen. I know they want to look scary and parental, but they just look pale and scared. And devastated.

"Where have you *been*?" Mom repeats. "Your guidance counselor called us this afternoon and told us you were talking about *killing* yourself?"

"Now, Lara," Dad says quickly. "She did say she didn't think Parker meant it—"

"It doesn't matter—*you don't go around making jokes like that!*"

She loses it for a second. Her face crumples and she cries and Dad wraps an arm around her. Bailey paws at the carpet nervously.

"Now, Lara, calm down—"

"Where *were* you?" She sniffles. "You know you have a curfew and you break it on the same day you're making *suicide* threats? Do you know what went through our heads when we got that call? We got you a dog, we thought you were doing better, you were doing your homework and now you want to *kill* yourself?"

They stare at me, waiting for an answer.

"I was at the mall," I say. "And now I'm going to bed."

"Jim," Mom says.

Dad steps in front of the stairs, blocking my path.

"Now just a minute, Parker. We're not finished here. What were you *thinking*, talking like that? Is this something we should worry about? I mean—" He squints, like he doesn't know who he's talking to. "If it's going to be like this, maybe we haven't been doing enough. Maybe we should get some *real* help here—"

"No!" Bailey scampers to the living room for safety. I count to three. "I'm doing my best, but you just need to back off a little, that's all. Everyone does. Just leave me alone, okay? That's what I want."

Mom reaches into her pocket for a Kleenex and blows her nose.

"And then what? You do whatever you feel like? No curfew? You run off to another motel two hundred miles away and end up in the hospital again—"

I really don't want to hear it, but she won't shut up, so I force my way around Dad, head to my room and slam the door as hard as I can. After a minute, I open it and call for Bailey. He comes barreling up the stairs and down the hall and I sit on the bed and pet him. As tired as I am, I'm too wired to sleep now because all I can think about is that chintzy seventies-style wallpaper at that motel, the last thing I saw before I closed my eyes, and when I opened them again the walls were white. Hospital white.

Because I had my chance and I blew it.

ten

On Thursday, I sit through a meeting with Henley, Grey and my parents.

A few things are decided.

Instead of having to suffer through an entire math unit, I'll sit for a special test and we'll consider me all caught up and isn't that *great*?

Friday meetings with Grey are still on.

Henley shares Chris's concerns that I might have come to school hungover that one time, and I don't confirm or deny it.

I don't say anything at all, actually.

Mom and Dad fall all over themselves apologizing for the trouble I cause.

The school is too good to me, they say.

I don't think they realize how it sounds.

Friday, after history and before art, I find my name on the Honor Roll plaques hanging in the entrance corridor. Right at the top. Three years running, with distinction.

My parents used to love to tell everyone the story about the time I was in kindergarten and the whole class was coloring these pictures of flowers and every time I went outside the lines I demanded a new picture to work with. I was going to do it *right* even if it killed me. Fifteen attempts later, I had the best-colored picture of everyone. I still remember being hurt when the teacher made as big a fuss over my classmates' lesser efforts as she did over mine, which was perfect. Or maybe not as perfect as I thought.

Talk about your self-fulfilling prophecies.

"Parker? Is that you?"

The air leaves my lungs. This horrible feeling settles in the pit of my stomach and I decide I'm in school, but I am dreaming this. And then I turn really, really slowly and everyone else in the hall disappears. I'm not dreaming it.

Evan.

He stands before me, still as pale and anorexic as he was the day I saw him, but at least he didn't know I was there then, and now he's here in front of me and I can't speak. He pulls me into a hug and I feel his bones poking through his shirt and I think I'm going to be sick and—*God, let me go.*

He lets me go.

"Oh my God, Parker, it's so good to see you." He brushes a few strands of ratty black hair from his face. "How are you? Chris called me a couple times and he told me—I mean, are you still hanging in there and everything?"

I try to swallow, but my throat is totally closed and my mouth is unbelievably dry. I can't believe how long his hair is now or how awful he looks this close up.

My palms start sweating.

"Holy *fuck*!" a voice cries behind me. "*Evan?* Is that *you?*"

Chris and Becky hurry down the hall toward us and I think that means their "break" is over, but that's hardly surprising. Becky would never give up the most popular guy in school that easily. Her face darkens when she spots me, but she forces a smile and lets Chris drag her over by the hand.

"Oh my God—how've you *been*?"

Evan laughs and Chris gives him one of those jock hugs, one of those violent squeezes that end in a brain-rattling pat on the back. I expect Evan to break. He doesn't.

"I can't believe this! Parker said she thought she saw you the other day! How long are you here for? Is it temporary? Are you going back to your aunt's or—and what the fuck happened to your *hair*?"

"Grew it out, man," Evan says, laughing self-consciously. Becky bounces up and throws her arms around him. They hug for a long time and I can see him breathing her in. I try to breathe in, but I can't. "God, Becks. Wow. You look great."

"So do you, Evan."

I can tell she doesn't mean it. And I know what she's thinking. She can't believe this is the guy she used to throw herself at all the time and he was always fending her off. Chris makes a few more exclamations of disbelief.

"So are you back?" Becky asks.

Evan shifts from foot to foot and smiles tentatively.

Oh no.

"Uhm, maybe. I mean, yeah. I had the time away that I needed and I've got an appointment with Henley and we're going to talk about me finishing out the year here. If I get the good-to-go, I'm coming back."

Chris whoops and claps his hands together and my head feels like it's going to burst and I can't breathe, so I just walk away from them and head to art. I'm the first person in the room. Norton isn't even here. I sit down at my usual spot, gasping. Get a grip, Parker. Just forget it. In. Out. The bell rings. Students start filing in. I bolt from my seat and wander over to the supply closet and pretend I'm looking for something. If I can do this to myself, I can make myself stop. It should be easy. Stop.

I'm coming back.

"This is humiliating."

"Trust me, this is hardly humiliating," the school nurse—Mr. Grant—says, as he takes my blood pressure. "And I can tell you about humiliating. You wouldn't believe some of the things I've seen here. This hardly registers."

"It was pretty funny, though," Jake says from his spot by the door. "Never pegged you for the swooning type."

"Fuck off. Why are you still here, anyway?"

"Hey now, enough of that." Grant gives me a hard look. "Okay, Parker, question time: did you eat breakfast today?"

I sigh. "Yes."

"But isn't crabbiness a sign of low blood sugar?" Jake asks. "No, I know what it is! It's okay, Parker; don't be ashamed. You're not the first victim of my dashing good looks. Girls take one look at my sexy face and it overloads their circuit boards. Should you write that down, Mr. Grant? She was looking at me when it happened."

Grant ignores him. "That time of month?"

"Agh!" Jake covers his ears.

I roll my eyes. "No."

Grant asks a slew of personal questions while Jake's ears are still covered, so that kind of works out. When Grant's finished, he fixes me up a Dixie cup full of water.

"So it's just one of those things," he says. Jake uncovers his ears. I nod and the lunch bell goes. "I want you to stay here until lunch is over and we'll see how you feel then." He turns to Jake. "Can you stay with her?"

I shake my head while Jake nods his head.

"I can do that," he says.

"Good. I'll be back shortly. I have to inform Mrs. Henley of this, Parker. They keep pretty good tabs on you, you know."

I stare into the Dixie cup. "Lucky me."

As soon as Grant's out of the room, I set the water down, head for the sink, grab a swath of paper towels, wet them and work on getting the yellow paint out of my uniform. Of course it wasn't enough for me to just pass out in class—I had to take a jar of yellow paint down with me.

"Maybe you should just sit for a second," Jake says, watching as I furiously scrub my skirt. The paint had better come out.

"I don't need to sit."

"I was joking before. It wasn't actually funny," he says. "I think you scared the hell out of Chris. Norton didn't know what to think."

I wish he'd stop talking. The paint isn't coming out. I toss the sopping towels into the sink and kick the cupboard underneath it, leaving a black shoe mark in the wood.

This is so stupid.

Jake stares. "It's not that bad, Parker."

I don't even want to dignify that with a response, but I do give him a look he shrivels under. I breathe in. At least I can breathe in now.

"My—" I head back to the cot and sit down. I can't bring myself to look at him. "My skirt didn't—it didn't, like, go *up,* did it?"

It takes him a minute to register that.

"You didn't flash anyone."

"But you do look like shit," a familiar voice says. Chris.

I flop back on the cot.

"Where's Becky?"

I make sure to say it in a supersnotty voice, hoping it'll make him leave faster.

"Cheerleading practice." I can't believe he hasn't given up on her yet. He studies me and frowns. "I had this funny thought while I was coming down here and now I have to know: is this about Evan?"

Jake looks from Chris to me. "Who's Evan?"

"He's—" Chris stops abruptly, backs halfway out of the room and glances down the hall. "Henley's coming."

I groan. "Someone *please* put me out of my misery."

The sound of Henley's high heels clacking along the floor momentarily precedes her, and when she enters the room she's got this look that says it all: she is tired of seeing my face. The feeling is so mutual.

"I heard what happened in Mr. Norton's class," she says. "Drinking in class again?"

"No."

"You wouldn't be lying to me now, would you, Parker?"

I cover my face with my hands. No one says anything. I hate that Jake and Chris are hearing this because it's none of their business and Henley should know better. I bite back the urge to tell her to do her job *right.*

"She wasn't, Mrs. H.," Chris says. "I mean, not that I could tell."

"Gardner?"

"It was—" He stops. I uncover my eyes while Jake gets all sincere on Henley. "It was an anxiety attack. I didn't see her drinking."

I know he thinks he's doing me a favor, so I try not to death-glare him.

"An anxiety attack?" Henley repeats. I can't tell if she's disappointed or not. "Well . . . that's something you can talk about with Ms. Grey on Friday, Parker." Thank you, Jake. Thank you *so* much. "Now if you'll excuse me, I have to get back to the teachers' lounge."

I snort. I bet they keep the good booze there.

Henley reads my mind and glares at me, but she goes.

"So it was Evan," Chris says thoughtfully. He laughs, kind of. "Jesus Christ, Parker. When do you think you'll stop kidding yourself, huh?"

"Oh, fuck off, Chris."

"Who's Evan?" Jake asks again.

I lie down, turn my back to them and stare at the wall.

"Just this guy we know," Chris "explains." "Anyway, I'd better get to the gym. Becky's waiting for me. Are you coming, man?"

"I told the nurse I'd stay here with her until he got back."

"All right, well. See you guys later."

"Chris, wait—" I sit up. "Since when do you have an alarm system? I saw the sign on your lawn."

He blinks, surprised.

"Some jackasses broke my mom's favorite bird fountain."

"You got an alarm and surveillance system for that?"

He shrugs.

"Dad's been looking for an excuse for ages."

Exit Chris. Jake turns back to me.

"Who's Evan?"

I stretch and yawn.

"Anyone ever tell you that you have a one-track mind?"

"Do you want some more water or anything?"

"No."

"So who's Evan?"

I gesture for him to come close. He hesitates.

"It's okay," I say. "Just come here."

He crosses the room slowly, and when he's close enough I reach out and grab his hand. He tenses. For someone who supposedly likes me, you'd think he'd be over the moon because I'm touching him, but no, he's suspicious.

I turn his palm up and trace my index finger over what I think is his life line. It's alarmingly short, if you believe that sort of stuff, and I don't. His breath catches in his throat. I hear it. I'm just fucking with him.

I let go of his hand and pat the spot beside me. He sits.

"I could like you, Jake." I can't believe I'm saying it. "But the more you know about me, the less interesting you become."

I'm not so steady on my feet. It's fifty minutes into the party and too much of the vodka is gone, and if I walk without leaning against the wall I'm afraid I'll do something dumb like fall over in front of everyone. Apparently my overwhelming fear of looking sloppy and stupid in front of the entire school is not as drunk as the rest of me. Next time Chris tells me to loosen the fuck up, I'm going to tell him to fuck the fuck off.

And I haven't seen Chris since he got the music going. I make a mental note to talk to him about that—it's too loud. The beat makes the house rock back and forth, or that could be the vodka, I don't know. I inch my way down the hall. I'm going to hide out in his parents' room and die on their bed. Someone can resurrect me in the morning.

"There you are!" Chris yells. Great. I turn really slowly and after a second the rest of the room turns with me. "I've been looking for you."

I give him a closed-mouth smile because I'm afraid to talk. "Hmm?"

"Let's go outside; the music sounds awesome out there," he says. "We can start off the poolside dancing."

"Uh . . ." My mouth is total sandpaper, thick. "Well—"

"Uh, well," Chris says, imitating me. "Don't think about it; let's go!" He pulls my hand. I reach out for the stair banister to my left.

"Go without me." I think I sound okay. "I'm going to stay . . . here."

"What?"

"Go; just go," I say slowly. Maybe he can't understand me. I can understand me. "Without me. Poolside dance. Without me. Go."

He stares at me for a good minute.

"Parker, are you hiding something from me?"

"Uh—well." I swallow and let go of the banister, but the room lurches to the left and I have to grab it again. "No. . . ."

"Okay," he says. Phew. Then he grins. "Parker, you're drunk."

"I'm—" so not in the position to deny it, so I give him an accusing glare. "You told me to loosen up."

He laughs. For, like, five minutes he just stands there laughing at me.

"Not funny!"

"It is so!" he insists. "You know what this means, don't you?"

I shake my head.

"It means it's now my responsibility to make sure you have the most amazingly fun drunken time of your life or I'll never hear the end of it." He grabs my hand again and pulls me down the hall. "Come on! Pool-side dancing!"

"No, Chris—" I dig my heels in. "Chris."

He turns. "What?"

"I don't want anyone to see me like this. Let me hide out in your parents' room, please—"

"You are the most sober drunk person I know." He says that like it's a bad thing. "Relax. It's a party. In another hour you're not going to be the drunkest person here. Becky will be. No one's going to think less of you."

"But I'm cheerleading captain."

"So what? Come on; the fresh air will make you feel better."

He says it with such authority I let him drag me outside.

"Besides," he adds, as we step through the door, "I won't let you do anything really stupid. Look at it this way: it could be the best night of your life."

I look up. The sun gets in my eyes.

Everything goes white.

eleven

"I think we should talk about what happened yesterday," Grey says, squinting at me over her Parker notebook. I wonder what she's written about me so far and hope it's something lost cause–y. "Tell me what got you so upset."

I press my lips together.

"Did someone say something to you?"

I keep my mouth shut.

"Maybe I didn't give you enough credit when you told me you felt overwhelmed. Maybe none of us did. I'm sorry, Parker."

If she seriously believes *that's* going to get me to talk, I'm kind of offended.

She sighs.

"Is this how it's going to be?"

I glance at the clock and watch the minute hand snail forward. If I wasn't so committed to this silence, I'd say something like, *I don't trust you, remember?*

"Uh, what are you doing?"

"What does it look like I'm doing?" Jake asks, settling into the seat beside me. The bus jerks forward. "I'm sitting beside you."

"No, you're not. Your seat is in the middle. Nice try, though."

He has the audacity to ignore me, sets his book bag on his lap and rummages through it. After a minute, he pulls out a folded sheet of paper and hands it to me.

I unfold it. "A love letter? How sweet."

"No." He turns pink. "It's just something I found on the Internet—"

"Porn? You shouldn't have."

"Just shut up for five seconds. It's breathing techniques, to get a handle on your anxiety. I thought you might find them helpful." I stare at him and he turns even pinker. "You know. So you don't pass out in class again—"

"I got it, Jake. About five sentences ago."

I know a thank-you would probably be more appropriate, but what happened yesterday continues to humiliate me, so never mind. I guess he can sit here just this once.

"Anyway, we've really got to start thinking about our art project," he says. "A lot of people have already started painting. We should probably be doing that."

"Got any ideas?" I ask. I don't. I barely think about our project when we're in class working on it, let alone out of class, on my own time.

"Not a sweet fucking clue." And then he rushes headlong into what he says next: "Do you want to brainstorm together at that coffeehouse on Victoria Street today, after school? It looks really good. I've wanted to try it ever since we moved here—"

"Are you asking me out?"

He blinks. "Am I?"

I lean my head back and stare at the bus ceiling where a huge wad of pink gum has attached itself. Gross.

"Well, say you *are* asking me out. That means you'd have to get off at my stop and we'd go from there, right?"

"It seems that would be the most convenient way to go about it."

I unfold the paper in my hands. *HOW TO BREATHE.* I fold it back up again.

"You'd have to meet my parents," I say carefully. "I've sort of freaked them out lately and they don't really like me going out when I can't be supervised, and since they've never met you they'd probably say no *and* I'd probably have to be back before my curfew, which is seven thirty. . . ."

I look him directly in the eyes.

"I mean, you know how it is. You chase a bottle of sleeping pills with a bottle of Jack Daniel's and life's never the same, no matter how many times you try to tell people it was an accident."

"Is that a no?" he asks. "If you don't want to, just say so. You don't have to be such a smart-ass about everything."

I want to laugh, but I don't. There's something unsatisfying about what just happened here. I set the paper down.

I could have a good time if I went out with Jake. But that doesn't mean I should.

"*Are* you asking me out?"

"Yeah," he finally says.

"Mom, Dad—this is Jake Gardner."

After they get over the initial shock that I still have a friend to bring home, my parents play twenty questions with Jake. They're straight out of The Parent's Handbook and they're so standard it doesn't even matter who's asking them.

> MOM/DAD: Well, it's nice to meet you, Jake! Gardner,
> Gardner . . . that wouldn't be any relation to the Gard-
> ners down on Marriott Avenue?
>
> JAKE: Thanks, nice to meet you, too. It might be. See, my

family just moved here from the West Coast not that long ago.

MOM/DAD: Oh, wow! How exciting! Welcome to Corby! So how do you know Parker? Do you two share a class together?

JAKE: We have art together. We're partnered for a big project due at the end of the year.

MOM/DAD: Oooh. Aaah.

At this point I go upstairs and change out of my uniform. When I go back downstairs, wearing something more casual, Jake and my parents are winding it up.

MOM/DAD: And your parents—what do they do?

JAKE: Well, my dad's in tech support down at that call center in Belton, my mom's a zoologist and my stepmother does voice-overs for commercials. You've probably heard her. She did the one for those crazy mop-broom hybrids. The Bop?

MOM/DAD: My mother-in-law *loves* the Bop! Wow! That's great, Jake! You're welcome here anytime!

We decide not to go to the coffeehouse right away, opting to wait for the school day to settle first. And Bailey needs a walk, so we take him to this patch of park where people bring their dogs to interact with other people's dogs and chase Frisbees and things.

"Here, Bailey." Jake grabs a stick off the ground. Bailey hops around lightly as Jake swings it back and forth. "Fetch, boy!"

Jake throws the stick. Bailey goes lunging after it and lets out a startled yelp when he's jerked back by the neck, and that's when I realize his leash is wrapped tightly around my hand at a painfully short length.

"Shit!" I say. "Oh, Bailey—I'm sorry!"

He gives a pitiful whimper and I crouch down and gesture him forward. He tiptoes up to me with this big Sad Dog expression and it makes me feel guilty. I wrap my arms around his neck because I don't know how to apologize to a dog, but this one always wants me to pet him, so a hug should be, like, huge.

"I'm sorry, Bailey. I didn't do it on purpose."

"You're obviously unfamiliar with the game of fetch," Jake says behind me.

I ignore him and pat Bailey on the head until he looks less pained and more adoring and for a second I think I'm going to do something I haven't done—and genuinely meant—in a long time.

Cry.

Chris is crying over my hospital bed the second time I wake up. The first thing I think is I can't pay him back. It's the first thing I say, too.

"Good boy." Bailey wags his tail. I turn to Jake because I can't shake this stupid sad feeling in the pit of my stomach. I snap my fingers. "Do you think he hates me for that? I mean, do you think he understands it was an accident?"

"He's a dog," Jake says. But then he looks at my face. "But sure, yeah. I bet he understands. He's clearly smitten with you."

"Clearly," I echo. I shove my hands in my pockets. "You have a lot in common with my dog!"

"Har, har," he says, reaching for another stick.

"I don't feel comfortable letting him off the leash," I say quickly, and Jake drops it and then I start feeling even worse for some reason. I shouldn't be doing this with him. I should stop. "And I'm not hungry. We should skip the coffeehouse."

His face falls. "Sure, that's fine."

"But we can still do this, though," I say.

"What's this?"

It's a good question. We're just standing here, Bailey sitting between us and glad to do it, but it's not really anything and Jake wants something. So I think about kissing him, but then I don't because that would be really stupid.

"I guess I'll just catch the bus home then, is that it?" he asks. "I wish you'd told me you weren't really into this, Parker."

"It's not that—"

"Then what is it?"

"Never mind. Let's just go to the coffeehouse."

He laughs. "Right, yeah, we'll just do that when you've already said you don't want to. You know, this is so typical—"

"No, I do! I asked you if you were asking me out and you said you were and I agreed to it, so we're going to eat and we're going to talk about our stupid art project, okay? You cancel a date before it happens, not during. So we're going to the coffeehouse. That's what we're doing."

"Fine, Parker. Whatever."

We drop Bailey off at home and go to the coffeehouse and I order a bagel and a black coffee and Jake orders a chicken salad sandwich and a black coffee and neither of us says anything even though we're supposed to be talking about our art project.

"If I knew why you liked me," I say after the waitress drops the bill on the table, "I could probably handle it a lot better."

"That makes two of us." He hesitates. "Do you even like me at all?"

"I don't know. It freaks me out. I try not to think about it too much."

Jake sighs, grabs the bill and stands. I do the same. And then I start thinking of the dog and I feel guilty all over again and I want it to go away and snapping my fingers doesn't help, so I do that really stupid thing.

I lean over the table and kiss him.

twelve

Chris wants to talk.

In homeroom, he hisses my name, but I ignore him. In art, he tries to start a conversation and I ignore him. After the bell goes, he tells me to meet him in the gym and—ignored. He either knows about Jake or wants to talk about Evan and I don't want to talk about either, so I have to find somewhere else to spend my lunch hour, somewhere that's relatively peaceful and not totally crowded.

Like the chapel.

Why didn't I think of it before? If I'd thought of it before, I never would've tried the nurse's office or made a habit of "hiding out" in the gym. The chapel. It's only a Catholic school. No one goes to *the chapel*.

But I'd forgotten just how awful and uncomfortable the place makes you feel until I push through the doors and step into the little God's House adjacent to the caf. It's like the walls know I'm a bad person. I stand before the altar, cross myself—force of habit—and try to pick the best pew of the lot, settling for one in the middle on the left-hand side. I could sleep away my afternoon classes and no one would ever think to look for me here.

"Parker?"

I groan.

"Oh my God. It's true."

"Go away," I mutter. "I'm not talking to you."

"You're a mess."

The thing about being drunk is people want to congratulate you for it, often in the form of giving you more to drink.

Or maybe this anomaly is only true of people in my high school.

Chris drags me out to the pool and for the next hour all anyone can talk about is how Perfect Parker Fadley is actually drunk, and then they slap me on the back and they say "way to go" all admiringly, and next thing I know, someone's pressing a red plastic cup into my hand. And because I start feeling that rush I usually feel when I've done something perfectly and everyone knows it, I drink whatever is in the red plastic cup.

And then I get props and another red plastic cup.

Four or six red plastic cups later, I have:

Danced horrendously in front of everyone, even though Chris assures me I looked sexy and plenty of guys want to "tap" that, nearly fallen into the pool, told several people I loved them, apologized to most of the cheerleading squad for being a Nazi—except for Becky, fallen down and cried, was helped up and laughed, threw up, cried again, told Chris I hated him for doing this to me because I was being stupid and he promised me I wouldn't and stumbled away to the front lawn, which is where I'm lying now, flat on my back with perfectly manicured blades of grass pressing into my legs, hands and neck.

Chris is probably searching for me all over the house and backyard where the party is, which is why I'm out front, where the party isn't. The remaining minuscule sober part of my brain refuses to let me make a fool of myself in front of everyone any more than I already have and the remaining minuscule sober part of my brain says the only way I can do this is if I stay the fuck away from people altogether.

"Do you need help up?" Jessie asks. "If I get Evan and Chris and

maybe Becky, I'm sure we can drag you up to Chris's parents' bed-room."

I throw my arm over my eyes.

"Go away."

She doesn't. She sits down on a patch of grass close to my head.

"Still pissed at me over what happened at practice, huh?"

"Go." I uncover my eyes and give her my best death glare, which I'm pretty sure is totally compromised by my total drunkenness. "Away."

She smiles. "Nope."

"I work really hard!" I struggle to sit up. "And you made a fool of me—"

"You made a fool of yourself by having a brain aneurysm in front of the entire squad," she interrupts. "You should've seen your face. You were going apeshit over the stupidest things, like, oh my God, we missed the beat. We'll get it. We always do."

"I wasn't having a brain aneur-an-any—" She laughs. I want to kill her. "Thing."

"And Chris is worried about you," she says.

I groan. "Shut up."

"He actually came to me; that's how worried he is. He's afraid to talk to you. He thinks you're fixing for a breakdown because you're, like, obsessed with perfection." She says this as breezily as someone re-lating the weather. And then: "So I told him about the panic attacks."

My heart stops. "You didn't."

She leans over me. Her face blots out the sky, and a strand of long blond hair hangs in front of my face, tickling my nose. I turn my head.

"It's the end of the year, Parker. Things are supposed to be winding down."

She makes me tired.

"Give Becky captaining duties until the year's over," she continues. "She's always wanted to do it and you can let her and say you did some-

thing nice. I've talked to the squad; they said if you do that, they'll want you back next year—"

This sobers me up completely for about five seconds.

"No. Are you out of your mind? Becky will do the loser cheer and we'll be a laughingstock—"

"It doesn't matter! Everyone hates you right now. You're an anal-retentive control-freak perfectionist and they need a break and so do you. And so do I—I can't do damage control for you anymore!"

"They only hate me until they give the best performance of their lives thanks to me and then they love me!"

She snorts.

"That's true and you know it," I mutter. Everything spins and I close my eyes. "I'm that good."

"Yeah, and the sooner you make a mistake and learn to live with it or let them make mistakes and learn to live with it, the better. Until that actually happens, I really think you're going to give yourself a stroke. You're not responsible for everything, Parker. You can't control the way things end up. Stop trying."

"Then it's my fault either way. Me, them. Everyone knows I do everything, so if they fuck up, it's my fault, and if I fuck up, it's my fault and—" I can barely think the words before I say them and start losing my thread. "The way it is, that's good. I'm a good person because it's the outcome that matters and I always do things that are right in the end—and that's how you get away with being a control-freak perfectionist, because in the end you're right . . . and there's no excuse for anything less. I am not going easy on them—"

"I'm getting Chris. You are so wasted it's unbelievable."

And she's right, but only about that. I'm right about everything else. A second later, I feel her brushing a strand of hair from my face. I push her hand away.

"Go, please. . . ."

"Look, Parker, I'm telling you this as your best friend. You're freaking

everyone out. If you don't step down, I'm going to do everything I can to
get you off the squad for your own sake, and Chris has agreed to help."

It takes everything, but I push myself up from the ground and pitch
forward. Jessie grabs me by the elbow and helps me regain my balance,
but I don't want her help. I jerk my arm from her grip and fumble side-
ways, reach out, rest one hand against the side of the house and wait for
the world to right itself. This is cheerleading. Serious business. My rep-
utation's on the line and, and, and they know . . . they know I'm not—

"I can't believe you went behind my back."

"Parker—"

"Evan's cheating on you with Jenny Morse. They're fucking."

I slide down the side of the house until I'm sitting. Jessie looks like
she's underwater, wavery, discombobulated, but I can still make out
her expression: openmouthed, white-faced, hurt. I didn't want to tell her
like this, but she deserves it. She shakes her head, totally shocked, and
marches past me so she can break up with Evan, give him hell, ask him
if it's true, whatever. I don't care.

"I'm only telling you this as your best friend," I call after her.

"Parker?"

The voice comes as a total surprise.

Maybe if I stay really, really still she'll go away.

"Parker, I know you're there. I can see your feet."

I heave a colossal sigh and sit upright.

"This is unexpected, Becky," I say. "What do you want?"

She marches up the aisle in an annoyingly self-assured way, a
brown paper bag clutched in one hand, and sits beside me.

"Chris has been going crazy trying to talk to you, but he said
you're avoiding him. So I said I'd talk to you because I know you
won't avoid me. And we should probably talk, shouldn't we?"

"What about cheerleading practice?"

She shrugs. "Postponed."

"I never postponed for anything."

"This is important."

"So self-sacrificing," I sneer. "I bet it really turns Chris on. I bet he's thinking it won't be so bad being your boyfriend after all. Actually, I know he's thinking it. And so do you. That's the only reason you're here."

She inclines her head, like we're playing chess and I made the first move and it wasn't a bad one.

"I really wanted to start over with you after everything happened. I thought it was possible." She stares at the wooden cross mounted to the wall. "For about five minutes, I almost felt like there was this mutual respect thing going on. . . ."

I laugh. "While you were wasting time feeling things, I was stealing your *Beowulf* essay and passing it off as my own."

She clenches her jaw. "At least after *I* saw Evan I didn't lose it."

"I'm disappointed. That's the best you can do?"

"Yeah, it is." Becky nods. And then she nods again, like she really means it. "You know who feels sorry for you? Chris. That's pathetic."

"Yeah, it is pathetic that he's still in love with me."

She rolls her eyes.

"Do you feel sorry for me?"

It's one of those questions I ask before considering whether or not I really care about the answer. Who am I kidding? It's Becky. Of course I don't.

"You've made a choice and it's so obvious. I see it; I accept it," she says. "Even if no one else can. You want to rot and I want to let you."

If I was feeling generous, I'd congratulate her. The only person standing in the way of ultimate popularity—me—had stepped aside and she snapped up the position before anyone else even realized it was available. She probably watched me all year, waiting to see how my calculated fuckups could benefit her, and figured out my motivations in the process. That takes talent. She'll make a great sorority sister after she gets out of here.

"Who would've thought that you of all people would be smart enough to get me?"

"Yeah, weird, huh?" She hands me the bag. "Consider that my contribution."

I peer inside of it. "Becky, if I'm drunk in school again, I'm expelled. I still want to graduate."

"Do you really?" She stands and stretches. "I'd better go. Chris is waiting for me. Is there anything you want me to tell him?"

"Nothing I wouldn't tell him myself."

She heads back down the aisle and I stretch back out on the pew, holding the paper bag to my chest, the bottle of Jack heavy inside it. The door creaks as Becky opens it and I wait for the click, the noise that tells me it's closed and I'm alone again, but it doesn't come. And then, her voice:

"You know, it's not any harder on you than it was for the rest of us."

thirteen

"Uh . . . what are you doing?"

"What does it look like I'm doing?" I ask, settling into the seat beside Jake. The driver shifts gears, the bus shakes and our shoulders bump. "I'm sitting beside you."

"No, you're not. Your seat is at the front," he says. They say imitation is the sincerest form of flattery. I'm so flattered. "Nice try, though."

It's weird sitting in the middle of the bus, but it's my peace offering to Jake for flaking out on him since the kiss. By "flaking out" I mean I may or may not be avoiding him or pretending to be deaf when he talks to me, unless it's something to do with our art project, and then I pretend to be hearing delayed and wait, like, five minutes before responding, which I decided last night wasn't very nice of me.

"I'm not moving," I tell him.

"Evan—" He clears his throat. "Evan is Chris's best friend. He left before senior year because he had a breakdown or something. Chris told me."

"Very good, Jake," I say, nodding slowly. "And can you tell me why he had a nervous breakdown?"

"Nope."

"Well, if you can't tell me that, you can at least tell me what any of it has to do with me," I say.

"Chris said he'd tell me what everybody already knows," he says. There's an ungodly pause because we both know what's coming next. "You *did* try to kill yourself."

"It was an accident."

"Oh, right." He doesn't believe me. "That's why you meet with Grey, isn't it? And that's why no one leaves you alone and you're not popular anymore and Evan fits in there somehow. That's your big secret, right?"

"Congratulations, you figured it out. So how 'bout them Mets?"

He blinks. "What?"

"Does every conversation between us have to be like this, with you prying into stuff that's none of your business? So tell me: How 'bout them Mets? What do you think?"

"Oh, they're just great," he mutters. "So are you depressed—"

I groan. "Jake."

"Okay, okay," he says quickly. "Never mind."

"Do you think I'm depressed?"

"I think it'd explain the bravado."

"You think this is bravado?" I shake my head. "Actually, you know what? You're right. I sit at the front."

I grip the seat ahead of me and stand, but before I can step into the aisle, Jake reaches out and grabs my wrist. I give him a look that says, I don't have time for this.

"You kissed me," he says.

"So?"

"Would you please sit down? I want to talk to you."

I do it.

"Look, I'm sorry that you—" He doesn't finish and I'm glad because he'd only embarrass us both if he started apologizing for something he knows nothing about. "Why did you kiss me if you were just going to shut me out after?"

I shrug. "Had to fill the moment at the coffeeshop somehow."

"Ouch."

"You were expecting something more?"

"Yeah, I guess I was."

"Why would you do a stupid thing like that?" I chew my lip. "The way you feel about me freaks me out. I've told you that."

"Maybe the way *you* feel about *me* freaks *you* out."

"But I don't know how I feel about you. I try not to think about it. And I've told you *that*."

I guess he knows I could run us in circles forever, so he leans in and gives me a kiss, all soft and hesitant, and I think it's supposed to make my heart beat faster and my head feel lighter, but it doesn't. It steals my breath and makes the tips of my fingers tingle and I start thinking I'll have an anxiety thing again, here on the bus while his mouth is against mine, and how awful that would be. A funny thought occurs to me at the same time Jake brings his hand to my face: I couldn't do this even if I wanted to do this.

"Stop telling Jake things about me."

Chris slams his locker door shut. "You're talking to me now?"

"Why did you tell Jake I tried to kill myself?"

He pretends to think about it. "Because you did?"

"I didn't." I rest against his locker. "That's what you think I did."

He does that lean guys do with their girls. I'm against his locker and he rests his hand just above my head and tilts forward so we're close. He doesn't even think before he does it; it's second nature. We used to stand like this every day between classes and he'd give me a kiss when the bell went. Sex is one thing, but I always thought that stupid lean meant intimacy. Because I was dumb.

"You drank a bottle of Jack Daniel's and downed a bottle of sleeping pills. I don't think you tried to kill yourself, Parker; I know it."

"You obviously know nothing and now Jake's getting the wrong idea about me."

"What do you care what Jake thinks about you?" He rolls his eyes. "Okay, you tell me what you think happened and if I think it has merit, I'll find him and clear things up. Sound fair?"

"I got drunk first," I explain. "And then I miscounted how many sleeping pills I needed to get through the night. It's hard to count when you're all fucked up."

"Well of *course!*" He slaps his forehead in disbelief. "That explains *everything*. How could I have been so stupid?"

"I'm serious. Stop telling Jake things."

"I don't tell him anything everyone doesn't already know. That's fair game." Chris finally becomes aware of the way he's standing and how close we actually are. He straightens and rubs his hands on his shirt. "He really likes you, huh?"

"I guess. Why do you think that is?"

"Damned if I know. That's not exactly the type of conversation you want to have with the ex. But I picked up on it, took pity on the guy and told him about that one time you tried to kill yourself."

It starts making sense. "You wanted to scare him away."

"No, I thought I'd let him take comfort in the fact that when you're fucking with other people, you're really just fucking with yourself. Becky and I had a talk about it and she threw that theory out there, and I gotta say it makes so much sense."

"Becky is becoming a real pain in my ass."

"Becoming?" Chris studies me. "You like him, don't you?"

"Would that bother you?"

"Even if it did, I've resolved not to let it ruin a good time with Becks."

"*Becks?*" I shake my head, disgusted. "But you don't love her."

He shrugs.

"You love me," I say.

He shrugs again.

"Oh, come *on*—this from the same guy who blackmailed me into kissing him in the change room because he missed me so bad? You've *never* liked Becky—"

"I didn't really know her before. And believe it or not, Parker, things happen around you that have nothing to do with you even if they start out that way. She's not that bad. By the way, Evan's back in two weeks. He has to get all his shit from his aunt's and cut his hair, but you should prepare yourself."

It throws me. I need a second.

"So he just cuts his hair and he's back?" I ask. "Everything's like it was?"

"Yeah, hopefully. Are you going to be okay? I worry—"

"Don't."

I head in the opposite direction, to my locker, open it and grab my English books. The bottle Becky gave me is sitting on the top shelf, face out, so everyone will see it, but no one sees it. I'd like Chris to see it. And I'd like him to ask me where I got it.

"Hey, Jake! Stop!" I manage to catch him between third and fourth period heading to whatever class it is he heads to. He waits for me to jog over.

"What's wrong?" he asks when I reach him.

I untie my ponytail and retie it. I'm not sure how to do this.

118   courtney summers

"I'm sorry," I finally say.

He raises an eyebrow. "You're sorry?"

"Yeah." I untie my ponytail again. "I don't know."

"You don't . . . know?"

"And even if I did, I wouldn't know how to say it."

"Parker, what are you talking about?"

My stomach twists. "I think you're okay, but I know you deserve better."

He looks totally confused now.

"You're making my brain hurt—"

"So now you can't say I didn't warn you."

He stares at me a long time. And then I see a light go on. Vaguely.

"Does that mean you—"

My stomach twists again.

"Don't call it anything yet," I say.

He nods slowly.

"I have to go."

I leave him in the hall and run to the girls' washroom, where I push through the closest stall door and throw up.

"You're like Jake in dog form," I tell Bailey after I mark the day Evan is coming back on the calendar above my bed. I sit down beside him and pet him. "I wish we hadn't gotten you."

Bailey gives me this uncomprehending, painfully loyal look.

"You make me feel bad," I clarify.

I reach for my math book, open it to the unit I never did and start reviewing. I have that test tomorrow and I need to pass it because I want to graduate, I guess.

I guess.

So I can get out. They can all leave me alone forever. Right.
I stare at my calendar. At that big red *X*.

"Wow."

Mrs. Jones looks up from my test, all startled. I insisted she
mark it as soon as I scribbled down the answer to the last question and watched her eyes grow wider with every red checkmark.
I'm not nearly so surprised; I stayed up all night studying like I
used to. Sometime after midnight it became imperative to me that
I show everyone I still possess those wonderful qualities that helped
separate me from everyone else.

Because it makes the way I am now that much more frustrating for them.

Jones shakes her head in total disbelief as she scribbles a
bright red *100%* in the upper right-hand corner of the paper.

"Congratulations, Parker."

"This demands celebration," Chris says, holding up the test and waving
it around. Jake laughs and Becky gives a tight-lipped smile.

I rip it from Chris's hand. "It does not demand a celebration."

Suddenly, we're a group. Jake caught me outside of math, saw
the test score and told Chris, who was with Becky, as we passed
them in the hall. And here we are.

"You're right," Chris agrees. "I'm just looking for an excuse to
party."

"Party?"

"Hang out." He chews his lower lip. It's what he does when
he's thinking. He doesn't do it very often. "Why don't we all go to

my house after school and rent a movie or whatever? My parents won't be home."

"Sounds good," Jake says.

"Because I got a perfect score on my math test?"

"If there's got to be a reason, that can be it," Chris says.

"Can't. My parents wouldn't like that." And for the first time in my life I'm happy to say this: "You know, because of my curfew and all. And it's a school night."

"Well, let's try them," Chris says. He wanders over to the pay phone, sticks a quarter in, dials my house and hands me the phone.

"Oh, fuck you," I say, pushing it away.

He brings it up to his ear.

"Hi, Mrs. Fadley? This is Chris. . . ." He pauses and winks at me. "I *know*, it's been way too long. . . . Yeah! I'm great. Yourself? . . . That's great. . . . Uh-huh—oh no, it's nothing like that. Parker's fine."

Becky and Jake stare at me. I pinch the bridge of my nose.

"I'm calling because a few of us are getting together at my house after school. We're going to rent a movie, that sort of thing. . . . Yeah. I was wondering if Parker could join us. She mentioned a curfew and it might be a little late by the time we're done, but I'd drive her home and—yeah, my parents will be home. . . . Uh-huh, yeah. Just a sec. . . ."

He hands the phone to me. I give him a death glare.

"Hi, Mom."

"Why couldn't you ask me that yourself?" she demands.

"I don't know. But I got a hundred percent on my math test."

"Are you being serious or are you joking?"

"I'm not joking. I can show you the test later tonight."

"You're not going to be drinking over there or anything, are you?"

"No, Mom. Chris said his parents will be there."

"Well, you know the Ellorys. They may be *there,* but they're not—"

"Okay, forget it. I'll see you after school." Yes.

"No, no, no," she says quickly. "Go and have a good time. I'm proud of you, Parker—for the test. And I didn't know you and Chris were still on speaking terms. That's good—these are good things. Go have fun. Your father and I love you."

I close my eyes. "Bye."

fourteen

I can't figure out what's stopping me from just ditching Chris, Becky and Jake and going home while they stand in front of the shelf full of new releases, trying to decide what movie to rent. Suddenly, we're a group. It makes me sick. I head over to the horror section and try to remember how to breathe and that's where Jake finds me ten minutes later, my eyes closed, snapping my fingers.

Breathe in.

"We've picked the movie," he says. Out. "Chris is paying now."

"Okay." In. I open my eyes.

He extends his hand, like for me to take, and when I don't, he drops it and it's awkward. That's what happens when you sort of tell someone it's okay if they've kissed you and it's okay if it happens again, but you don't tell them if it's okay to do couply things like hold hands and, I guess, care.

"Okay," I repeat. "Let's go."

"Wait."

"Stop following me." Slam. *"I said get away from me!"*

I turn my head in the direction of the noise. It takes such an effort, I think I must be dying. I feel like it. I blink slowly, several times, until I can sort of focus on a pair of people silhouetted by the moonlight filtering in through the window blinds.

"Nothing is going on between me and Jenny Morse—"

"That's not what Parker said!"

I close my eyes.

"What? You're taking Parker's word for this? She's drunk off her ass! When we dragged her in here she was telling us what a beautiful person Becky is! I am not fucking Jenny Morse!"

"Oh, really? Because that's not what Jenny Morse told me and she wasn't drunk off her ass when she said it!"

She starts to cry.

"Oh, Jesus, Jessie. Don't cry, please. . . ."

"I can't even look at you right now. Get out."

"No, please, Jess—we can figure this out. I'm not leaving this room until we do. Don't do this. Please."

"There's nothing to figure out, Evan."

"What does that mean?"

Silence.

"I asked you what that meant."

"What do you think it means? I don't want you here. Get. Out."

All of a sudden I'm being jerked upright. My stomach lurches. I try to tell whichever one of them it is to stop and leave me alone, but I can't move my mouth.

"Parker, sit up. You can't stay on your back because if you get sick—" Jessie sobs and taps my cheek, once, twice, three times. Stop. I want to sleep. "Parker, come on."

"I hope she chokes."

"Nice, Evan. Would you just leave?"

"Not until you talk to me about this."

"If I talk to you about this now, I'll just say something that you really won't like—"

Their voices disappear and so does everything until seconds, minutes, hours later, I don't know, Evan's shaking me, grabbing me roughly by the shoulders.

I try to push him off me, but my arms don't work. I think he's crying.

"*—Because you couldn't keep your goddamn mouth shut—*"

"Jessie."

I open my eyes. I'm pressed up against Jake's left side and the flat screen mounted to the wall is rolling the end credits for the movie I didn't watch. I rub my eyes and straighten up. Chris and Becky stare at me.

"Welcome back," Jake says.

"Trust you guys to pick the most boring movie in the whole store," I grumble.

"It kept the rest of us awake."

I lean forward, rest my head in my hands and try to shake the sleep off.

"Who were you dreaming about?" Chris asks.

My eyes travel from him to Becky.

"Nothing. No one." I stand. "I'm going to get some air."

"Come back in soon," Chris says. "We're popping out the bubbly."

"Really?"

"Coke's bubbly, isn't it?"

Becky giggles and rests her head against his shoulder. He puts an arm around her.

I've never met a girl so content to be a growth.

Outside, I stand in front of the woods, but I don't go in. All I can think about is getting caught, the cameras that could be recording my every move, that memory-dream and Bailey's my dog and Evan's coming back and there's a bottle of Jack in my locker Becky gave me and Jake's allowed to kiss me and this isn't at all how things are supposed to be going. I wanted to be alone. It's safer that way.

After twenty minutes or so, I hear footsteps behind me.

"I've kissed Jake," I say.

"I know."

I turn and there's Chris, all washed-out in blue moonlight.

"He told me because he felt guilty," he explains. "I told him to go for it."

"I don't like you with Becky. She's not a very nice girl."

"I don't like you with Jake. He's not me."

"Do you remember that party at the end of junior year . . ."

I trail off and look up. The stars are out tonight, full force. They're pretty.

Of course he remembers.

"How could I forget?"

"I'm a different person now."

He regards me for a long time before he says, "No, you're not."

"Yeah, I am. I am so, *so* far away from all of that." I don't even know why I'm saying this. It just feels like I should. "It's all totally behind me."

"Whatever you say." He holds out his hand. "Let's get back to the house."

"She's nicer than me, though."

"Who?"

"Becky."

"Come on, Parker. Let's go in."

"Wait; I—"

I turn back to the woods before I realize what I'm doing. I didn't even get to—

"Are you okay?"

"No. What?" I want to shake myself. Stop looking over there; you can't go over there, so stop. I run my hand over the bracelet on my wrist. There's nothing else there that I don't have. "I mean, yes. I'm just tired. I was hard on you, wasn't I? I never let you get away with anything."

"Yeah, but you never let anyone get away with anything."

"You were worried about me."

"I worry about you."

"You know, even when I was really hard on people and not very nice, they always thanked me afterward because you couldn't argue with the results." I kick at the ground and give a bitter laugh. "Couldn't argue with perfection."

"You were running yourself into the ground."

"I didn't want anyone else's mistakes jeopardizing my track record. And God forbid I made a mistake. Because if it ever turned out wrong, what would that say about me? I mean, what would happen?"

"The world would end. You wouldn't even know how to cope," Chris says lightly. "And that's what did happen."

"No, it didn't." I shake my head. "That's what I'm trying to tell you: I'm not Perfect Parker Fadley anymore. I never was. I know who I am now and I'm more in control of my life than I've ever been."

"You're a perfect mess. You even have to do *that* perfectly."

"Look, I'm trying to tell you not to worry," I say impatiently.

"I'll do what I like." He sighs. "We should really go in."

Becky and Jake are talking happily when Chris and I return to the house. They each have a glass of Coke. Chris pours one for me.

"So," Becky says as we crowd around the island. It feels like those moments after everyone has left the party and before you start cleaning up. "Ms. Abernathy told me all these old cheers the squad used to do, like, way back in the day, so at the next game, we're going totally retro. Old-fashioned music, chants, everything. I think it'll be great, like nothing we've done before."

"What about the outfits?" Chris asks. "You're not going to go retro with those, are you? When Abernathy was a cheerleader the skirts went down to the ankles."

The guys laugh like Chris has told an amazingly funny joke.

"Oh, don't you worry, Chris," Becky says, touching his arm. "You'll be able to see our gitch. Gitch? Gitches? Is it 'gitches' in plural?"

I raise my glass. "Whatever it is, it's classy."

"I know." She eyes me. "What do you think, really? Think it's a good idea?"

I shrug. "Can't be any worse than the cheers you've been doing lately."

"I can't believe you were cheerleading captain," Jake says to me.

Becky smirks. "Cheerleading Nazi."

I set my glass down.

"Jake, walk me home? That way Chris doesn't have to get the car out."

So he does.

"It's nice out," he says, as we tromp down the driveway. "I mean, it's definitely getting warmer out."

"Yeah. . . ."

"My mom doesn't talk to me."

"What?"

"My mom doesn't talk to me," Jake says. "Because I chose my dad. He cheated on her with Wanda. I guess she thought I'd stay with her because of what he did, but I've always had more in common with him."

It's the kind of thing that interests me, but I don't want Jake to think I'm interested, so I swallow the million questions fighting their way up my throat until I can't.

We're pretty close to my house at that point.

"So do you forgive him?"

"Yeah, I guess so," Jake says. "I mean, he's sorry."

"Do you forgive your mom?"

"I didn't think I needed to."

"She should talk to you. You're her son."

"Yeah, but it's more a case of her having to forgive me, isn't it?"

"But are you sorry?"

He pauses. He looks sad. "No."

"Why are you telling me this?"

"Because . . ." He shrugs. "I don't know. Because I want you to know we've all got something?"

"Oh, Jake. You're so melodramatic and angsty."

"Yeah, we have a lot in common." He shoves his hands in his pockets. "Did you mean what you said before?"

"What did I say before?"

"The more I know about you, the less interesting I am. . . ."

"I guess not," I say. "Lucky you."

"Lucky me," he repeats. "I'm going to kiss you."

So he does.

fifteen

Something's not right.

I set my book bag down and listen. There are the usual sounds coming from the kitchen; Mom puttering around, getting dinner ready maybe. That's normal, almost welcome. But something's missing. Not right.

I round the corner. My perfect test is stuck to the face of the fridge, the way my childhood drawings used to be. Mom's gearing up to do the dishes, but Dad's not at his usual spot at the table.

And Bailey didn't run to greet me when I stepped through the door.

"Where's Bailey?" I ask.

Mom looks up.

"Your father had to take him to the vet."

"What happened?"

"He got into a fight with another dog at the park."

"Is he hurt?"

She nods. "He might need stitches."

"He's not—" I swallow. "He's not going to die, is he?"

She gets all hopeful around the eyes.

"Are you worried?"

Why do people do that? Turn nothing into something?

"I couldn't care less either way."

She flinches and turns back to the sink. As soon as I leave the room, she might cry about how much she doesn't understand me anymore, how much she wants her old daughter back, but she's not coming back. I went too far, but sometimes you have to.

"He's not going to die," I say.

But she doesn't look at me and Bailey comes home with stitches on his hip and a lampshade around his neck so he won't gnaw at them. I take pity on him and I let him sleep in my room.

"Are you going to the dance?"

I slam my locker shut.

"What are you talking about?"

"You know. . . ." Chris wiggles his hips in a poor imitation of dancing. "The dance this weekend. You going?"

"I'm not following."

He rolls his eyes, grabs me by the hand and drags me down the hall to the entrance corridor. There, on the wall, is a bright pink poster advertising the semi-formal this weekend. Be there or be square.

"There are only, like, a half a million of these all over the school," he says.

"Semi-formal already," I say, staring at the poster. "How about that."

"So are you going or what?"

"Well, I *would*, but no one's asked me." I jut my lower lip out, but his eyes light up, so I drop the expression and snort. "Are you kidding me? Of course I'm not."

"I have it on good authority that Jake's going to ask you, though."

"Why does Jake insist on breaking his own heart?"

"Just go," Chris says, groaning. "I'm taking Becky. We'll all go together, leave together. It'll be fun times. Supervised fun times. How can you resist?"

"Easily. Contrary to popular belief, Chris, I don't like spending time with you, Becky or Jake. Especially Becky. In case you've forgotten, she annoys the fuck out of me. She's not a good argument for my going to the dance."

"So show her up!"

"What?"

"Wear that really nice black dress you've got, fix your hair up all nice and show her up. She'd hate that."

I can't help but laugh. "She *hated* that."

"There, see? I just gave you a reason to go."

"If Becky knew you said that, I don't think she'd like you very much."

"You won't tell her," he says. "And I think you should go."

"Why do you care?"

"Because I'm still in love with you, of course. What else could it possibly be?" Before I can say something snide, he laughs. "Haven't you done the whole Alienate Everyone thing long enough? I mean, how much longer are you gonna keep at it?"

"Uh, I don't know—until it works?"

"You used to like going to dances," he reminds me. The bell rings and we head for homeroom. "Bet you still do."

"I can't take this anymore."

"Can't take what?" I ask, even though I know.

Jake and I are so done with the sketching part of our landscape, but because we haven't figured out what to do next we spend most

of the period taking turns tracing the same set of rocks. I don't
know why he's so freaked out about it. It sure beats working.

He gestures to the paper.

"Unity and disparity. We need a plan."

I rest my head on the desk. "Why?"

"Because that's the project!"

"Head up, Fadley!" Norton yells. "Nap time's not for another
fifteen minutes!"

Everyone snickers. I raise my head.

"So-o-o . . . ," Jake says, and I can tell by the way he protracts
the *o* he's getting ready to ask me to the semi-formal. Sure
enough: "What are semi-formals like at St. Peter's?"

Why are guys so predictable?

"And what's a *semi*-formal, anyway?" he asks quickly, before I
can answer his first question. "Does that mean dress nice from the
waist down?"

"Something like that, yeah," I answer.

"Are you going?"

"I'm probably not allowed."

"That's convenient."

He stops tracing the rocks and I pick up where he left off.

"No, really," I say. "I'm not sure if I'd be allowed. I'm not even
allowed off grounds for lunch, remember? Grey and Henley
would probably have to okay it, not to mention my parents. It's
not as simple as me putting on my best dress and going to the
dance, you know?"

"And if it was?"

"It's not."

"Would you go to the semi-formal with me, Parker?"

I look up from my rocks. Chris is watching us from across the
room. He winks and turns back to the landscape he's working on
with his partner.

I hate him for enjoying this.

"Uhm." I focus on the rocks. "I guess."

"I'm twenty dollars richer, thanks to you!"

I shut the door to Grey's office and try to figure out what she's talking about. And then I roll my eyes. She just grins.

"The math test?" I guess.

"Principal Henley didn't think you'd pass, but I knew you would."

I lean against the door. I should be sitting so we can have our weekly session where I pick the lint off my skirt and determinedly maintain my silence while she stares at me, except today I have to break that silence. And all for a boy, too. How degrading.

"I want to go to the semi-formal tomorrow," I announce.

Grey blinks.

"What do your parents think about that?"

"They think it's a great idea."

She raises both eyebrows. "Really?"

"Call them and ask."

It's sort of true. Mom and Dad think going to the semi-formal with Jake and the gang is a great idea, but only because I've already told them it was okay with the school. I wait until Friday to spring it on Grey because I don't want to give her or Henley all the time they need to think up the reasons why it's probably not a good idea.

And they would, too, since the last dance I showed at was a disaster.

"Jake Gardner asked me," I continue. "They think it would be good for me."

"You don't have any plans to spike the punch again, do you?"

She gestures to the seat across from her and I sit.

"No. I'll just be there to look pretty and dance."

"I'll have to check with Principal Henley. This is very short notice, Parker—"

"But if you tell her you're okay with it, there shouldn't be a problem. Henley—*Principal* Henley's too busy to take a long look at a Pros and Cons list for my attending one semi-formal. You only have to give her the word."

"But I'm not too busy for that list." Grey smiles in a way that doesn't thrill me. "And we have thirty minutes of this session left. So how about you talk to me, *really* talk to me, and maybe you can attend the semi-formal."

"Ms. Grey!" My eyes widen. "That's dirty pool."

And it's really not worth spending an evening with Jake in an auditorium decked out to look like something special with a bunch of people I can't even stand being around on a good day.

But my parents think I'm going.

"Fine," I say, opening my arms. "Ask me anything."

She puts her best Movie Guidance Counselor face on and leans forward.

"How are you?" she asks after a beat. Oh my God. "How are you *really*?"

When I wake up, I'm still drunk.

I'll remember this as the longest, most miserable night of my life. Chris's living room is empty, no trace of anyone having been here, but the party is still going strong outside the door because it isn't that late, I just got smashed that early.

My shoulders hurt where Evan shook them. I hold my hand out. It feels like lead, but at least I'm not cemented to the couch like before, which is good because

I'm going to be sick.

I force myself off the couch, and fumble my way to the door, trying to remember which bathroom is closest to the living room while at the same time vowing never to drink again because I've been here a million

*times and I should know which bathroom is closest to the living room,
but my head feels awful and I just can't think.*

*I push through the door and bump into God knows how many peo-
ple as I weave down the hall. Mostly all of them laugh at me, or maybe
they've just hit the Feel Good Stage of the party where everything's
funny. Who knows. My stomach flip-flops.*

I cover my mouth.

*The closest bathroom is occupied and there's a lo-ong line and there
are three bathrooms upstairs, but I don't think I'll make it to any of
them in time. The music is so loud it forces any other potential plans
of action right out of my brain and I stumble through the kitchen, head
outside, take a few uncertain steps toward some bushes and throw up
until there's nothing left in my stomach to throw up.*

And then I start dry-heaving, which is worse.

*When it's over, I sit back on the grass, trying to ignore the sour taste
in my mouth and wondering how I'll make it back to my safe haven in
the living room. And that's when I spot Jessie by the pool, Jessie laughing it up with some guy I don't know. He looks older than us and she's
in full party mode, probably buzzed, and the way she leans into him is
all wrong because it's how she leans into a guy when she wants to fuck
him. This is wrong. I did this. I focus on getting upright again. I have to
fix it.*

"Parker?"

"I'm getting by," I tell her.

What else am I supposed to say?

"Well, that's good. Because things are happening, aren't they?
Evan Corman is coming back. That must be nice for you and your
friends." Grey's voice is like nails on a chalkboard. "I saw him
when he met with Principal Henley. He seems eager to get things
together. You two could help each other."

"How?"

"Well, given the circumstances . . ."

"You mean because he tried to kill himself, you think we can help each other?" I can't believe I'm sitting through this for a *dance*. "It won't help."

"Why not?"

"Because Evan didn't really want to die. And mine was an accident."

"Evan didn't want to die?" she repeats slowly. Stupid. "The evidence certainly suggests otherwise."

"He didn't," I say. "He planned it right down to getting caught."

Stupid, stupid. And then I decide to give it to her because when people are this stupid they should be told every once in a while.

"When he got in the bath with the razors, he knew his mom would find him before he bled out," I say impatiently. "It was more a gesture than anything. Like, 'This is how far I would go for absolution,' and everyone was like, 'Wow, fine, you're forgiven.' And that's how he lives with himself. He did his bit and he goes on like before. Which doesn't help *me* at all."

"And is this—" She makes this sweeping gesture around the room, like she's gathering up all the things I've done. "Is this your bit?"

God, she's so *stupid*.

"Look, can I go to the semi-formal or not?"

She stares at me a long time.

"Wait here."

She leaves the room. I sit in the hard plastic chair and wait, wait, wait for, like, ten minutes and then she comes back.

"You can go to the semi-formal," she says, shutting the door. "You can go to the semi-formal, but if you're on anything less than your best behavior—"

"I know; I know. I won't graduate."

"That's right. You won't."

The bell rings. I head for the door.

"Thanks," I say without looking at her.

"English homework," **Becky** says, handing me a piece of paper. I grab it and she heads on her merry way. "See you Monday or something."

"See you tomorrow," I call after her.

She stops, turns and gives me a hilariously quizzical look.

It could be worth it for this alone.

"What?"

"I'll see you tomorrow. For the semi-formal? You, me, Chris and Jake." I force a big smile at her. "I'm really looking forward to it."

I'm such a bitch, but Becky makes it so easy.

sixteen

Hair.

I stand in front of the full-length mirror mounted on the back of my closet door and try to figure out what I'm going to do with my hair. Jake won't be here for another two and a half hours, but any girl knows you need at least three to look your best for a semi-formal. And I haven't even showered yet.

So I do that.

And then I stand in front of the full-length mirror mounted on the back of my closet door and try to figure out what I'm going to do with my wet hair.

Blow-dry it, probably. For starters.

So I do that while vaguely recalling a time I made checklists on dance nights. I reduced getting ready to a list of tasks, all of them allotted certain amounts of time for completion. As I checked off each one, I got to enjoy a warm feeling of accomplishment for an allotted 1.5 seconds.

But not tonight. The lack of structure disorients me. I decide to leave my hair down and curl the ends. While I wait for the iron to warm, I pick out my best black dress from the closet. It has off-the-shoulder short sleeves and stops just before the knees. Decent, but sexy, and miraculously uneaten by moths. I have a feeling it's not going to fit what with the ten pounds I've gained and the fact that I haven't done anything remotely physical since I quit the cheerleading squad, but unfortunately it does fit. Kind of. My boobs look desperate to break free of the soft satin material that binds them, and if I sit I have a sneaking suspicion the whole dress could split down the back. But if that happens, then hey, at least I'll have an excuse to leave early.

The dress (barely) on, I begin to work on my hair, which is a longer process than I'd like it to be or ever remember it being. It's because I don't have a list.

And the makeup. That's another beast entirely.

How did I do this every day for school? I didn't need a checklist then. The routine was so ingrained in me because it was so important because—*why?*

Because I had to look perfect, of course.

I pick through the collection of makeup on my desk. Foundation, under-eye concealer, lipstick, lip gloss, eyeliner, eye shadow, mascara and blush. I settle for clear gloss and mascara and then stand in front of the mirror and inspect myself.

It's good, I guess.

"Parker!" Mom shouts. "Parker, they've just pulled up!"

I grab my black clutch and hear Mom cooing all three of them into the house before I'm halfway down the stairs. I've barely stepped into the living room when Bailey comes bounding at me, lampshade tight around his neck.

"Bailey, stop!" I say before he can jump up. He comes to a screeching halt and I reward him with a pat because I can't help it, he looks that ridiculous. "Good dog."

"Look at that! You know, he doesn't even fetch my slippers anymore," Dad says from his recliner, smiling. "You look beautiful, honey."

I bring my clutch up to my chest. "Dad, don't."

"Well, you do. Have fun at the dance." He gives me a look. "And behave."

"I wouldn't dream of doing anything but."

I give Bailey one last pat on the head and make my way into the kitchen, where Mom's having an animated conversation with Jake, Chris and Becky. She has the camera out. Joy. I clear my throat. They stop talking and look at me.

"Oh, Parker!" Mom cries. "This is the best you've looked in *ages!*"

Becky smirks, but not for long. We simultaneously ascertain that I look better than she does, even packing weight. Just because one is an affinity for pink doesn't mean she should wear it, but boy, is she. Pink hair accessories, jewelry, makeup, dress, shoes, clutch. It's one those hard, bright pinks, too. Not the soft, pretty kind.

I mean it's blindingly awful and awfully satisfying all at the same time.

"I just want to get a picture of all of you, really quick! You look *so* nice!"

Mom ushers us into a line and places me between Chris and Jake, who both look very handsome. They've opted for black suits. Chris's hair is slicked back and Jake's is loose, like it always is. Chris smells like pine; and Jake, like paper. For a minute, I can't remember whom I'm supposed to be spending the evening with.

Jake.

Mom raises the camera to her eye and says, "Smile!"

"Thank God that's over," Becky says as we cross the lawn to Chris's car. She glares at me. "Your mom is such a freak, Parker."

"Well, I think it's sweet that she wanted to get a memento of this grand occasion," Jake says cheerfully. "Your mom didn't take any pictures, Becky."

She snorts. Chris opens the driver's side door and gives me this look.

"I've seen that dress before," he says, letting his eyes travel over me. "But I don't think you've ever worn it quite like this."

I glance at Becky. She clenches her jaw, climbs into the passenger's side and slams the door shut. The night can only get better from here.

"I've gained weight," I tell him. "All in my boobs."

"Looks good on you," Chris says as he gets in the car.

Jake opens the back door for me. What a gentleman.

"You look really beautiful. I like your hair."

He says it in a voice I don't really deserve and it catches me off guard. I feel my face heat up and bring a hand to one of my curls. It's a weird moment.

"Thanks. You look nice." I reach out and push a stray piece of hair away from his eyes. "I like your hair, too. It looks very complicated."

We smile at each other and get in the car.

The dance has a ten-dollar entrance fee, the music is loud and bad and the auditorium is sparkly, purple and hot. Chris gives me a longing look as Becky drags him over to the popular corner. Just because we came together doesn't mean we stay together, especially when I look a thousand times better than Becky does.

And I get the feeling by the way everyone is staring at me that I look *great*.

Or a boob has popped out or my dress has split down the back.

I spin for Jake, just to make sure.

"Everything in place?"

"Do that again," he says, so I do. "Yeah, everything's in place. Now do it again."

"Maybe later, but only if you're good." I scan the room.

Everyone's in various stages of spaz-dancing to the spaz song piped through the mega-speakers onstage. "I don't think I can dance the fast ones in this dress, Jake. Sorry."

"We could have one continuous slow dance instead "

"Now why didn't I think of that?"

"Because you can't see your chest the way I'm seeing your chest. It gives me thoughts. . . ."

I stare at him. "Feeling confident?"

"I'm matching wits with you or something."

He smiles and holds out his hand. I take it and we step onto the dance floor and make a mockery of slow dancing by pressing up close and swaying back and forth. I rest my head on his shoulder and think of Evan, who will be here soon, and what that means and I think of Grey and all the stupid things I said to her just to get to this moment.

He did his bit and he goes on like . . . before.

Have I done my bit and that's why I'm letting myself be here? The answer comes to me quickly: no. I can't lose everything I've worked so hard to give up. I'll have to make up any good parts of the night later. So I'd better enjoy myself while I still can.

I trace a circle on the back of Jake's neck with the tip of my finger.

"I want to have a nice time tonight," I say.

"Me, too," he replies, his voice cracking. I stop tracing. "But what's a nice night for Parker Fadley? Just so we're clear."

I have to think about it. "I won't say anything mean, you won't ask questions I don't want to answer and I might let you kiss me. You'll make me laugh at least once before the night is over, preferably by making fun of Becky. We'll dance and have punch and on Monday we won't talk about it."

"Okay."

"What about you? What makes a nice night for you?"

He leans his head back and stares at me. "Everything you said, but maybe you'll tell me something that makes me understand you better, or where I stand with you better, and I'd like to see where we are on Monday and go from there."

"Forget about Monday," I warn him.

"We'll see."

"Please don't set yourself up for disappointment."

"Be quiet," he says. "I'm trying to think of something disparagingly clever to say about Becky and I'm coming up short."

I laugh.

"Wait, does that count? I made you laugh! That counts!"

"You didn't make fun of Becky, though; you totally failed."

"She's a bitch . . . face?"

I bite the inside of my cheek. "Points for trying, I guess."

The fast dance stops and a slow one starts, but I'm tired of this, so I gently extricate myself from Jake, and we wander over to the punch, where he fills up two cups. We lean against the wall and watch Becky, Chris, their posse and the peons try to turn a poorly decorated room into an event and I try to let myself feel happy because I'm not one of them anymore—but I'm not really happy about it tonight. I *did* used to like dances. I raise the cup to my lips and sip slowly. It's just punch. Boring.

"Nice bracelet," Jake says suddenly. "You always wear it. Was it a gift?"

"Uh . . ." I stare at the thin gold strand. "Yes and no."

And then my chest feels tight because of all the moments for him to bring it up, he'd pick this one. I snap my fingers, desperate to head off the bad feeling before it starts.

"Do you want to do something fun and not allowed?" I ask.

He eyes me warily. "And what would that be?"

I lead him around the edge of the dance floor. Grey, Henley and Bradley are clustered in one corner "supervising." They should be ashamed of how easily we sneak by them and find ourselves in the middle of the darkened halls, which is against the rules.

We have the whole school to ourselves.

"There's this rumor the skeleton in the lab glows in the dark," I lie. "I've always wanted to see if that's true."

Jake smiles. "Lead on."

The way our footsteps echo down the hall is pleasantly creepy. When we peer into the lab, Jake notes with a hint of sadness that the skeleton doesn't actually glow. Despite this, I open the door and step inside. I love the lab. The right wall is mostly made up of windows, big ones that let in lots of light. Moonlight, in this case.

Jake follows me in and shuts the door behind us. He wanders over and sits on top of one of the tables. I sit beside him—very carefully, so as not to break my dress—and swing my legs back and forth. It's quiet for a while, peaceful. I like that.

Then he speaks: "So I think I've finally figured out why I like you."

"Do tell."

"It's really unoriginal, but . . ." He clears his throat. "I've never met anyone like you before."

"Ah," I say. "You're right. That is really unoriginal."

"Well, I think you're—you're not nice. And you're definitely self-absorbed, but . . . you interest me." He pauses. "You know how when you meet someone and they just give you the impression they're living on this entirely different planet from everyone else? That's sort of how I felt when I met you. I thought, 'It must be something to know the girl who tells you that you want into her pants like five minutes after she meets you.' I mean, after I stopped being pissed off."

I force a smile. "And is it something?"

"It's difficult," he says. "You're very difficult."

"I don't mind you, Jake," I say after a second. "There. That's what you get from me. And you get tonight and on Monday you get nothing."

He stares at me.

"You really mean it, don't you?" he asks. "Do you think you're doing me a favor? Because—don't."

"I'm doing *us* a favor. Let's get it out of our systems."

"Why don't you just want to start something with me, seriously? Like maybe a date that doesn't end weirdly, like seeing a movie. . . ."

He runs a hand through his hair.

"Because this way is better," I tell him.

"But what if we did it and you found out you really liked me?"

"I could make myself get over it."

He winces. "Do you do that a lot?"

"Yeah, I'm great at it. And you're ruining this."

"Sorry."

And then he kisses me, just forces his mouth against mine, and I'm surprised by how rough it is, but that's fine, if that's how it has to be. I bring my hands to his face and press my fingernails into his cheeks hard, and he pushes me back against the desk and I'm lying down and some small part of me thinks this is funny; we're going to do it in the lab.

I reach down, push his jacket aside and fumble with his belt. Jake runs his hand up my thigh and nibbles my lower lip while I unbutton his pants. His fingers drift over my chest and his mouth moves down to my neck. I pause and enjoy the feeling of his lips against my skin. He's really good. And then he stops.

"What?" I ask. I'm short of breath; he's short of breath. He leans back, but his face is still close enough for me to give him a light kiss on the lips. "Why are you stopping?"

He stares at me a long time and then he skirts off the desk, red faced, and starts buttoning and buckling up.

"I don't want to do this," he says. He doesn't sound like he means it.

"Yes, you do." I sit up. "You're a guy. It's what guys do."

"Not—not . . ." He takes a deep breath. "No."

"Why?"

"Because it's a bad idea," he says, tugging at the edges of his jacket. "Because I don't see Monday going all that well if I fuck you in the school's science lab tonight and pretend it never happened. Which is pretty stupid, since I have a feeling this was the closest I was ever going to get."

"You're right," I say.

He groans and rubs his eye.

"You're so frustrating, you know that? You want everything and none of the—are you scared?" He shakes his head. "Is that it? I think we could have a great time."

"We could still have a great time—"

"Except forget it happened on Monday, right? And I can kiss you, but I don't know if I can hold your hand. And I can kiss you, but I can't ask you questions. Forget it, Parker. If you're too afraid to start anything, just forget it." Pause. "*Are* you afraid?"

I keep my mouth shut. We crossed a line here. Even if we didn't do anything, we really crossed a line. He sighs and opens the door to the lab.

"Whatever," he says. "We should get back."

I edge off the table but make no move to leave. I feel guilty. I hate that feeling. It's like when Bailey's looking at me and he loves me and there's nothing I can do to convince him he got such a raw deal being stuck with me.

"Are you coming?" He sounds impatient.

"I'm sorry," I say. I focus on the wall above his head because I can't look him in the eyes. "I had this plan before you got here and it's hard for me. I mean, I'm afraid—"

I hate being honest. It feels gross.

"Anyway." I swallow. "I am sorry."

It was supposed to be a nice night.

Sneaking back into the auditorium is slightly more complicated than sneaking out, but we manage. We head over to the uncomfortable metal chairs lined against the wall and sit down. It's hot, stuffy. I try and fail to spot Chris and Becky amid a throng of dancing students. Jake leans his head against the wall and closes his eyes.

The music goes fast, then slow.

"Want to dance?"

He opens his eyes. We're back where we started.

"Sure."

We dance. He wraps his arms around me and our foreheads touch and I decide this is the nice moment; this is what I'm allowed to have. I like the way he feels next to me, and if I were someone else I could be his girlfriend. And then I pretend to be her and tomorrow doesn't worry me; two weeks from now doesn't worry me. Everything is fine.

And then the dance ends.

When I get home, I realize the bracelet is gone. I imagine it slipping off my wrist in Chris's car, in the lab, on the dance floor, on the ride back.

I cut off my hair.

seventeen

Evan steps into the entrance corridor like a ghost.

People pass him without a backward glance, none of them aware of this new old addition to the halls of St. Peter's High. I watch—from a safe distance, of course—as he takes the school in like he's never seen it in his life. His hair is short, clean-cut like before, like Chris said it would be, but he's done nothing for his weight.

Leave.

I think it as hard as I can, but Evan's skull is so thick it'll probably never get through. Still. *Leave. You're not wanted here.*

I do not want you here.

My chest gets tight and I try to focus on all those techniques on the paper Jake gave me, but it doesn't work because I don't remember them, and besides, they'd never work. When my hands start shaking, I know I have to get away. I give Evan one last look and head in the opposite direction. So I can't be around him at all; that's fine. St. Peter's is a big school. I could avoid him easily for the next few . . . months.

The bottle in my locker is begging me to open it.

But I want to graduate. I want to graduate.

"I want to graduate."

I don't mean to say it out loud.

"What?" Jake looks up from our landscape. "What did you say?"

"I want to graduate. It's my new mantra."

"Oh." He turns back to the paper.

"No congratulations? It's a very positive mantra for me."

"Nope."

Things you can't do with someone without fucking up the weird enough relationship you already have:

1. Almost have sex with them in the school's science lab.
2. Give yourself a really bad haircut?

Actually, I'm not sure the haircut has anything to do with it. He hasn't said a word about it. Chris freaked, Becky laughed—she's finally better looking than I am—but Jake, Jake was quiet. He's been quiet. I can't even pretend to know what he's thinking about now and I hate that. It messes me up.

"Fadley! Gardner! In the name of our Lord Jesus Christ, *when* are you going to start painting that thing?"

I jump. Norton got us from behind. I turn and give him my sweetest smile, but he only raises one very unimpressed eyebrow at me. I think my haircut has actually compromised the manipulative properties of my face.

"You of all people should know real art can't be rushed, Mr. Norton," I say.

"If *that* is real art, Fadley," Norton says, nodding at our paper, "then please direct me to that ravine so I can throw myself into it."

Jake stares determinedly at our landscape. It's not *that* bad.

"Art is subjective," I remind Norton.

"That it is, Fadley. Nevertheless, I suggest you get a move on. Your landscapes are due at the end of this week."

The room explodes. This is news to everyone. Jake's mouth

drops open and several students make a mad scurry to the supply cabinet to get more paint. I ignore the voice in my head telling me to vomit. I want to graduate. I want to graduate. I want to graduate. Or else I'll be stuck here forever.

"Oh my!" Norton looks around the room in mock surprise and genuine delight. Old bastard. "Did I forget to tell all of you?"

"Okay, that's it," Jake says. "We need a plan and we need it now."

"I can't think," I say. I really can't. What if this is it? What if this is the stupid thing that keeps me from graduating? Unity, disparity. Unity. My fingers start tingling. I press my hands flat on the desk. Don't think about it.

"Come on, Parker," Jake says desperately. "Give me something, anything."

"Jake, shut up. I can't—"

"Why am I not surprised?" he snaps.

He wanders to the back for the paint, returning with five or six different colors, but by the time the period ends, neither of us has attempted a start.

I zombie-walk to the gym, completely forgetting about the chapel, and when I get there the cheerleaders are preparing to practice and Evan is preparing to play basketball and everyone sees me come in, so I can't leave.

Chris walks over.

"How did you get here?"

"I walked," I murmur, staring past him. I can't lose sight. I have to fix it.

"Come on; let's get you back inside. You can crash in my room."

"No—" I blink and Jessie and the guy she's with have gone. Disappeared. They were by the pool and now they're not and I haven't fixed it. I turn to Chris. "Where did they—where did they go?"

"Where did who go?"

"They—" And then this song starts up, really loud. I can't think. If I can't think, I can't find Jessie; I can't fix it. I have to find Jessie. "Chris, this music makes me feel like, it's like—"

He laughs.

"Okay, when you start talking about how the music makes you feel, maybe it's time for you to go to bed. Come on, Parker."

He tries to force me toward the house, but I jerk away.

"You're not listening to me! Just listen to me—"

"Okay, just—it's okay." But he's patronizing me. He has this stupid patronizing, condescending voice on and he thinks I'm too drunk to hear it. "Where are—"

And that's when she reappears, that strange guy beside her. No. A different guy. I relax. They start dancing and she stands on her tiptoes and kisses him, this new guy, and my stomach turns because I did this.

Evan removes himself from the basketball game before it really starts. He jogs across the gym, to the bleachers where I'm sitting, and the vice around my heart gets tighter and tighter, but I think I'll be okay as long as I focus solely on breathing. But if he starts talking to me I'm worried I won't be able to talk back and breathe at the same time.

"Hi, Parker," he says, sitting beside me. "I've been hoping to talk to you."

Inhale. "Oh?" Exhale.

Okay, maybe I can do this after all.

"Yeah. We haven't really talked. So, I mean . . ." He shrugs self-consciously. "Like, how are you? How've you been?"

Inhale. "You're missing the basketball game." Exhale.

"Not really. I'm so out of shape, passing the ball takes up most of my energy. Two minutes in and I'm on my third wind." He cracks a smile. I edge away, but he doesn't notice. "Not much changes at St. Peter's, huh? I mean it's like I never left."

"I wouldn't say that."

"Oh." That doesn't slip past him. "Okay."

"Yeah."

Oh, right—inhale. Exhale. I clench my hands into fists and glance down the court. Chris and Jake are involved in the game, but every so often one of them looks my way.

Call Evan back. Call him back and get him away from me.

"Man, I was hoping it wouldn't be like this," he says. "I wanted to talk to you."

I close my eyes.

"I have nothing to say to you, Evan."

"Hey, Parker!"

I open my eyes. Becky's staring at me expectantly, arms crossed. I can't even begin to imagine what she could possibly want with me.

"What?"

"Would you come down here and stand in place for Ellie? She's sick and I want to see the formation from the front without a big gaping hole in it. You don't have to do anything, just stand there."

"Sure."

I jump up and jog over to the squad. The girls are already in formation. I take a quick look back and Evan's where I left him, staring at me. I don't like that.

"Where do you want me?" I ask Becky.

"Over there, between Sarah and Hannah," she says, pointing. "Are you okay?"

The girls stare at us, awaiting instruction. Robots.

"Why?"

"You look weird." She smiles. "And *not* just because of the hair."

I wipe my palms on my skirt. Block it out. He's not there.

"As former captain, I'm trying to get over my disgust that you can't use your imagination to pretend Ellie's in her usual spot," I say. A couple girls gasp. "I did that for all of those practices *you* managed not to show up for."

Becky scowls. "Are you going to help me or not?"

"Oh, I'm not helping you, Becky. I'm here for my own amusement."

With that, I flounce into Ellie's spot, and Becky climbs a little way up the bleachers to inspect us.

"Okay, it's good," she shouts. "Parker, stay there. The rest of you show me what victory looks like!"

The girls stretch their arms into the *V*. Evan's still looking at me. I want him to stop. They move onto the *I*. I glance down the court again.

Come on, Chris. Call Evan back.

Make him stop.

I pull at my collar. It's hot in this gym; it's—*T. O.* I realize I'm not breathing again. I'm not breathing and it's hot. The scene turns to mush. I try to blink it back into focus. The girls are moving in slow motion but not really, but they *are* standing too close and if Evan doesn't stop staring at me I'll—

"Somebody get Henley or something."

I don't want to open my eyes.

"Just wait. Parker? Can you hear me? Parker?"

I am not going to open my eyes. I'm going to lie on the court until I die, and I hope that happens soon, because I want to die.

"Okay, someone get Henley."

After a minute, I open my eyes. Chris notices first.

"Hey," he says.

Jake glances at him. Then me. He exhales, relieved.

"You're okay."

If he says so, it must be true. I stare at everyone staring at me. The entire stupid cheerleading squad and all of the brainless hard-core jocks. This is great.

I will the floor to open up and eat me alive.

"Hey, let's give her some space. Get back to the game, guys," Chris says. Thank God for him, just this once. "And cheerleading. Get back to that, too." No one moves. "Okay, fuck off, basically, is what I'm saying. Fuck off!"

Everyone mumbles in assent and scatters back to opposite sides of the court. That's what it's like to be popular. Becky lingers a minute before remembering she's captain and Jake helps me into sitting position and I try to think of something clever and smart-ass to say, but I can't and it freaks me out.

Chris crouches down and hands me his water bottle.

"Drink that." He looks so concerned I want to die. "You'll feel better."

I take a small sip and hand the bottle back. Maybe the first words out of my mouth don't have to be totally smart-ass. Just normal.

But I have nothing.

And that's when I notice Evan's not around. Gone. And then I wonder if he was ever here at all and my hands start shaking because seriously, what if he wasn't and I'm losing it? I try to hide my hands, but Jake sees and he gives me this look and I *still* can't think of anything to say and it's quiet.

And then Henley comes in and Evan is with her. Oh.

"What happened here?"

I wish for once she'd look surprised to see me. I move to get up, but Jake puts a hand on my shoulder, stopping me, while Chris explains the situation to the best of his limited vocabulary. I meet Evan's eyes and I guess I'm sending out the right *go away* vibes, because he skulks off to play basketball with the rest of the guys.

When Chris is finished, Henley regards me carefully. Even she has more couth than to ask whether or not I've been drinking or whatever in front of everyone. But it should be painfully obvious I haven't, because I don't look happy.

"Nurse's office," she says. "Can you walk, Fadley?"

I get to my feet with Jake's unneeded assistance.

"I want to go home," I say.

Except my voice cracks and just like that I'm totally overwhelmed by how stupid this feels and the edges of my mouth start pulling themselves down like they always do when I'm about to cry and then I realize *I'm about to cry*. I cover my eyes. *Don't cry.*

Don't cry.

"Fadley?"

"I—" If I don't lower my hands, they'll think I'm crying anyway, and I can't let them think that so I drop my hands to my sides. "I don't want to go to the nurse's office. I don't feel well. I want to go home."

Jake and Chris stare at me funny. Maybe they think it's a crock.

I mean, even Henley doesn't really seem convinced, but she never does.

But Bailey believes me. I spend the evening sitting in a chair by my window and he guards me diligently, ready to ward off any intruders that dare disturb me. He actually growls a little the first time my bedroom door opens, but he wags his tail when he sees it's Mom. It's Mom, even though I told her to leave me alone because I know I make her feel the worst when I make her feel useless.

She tugs at a strand of my hair and sighs.

"At least let me even out the edges, Parker."

I rub my wrist. I wish it was there. The bracelet.

"If I do, will you let me stay home from school for the next two days?"

She's quiet for a long time, debating it.

"Fine," she finally says. "I'll get the scissors. Meet me in the kitchen."

Bailey follows me downstairs, where Mom's set up barbershop—a chair atop scattered newspapers in the middle of the room. She stands behind it, waiting, scissors in one hand. I sit.

"I worry about you, Parker," she says, gently pushing my head forward. I want to tell her to join the club and then I want to tell her how boring that makes her and to not be so tedious. But I don't. Snip, snip, snip. "You used to talk to me."

But I never *said* anything.

"You were so . . ."

Perfect. She never finishes, but I know if she had, that's what she would've said. *Perfect. You were so.*

When she's finished evening out my hack job, my hair that used to fall past my shoulders now stops at my chin. And it looks horrible.

Which is good, I guess.

eighteen

"**Hey, Parker?**"

I slam my locker shut. Evan.

He's incredibly in-my-face for a guy who knows I want nothing to do with him, but at least I'm more capable of handling myself now. During my two-day vacation I did a little cognitive behavior therapy and taught myself this anxiety transference trick, where I effectively turn the feeling that my heart wants to claw its way out of my chest into sheer annoyance and total anger every time I see him.

Which means my hands might still shake, but the difference is that it's not going to end in total nervous collapse.

Here's hoping it works.

"What." It's not a question; it's a statement. And I spit it at him.

He cringes.

"I'm sorry, I know you don't want to . . ." He shifts and just blurts it out: "Look, do you remember that party last year, I mean, like, at all?"

"Why?"

"Because—" He takes one look at my face and shakes his head. "You know what? Never mind. Chris said you didn't."

"Well, don't take him at his word or anything; he's only your best friend." My voice oozes sarcasm. In our old lives, Evan and I didn't like each other very much. This feels like slipping on a pair of comfortable old shoes. "Thanks for wasting my time."

"I had to ask," he says, but he doesn't go.

"I barely remember it," I lie; if anything, I remember it too well. Then I pretend to spot someone over his shoulder. "Oh, hi, Jenny! Have you welcomed Evan back yet?"

He turns white and whirls around. Jenny's not there, of course, and he should know that, but when he faces me, furious patches of red decorate his pale face.

"If anything, you're an even bigger bitch than you used to be," he mutters. He storms off, not knowing how reaffirming it is to hear that. I feel steadier on my feet than I have in days. Still got it.

I put on a radiant smile for art and sit next to Jake.

"So, I think I've finally got an idea for our project," I say without adding *you know, the one that's due tomorrow?* "We might have to put in some time after school, but I didn't think you'd mind very much."

"Forget it," Jake says. "I already handed it in."

"Okay, so what we do is—" I stop and process. "What?"

"While you were gone, I just did it. I took it home and I did it. Handed it in yesterday. You don't have to worry about it."

"Oh."

"Norton seemed to like it. So we've got the period to draw whatever we want."

I nod slowly. "Okay."

I get us paper from the supply closet and my mind is going a thousand thoughts a second but never settles on one. I used to be good at improvising.

I set the paper in front of him.

"Why would you do that?" I ask.

"I figured you had enough to deal with."

"You mean you felt sorry for me."

"Did I say that?" He grabs a pencil and starts doodling. "I don't feel sorry for you, but do you really think you could've gotten yourself together enough to help me get our project finished? But be honest when you answer."

"That's not fair."

"You're the one who disappeared for two days."

I snap my fingers.

"You know, you were acting strange on Monday," I finally say. "Like, weird. I *knew* I shouldn't have gone to the dance with you—"

"I was acting like how *you* wanted me to act," he points out calmly.

"Yeah, and then some."

"What's it to you?"

"It's—" Goddammit. I snap my fingers again. "Are you trying to back me into a corner so I'll date you or something? Because here's a little advice for you: girls don't like being emotionally blackmailed."

"What am I blackmailing you with? I don't have anything you want."

"I—"

"Look, I made this decision after the dance," he says. "I don't want to screw around since you've made it pretty clear you're not interested in actually starting anything. You should be happy. It works out for you better this way."

"I like it the other way," I say stupidly.

"Too bad."

"You can't just *not* like me. Feelings don't go away like that. Ask Chris. He's still totally in love with me and it's been months and months."

But it occurs to me I don't know if that's true anymore.

"I'll get over it," Jake says, his eyes meeting mine.

"Fine, fine, fine," I say quickly, still snapping. I don't know why I care, but I don't like him getting to decide this. It's mine to decide. "If that's the way you want it, let's go out. Let's go out tonight. I'll take you out. How about that?"

He falters. I can tell.

"I can't. I'll be at Chris's tonight."

"How about after? Or are you staying the night?"

"I'm staying. We're going to Whitney tomorrow, to this old car exhibit."

"Is Evan going to be there?"

"Not that I'm aware of."

"Why?"

He shrugs. "Ask him yourself."

I corner Chris on his way to his last class.

"Aren't you still best friends with Evan?"

He blinks. "I like your hair. I'm getting used to it."

"How come you didn't invite Evan to that stupid old car exhibit?"

"Because Evan's not into stupid old cars?"

"Evan wasn't into a ton of stuff you liked and you made him do it anyway. So are you still best friends with him or what?"

"Why?"

"I have to know."

He glances at his wristwatch.

"I don't have time for the 'things change' speech, Parker."

"So give me the CliffNotes version."

"Okay. You ready?" he asks. I nod. "Things change."

"*Chris.*"

He makes an exasperated noise.

"He just got back and there happens to be this event in Whitney that I think I'd probably have a better time at if I took Jake along. Over Evan. Satisfied?"

I shake my head. "No."

"Why?"

"I don't know." Everything feels wrong. I start snapping my fingers again. "But what about me? How do you feel about me? You're still hung up on me, aren't you?"

"Parker—"

"This is your fault," I say. "You made me go to the dance."

His mouth drops open.

I go to the girls' washroom and pace because my brain is telling me to do something and this is it. Pace. This is *so* annoying; last week I had the whole school and everyone in it and now things are different and I hate it. The door opens, but I pace in spite of it. Anyway, it's Becky, so it doesn't matter.

"Oh," she says when she sees me. She walks over to the sink, pencil case in hand because that's where she keeps her makeup. "Hi."

I watch, still pacing, as she takes out her lipstick and gets to work.

"What do you and Chris talk about?"

The lipstick hovers above her lower lip. She stares at me in the mirror.

"None of your business?"

"Do you talk about, like, the deep stuff? Important stuff? Or just basketball and cheerleading? Or is it a sex thing and you don't talk at all?"

She does her lips and caps her lipstick before she even dignifies that with an answer, which drives me crazy.

"What did you and Chris talk about?" she asks.

"Everything," I say quickly. "Our conversations were deep and profound."

"Would you quit pacing?"

I can't stop. I want to tell her that, but I don't.

And I wouldn't stop anyway, now that I know she wants me to.

"Do you talk about Evan and stuff?"

"And stuff," she repeats faintly, smiling a little. "And stuff? Yeah, we talk about Evan 'and stuff.'"

"Do you talk about me?"

She crosses her arms. "What is *wrong* with you, Parker?"

"Is Chris over me? I mean—" I stop pacing. "Is he?"

"Your name doesn't come up so much anymore."

I snap my fingers. Both of them. Again and again.

"Just like that?"

"Just like that."

"I don't believe you."

I leave the washroom as the bell rings, Becky calling after me.

I've got my usual meeting with Grey, and for once in my life I'm glad. Finally, someone I can predict. I enter her office, sit down, and we say nothing and I feel a little better. At least there's still one person in this school who can be counted on.

After the first fifteen minutes of quiet, she starts flipping through a magazine.

I blink.

I'm on the lawn, by the bushes where I threw up. I blink again and I'm next to Chris. I blink again and Jessie's dancing, making out with a new mystery guy, different from the last one. Where do they all come from? I blink again and Evan's there, screaming at both of them. I blink again and someone's pulling Chris away because something's broken, a lamp or a vase.

I blink again and I'm alone, in front of the drinks table set out on the lawn. I'm here because I'm thirsty. My hands drift over the booze and go straight for the bowl of punch for the designated driver. I fill up a cup with shaking hands and drink it, then another.

It's passion fruit or strawberry Hawaiian something and it tastes good.

Then, a voice behind me:

"Someone spiked that, like, an hour ago."

I drop the cup and moan.

"Oh, God."

Becky laughs. "Good one."

I shuffle over to a soft patch of grass and sit down. Someone will probably have to peel my alcohol-bloated corpse off the lawn come morning.

"Chris wants me to get you inside," Becky says, grabbing my arms and pulling. She stumbles forward and giggles, her face in my face, beer on her breath. "Come on."

"Where's Jessie?"

"Somewhere. I was just talking to her," she says brightly, pulling on my arm again. She gives up and sits beside me. "She and Evan are so over, by the way. Well done, Parker. I should console him."

"You would."

Then I remember it's my mission to fix what I did, because it's wrong and I don't do things that are wrong. The goal swims in front of my mind and starts to drift away, but I try really hard to hold on to it. And then I close my eyes.

Maybe after I sleep.

"Did you see them fighting by the pool? So over," she says again, giggling. My head snaps up. "Big surprise. Me and Evan, we'd make a much better match."

"Parasite," I say. I blink several times, trying to snap myself out of this fuzzy place. "It's never going to happen."

"It will. We have tons in common." Tipsy Becky is a thousand times more annoying than sober Becky, and that's saying something. "So when are you going to relinquish captaining duties to me, anyway?"

"Fuck off and die first and then we'll talk," I mumble, feeling my *head go forward. It wants to sleep. No. I jerk upright. It doesn't really help.*

"I'll be captain in a week." Her voice is hard, too hard, and it dawns on me through the murk that she's only pretending to be drunk, which is one of her favorite party tricks because she's under this bizarre delusion it's cute. *"You'll finally snap or the rest of the girls will vote you off the squad. Whichever comes first."*

"Brave to say so in front of me." I struggle to push myself up from the ground, but it's just not happening. *"I could ruin your life."*

"You won't remember any of this," she says.

"What makes you think you deserve to be captain?"

"I'm nicer than you, for starters." She goes quiet for so long I think that's it, I can pass out, but no, she starts talking again. *"I'm nice to everyone and no one gives a damn. You tear people down and act like you're doing them a favor and they act like you're Jesus because they're stupid enough to believe it. At least they're starting to catch on now. Not even being Chris's girlfriend is helping you. And I'm so looking forward to making everyone realize how much better they could've had it with me."*

"That's really pathetic." I have to force every word through my teeth. *"And I'll remember this, Becky."*

She snorts.

"Where's Jessie?" I use Becky's shoulder to get into standing position. The world tilts. For a second, I think I'll be sick, but I'm not and I'm standing and it's a miracle. *"Becky, where is she?"*

"I talked to her for a minute, after she and Evan fought. She was crying her eyes out. She said she was going to run away. Drama Queen." Becky looks up at me and smiles. *"Nice going, Parker."*

"Where did she go?"

Becky points in the direction of the woods.

nineteen

They could be talking about me, like, right now.

Chris and Jake.

I hate that.

So after I choke down dinner I decide to take Bailey for a walk. I slip on my shoes, call him from the living room and hook him up to the leash. He figures out what's going on and squirms and slobbers all over me.

"I thought dogs were supposed to mellow with age," I tell him. He flicks his tongue at my face and I back away just in time. "Jesus, Bailey."

"Parker, don't talk like that in the house," Mom says. "It's disrespectful."

Jesus, Jesus, Jesus.

"I'll see you guys later."

"Have a nice walk, sweetheart." Dad.

"Be home by nine." Mom. I don't say anything. "I mean it, Parker."

"Yeah, sure," I say, and then, for good measure: "Whatever."

So I leave and we walk, and it's an okay walk. I steer Bailey onto Chris's street without realizing it. Actually, that's a lie. I know what I'm doing.

I know what I'm doing and it's stupid.

But Bailey pulls me forward at a happy trot, his tongue always and forever hanging out of his mouth. The closer we get to Chris's house, the more uneasy I feel, but maybe I'd feel better to pass it once and then go home.

So that's what I'll do.

We're practically there when this string of cars go by, one after the other, and I feel criminal, caught. It makes me want to turn back, but I can't because the thought is there, that I should pass the house. So I have to.

This is *so* stupid.

And then this explosion of sound fills the street, like a small bomb going off—an engine backfiring—and Bailey yelps and tears loose because I'm not holding the leash tightly enough. He runs into the road and before I can call him back or go after him, there are all these other sounds, smaller sounds, this dull thud, squealing tires.

And then silence.

Just like that.

He lies in the middle of the street, his legs splayed out before him the way they are when he sleeps on the living-room floor. I go to him, kneel down in front him. He stares up at me, pitiful but alive. But what kind of—

What kind of asshole *hits a dog and drives away*?

Bailey shudders.

"Bailey. Bailey—Bailey . . ."

I spew his name. I say it a thousand times in three seconds. I rest my hand on his stomach and it comes back red and he makes a noise, this awful whimper.

"Stop that," I snap. "You're fine. We'll just get you off the—"

I wrap my arms around him so I can drag him off the road, but I don't have the strength to lift him and my shirt gets red. I have to let him go.

I wasn't holding the leash tightly enough.

"Don't," I tell him. "You're fine. I'll get someone. I'll—"

I stand. I don't have a lot of time. I need—

Chris. Chris can fix this; he's rich.

I run to his house and pound on the door and ring the bell at the same time and it seems like hours before the door actually opens and there he is.

Chris.

"What the fuck—" He stops, his eyes traveling from my face to my hands to my shirt. The parts of me that are red. "Parker, what happened?"

"My dog got hit by a car. I don't know what to do."

He stares at me uncomprehendingly and then Jake appears behind him and gives me this surprised look and Bailey is dying.

"What's going on?" Jake asks.

I don't have time for this. I'm wasting time. I run back down the driveway and they both follow after me, calling my name.

But they quiet when Bailey comes into view.

"Oh God," Chris mutters.

My pulse is in my ears, loud and insistent.

When we get to Bailey, he's still.

"I'm so sorry, Parker," Jake says.

For a second, I think my heart is going to explode.

But then the feeling goes away.

"This engine backfired or something; it really scared him." I stare at Bailey's body. It doesn't even look real. "I wasn't holding the leash tightly enough."

"Did you see who did it?" Jake asks.

"No—I thought there'd be time to do something for him," I say stupidly. I wish his eyes would close. Bailey's. "Sorry for dragging you out. . . ."

"It's okay," Chris says.

"No, it's not. I should really go."

I stand and start heading down the street without looking back at either of them. I want to get far away from Bailey's body. Take a shower. Get his blood off of me. I pull at my shirt. Off of me.

"Parker, where are you going?"

I stop and turn. I hear the question, but . . .

"Your house is that way." Chris points in the opposite direction.

"I'll get there eventually."

"Why don't you come inside and I'll make tea or something."

"No thanks."

"I know you," he says. "You won't go home."

"I *can't* go home."

"You can stay at my place tonight."

No.

"You have that car show."

"Forget it," Jake says.

Chris holds out his hand.

"Come on."

"I wasn't holding the leash tightly enough."

I don't know why I say it again. They look at me funny. And then Chris takes me by the elbow and the three of us walk up to his house.

I can't feel my feet.

I can't feel my feet and the night has all caught up with me, but I soldier on. The farther I get from the house, the louder the music sounds. A heavy bass line and an earsplitting drumbeat winds its way into the woods from Chris's open bedroom window. And then there's the splashing sounds from the pool and everyone's laughing and talking and shrieking and having a good time.

Because Chris's parties are the best except when they're not.

Twenty-five steps into the woods, I think about lying down or turn-

*ing back. I can't feel my feet, I can't feel my legs, anything, and my
head is barely attached to my neck, but I've got to fix this because I'm
supposed to be better than this and what if everyone finds out I'm not.*

A few more steps. I hear something and I stop.

"Go to the guest room, take a shower and grab a nightshirt.
You know where everything is," Chris says, closing the door behind us. "Come down and we'll have . . . tea."

"Tea," I repeat faintly. "Do you even know how to make tea?"

"It can't be that hard," he says, heading for the kitchen.

I go upstairs. I sit on the bed in the guest room. I don't even
feel like showering anymore. I just want to sit here with Bailey's
blood on me while he's splayed out on the middle of the road.

He can't stay there forever.

After a while, I tiptoe down the hall to Chris's parents' bedroom, steal into their bathroom and turn on the light. I stare at
myself in the mirrored cabinet. I look really bad. I open the cabinet and stare at the prescription bottles inside.

Chris's mom was a desperate housewife before it was cool.

I grab the bottle of pills that make you happy and let you go to
sleep, open it up and empty them beside the sink. I start counting
them out, and when I've done that I arrange them in neat rows of
six.

*I can make out two shapes in the darkness, on the ground. On a bed
of pine needles. My heart sinks. I inch forward quietly and hold my
breath. If she's fucked him, this is—this is harder to fix. Jessie's fucking
him.*

"What are you doing?"

My hand jerks into the rows of pills and some of them scatter
into the sink. I scramble to prevent as many of them from going
down the drain as I can, but it's futile, they all go, and anyway, it
doesn't matter.

I start putting what's left of them back.

"Why don't you tell me what you think I'm doing?" I ask.

"I don't even want to say it."

I rub my hands on my shirt.

"I just wanted one to sleep. Your mom has the good stuff."

"A whole bottle is hardly one."

"I wanted to pick the right one."

"Oh, duh. I should have known."

"I—" I force myself to look Chris in the eyes. "I have to take that shower."

"Fine. But if it takes longer than ten minutes I'm coming back up to get you."

I take the shower, but I make sure it's a long one just to see if he'll come in. He doesn't, like I knew he wouldn't. Because the air is different now. I'm far away from the pills and they're far away from me, but Bailey's still out on the road, dead, not far away at all, and he can't stay there forever.

I come out of the bathroom and change into one of the nightshirts they leave for the guests and wrap myself up in one of the guest housecoats.

And then I put on my best face and head downstairs.

"—But we have to move him," Jake's saying. "Should we get Parker?"

"She's upset. We could do it for her," Chris says. Pause. "I don't know. Maybe she wants to be there for it. Maybe we should get her."

Silence.

"Well, which is it?"

"I don't know," Chris says again. "I hate this."

It gets heavy quiet. I sneak out the back door, putting as much distance as possible between me and the house. I thought I knew why I was coming out here, but now, between the road and woods, I'm not so sure.

I head for the woods.

It's extremely quiet. No matter how close I get to all the trees, even memories of sound are hushed by the death out on the street.

And then I'm in the woods. In them. Just far enough in.

I get down on my hands and knees and start brushing pine needles aside. Maybe the bracelet will show up again. Maybe I'm supposed to lose it every so often and then I'm supposed to find it again and Bailey was supposed to die because it's here for me, like it was before. And then I can wear it around my wrist, for both of them—

Bailey.

I can't do this. What am I doing?

I leave the woods and make my way to the road, to do what I should've done in the first place. He's still there, all broken and stiff, and I think I hate him for it. I kneel in front of his body and rest my hand on his chest, hoping for a heartbeat even though I know there won't be one.

Or maybe . . .

I rest my head against his chest and listen. His fur is scratchy and unpleasant against my skin, not soft like it was, the blood on it caked and flaking.

I close my eyes and I really listen.

Come on, Bailey, you stupid dog.

Come on.

Please.

"Parker?"

It's Jake.

"My dog's dead," I say. He kneels beside me, but he doesn't say anything, so I keep talking. "I knew this would happen."

"You couldn't have predicted that car."

"Yeah, I could have," I say. "Because that's what I do to people.

And now dogs. I just fuck them up. And it's always spectacular how I do it, too. But—maybe not before. I wouldn't have predicted it *before*. But now I can."

He stares at me, concerned. I feel off my head.

"What do you mean?" he asks.

"Before I thought I was above letting these kinds of things happen, but now I know that's not the truth. Now it's just a matter of time before they do. And I knew if Bailey—" I gaze at my dog's prone form. He was my dog. "I knew it would end like this. And here we are."

"Here we are."

"It shouldn't upset me that you guys are done with me," I say. "Because that's what I want."

"Really," Jake says. "That's what you want?"

"Yeah. I just forget it sometimes, I guess. I don't know."

"You don't know?"

"You're echoing everything I say." I meet his eyes and I can't believe how it wasn't that long ago he was just this new kid and I kind of scared him and somewhere along the way I got lazy and let him get close, so I guess that means he'll get hit by a car or something, too. "I like certain things a certain way or it's not right. But I've been forgetting."

"I'm sorry," he says.

"But he was a good dog," I say after a minute, running my hand over Bailey's head, the way he liked it when he was alive. Alive. I swallow. "And I have to move him. I can't leave him here."

"Parker, I can . . ." He hesitates. "Do you need help?"

My answer gets stuck in my throat and stays there, never passing my lips.

It doesn't matter.

Together, we move Bailey off the road.

twenty

Mom decides we should bury Bailey under the maple tree in the backyard. She asked me what I thought about it and I said I didn't care, but she just kept at it and kept at it and I just wanted her to shut up, so in the end I had to remind her about the time I told her I couldn't have cared less if Bailey died, and it worked. She shut up.

And she hasn't really spoken to me since.

"It felt like we had him longer." Mom wipes her eyes. Dad nods and wraps an arm around her. "We should have had him longer."

That's a dig at me.

"I guess it was just his time," Dad says after a while.

"Lucky him," I say.

It just slips out.

"What did you say?" Dad's voice is sharp. He gives me this look. I shrug and march away from the whole scene, but he keeps talking. "Parker, get back here and tell me what you said—Parker!"

"What did she say?" Mom asks.

And of course they can't just leave it at that. On Monday, on my way to catch the school bus, my little slip-of-the-tongue turns into this:

"Make sure you come straight home after school."

I pause at the door.

"Why?"

"Because your mother and I need to talk with you."

Think quick, Parker.

"I can't."

Dad lowers the paper and looks at me, like, I don't know.

"Why?"

"I promised Becky I'd give her some tips about these new cheerleading routines she's planned. She's not feeling so confident about them. And then I was going to . . ." I fumble for the words. "I was going to stay the night. I forgot to ask. Sorry."

He frowns and thinks about it. Doesn't even notice I don't have an overnight bag or anything, but doesn't want to believe that after all this I would still lie. It's sad.

"Fine," he says, returning to the paper. "Tomorrow then."

"Death freaks me out," Jake says suddenly.

It's going to be one of those days.

"Thanks for sharing," I say. I'm filling my blank sheet of paper with circles and he's drawing a tree. Art is back to normal, as in no one really cares. "I don't know what I ever would have done had you not told me that about you."

He frowns.

"I don't like it. It always makes me take stock. And then I have to go through this process where I have to decide how important things are and if I'm doing enough about them. That freaks me out, too. Does that happen to you? . . . Did it happen to you?"

"Nope."

"So I called my mom."

I stop drawing and give him my full attention because if we're talking about this we're not talking about Bailey or me.

"What happened?"

He squints at his paper.

"She thought I was calling to beg to come back home. It didn't go so well when she found out I wasn't."

"That sucks."

"Yeah."

"So what are you going to do about it?"

"What can I do about it?" He shrugs. "She's decided; I've decided. I called her and she shut me out."

"Does it make you feel worse or better?"

He thinks about it for a second.

"I thought I'd be happy for the closure. But it's worse, actually. I feel guilty."

"So what happens next?"

He shrugs again.

"I keep going from here?"

We reach for the white gummy eraser sitting between us at the same time. His hand brushes over mine and then lingers there and I freeze.

"Your hand is on my hand," I say in this completely stupid voice.

And then Chris struts over under Norton's disapproving gaze, but since the sun is shining and it's nice out he's feeling lenient enough not to shout Chris back to his seat.

"Hey, Jake. Rain check tonight."

"What?" Jake turns around. "What the fuck?"

"Sorry," Chris says, glancing at me and looking away. "It's just that Becky's got romantic-type plans."

I roll my eyes. Becky's idea of "romantic" is no underwear.

"So?" Jake asks.

"So," Chris says slowly, leaning forward, "I can either fuck Becky or dick around with you. What do you think I'm going to choose?"

"Oh, fuck off," Jake mutters. "Asshole."

Chris punches him in the arm.

"Thanks, man. I knew you'd understand."

"You've got until I count to three to get back to your seat, Fllory," Norton says lazily from the front of the room. "One . . . two . . ."

Chris scurries away.

"Plans tonight?" I ask.

"Not anymore," Jake grumbles. "I'm on a two-day vacation from my parents. It was going to be a guys' night in, blow off school tomorrow. We've been planning it forever."

"Sounds pretty hot."

"I was hoping," he says, grinning. "I mean, look at him. He's so built."

"You're preaching to the choir, Jake." We draw in silence for a little bit and I'm thinking, thinking, thinking. I know how to take advantage of every situation and I've got nowhere to sleep to-night. "If you ask me over right now, there's a ninety percent chance I'll say yes."

Jake stops drawing, but he doesn't look at me.

"Are you serious?"

"Eighty. It's eighty percent now." Pause. "Seventy . . ."

"Come over?"

I stare at all the circles I've drawn.

"Yeah."

On the bus ride there's only quiet between us. Jake leads me off at his stop and we walk up Trudeau Road, to his house near the end of it. I recognize the place. It's a small bungalow with a neat front lawn and a cute little garden along the path to the front door. The shutters are faded pink. It's the kind of house that might as well have a sign that says GOOD PEOPLE LIVE HERE mounted in front of it.

"How did you finish our art project anyway?" I ask while Jake unlocks the front door. "What did you do in the end?"

"Oh," he says, pausing, "I painted half of it and let the other half stay unfinished. I don't think even Norton knew what he was talking about when he said all that bullshit about unity and disparity. He was just fucking with us. But he enjoyed the picture. Said the right side reminded him of you."

I'm not expecting that.

"Why?"

"It was the unfinished side. He was totally on to us."

I smile. "Seriously?"

"Yeah." He opens the door and steps aside. "But he still gave us an A, so it's all good."

The front door opens into the kitchen, which is a small, neat little room with a tiny breakfast nook that must serve as the lunch and dinner table as well.

"Nice place," I say automatically, because that's what you do.

"Thanks," Jake says. He sets his book bag on the floor, so I do the same. He makes a beeline for the fridge, totally relaxed. "Are you thirsty? Hungry?"

"Thirsty."

"Water, Coke, OJ? . . . Heineken?"

"Water, thanks."

He hands me a bottle, takes one for himself and leans against the kitchen counter, staring at me. He gets the upper hand because it's his house. I should've thought of that before I wrangled an invitation out of him. I twist the cap off my water and sip.

"Sure you're not hungry?" he asks after a minute.

This is weird.

"I'm sure."

"Well, I'm starving and I have to do something about it." He heads back to the fridge, rifles through it, and pretty soon he's got all the ingredients needed to make a sandwich massive enough to feed ten men or one teenage boy. "Hey, First Friday Mass is this Friday."

I groan. "Don't remind me."

"Yeah, tell me about it. What a waste of time." He looks at me. "Is that blasphemous? I don't know how you crazy Catholics operate."

"It's probably blasphemous."

He goes back to the fridge, retrieves an apple and tosses it to me.

"I never see you eat lunch," he says. "Eating is good for you."

I sit at the table and roll the apple along the varnished wood surface.

"You go to church a lot?" he asks, throwing everything imaginable between two thin slices of bread. For the first time since we got here, he sounds awkward. I don't want things to be awkward when we have the whole evening stretched out in front of us.

"Not outside of school, no."

It goes quiet, which makes everything else get loud. Jake finishes making his sandwich and the sound of his chewing is amplified by our silence, weirdly punctuating the moment. I stop rolling the apple and take a bite. It's so sweet, I almost gag.

"I miss my mom, though," Jake says randomly. "Before my dad fucked around on her she wasn't as bitter and crazy as she is now."

"Gee, who would've thought," I say.

He laughs.

"She really thought I was going to stay with her. Like, she really—" He breaks off and shakes his head. "Anyway, that's the worst thing I've done. Chose my dad."

"That must be a relief for you," I say, setting the apple on the table. "Imagine if you'd done something really, really bad."

He stares at me, bemused.

"What's that supposed to mean?"

"She's your mom. She'll forgive you. You'll forgive her."

"It could be years from now."

"So you lose a little time. You still get to fix it."

He sips his water.

"What's the worst thing you've ever done?"

"None of your business." I run my finger along the ragged edges of the apple where I bit it. "Nothing that can be fixed."

"It can't be that bad."

"You don't know that, though, do you?"

"Okay. . . ." He chews his thumbnail. "It can't be fixed, so let it go."

"I'll just do that."

He's forgotten his sandwich. He tilts his head back and closes his eyes and stays that way for a minute. Then he opens his eyes and stares at me.

"How do you get to be an eighteen-year-old who's done something so unimaginably horrible it can't be fixed? I mean, seriously?"

"Where's your bathroom?"

He blinks.

"Through the living room, down the hall," he says, pointing. "It's the second door on the right."

I wander through his living room, which is sort of quaint and cozy, and down the narrow strip of hall with doors that offshoot into bedrooms, closets and bathrooms. The room opposite the bathroom catches my attention. It's unmistakably Jake's room, from the clothes piled on the floor to the unmade bed. I check to see if he's watching me from the kitchen. He's not.

I cross the hall and enter his room.

You can tell a lot about a person from their personal space, go figure. The posters on the wall make Jake's homesickness more evident than he ever would. There are no declarations of love for a particular band or movie, only shots of buildings in a city by the sea. I move to the bulletin board hanging over his desk and study the photographs tacked to it. Jake is in every single photo, naturally, and he's always surrounded by people and he always looks happy. I lean forward and peer at a photo of him wedged between two people who I'm guessing are his parents, pre-divorce.

He looks a lot like his mom.

"My yearbooks are on the bookshelf, if you're curious. And, uh, that's my underwear drawer over there and of course there's my closet. Snoop away."

I try not to let on he's startled me.

"Nice room," I say.

"It does the job." He's right behind me, really close. "You never answered my question."

"Don't you ever get tired of asking me questions?"

"Have to fill the moment somehow," he says.

I turn. We're close. Like, I Could Kiss Him close. I skirt around him and sit on the bed. He sits beside me and clears his throat.

"I just wonder what you're punishing yourself for, that's all," he says.

"I . . ." I clench my right hand, my fingernails digging into my palm. "I did something really wrong and I knew it was really wrong while I was doing it and I did it anyway."

"It happens."

"Not to me."

My eyes hurt and my throat is tight. But I don't want to cry in front of Jake because there's nothing in it for me.

"Oh hey," Jake says, alarmed, when the first tear gets by me. "I'm sorry."

Goddammit.

"You should be."

If my life were a movie, this would be the scene where I start blubbering and tell Jake to stay away from me or he'll just end up hurt or dead and, I don't know, maybe we'd kiss and try it anyway. But as fast as the tears come, they stop.

"Was it when—" He clears his throat. "Was it when you tried to kill yourself?"

I don't say anything.

"I mean . . . what was that like?"

I snort. "Well, it was obviously a very happy period in my life."

"Why are you doing that?"

"Doing what?"

"Snapping your fingers."

I look down. Sure enough, I'm snapping. He reaches over and grabs my hand. Holds it. I try to act like it doesn't bother me.

"I shouldn't have asked," he says.

It's just getting more and more awkward. There are *hours* until tomorrow.

"I stole a few hundred dollars from Chris and I got the hell out of Corby," I say after a minute. I've never talked about it like this before. "And I got a big bottle of booze and a big bottle of sleeping pills. And I downed both. And then I got found. And then I got my stomach pumped."

"How close were you?"

"I don't know."

Not close enough.

The phone rings from some other room. Jake clears his throat and the moment is over. I wonder how people lived with each other before they could learn to count on these types of inconveniences.

"I should get that," he says.

He leaves the room and a minute later his voice wafts into the bedroom from the kitchen and I can't think of anything to do, so I start rifling through his nightstand. I wouldn't do it if I knew he'd have a problem with it. Or maybe I would. Cough drops, condoms, old movie stubs and loose change. By the time Jake gets back, my hands are folded in my lap. He stands in the doorway, a silhouette.

"Parker, why are you here?" he asks.

"Do you want me to go?"

"No, no. It's—" He steps into the room and sits back down beside me. "I was just wondering why you're here. I mean, I'm *glad* you're here, but—"

I kiss him then, not to shut him up, but because I want to and because no one says things like *I'm glad you're here* to me anymore, which is mostly my fault, and I don't know, I don't want to keep coming back to him because it's better if I don't.

So I should get this part over with.

Jake kisses back. His lips are soft. My fingertips drift over his cheeks and I want this and I'm so caught up in how nice he feels and how nice he smells and the way he's touching me, I can almost pretend it's okay that I want this.

It's okay to want this. Everything's . . .

His mouth moves from my lips to my neck. I close my eyes.

"I'm glad I'm here," I murmur.

"What?" His voice tickles my skin. He heard it. I know he did.

"Nothing," I say, and his lips are on mine again.

I don't remember lying down, but we're lying down.

His hand slides up my shirt. He hesitates and I like the way his fingers dance around my skin, unsure, before his hands are all over me and mine are all over him and I half-expect to check out, but I'm really there for it. It's not like at the dance, angry and forced. It's terrible in its gentleness and he's just wasting it on me.

twenty-one

"Leaving?"

Jake sounds disappointed and I don't turn around because I don't want to see it on his face. I finish off my glass of orange juice and set it in the sink.

"I can't skip," I say. "The school will call my parents, my parents will find out I lied about where I was, there will be a freakout of epic proportions from both parties and I won't be able to graduate. You know how it is."

"You could've woken me up," he says. "I don't have time to catch the bus now."

"You should enjoy your day off," I say. "You planned it."

I finally turn around. Jake stands there, rumpled and sleepy eyed, hair sticking up at all sides. He smiles at me, crosses the room and gives me a kiss on the cheek and then the mouth. I count until it's over. It doesn't last very long. I mean, I'm not moving my lips or anything, so Jake can tell something's wrong.

"What?" he asks, pulling away.

"Nothing."

He studies me.

"This isn't going to end well, is it?"

"Well, now that you mention it . . ."

But I can't think of what else to say. I want to be biting about this, but it's harder once you've had sex with a person. Twice.

"Just say it," he says.

"It doesn't change anything," I tell him. "What we did."

"Yeah, it does."

"Okay, it does. But not the way you want it to."

"Oh, come on, Parker," he scoffs.

"I don't want a . . ." I struggle with the words. "I don't want to be with you."

"Why?"

"Because. I don't want be with you," I repeat slowly, making sure to look him in the eyes. "Especially not now that I've been with you."

It's the best I can do. He swallows. He's probably not taking it the way I mean it, and the way I mean it is that last night, after the first time we did it and I let him hold me, I knew I could ruin him. And I know I'm ruining him now, but it's different.

It's less.

"Is that it?"

"Yeah, that's it."

"You'll miss the bus," he says.

He pads out of the room and I feel empty and kind of surprised that for once in my life things would go the way I want them to. Because this is what I want, isn't it.

On my walk to the bus stop, I pass a dog stretched out on a lawn. It stares at me sort of accusingly.

It looks exactly like Bailey.

twenty-two

I'm avoiding Jake and Chris, and Mom and Dad have decided to send me to a real live shrink. Like, they've set up an appointment and everything, even though I still do my homework and I haven't missed one goddamn day of school. I can't figure it out. It's not like I binged on crystal meth, went crazy and shaved my head.

I cut my hair and our dog died.

So I trail Evan through the halls because I want to know how he does it. I'm not fooled for a second, not even with the haircut. The guy's practically dying in plain sight and everyone leaves him alone. I want that.

It takes three days for him to realize he's being shadowed. It all comes to a spectacular end when he makes a rough left turn and a sudden stop in the middle of the hall and I crash into him and my history books scatter all over the floor. The jig is up.

"Why are you following me?" he asks, bending down to retrieve my books. I rip them out of his hands. "Why have you *been* following me?"

"I—"

Wish I had liquid courage. My heart thuds in my chest and I can't even do that neat thing where I make myself get angry instead of anxious.

He stares at me, wary and expectant.

"Why are you back?" I finally manage.

"Why do you care?"

The only thing I can think to do is shake my head at him, and he's not interested in letting me waste his time, so he turns and goes the other way and I've got more pride than to chase after him, so I head back the way I came and crash right into someone—second time today my history books go flying.

"Jesus."

Not Jesus. Jake. He bends down and grabs my books.

"Great, thanks," I mutter, avoiding his eyes. Figures *now* all that anxiety would turn straight to rage. "What were you doing, following me? Were you just waiting for the opportunity to—"

He holds out my books without a word.

I grab them, but he doesn't let go.

"Let go," I say, tugging at them. "Give them to me."

His grip on my books tightens. His knuckles go white. I grit my teeth and make myself look at him because that's what he wants.

"It's not going to work," I say.

He releases the books. I clutch them to my chest and let him be the one who moves on. He passes me, close. I can smell him and for a second I think I'm in his bedroom again and his hand is trailing my cheek, my neck. In his bedroom where he kisses me and I sort of forget everything that came before it and everything that will have to come after. In his bedroom where I enjoy every single clumsy kiss and it surprises me, how I feel about it. Him. By the time we finish, it's not that I'm—I mean, I don't know what I am, so we do it again and later I realize it wasn't that I was happy, it was that I wasn't heavy, that there were these brief moments where the thing I make sure I live with wasn't in every breath in and out. And that scares me because it's not supposed to be that easy. Because that's wrong. I'm supposed to be paying for this for the rest of my life.

Because that's right.

"I don't want to see this shrink," I announce. "I won't go."

Dinnertime. Dad's at one end of the table, Mom at the other. My declaration causes Mom to stop sipping her drink and Dad sets his fork down and rests his chin in his hands. Their eyes meet and they have a telepathic conversation about it.

I hear every word and I don't like what they're saying.

She's going to the shrink, right?

Of course she's going to the shrink.

We're good parents.

And then they both look at me like I'm—I don't like the way they look at me.

Dad sighs and picks up his fork again. "You have to see her."

"I see Grey. I see Grey once a week. That's enough."

"She says you're uncooperative," Mom says. "She says you never talk."

"I'm not seeing a shrink. I'm not. I don't—"

"Her name is Georgina Bellamy," Dad interrupts gently. "She's an excellent psychiatrist. She specializes in talking to teenagers who need help."

"I don't *need* help." They don't say anything. I push my plate away and cross my arms. "I'm not going. I'm not going to say it again."

"We should've done it sooner," Mom says to Dad, like I'm not even in the room. "The first time she got in trouble after—"

"I'll hate you for it," I say over her.

Dad turns to me. "If that's what it takes to get you back—"

"Oh, *please.* That's so pathetic. *This* is pathetic. Is this because

of . . . is this because of what I—" Calm down, Parker; calm
down. Calm. "Is this about Bailey? Because I didn't want him to
die; I just said that—"

It gets really quiet. And then Mom speaks.

"You know, after we buried Bailey, I came in and I thought—I
don't even *know* you anymore. I don't even know my own daughter. You're not the *same*, Parker." She starts to cry. "You're not the
same."

"I'm going to bed," I say, standing. I have had enough.

But Dad stands, too. He stands between me and my only way
out of the room.

"You should just give up," I tell him, but it comes out sounding
like a plea and he looks so worried from behind his glasses I want
to break something.

And then he makes his way over to me and wraps me up into
this hug and I feel myself go rigid. I let my arms hang at my sides.

"Don't say that," he says. "Don't even think it."

This is unbelievable. They still have hope for me.

I have done something wrong if they still have hope.

twenty-three

I open my locker and stare at the bottle of Jack resting on the top shelf.
It feels like it's been there forever, and every time I retrieve my books I'm always a little surprised no one's noticed the attractive, almost demure square bottle full of pale amber liquid, half-hidden by the black label with boastful white lettering I've never read beyond the name. All I need to know is how hard it messes you up, and Jack Daniel's has a tendency to do that like nothing else. I was a vodka girl before, because it was easier to hide in school and didn't make me as sick, but Becky obviously wanted to see me fall on my face when she gave me that paper bag in the chapel.

And today I am going to make her a very happy girl.

I reach for the bottle at the same time a low rumble of sound travels through the hallway the way a ripple crosses a pond before hitting the bank and going back in on itself. I feel this disturbance—this strange interruption of peace—in the pit of my stomach when I think I hear a name.

I forget about the bottle and follow the undercurrent of sound. The people I pass look at me like they know something, but how can they know anything? It's too early in the morning to know anything. An invisible thread leads me down the hall and around the corner where a group of people are clustered around a sobbing girl.

I get closer. It's Becky. She's the one crying. She's consoled by Chris, who stands at her right side, and Jake is at her left, looking out of place and awkward.

And I walk right past them, but Chris calls me back.

"Parker."

I backtrack slowly and face them, not just the three of them, but three plus an audience, because I don't deserve less. I clench my hands into fists, digging my nails in, and wait for one or all of them to speak. Becky stops crying long enough to raise her head from Chris's shoulder, and get ready for it, Parker, because this is it.

The party starts at eight, but I show up early so Chris and I can have sex. We go to his bedroom. He kisses me and I kiss him back and then, I don't know, I kind of seize up.

He flops back on the bed.

"You should loosen the fuck up every once in a while; the world wouldn't stop. No one would die."

We come downstairs looking like two people who've spent the last thirty minutes having sex. Chris gets to work on the tunes and I wind my way through the house and spot Evan in the kitchen kissing Jenny Morse. I clear my throat.

"Parker," Evan says nervously. He runs a hand over his prickly black hair and holds out a bottle of vodka and a shot glass. "Uh—shot?"

Jenny flees from the room. I take the bottle and the glass and move to the kitchen counter, pour a shot and knock it back. Then another.

Evan watches. Hesitates.

"You're not going to tell her, are you?"

I leave him there. When I step into the foyer the music is going proper, really loud. The party has begun.

Fifty minutes later too much vodka is gone.

"*There you are!*" *Chris yells. I turn really slowly and after a second the rest of the room turns with me. "I've been looking for you. Let's go outside.*"

"*Go without me. I'm going to stay . . . here.*"

He grins. "Come on; the fresh air will make you feel better."

I let him drag me outside. I look up. The sun gets in my eyes. Everything goes white.

"*Oh my God, it's true.*"

"*Go away.*"

I'm flat on my back. Perfectly manicured blades of grass press into my legs, hands and neck.

"*The sooner you make a mistake and learn to live with it, the better. You're not responsible for everything. You can't control the way things end up.*"

"*Evan's cheating on you with Jenny Morse. They're fucking.*"

All of a sudden I'm being jerked upright. My stomach lurches. I try to tell whomever it is to stop and leave me alone, but I can't move my mouth.

"*Parker, sit up. You can't stay on your back because if you get sick——*"

"*I hope she chokes.*"

"*Nice, Evan. Would you just leave?*"

"*Not until you talk to me about this.*"

"*If I talk to you about this now, I'll just say something that you really won't like——*"

When I wake up, I'm still drunk.

I stumble through the kitchen, head outside and throw up in some bushes until there's nothing left in my stomach to throw up. When it's over, I spot Jessie by the pool, laughing it up with some guy I don't know. He looks older than us and she's in full party mode, probably buzzed, and the way she leans into him is wrong because it's how she leans into a guy when she wants to fuck him.

*I blink. I'm on the lawn. I blink again and Jessie is making out with
a new mystery guy, different from the last one. I blink again and Evan's
screaming at both of them.*

*I blink again and I'm in front of the drinks table set out on the lawn.
I go straight for the bowl of punch, fill a cup with shaking hands, drink
it, then another.*

Then, a voice behind me:

"Someone spiked that, like, an hour ago."

I drop the cup and moan.

"Where's Jessie?"

*"She was crying her eyes out. She said she was going to run away."
Becky looks up at me and smiles. "Nice going, Parker."*

"Where did she go?"

Becky points in the direction of the woods.

*I can't feel my feet, but I soldier on. The farther I get from the
house, the louder the music sounds.*

Chris's parties are the best except when they're not.

*Twenty-five steps into the woods, and my head is barely attached to
my neck, but there's something I have to fix, so I keep moving.*

A few more steps. I hear something and I stop.

*I can make out two shapes in the darkness, on the ground. On a bed
of pine needles. My heart sinks. I inch forward and hold my breath.*

Jessie's fucking him.

Except that's not what it is at all.

*I breathe in. The air is stagnant from all the people wandering
around the property dancing, drinking, smoking. These dirty scents
mingle with the damp summer air and fresh-cut grass and there's Jessie
and that guy, this clean-cut frat boy with an ugly mouth and dead eyes,
and she's crying and it's not sex; it's a rape. He forces her to her feet and
drags her away and I'm alone and then Chris is taking me back inside.
And the next night I'm sick and Mrs. Wellington calls and asks us if
we've seen Jessie, if she's with us, and I don't say anything and when*

she becomes a missing person and the police start asking questions I tell them I don't know anything and everyone vouches for me because I was drunk and stupid and when I find her bracelet in the woods two weeks later I think it's there for me because I killed her and I take it and I wear it so I never forget even though I'll never forget and I never say a word to anyone because if I hadn't said anything in the first place none of this would have—

JESSICA WELLINGTON. MISSING.

I rip the poster off the wall.

twenty-four

"I'm sorry," Jake says.

I crumple the poster, walk over to the garbage and get rid of it. If I don't get rid of it, no one will, and if no one gets rid of it—

Once my hands are empty, I don't know what to do with them, so I snap. My fingers.

"Chris said she was your—your best . . ." He trails off like the gravity of the situation has hit him full on, like he knew Jessie, and it's funny watching that happen on his face. Better his than mine. "I'm so sorry."

I tilt my chin defiantly, still snapping.

"I bet you—" I have to wait three finger snaps before I can speak. "I—"

And then I'm walking down the hall, away from him, walking down the hall as fast as I can, as close as I can get to running without actually doing it. People pass me on their way to classes or to Becky, who's always been a kind of celebrity because everyone thinks she's the last person who saw Jessie alive and Jessie told her she was running away and everything and Chris is probably holding her through it, because that's traumatizing, you know, and I feel like I'm going to throw up.

I'm really going to throw up.

I push through the back doors, outside, at the same time Henley announces a special assembly in the auditorium. I gag on the fresh air and let the thought take over: Jessie's dead Jessie's dead she's dead she's dead. I end up on my knees, but I don't vomit. I dig my fingers into the pavement until the fingernail on the index finger of my right hand snaps back and there's red.

"Shit."

I suck on my finger and taste my own blood. It hurts. I want to scream.

Instead, I get calm.

Like, leaving-my-body calm.

I stand and brush bits of gravel and dirt off my skirt and knees at the same time the doors behind me open. It's Evan. His mouth is a terrible *O* and he makes these gasping noises, fish-out-of-water sounds. He's heard.

"Jessie's dead," I tell him.

He lets out this groan, curls his hands into fists and presses them into his eyes and sobs. The calm that's enveloped me never falters. I wonder if I should be worried about this.

I should be worried about this.

"I can't believe it." He wipes his eyes with the back of his sleeve. "I can't. I—"

"You didn't actually think she was coming back?" I always make it worse. "I called it ages ago. Dead."

He chokes. "Bitch."

"Fuck you."

"Fuck you." His neck and face turn red. "Show a little respect. She did more for you than you ever did for her."

"Fuck you."

We could probably do this all day. And Jessie's dead. I pinch my arm.

"I should get back in," he finally mutters, sniffing. His eyes well up again. The closer he gets to crying, the further I feel from it myself. "Chris will be looking for me. I should go back. . . ."

"What's stopping you?"

"Becky."

"What?"

"I can't stand being around her. She—" The tears spill over. He buries his head in his hands, and if it was anyone but me next to him he'd be comforted. "I mean, I don't like you, but if you told me you were running away, I'd stop you. I'd talk you out of it. Becky didn't even . . . I mean—"

"Bullshit," I mutter. "You would've driven me home, helped me pack and given me enough bus fare to get out of town."

"So that's what you think of me. You really think I—"

He stops. He cheats on his girlfriends. He knows what I think of him.

"Why did you come back?" I ask. "Why would you come back to this when everyone thinks it's you—that you made her run—"

"Because," he says. "It's what I deserve."

I swallow. "What did she say to you?"

"What are you talking about?" He stares at me. But he knows what I'm talking about. "Why are you asking me all these—I have to . . . I have to go inside."

He brushes past me.

"At the party," I say at his back. "She said something—she said she was going to say something you wouldn't like."

"You said you didn't remember the party," he says slowly.

"Like I'd tell you otherwise." I wrap my arms around myself. "I remember."

The parts I'd like to forget.

He faces me.

"She said she'd never forgive me and that she—" He chokes on the words. "That she hoped I was guilty for the rest of my life, but I didn't know she was planning to—I didn't—"

And he's crying again.

"Oh, give me a break, Evan," I snap, because I'm annoyed by the sound of it, the idea that he would make himself guilty because Jessie said she hoped he would be. She wasn't like that. "She wasn't that type of person and you know it. She would've forgiven you."

"But that's what she said and then she ran away so I would—"

"She was a good person."

"No," Evan says, crying even harder. "She said she would run away and she did it to get back at me—" Shut up. Shut up. *Shut up.* "But she wasn't supposed to—she said she was going to run away and now she's—"

"She didn't run away!"

His tears stop and my heart is going crazy in my chest because it wants out of me and I want out of me and I hate him, I hate Evan, I've always hated him because it's my fault he's ruined and it's all I think when I see him, it's my fault and I could fix him, but I don't want to give that to him because if I do, I have to tell and I've never told anyone *it's my fault.*

"She ran away," he says.

"She was in the woods. She was with—" I shake my head. I want it out of my head, but I don't want to say it. "No, you're right. She ran away—"

I start walking, put some distance between us. I don't even know where I'm going. He grabs me by the arm and pulls me back.

"Parker, who was she with?"

I shrug him off.

"Some guy. Leave me alone, Evan, I have to—"

"This was after Becky saw her? After she told Becky she was running away?"

"I have to go," I say, moving again, and he grabs me again. "I have things I need to—I have—"

"Parker."

I close my eyes.

"Yes."

"Who was she with?"

"I don't know."

"What happened?"

So I tell him.

"You didn't . . ." He stares at me like I'm some kind of monster.

My mouth is dry, parched. I feel slightly sick again but beyond that—nothing.

"Why?" he demands.

"I don't know. I don't—"

His hands come out and he shoves me hard and I fall back and hit the ground hard and I want to stay there, but he's on me, clawing at my arms and my shirt, anything he can get a hold on, trying to get me up again, and all I can think is *yes* and he's screaming at me, "You bitch, this is your fault, I thought it was me this whole time," and his fingernails dig into my skin and I keep saying, "I know, I know, I know," but I can't feel anything and then Chris is there and he's pushing Evan back, and he's screaming, too, "What the fuck are you doing, man? Get the fuck out of here!"

I scramble to my hands and knees, gravel digging into my skin. As soon as I'm on my feet, Evan makes another lunge at me, but Chris pushes him back.

"It was her! I thought it was me!" Evan's voice is hoarse. "It was her—"

"Get the fuck out of here, Evan!"

Chris gives Evan one last shove and Evan swears and stalks across the parking lot. There are angry red fingernail scratches up and down my arms, a little blood here and there. But it feels like nothing. Chris turns to me, furious.

"What did you say to him?" he says. "What the *fuck* did you say to him?"

"Chris," Becky says, "don't—"

And then Jake asks if I'm okay, but I shrug, shrug, shrug them all off. This is so stupid.

"Get away from me."

This is *so* stupid. I have plans and I'm not letting this ruin them because Jessie's been dead forever and I'm still alive and I still have things to do.

I head back inside, straight for my locker.

I wait for the JD to settle before I exit the stall. I wait until I know I'm good and wasted and everyone would know it to look at me, just like old times, and I walk unsteadily across the washroom floor and I fumble with the door for a minute before I pull it open and I step into the hall and crash into someone.

I hope it's Grey.

Or Henley.

twenty-five

Jack Daniel's is a more unsavory color coming up than going down—it always is— and I'm hunched over a toilet I don't recognize, puking my guts out.

I don't know where I am.

I hope I'm so wasted I can't tell I'm actually at home. After I'm done puking—it feels like forever—I float to my feet and a pair of hands guides me to a bed that swallows me alive. It's not my bed. I'm definitely not at home.

Maybe the hospital?

I inch my eyes open and the room goes in and out of focus. I catch a glimpse of a photo on the wall I've seen before. I'm at Chris's house. Saved again. But I don't want to be saved. I try to say it, but I can't get the words out of my mouth, only garbled sound. Someone says something to me in a soothing tone and I mumble something back, but I don't know what I'm saying, hearing, anything.

I don't know how to live with myself.

Even before Jessie disappeared, I never understood how I was supposed to work as a person or how I was supposed to work with other people. Something was really wrong with me, like I felt wrong all the time. I longed for some kind of symmetry, a balance. I chose perfection. Opposite of wrong. Right. Perfect. Good.

I get caught up in outcomes. I convince myself they're truths. No one will notice how wrong you are if everything you do ends up right. The rest becomes incidental. So incidental that, after a while, you forget. Maybe you are perfect. Good. It must be true. Who can argue with results? You're not so wrong after all. So you buy into it and you go crazy maintaining it. Except it creeps up on you sometimes, that you're not right. Imperfect. Bad. So you snap your fingers and it goes away.

Until something you can't ignore happens and you see it all over yourself.

And there's only one thing left to do.

I throw myself at Chris, wrap my arms around him and press my lips against his, something I haven't done in a long time. He holds on to me, surprised, and I reach into his pocket and grab his wallet. It snags on his jeans and I give it a little tug. Maybe he feels it and pretends he doesn't. Two hundred miles later, he's three hundred dollars poorer and I'm at the Morton Motel getting ready to die.

I debate leaving a note, but it comes out like a legal waiver.

I unscrew the bottle of pills and the booze, and with every bitter swallow I'm less afraid of myself. I'm finally doing the right thing. Except I fuck it up and I end up in the hospital where I get my stomach pumped and I live. The first time I wake up, I think I've died and I think it's heaven.

The second time I wake up, I know I'm in hell and Chris is crying over me.

"*I can't pay you back,*" *I murmur thickly.*

"*Are you awake?*"

I take a deep breath in. The air is sweet, dead-flower sweet. My stomach turns and I think I'm going to throw up, but I don't. A minute later, I open my eyes. I'm in Chris's guest room and he's sitting on the bed, peering at me. The lamp on the nightstand is on, casting a weak yellow wash over both of us, and the window reveals a black night sky outside.

My head aches.

"I know that face," Chris says quietly. And then he starts explaining, like I asked, like I even care. "Becky found you, and Jake and I got you out of school by—by the grace of God, I think."

My mouth tastes vomit sour.

"Because we were looking all over for you after Evan . . ."

He edges up the bed until he's close enough to hold my hand and then he does it and I wish he wouldn't. And I wish he'd shut up.

"She's been dead awhile. Jessie." He says it like he can't believe it. His voice breaks. "I mean, a long time ago. I heard it on the news this morning, before I came to school. I guess they found her over the weekend. That was on the news, too. But they didn't say who it was because they had to . . . they had—it's crazy, isn't it? I mean, when you think about it. It doesn't feel real."

"Chris." My voice comes out splintered, gravel. "Stop talking."

"But no one thought she was alive anyway, did they."

He stares at the wall, his eyes bright. He swallows once, twice, three times, his Adam's apple going up and down. A couple tears slide down his cheek and he brushes them away.

"Jake said you told him you wanted to die." He turns to me and the look in his eyes reminds me of Bailey on the side of the road. "I went downstairs to get water and you told him you wanted to die."

"Anyone would say that after a bottle of Jack Daniel's," I say.

"That's not how you meant it and you know it." He keeps looking at me until I'm the one who has to look away. "Why?"

I want to sit up, but I can't guarantee my stomach won't revolt and it's a miracle I haven't already puked on the white duvet.

"I want to die, I guess."

It gets so quiet.

"Why?"

But I've had enough. He wasn't even supposed to find me. Henley, Grey—*they* were supposed to find me and kick me out of school so my parents would give up on me and then everyone would give up on me and I wouldn't have to worry anymore. I push the duvet off, swing my legs over the bed and stand.

"I'm going," I tell him.

"Parker—"

My legs are shaky, but I make it across the room and then I get to the door and I puke. I mean, I feel it coming up, clamp my hand over my mouth and reach the bathroom just in time. My stomach muscles scream. A few dry heaves later, I'm propped up against the wall, panting. I rest my head against my knees while Chris stands in the doorway, watching. A bead of sweat trickles down the back of my neck and under my shirt collar. I gulp air like it's going out of style.

"You think I ever stopped wanting to die after the motel?" I ask. "You think a feeling like that just goes away?"

He steps forward and steels himself like he's about to give a speech to a room full of people. He probably thought one up the whole time I was out, just waiting for me to wake up so he could say it and we could have A Moment That Would Turn It All Around. But if you learn anything by the time you're eighteen, it's that those moments don't happen in real life. Ever.

"I don't want you to die," he says woodenly, but the funny thing is, he really means it. "I don't want to go to your memorial service."

"Memorial service," I repeat. "When's Jessie's memorial service going to be?"

"Are you even listening to me?"

I groan, rest my head against the wall and close my eyes.

"I'm just tired, Chris. And my stomach hurts and I have a headache and—" My voice breaks. She's dead and I am not going to cry. "I'm tired."

"Then you should sleep," he says.

I find my way to my feet and head back to the bedroom. Chris follows close behind. I crawl under the covers and he pulls the duvet up around me.

"It shouldn't be like this for you," he says. "You need help."

"What I need is for everyone to leave me alone. That's what I want."

"Parker, you don't want that. Everyone's on to you and you don't even know it. You have to stop this; you have to—" I think he's crying. "I don't want you to die."

I roll over so my back is to him.

"It's just Jessie," I say into the pillow. "I'm just shocked about it. That's all."

But the truth is, I haven't felt a thing since Evan.

"Yeah, but you've always needed help," Chris points out. "Even she knew it. I think she'd want that for you."

"And I don't think we should be talking about me."

I close my eyes.

twenty-six

"How are you doing?"

It's not like when someone who's there one minute is gone the next.

It's worse.

"I'm great."

"So," Jake says, staring at me expectantly. "Are we going to stand in front of the school all day or are we going in?"

I stare up at the concrete building. The memorial service is to-day.

"You could always go in without me," I tell him. Before he can say anything, I ask, "Do you think if I'd told you it would've made a difference? About how I knew Jessie?"

"Between us?" he asks. I nod. "Probably not, unless you had a completely different personality or something. But then I doubt I'd have found you as interesting."

"Sounds like I was destined to screw you over, then."

"Doesn't it."

At least I didn't have to stress over what I was going to wear to the service. Thank God for school uniforms, just this once. But I couldn't find my dress shoes, so I'm wearing muddy running shoes. And I forgot to brush my hair.

"Too bad it couldn't have been different."

He shrugs. "It can always be different."

It's weird the way all of this has dulled the fact we had sex and I ran. My parents have forgotten about Bailey. Henley and Grey don't care about me skipping afternoon classes. It's okay I spent the night at Chris's. It's okay because Jessie's dead.

Because they don't know what I did. Didn't do.

"Are you ready to go in?" Jake asks.

"I can't go in."

"Chris will be there and I'll be there." He clears his throat. "Uh . . . and Becky will be there, too."

"Well, if *Becky's* going to be there . . ."

A few cars pull into the parking lot. I recognize Mr. and Mrs. Wellington's Saab right away. My chest tightens.

"I can't go in," I repeat. I snap my fingers. "Make an excuse for me. Please."

"I can do that for you," he says. I must sound desperate enough. He pauses. "What was she like?"

My stomach ties itself into little knots and I keep snapping my fingers.

"You have this knack for asking questions I don't want to answer."

"You don't have to answer it."

"She was like . . ." I raise my head and look to the sky and try to think of a way to put it. "She was like a buffer between me and the rest of the world. Nice. Good."

He reaches out and gives my shoulder a squeeze before heading into the school without me.

After a while, Evan shows up.

Or maybe he's always been there, watching from his car in the parking lot or behind the sole maple tree they planted in front of the school to make it look less like a concrete penitentiary; I don't know. He's just here, which means I have to leave.

I hurry up the steps, wrench the front door open and—

Except I can't go inside.

"I just want to talk," he says.

"Is that all? Sure you don't want to attack me again, too?"

He sighs.

"I shouldn't have done that. I—"

"Evan, I don't care."

"Oh, right, I get it," he says. "You're right back into it, aren't you?"

"Back into what?"

The wind picks up, pushing my hair in my face. I shiver, brush it away and face him. I try to read what's in his eyes, but there's nothing there. I remember when I caught him with Jenny. How scared he was. And I was happy because I wanted to hurt Jessie for caring that I spent junior year hiding out in the girls' room between periods, hyperventilating. She wanted to help me and I wanted to hurt her for it because I didn't want anyone to know because it was important because . . .

Perfect people don't break.

I can't remember what was running through me when I saw her face pressed into the ground with that guy on top of her, I was so out of it, but I can't convince myself it wasn't bad. All I know is I went to a party and I was the catalyst for every horrible thing that happened there and after and I don't know why I didn't say anything when I saw her and I don't know why I didn't say anything later and I don't know how to fix it and I'm afraid of what happens next, so I have to keep doing it this way until it's right again, but I don't know how to make it right again because I'm always wrong.

I'm a bad person.

"You'll just go on until the next party," Evan says.

"Fuck you."

I'd rather be in school. I turn around and open the door, but I can't go in.

"It wouldn't have made a difference."

The handle slips from my grasp and the door clicks closed.

"What?"

I face him slowly because I'm afraid of what he said. What I think he said.

"I run it through my head every single fucking day, trying to figure it out—and there was a . . ." He pauses. "There was a group of college guys; they crashed it. And Jessie was all over them to get back at me. And I . . . I was there when Chris carried you out of the woods, after you must've . . . after you saw it happen and you were . . . you—"

He shakes his head and squints up at me.

"You couldn't have changed anything."

"You don't know that."

He makes a face like he wants to hit something or scream. And then it disappears and he's just tired looking, old. But I still don't believe him.

"They're pretty sure she was dead before the night was out." He clenches his hands. "And I *wish* it was your fault. If I could make it your fault, I would."

"It is. If she hadn't known about you—and I let everyone think she ran away—"

"You should've told," he agrees. "But it wouldn't have made a difference."

"Why are you telling me this?"

"Because last night I was thinking about it and I just knew—" And then he starts crying. God, he's always crying. "That she wanted me to."

I bring a shaking hand to my eyes.

"You can't know that," I tell him. "You're wrong."

This strange and horrible feeling takes up residence in the middle of my chest and spreads through the rest of my body. Something insides me caves and I'm afraid this is going to be the panic attack that kills me.

The one where my heart beats so fast it disintegrates.

I pull open the door and stumble into the school and I think he calls me back, Evan, but I don't care. I walk past the doors to the auditorium; I'm walking blind and everything hurts. I want to cry, it hurts so bad, but I promised myself I wouldn't cry because I don't deserve to cry over her. And I want to believe what he's saying is true, but no one can say it's true and it doesn't matter because it doesn't *change* anything because she's dead and she's never coming back and it's my fault and I miss her, *I miss her so much.* I can't breathe. I can't. I reach out for the wall and force myself to keep moving because I hear voices coming from the auditorium. It's over. The service is over.

So I have to get away.

Walk, Parker; just keep walking. Just keep—

"Parker?"

I blink.

I'm looking into a sparrow's dead eyes.

And then I look at my hands. I'm sitting on the floor and there's a crowd. And then I spot Bailey in the back and he's staring and he looks sad, but I don't—

"Parker?" the sparrow says gently. "Parker, can you hear me?"

I don't want to do this anymore, but I don't know what else to do.

I've never done it any other way.

twenty-seven

"Clearing out, huh?"

Chris and Becky walk up to me, holding hands. If the events of the last few weeks have done anything, they've made them a stronger couple. So strong, in fact, it doesn't really matter they have nothing in common because they're really, really serious about each other now. I wasn't there when it happened, but I think it means he's over me.

I reach into my locker, pull out all of my books and set them on the floor next to the garbage bag beside me. I don't know how such a small rectangle of space could hold so much crap, but there it is.

"Yep," I say. Wedged in the very back of the top shelf is a T-shirt I thought I'd lost ages ago. I toss it into the garbage bag.

"Will you have to repeat the year?" Becky asks.

"Would that make you happy?"

"I just wondered."

"Grey and Henley are working something out. I'll be graduating; I just won't be . . ." I toss a few crumpled pieces of paper into the garbage. "I just won't be here."

"I'll miss you," Chris says.

My locker is empty. They didn't want me to come back and

empty it, but I insisted. I didn't want anyone else touching my things. I tie up the garbage bag and brush my hands on my jeans.

"It's not like I won't still live two streets away," I tell him.

"Yeah, I know," he says. "I just thought it was worth saying."

So this is it. These things happen fast, I guess. From the moment in the hall to telling Grey the truth to her creaming herself and telling my parents to them crying to the news slowly traveling through the school and not everyone thinks it's my fault, but no one can say anything for sure. And I'm supposed to know what to do with that. Just like that. The Jessica Wellington murder is all over the local news and sometimes I make myself watch it for hours. They're calling it a kind of nervous breakdown. I don't know. I've had a couple appointments with that shrink. It was okay.

"Big game against St. Anthony's next weekend," Becky says tensely, changing the subject. There's something validating about the fact she still sees me as a threat, even like this.

"Decide on the cheer?" I ask.

"Not yet."

"Do the 'win, lose, it's all the same' one."

Her eyes light up. "You think?"

I nod. "I think."

She studies me. "You're not serious."

"I am," I insist. "I'd even come to the game just to watch everyone laugh at you."

She turns pink.

"Maybe you should see if they can't do something about your personality when they're fixing your brain," she snaps.

"Anyway," Chris says quickly. He gives me a hug. "We've got to go. We're meeting Evan for lunch. You need a ride or anything?"

"My mom's picking me up." I give him a small squeeze back. "But you can do me a favor and toss the garbage in the Dumpster outside."

"Sure." He hesitates, like he wants to say something else but doesn't know how to say it. Then he brings his mouth close to my ear and murmurs quietly enough so Becky can't hear, "I love you."

But it's different now.

"I'm sorry," I say.

"I know. I knew it before you did."

He leans back and smiles at me while Becky scratches her head, oblivious to the whole exchange. And she's going to live out the rest of her life like that, but good for her. Chris picks up the garbage bag and swings it over his shoulder.

"Jake's around here somewhere," he says.

"How about that."

I bend down, gather my books and shove them into my bag.

"See you, Parker," Becky says.

"You can call anytime," Chris says over his shoulder. Becky holds out her hand and he takes it. "If you want."

I wait until they're gone before I heave my book bag onto my shoulders and straighten up, the bones in my arms and legs crackling in protest. I make the slow trek down the hall. The lunch bell rang twenty minutes ago and it's mostly quiet but for the distant sounds of talking and laughter coming from the cafeteria.

I run into Jake outside of art. He's leaning against the door, his arms crossed.

"Hey . . . hey, you—girl," he says.

It almost makes me smile, but I can't. "Hey . . . hey, you—New Kid."

"You're really leaving?"

I nod and adjust my book bag.

"Yeah. I'm going to get my head screwed on straight and everything. Figure out what's . . ." Even now, I hate saying it. "What's been wrong with me."

"Good," he says. "Is this what you want?"

"I think so."

He lets his arms fall to his sides. "I'm glad."

"I hear admitting you have a problem is half the battle."

He stares at me expectantly. I should apologize to him.

"Are you going to be around this summer?" I ask instead.

"Nope," he says.

"Why?" I hope it wasn't me. I know it was me. "I mean, it's none of my business. But I bet whatever you're doing can't be more exciting than the therapy sessions I'll be stuck in."

"Probably not," Jake agrees. "I'll be at my mom's."

My mouth drops open and he nods.

"Yeah, I know." He gives me a lopsided grin. "She doesn't want me to come, but I'm coming. Dad figures she'll let me in if I show up on her doorstep and if not, he'll foot the plane ticket back here. We'll see what happens."

"Wow."

"It was you," he says. "I wouldn't have done it, but after we . . ."

It hangs in the air between us. I swallow.

"And after summer it's straight to college, right?"

"Taking the year off, actually," Jake says.

"Oh," I say, surprised. "And then you're coming back here?"

"Yep."

"And I'll be here." As soon as it's off my lips I'm sorry I've said it. I'm just pushing my luck and I don't even know why. There's nothing to push. It's over. I clear my throat. "Anyway, good luck with your mom."

"Good luck to you, too," he says.

That's my cue to go, but my feet are cemented to the floor. He waits for me to move and I can't because I want everything taken care of before I can start taking care of everything. I know that's not the way life happens. There are no tidy resolutions. Ask me if I think it was my fault, if I think this heaviness will ever go away.

"I'm scared," I admit.

"That's because it's scary," he says. "But it'll be better this way."

If he says so, it must be true.

"I jerked you around," I blurt out. "I didn't give you a chance."

"Yeah," he says. "I know."

And it's awkward and I hate it, but I have to accept it because I'm supposed to be accepting things now and working with what's left. Because that's what my psychiatrist told me to do. So I almost hold out my hand to shake his, a symbol of acceptance and moving on, but even I'm smart enough to know how stupid that would be.

So I force a smile at him and continue my way down the hall.

"Hey, Parker?"

I pause.

"I'll see you in the fall," he says. "I mean, you never know, right? Maybe we'll actually get somewhere this time."

I turn around and he's standing in the middle of the hall, smiling at me, but I can't think of anything to say. We stay like that for a minute until he inclines his head and goes where he's going and I'm alone, like I've wanted forever, except that's not really true because Mom's waiting for me outside and there's a shrink waiting for me in the city and there's nothing I can do about the past.

"Recovery" is going to be boring and painful and painfully boring, I can already tell. Which is good, I guess.

I hope it works.

some girls are

To Amy Tipton and Lori Thibert

*In Memory of Ken LaVallee
and Bob Summers*

acknowledgments

Endless thanks to my agent, Amy Tipton, whose tireless guidance, support, and hard work on my behalf continues to make all of this possible. She's a force to be reckoned with and I aspire to her levels of fierceness. Sara Goodman, my editor, is a rock star who has an incredible way of looking at words, and her sharp insights inspire and make me a better writer. It's an honor to work with both of these amazing women and their endless passion and enthusiasm for this book saw it to its very last page.

To my family, David and Susan, Megan and Jarrad, Marion and Ken, Lucy and Bob and Damon, whose unconditional love and support means everything to me: Thank you with all of my heart. So much of this is what you gave to me.

Thanks to all at FinePrint Literary Management for being so awesome, particularly Stephany Evans, Colleen Lindsay, and Janet Reid. Thanks to all at St. Martin's Press for putting this book together and making the finished product look fantastic. Thanks to my brilliant copyeditor, Kate Davis, for catching all of my mistakes, and to my publicists, Katy Hershberger and Vimala Jeevanandam, who are absolutely fantastic at what they do.

Thanks to Lori Thibert, who has been a constant friend, support, and inspiration to me. There aren't enough words to describe what an incredible driving force she is, but I'm going to e-mail her to tell her how much she rocks after I finish this sentence. I honestly couldn't do it without her.

Many hearts and thanks to Baz, Kim, Samantha, and Whitney, a talented, fab, and sparkly four, who mean very much to me. They can always be counted on to bring the -.* ., and the ~"~ makes all the difference.

Many thanks to the wonderful Daisy Whitney—I'm in constant awe of her drive, her generosity, her kindness, and her time-management skills.

For their support and friendship and for being oh so cool (!), thanks to: Alicia R., Annika and Will K. Briony W., Carolyn M., Damon F., Danette H., Emily H., Fiona H., Jessica S., Kelvin T. and Tristan H., Laura S., Mehmet E., Mur L., Nova S., Susan A., Thomas T., Ursula D., Veronique M., Victoria S., and WMC.

Special thanks to Allie Costa for all the work she does and continues to do online in support of children's and YA authors everywhere and to all YA book bloggers, whose passion and enthusiasm for YA novels has created one of the best online communities out there. Special thanks also to Verla Kay's Blueboards for being one of the most helpful and supportive places for writers online (extra-special thanks to its moderators and administrators!).

And to absolutely everyone I've been fortunate enough to cross paths with both online and off since all of this began, who have given me their time, encouragement, kind words, and support: Thank you.

before

Hallowell High:

You're either someone or you're not.

I was someone. I was Regina Afton. I was Anna Morrison's best friend. These weren't small things, and despite what you may think, at the time they were worth keeping my mouth shut for.

friday

Everyone is wasted.

Anna is wasted. Josh is wasted. Marta is wasted. Jeanette is wasted. Bruce is wasted. Donnie's always wasted. I'm not wasted. I had my turn at the last party, called shotgun in Anna's Benz after it was over. My head was out the window, the world was spinning. I puked my guts out. It wasn't fun, but it's not like there was anything else to do. Tonight, there's even less to do than that. Tonight, I'm the designated driver.

Boring.

"Okay, okay, just—" Josh fumbles into his pocket and pulls out a little baggie of capsules. He tips one, two, three, four into his palm while Charlie Simmons, a fat, cranky sophomore, waits impatiently. "I have to restock." He drops the pills into Charlie's piggy hands. "That's all I can give you right now, man."

Charlie sniffs. Fitting: All that Adderall is going up his nose.

"How much?"

"Oh . . ." Josh's eyes glaze over. "Forget about it. I like you, Chuck."

Charlie grins. "Cool. Thanks."

"Hey, *Chuck*, you're paying," I say, grabbing his arm. Instant scowl. "Bring the money on Monday."

"Bitch," he mutters.

He stalks off. Payment secured. I only strong-arm Josh's clientele when Josh gives his merchandise away, which is every time he gets this drunk.

"Jesus, Regina." He somehow manages to trip over his feet, even though he's just standing there. He wraps an arm around me. "Show a little respect, huh?"

"Fuck Charlie Simmons."

He laughs, and the ability to remain upright completely abandons him, forcing all his weight on me. I struggle to keep us standing, casting my gaze around the property for help. The lights are on, the music's loud, and I spot a few people puking in the topiary, but none of them are my friends.

Josh buries his head into my neck. "You look hot tonight." His blond hair tickles my face, and I push him back. It's too hot out to be this close. "I mentioned that, right?"

"Let's go inside," I tell him.

He laughs again, like *Let's go inside* is code for something it's not, but I guess he's right: I guess I look hot tonight. Anna loaned me a shirt and skirt, and everything she owns is nice. *I want you to look* really *good for once, Regina.* I've spent the last seven hours afraid someone's going to vomit all over me, because I can't afford to replace the labels I'm wearing.

I help Josh up the path to his front door. He stops abruptly, opens his arms wide, and shouts, "Is everybody having a good time?"

He's met with scattered applause and cheers that barely make it over the music. He shakes his head ruefully, listing sideways. I wonder what would happen if I just let him fall this time, but he manages to regain his balance without my help.

"We're graduating in like, eight months," he tells me very seriously. "I'm going to *Yale.* Who will supply these poor kids while I'm gone?"

I roll my eyes and right him for the thousandth time, forcing him into the house, where it's a different kind of party-chaos—quieter, but just as corrupt. Music filters in from outside, clashing with the music playing inside. Four seniors are toking up at the kitchen table. Drinking games. People making out in the living room. It's boring—it always is—but it's all there is. I just wish I was trashed enough to be able to pretend to enjoy it. I *hate* being designated driver. It was Kara's turn this time, but she's at home, sick.

"Are we going upstairs?" Josh asks when we reach the stairs. Before I can answer, he crumples onto the steps in a heap, too heavy for me to pick up. He rolls onto his back and blinks twice, struggling to focus. "Is this my bedroom?"

"Yes," I lie.

I bend down and kiss his cheek.

The smoke wafting in from the kitchen is giving me a headache, or maybe it's the music—I don't know. I lean against the wall and check my watch. It's officially Too Late, but Anna says the designated driver doesn't get to decide when the party is over; everyone else gets to decide when they're over the party. And Anna—I lost her an hour ago. Her face was as red as her hair, and she was slobbering all over Donnie.

I sigh.

Jeanette lurches up from out of nowhere looking like a guarantied good time. Strung out. I can never tell when she's over the party; the party's usually all over her.

"I'm leaving," she declares. "With Henry."

"Is Henry sober?"

"Yes, he is," Henry says in my ear, startling me. He grins and points to Josh, sprawled out on the stairs. "You can't just leave him there."

I ignore him and turn to her. "Where's Marta?"

"Waiting in the car." She brushes her hair out of her eyes. "We're dropping her off at her house, and then me and Henry are going back to his place."

"Is Henry sober?"

"I'm right here," Henry says, annoyed. "And you already asked that."

"Do you *really* want to go to his place?" I ask Jeanette. Another of my duties as designated driver. If I can't prevent an undesirable drunken hookup, then why bother being here sober in the first place? Jeanette grins and nods.

"You know, I'm in the circle," Henry points out. "I get an automatic pass."

"But you're kind of an asshole," I tell him.

He smirks and laces his fingers through Jeanette's. They amble through the smoke. He glances back at me once. "Have fun babysitting, Afton."

Josh on the stairs. Marta in the car. Henry taking her home. Henry taking Jeanette back to his place. I don't care about Bruce, so that just leaves Anna and Donnie. I know they're in the den. They always end up in the den if Josh and I don't get there first. The den is off-limits.

But we're in the circle.

I bypass the living-room festivities, open the door to the den, step inside, and close it behind me. The party noises fade and the room is dim, moonlight slivering in through the curtain drawn over the glass doors that lead to the backyard. I close my eyes briefly, inhaling slowly, letting the semiquiet of it all kill my headache.

When I open my eyes, I spot Anna at one end of the room. She's curled up on the couch, a picture of six shots of Jack chased with one Heineken too many. She drinks too much around Donnie, desperate to keep up with him, like the difference between him staying with her and leaving her is her blood-alcohol level.

"I need a girlfriend who can hold her liquor," he says.

Maybe it is. Donnie's lounging in the chair at the opposite end of the room, looking as half awake as he always does. No matter how hard I try, I can't seem to talk Anna out of him. He has a *convertible*.

She'd kill me if I left her here like this, so I lean over her ear and say her name, loud and sharp: "Anna." She doesn't move. I pull on her arm, tap her face, shake her. Nothing. I make my way over to the pitcher of water sitting on the end table beside Donnie.

"Help me get her to the car," I say.

He stares at me. "Why? Where are you going?"

"Home."

"What about me? I'm in no condition to get myself back to my place."

"I don't care what happens to you. I'm going home and I'm taking Anna with me." I grab the water and pour a glass, cross the room, and try to get her upright enough to take a sip, somehow. "Anna, come on . . ."

She flops back on the couch. I rub my forehead—my headache's returning—and make my way back to Donnie with the glass.

"Would you give me a hand?" He stares at me and then grabs my arm. The water sloshes onto the table. "*Christ*, Donnie."

He keeps his hand on my arm, and I'm suddenly aware of how much skin Anna's shirt isn't covering, but I guess that's the point.

"Why don't you care what happens to me?"

He sounds as pathetic as he looks.

"God, you're drunk." I step back, but he keeps his hand on my arm. "Just crash here," I say. "I'm not driving you home." He digs his nails into my skin. I yank his hand off me. "Don't."

"Don't," he repeats in a soft falsetto, and then he grabs my other arm before I can move, gripping them both so tightly, I know I'll still feel his fingers tomorrow. He uses me to get to his feet, and then he's on his feet and he's close.

Too close.

I turned him down in the ninth grade. Anna likes to say we've been close to hate-fucking ever since, which is too gross for me to even contemplate. It's a gunshot kind of thing for her to say—a warning. The way she says it, it's like she can see it happening, and the way she says it lets me know I better not let it happen.

As if I'd ever let Donnie get that close to me, anyway.

Except now he's that close to me, and I think he's thinking the wrong things.

He is. He presses his mouth against mine, mashing my lips against my teeth. The inevitability of every party: Someone will kiss you and you won't want it. Except this is worse than that. Way, way worse. This is my best friend's boyfriend, and my best friend is passed out on a couch eight feet away, and she will kill me for this, and I really, *really* don't want it. I press my hands against his chest and push him back, trying to force *stop* out of my mouth and past his. He detaches himself and fumbles backward. I wipe my mouth on the back of my hand, trying to get the taste of him out. I need water. I need to spit. He grabs my arm. I try to jerk away, but he holds fast.

"You better not breathe a *word* about this to her—"

"Donnie, fuck off."

He keeps tightening his grip until I can't keep the pain off my face—it hurts—so I bring my foot down on his foot and watch that happen on *his* face. It bursts red and I'm free. I rush to the door, but before I can open it, he's on me, crushing me into place from behind and breathing so hard in my ear, I can't even hear the vague sounds of the music outside or in. What turns a moment into this—me against the door, him against me. He puts his hand on my shoulder and turns me around roughly, and I'm afraid.

I've never been afraid of Donnie Henderson before.

He forces another kiss on me, lips working overtime, trying to get something out of mine. I grab a fistful of his hair and pull. He shoves me, but I stumble past him. The brief space I put between us makes me think it'll be okay, that this is as out of hand as it gets, but it's too close or it's not close enough and he lunges for me and we both go down.

We're on the floor.

He pushes me into the carpet. I glimpse Anna, tangled red hair, eyes closed. *Anna, wake up.* What turns a moment into this—he's on top of me, panting, and my face is smashed against the rug. I focus on the strands of hair laid gently across Anna's face.

This isn't happening.

But he turns me over and slides his hand up my skirt, and this is really really really really happening.

"No—"

I reach out and grip one of the table legs. His hand up my skirt. One hand up my skirt. Touching me. And the other clumsily feeling every part of me it can. His mouth on my neck. I yank the leg. The table tips and the pitcher rolls off, vomiting water all over us. Wet. Hands all over me.

I grab the pitcher and bring it up and then down on him. It's hardly a hit, but he feels it. I raise it up again and he dodges me and I'm crawling away. Last shot, Regina. *Get out.* I grab the chair and pull myself to my feet while he tries to stand, but the last of his co-ordination is gone on his hand up my skirt. Anna's skirt.

"Anna!" I turn to her. "Anna, help!"

But she just lays there, and Donnie's blocking my path to the door, swearing, trying to stand, and my heart is trying to race me out of this room before that happens. I stumble over to the sliding glass door and yank it open. I step outside, into the heat, into the party, the last of the party, but the music is as loud as it was at the start of the night.

I need to tell someone, but everyone is wasted.

I walk fast. I walk forever, blind, numb. I wrap my arms around myself. I need to tell someone. I lick my lips and taste salt: I'm crying. How long have I been—

Kara.

I'm standing in front of Kara's house. My feet walked me here. Kara. Kara is someone. The walk to her door sets off the motion sensor, soaking me in artificial too-bright light. I knock and wait, fighting the urge to throw up. I wipe my eyes and pull at Anna's skirt. It's torn.

A minute later, the door opens. Kara's there, a fevered doll with blond curls hanging in front of her flushed face. She crinkles her snotty nose.

"Jesus, Regina. What part of 'designated driver' don't you understand?"

The contempt in her voice almost tricks me into feeling normal. For a second. And then she looks closer and I remember the skirt—Anna's skirt—and his hand up Anna's skirt. And I'm still crying.

"What happened to you?" she asks.

A million words fight their way up my throat, all lobbying to be first out of my mouth. They pile up, stuck. Only one manages its way out: "Help."

She lets me inside, and the rest of the words come, falling from my lips, a stupid, stuttering truth. By the time I collapse in a chair at the kitchen table, she knows what he did to me. And then it gets really quiet while I wait for her to tell me what to do.

I need someone to tell me what to do.

Anna always tells me what to do.

"God," Kara murmurs, pressing her fingers against the angry spots on my arm where he grabbed me. The skin is tender and marked, but by Monday it will be splotchy purples, browns, and yellows.

"The police?" I ask. My voice cracks. "Do you think? Do I go to the police?"

Kara stares at me, and then she stands and goes into the fridge and gets a bottle of water. I can't read her expression.

"You really want to put yourself through that?"

"I could put Donnie through that." I rub my forehead. But I don't really want to go through that. I don't want to talk to the police about his hand up my skirt. And then—my parents. It's not like you can do that and not tell your parents, and I don't want them to know. I don't want them to think of me on the floor, with Donnie's hands there. Kara sets the water in front of me. "Maybe Anna—"

"You're going to tell *Anna*?"

"She has to know—" I swallow. "That's her boyfriend. She won't let him get away with it." She'll take care of him. Me. She takes care of everything.

"If she believes you."

I open my mouth and nothing comes out. *If she believes you.* I should've known Kara would do this. There's a reason we hate each other. *If she believes you.*

"Look, *I* believe you," Kara says, reading my mind. "I know you hate Donnie, and I can see him doing something like this, but . . . Anna's always thought . . ."

You're like, this close to hate-fucking.

I pick at the hem of Anna's skirt. The jagged rip in it finally hits me. She'll kill me. She will kill me for ruining her skirt. "Shit." I stand and try to force the ragged sides together, like that's how you fix these things. "I need to—I told her I'd be careful—"

"Regina—"

"I told Anna I wouldn't—"

"*Regina.*" She snaps her fingers twice. I let the skirt go and sink back into the chair. I need to get it together. Kara stares at me, concerned. I never thought I'd live a moment that could exist outside our hate for each other. I could go my whole life without one. But this feels . . . safe.

"What do you—so what do I do, Kara? What . . . ?"

She sits across from me, quiet, for a long time. My stomach knots itself up while I wait for her to speak. If I have to live with this, I don't want it to be hard.

"Donnie's not going to tell Anna," she finally says. "And Anna's not going to believe Donnie would do that to you. She'd think you were screwing around behind her back. It's not fair, but that's Anna."

My best friend.

"I mean . . ." She taps her fingers along the table. "He was really wasted, right? It's not like he does that all the time. . . ." I don't say anything. "And I feel really bad for you, Regina . . . but there are some things worth keeping your mouth shut for."

"She's my best friend." A tear manages its way down my cheek. I wipe at my eyes. "I mean—"

"But you know what she'd do to you if she found out, right?"

I nod slowly. I know. And then I nod again: *I know, I know, I know.*

"And I'm totally here for you," she says. Kara. Totally here. Nothing makes sense anymore. "I'm not going to say anything."

"Thanks," I whisper.

Kara presses her fingers against my arm again.

Her touch is cool and strange.

monday

I wake up, and the bruises on my arms have turned really yellow and brown, so I have to wear long sleeves, even though fall is doing its best impression of summer and the air is sticky and hot. Anna decided we'll all wear tank tops and miniskirts for as long as the weather holds—before winter confines us to less revealing outfits— and I agreed, so I don't know what I'll tell her when she sees me today and asks what my deal is.

And I'll have to tell her something, because I can't tell her the truth.

I debate various lies over breakfast, a pale pink antacid with coffee. I'm a pretty good liar as long as I'm talking to an easy sell, but Anna is not an easy sell. If she finds out I'm hiding something, she'll want to know what. Maybe she'll be mad. Maybe she won't give a damn. Anna is funny like that.

I decide to tell her I'm having a fat day.

"Little warm out for that shirt, isn't it, Regina?" Mom asks, setting a plate of eggs and toast in front of Dad. Her comment draws his eyes up from the paper.

"You'll melt," he says.

I shrug and drain my coffee. "Whatever. I'll see you later."

Halfway to school, I feel like I'm going to throw up. I fan my face with my hand, and the air that meets my skin is hot. My shirt clings to my back, pressed uncomfortably into place by my book bag. A pay phone looms on the horizon, the closest thing I've got to a cell phone, because my parents kind of suck. I drop my bag and rifle through my pockets for change until I find a quarter. I use it to call Josh.

Pick up, Josh. Pick up. I imagine the song that plays when someone calls his cell, exploding from his pocket until he picks up, but he never does, which is weird because Josh always picks up, and he's always good for a ride. He's my boyfriend.

Hallowell High: The parking lot pulses with scantily clad life, and I'm in the middle of it all, wearing a sweater. My scraggly black hair is plastered to my forehead, and a couple people point and stare at me because I look that ridiculous, but I don't care. I'm still better than them. It's not hard. Hallowell is one of those in-between towns, stuck between a city and another city, and everyone here knows everyone else. It's too small for a social landscape more complicated than this: You're either someone or you're not.

I'm someone.

I'm Regina Afton. I'm Anna Morrison's best friend. These aren't small things, and Kara's right: They're worth keeping my mouth shut for. So I kept my mouth shut the whole weekend, and I'm still Regina Afton and I'm still Anna Morrison's best friend.

Friday never happened.

I wipe a light sheen of sweat from my forehead. Anna, Kara, Jeanette, and Marta usually wait for me at the front so we can enter school the Fearsome Fivesome. It's the only part of the day I sort of like, standing next to Anna, untouchable.

Everyone is afraid of us.

Today, they're nowhere to be found.

I scope out the parking lot just in time to see a black convertible pull in. Donnie. My stomach twists and I can't breathe. I feel wrong in all the wrong places. I have to get inside. Now. I navigate the cacophony of voices, drug deals and insults—

"—See you at lunch, okay?—"

"—I didn't finish it, but I don't think Bradbury will care—"

"—Wait up, I've got to get—"

"—For one pill? Fuck you! I can get them cheaper from—"

"—Slut! HEY, SLUT—"

—and push through the front doors, into the air-conditioned main corridor. I scan the halls. They can't be that far off. I just need to find them. I feel naked without them.

A flash of blond hair catches my eye.

"Kara!" She doesn't turn around. She must not have heard me. *"Kara!"*

She stops and I hurry over. Being next to her calms me a little; I'm not invincible yet, but it's better than nothing. And it's weird. I never thought we could be friendly, but she was nice to me. So I'll be nice to her. For a while.

"Have you seen Anna?"

But she stares at me like I've just told her to stab her eyes out with a pen, and even though she gives me that look a lot, I don't get it today.

"Uh, yeah?" Bitch-voice. Okay.

I readjust my book bag and clear my throat.

"Where is she? I want to talk to her. She called this weekend and I didn't pick up." I wasn't ready. "You know Anna. She'll be pissed."

"Yeah," Kara agrees. "You could say that."

"What? Did you talk to her?"

Kara shrugs and flounces down the hall, her golden curls bouncing off her shoulders as she goes. A bitter taste works its way up my throat in spite of the antacid I took. I follow her. She turns a corner. I turn it.

Jeanette and Marta are at Marta's locker. Kara prances over, and they enfold her into our secret huddle, the one I should be at the heart of, but my feet are cemented into place by some kind of animal instinct that tells me I'm not allowed over there. Marta spots me. My heart leaps. *Invite me over.* She murmurs something to the other girls. *Invite me over.* They laugh. *Invite me over.*

They turn their backs to me. No.

No way.

This is not a freeze-out.

But I have to find Anna to be sure.

She's not at her locker. I check her homeroom. She's not there either. I stalk the halls, and people are looking at me, whispering. But it's the sweater.

I detour into the girls' washroom, not because I think Anna will be there, but because my stomach is upset. I pop two more antacids and lean over the sink. My heart spazzes in my chest and my arms itch. I scratch along the outside of my sweater because I don't want to look at the bruises, even though I could close my eyes and see them.

I could close my eyes and see—

Don't think about it. Don't think about it. Don't think about it.

I stare at my reflection in the mirror. My hair is limp, dead, and my face is an unattractive overheated red. Anna would not approve. Anna doesn't want to talk to me because . . . Because. Because.

I haven't returned her clothes yet.

I ignored her all weekend.

Duh.

Anna doesn't want to talk to me, and the other girls are giving me the Cryptic Cold Shoulder until I apologize to her. I exhale. It's almost comforting in its familiarity. I've been here before and I can handle it. It's not fun, but it's easy.

It's not a freeze-out.

I'll find her. Apologize.

The first bell rings. Homeroom. I haven't even gotten my books. I leave the washroom and step into the hall, forcing my way past the whispers and stares.

It's the sweater. That's all it is.

And then I push through the crowd converged in front of my locker so I can get a good look at the word spray-painted across it.

WHORE

This is a freeze-out.

The scene fades out until it's me and that word and nothing else.

I step forward and touch my fingers to one of the letters. It comes back black. I rub my sleeve across the metal. The paint is fresh enough to ruin my shirt but dry enough to keep from smearing into an unintelligible mess.

"Is it true?" Someone asks. I touch the paint again. It's really there. "Did you really bone Donnie Henderson?"

The scene fades back in. Voices assert themselves over the sound of my heart pounding in my chest, and they're all saying something about me.

Me. Donnie Henderson. Did I really bone Donnie Henderson.

His hand up my skirt. Mouth on my neck.

I step back and end up on someone's foot. They swear at me. *Watch it, bitch.* I focus on not looking like a cornered animal and try to zero in on a face I know, someone familiar amid the slack-jawed rubberneckers.

Josh. My boyfriend.

He hovers just outside the mob. Our eyes meet.

He turns away.

"Oh, my *God*, here comes Holt." Another voice. "This is *so awesome!*"

The second bell rings. Principal Holt is there before I can escape, the decrepit old janitor trailing behind him. His face purples as he surveys the damage. He paces, yells, and makes such a fuss, a new crowd is born. He orders a temporary cover for my locker until the paint can be removed, and he vows the perpetrators will be brought to justice.

And then he asks me if I know who they are.

After homeroom, I'm gone. I'm at that pay phone again and I'm calling Josh. Again. I pick at the phone book dangling from a string, half torn away by some vandal with nothing better to do, while the sun continues its slow rise overhead. It's hot in this booth. I turn my back to the cars rushing past me, on their way to the main street.

I finally get his voice mail.

"It's me." A car goes by. I swallow twice and try to figure out what to say while the silence on the other end of the line waits for me to fill it. "Look, what they're—what they're all saying—what I—" I can't tell this to Josh. Not on the phone. ". . . You heard it from Kara, didn't you?"

I hang up. Kara.

Kara, Kara, Kara.

Kara Myers.

Kara.

I am such a fool.

tuesday

I'm used to everyone's eyes on me; that's nothing new. When you're Anna Morrison's best friend, people look. We're the kind of popular that parents like to pretend doesn't exist so they can sleep at night, and we're the kind of popular that makes our peers unable to sleep at night. Everyone hates us, but they're afraid of us, too. Anna thrives on it. She says the day people stop hating us is the day something is really wrong. She says I should look at it that way, but I can't. Everyone hates us, and it makes me a total wreck.

She hated that about me.

These people are nothing. *They don't matter. None of this matters. There's a whole world outside of this hellhole. God, Regina. You could at least* act *like you don't give a damn.*

So I do it like she does it: I square my shoulders and march across the parking lot, my jaw clenched and my eyes narrowed. I try not to let the heat touch me or flinch at the blast of cold air on my skin when I step through the school doors.

I'm ushered in by whispers and stares. Half the student body relishes it; they've waited a long time to show me just how much they hate me. The other half doesn't know what to make of it after spending four years fearfully revering me.

Principal Holt makes quick work of restoring my locker, but whoever repainted it doesn't know how to color-match. My locker has been painted red. Every other locker in this school is a bright, hideous pumpkin orange. It's a wash of a coat, too.

I can still see the WHORE forcing its way through.

I grab my books. Two girls go by, and I hear my name but not the context surrounding it. Probably something like. *Regina Afton is a slut who slept with Anna Morrison's boyfriend I know can you believe it pass it on.*

I will kill myself before I get used to this.

Anna catches my eye then, swaggering down the hall in the opposite direction. A dozen guys watch her as she goes; it's the way her skirt moves with her hips when she walks. She takes a sharp turn left, and I know where she's going. And she's alone.

This is my chance.

I take the same left, push through the pale blue door that opens into the girls' washroom, and there she is, admiring her reflection in the mirrors over the sinks. I don't blame her. Anna is beautiful, with her soft, fine auburn hair and the kind of body that brings guys to their knees. It's cliché, but she's a Siren. Impossible to fight, there's no better feeling than to hear her sing your name until she has you and eats you alive. The people at this school think it's hard enough living beneath her, but it's even harder being her friend. Anna.

The door swings shut. She stiffens and turns, and the air leaves my lungs. I'm torn between wanting to be far away from her and wanting to throw myself at her feet to beg forgiveness for something I didn't do. As long as it means we can be friends again.

I'm sorry. I'll never sleep with your boyfriend again, never, never, never. . . .

Maybe I should've thought this out better.

She takes me in slowly, one eyebrow arched. She wants me to feel like I'm not good enough to be acknowledged, and it's working. I'm suddenly aware of the sloppy ponytail tied at the back of my head and how dumb my outfit looks—jeans and a sweater on another sweltering day—but it doesn't matter. She's always been prettier than me.

"Nice job you did on my locker," I say.

We stare at each other, Western-movie-showdown–style. Several agonizing seconds pass, but Anna never draws her gun, which is good, because I'm totally unarmed. She turns back to the mirror and digs through the makeup bag in front of her.

"I didn't do it." She pulls out some lip gloss. "I had it done."

"I didn't have sex with him, Anna."

"Wow," she says. "You almost sound like you mean it."

"Kara's lying to you. She set me up—"

She snorts. "Don't even."

"She *is*. She set me up. You know she hates my guts—"

"How dumb do you think I am, Regina? You know the part that really makes me sick?" She tilts her chin up, eyes never straying from her reflection. "I was *right there*. Did you get off on that?"

"Anna, he—" The words come out of my mouth fast and stupid, because if I think about them too much, I won't be able to say them. "Anna, he tried to rape me—"

It doesn't go over well. She slams the gloss down and whirls around, her face as red as her hair.

"I cannot *believe* you just said that."

This is the air sucked out of my lungs, this is a punch in the stomach, this is a slap across the face, and *that* is *not* what she was supposed to say.

"I'm your best friend," I choke out.

"You were until you fucked my boyfriend."

"Anna, I *didn't*."

She drops the gloss back into her bag. "I've been saying it forever. You always acted like you hated him, and you tried every trick in the book to get me to break up with him, and when that didn't work, you waited. Now you're caught and you're scared and you're standing there telling me he tried to *rape* you? That is *fucked*, Regina."

"Wait—I'll show—I'll show you—"

I'll show her the bruises. I fumble with my sleeves, my hands shaking horribly, while Anna zips up her bag. The washroom door swings open, interrupting me, and when I turn around, it's Kara. She looks so different. Like, confident.

So this is really bad.

"Bell's gonna go," she says over me. "Are you coming?"

I turn back to Anna. She smiles at me. No, not *at* me—through me. She's smiling at Kara, through me, but this can't be over because I haven't had my say. In the movies, you get the time to make the speech that saves your life, and everyone wants to listen to you. She hasn't even seen the bruises yet.

"Anna, just wait—"

"Yeah," Anna says to Kara, over me. "Let's go."

"Anna—"

"You hear something?" Kara asks Anna, grinning.

"Anna, please." Anna gives herself one last look in the mirror, grabs her makeup bag, and passes me on her way out. The air that follows her smells berry sweet, and I beg after it. "Anna, Anna, *Anna—*"

"Fuck off, Regina," she says in a singsong voice.

And she leaves.

Kara doesn't. I feel her behind me; I feel every part of her enjoying this. I take Anna's place in front of the mirror, trying to ignore how sick it makes me that every part of Kara is enjoying this. I try to conjure the Regina she was afraid of. The one who put her in her place. Over and over again.

I can't.

"You talked me out of it." My voice breaks. "You told me not to tell."

"Well, it wouldn't have done *me* any good if you had," she says in that same singsong voice that Anna used, and then she leaves, and I bite my lip until I taste blood.

It hurts less than what just happened here.

For the first time in four years at this school, I'm aware of the cafeteria like I've never been aware of it before. Greasy, overcrowded, hot and loud.

I can see *everyone*.

Those teen movies that use the cafeteria to present the social hierarchies of high school, the ones where the lunch tables become little islands, spaces for you and people like you and no one else, where the overlap is nonexistent—they're all wrong. Hallowell High's cafeteria is *only* overlap. Cliques bleed into other cliques for lack of space, and there's only one exception: Anna's table. It's always been Anna and everyone else.

And now me.

This must be what the first day of ninth grade felt like for people who didn't have seating insurance. I scan rows of tables for an empty chair, but my gaze keeps drifting back to home base, where there are two—mine and Donnie's.

They're all watching me.

Fourteen pairs of eyes track this moment where I'm lost and it's obvious. I maneuver around tables with as much purpose as I can muster, pretending I've got somewhere to be until I find somewhere to be. I end up at the table at the back, the one next to the long line of garbage cans. It's the Garbage Table. It's Michael Hayden's table. It's nearly always empty because no one likes eating next to the garbage.

No one likes eating next to Michael Hayden.

He's hunched over a burger and Coke, writing in the Moleskine he's constantly carrying around. Michael Hayden: Unstable Emo Writer Boy.

I pick at my fingernails and debate how to do this. Michael probably doesn't want me to sit with him. We have phys ed together and I'm sure that's enough of me for him. It's enough of him for me, but when I look up, he's watching me. My face gets hot, but I go all fake-confidence on him and walk over. He closes the notebook and shoves it aside.

"Can I sit here?"

He doesn't say anything. Doesn't look at me. I decide it's an invitation and sit. I pick my nails while he eats. I don't actually eat lunch in the traditional sense; I dig into my pockets and pull out a pill. Everyone's eyes are on me. I can't imagine what they're thinking. This is Michael—longish, dark brown hair that always hangs into his pale blue eyes. His face is all sharp features, and he's tall, broad shoulders, sort of built. He moved here during ninth grade, when his shrink mother decided to set up a practice in town. He came here quiet—not shy, but removed, above it all. Like he just didn't care about us.

We tried to make him care. It didn't work. So first we told everyone he was a creep. Stay away. We couldn't even give a solid reason why, but because it came from Anna's mouth, that was good enough. He was a freak, and then his mother died in the eleventh grade and Anna was thrilled; she finally had a solid reason.

Michael now: We got everyone to believe his mom's death made him snap, and he's a torturing-small-animals kind of walking anger-management problem, that he's on meds, and his Moleskine holds school-shooting manifestos.

So this is going to be awkward.

I swallow the antacid dry. My throat is tight and it refuses to go down. I try again. The pill begins a slow dissolve over my tongue. I finally dredge up enough spit to force the thing down. The clock on the wall behind Michael's head tells me there are twenty minutes of lunch period left. I'm not obligated to wait them out here, but a small part of me wants to do it to prove that I can.

Michael steadfastly ignores me, radiating the kind of tension that makes me want to go in on myself and stay there, until he finally looks at me and then past me.

"They're watching you," he says.

"I didn't sleep with him," I say. I don't know why. "Donnie, I mean."

He stares at me like he clearly doesn't give a fuck and wants to know why I think he should. It's the kind of look that makes me feel every inch of my skin in a way that makes me want to claw it all off.

He hates me.

I twist around in my chair. The seven heads turned in my direction go back to their food, whispering. I can just guess what they're saying.

"So how come they're telling everyone you did?"

"I got set up." I say it casually, but I feel every word in my gut, and it causes the kind of upset a pill can't reach. "By someone who I thought was my friend."

Except Kara was never my friend. She was just one of those girls you have to throw a bone to because there's nowhere else for them to go, and you've known them for so long, you can't even remember how you met.

"Kara," I tell him, even though he didn't ask. Saying her name elicits a Pavlovian response from me. My hands twitch, overcome with the urge to strangle her to death.

"I guess that's what you get," he says.

Our eyes meet. He stares at me, and I can only take it for a second before I have to look away.

He looks like his mom.

"She used to be really fat," he says. "Kara."

"Your point?"

He shrugs. I know what he's implying. I don't care. It's no secret.

Everyone knows Kara used to be fat until the second half of tenth grade, when she learned how to stick her fingers down her throat and started popping diet pills. She had to wear a wig in her class photo because she was losing her hair; you can see it if you look really closely. It was the pills or the purging. And those were only suggestions, anyway.

It's not like I told her she *had* to do that to herself.

Michael goes back to his burger. I try not to watch him eat, but I end up watching him eat anyway. It always amazes me how people can relax enough in this place to do that—eat—and not care. He finishes it off with precious minutes of the period to spare. He uses those to study me, and I get that claw-my-skin-off feeling. I know he's trying to make me feel so uncomfortable I won't come back and sit here . . .

Tomorrow.

I have to do this all over again tomorrow.

"I knew your mom," I blurt out.

He blinks, surprised. I've surprised him. And then his eyes light up in the strangest way—like he hasn't heard the word *mom* in a long time. It's not exactly happy, it's sort of curious—like, *Mom. I know that word.*

"How?" he demands.

"We—" For a second my head is full of her office, the way it smelled—sort of like coffee—and the walls were this pale blue. Her voice was soft and kind. "We were friends."

I feel bad for the lie, but it's not like I don't want it to be true. I don't know if his mom ever thought of me as anything but her patient, but I really liked her and I wish we had been friends. It's horrible, but sometimes I'm relieved she died before she could ever find out what I helped do to her son.

"She never mentioned you," he says.

"We were friends," I repeat. He searches my face for the lie. I sweat it out until he concedes and says, "Maybe."

The bell rings.

"Can I sit here with you tomorrow?" I ask. It's humiliating having to ask permission to sit at the Garbage Table, and when he doesn't answer me immediately, I pose the question again with the kind of urgency that makes me sound totally pathetic. "Michael, can I sit here with you tomorrow at lunch?"

"What if I said no?" he asks. My mouth goes dry. *You can't.* The cafeteria is emptying. Ms. Nelson stands by the door, waiting for the last of us to leave, but I can't leave without this one thing and he knows it. "Regina, I don't care where you sit."

He grabs his things, gets up, and makes his way out. I stay, staring at the table until Nelson blows her whistle and tells me to "get out there."

BITCH.

Kara drops the note on my desk on her way to the board to do a few math problems for Mr. Brenner, and her wrist action is so subtle, he doesn't even see it and he's looking right at her. And that has everything to do with how short her skirt is.

I crush the note into a neat little ball.

"Well done," Brenner says, as Kara chalks down the answers to the last problem. He's staring at her legs like the skeeve he is.

Bruce waves his hand around.

"Excuse me, sir? I did the problems with Kara, and she got the last one wrong."

The silence is delicious. Kara reddens and Brenner blinks, totally caught.

"Maybe *you* got it wrong, Burton," he suggests, and waits for the rest of the class to laugh, like, *Yeah, maybe.*

We don't.

"I doubt it, sir," Bruce says.

That's when we laugh. Brenner tells us to be quiet, and we review the problem as a class, and sure enough, Kara got it wrong, so Brenner has to backtrack. He starts babbling about the "mathematical journey" and how the steps you take are sometimes more important than the destination, until he loses his ridiculous train of thought and sends Kara back to her seat.

I stare at the crumpled note, and when she's close enough, I wind my arm back and whip it at her forehead. She shrieks and Brenner totally sees it, so it's detention for me, shelving returns in the library after school.

There's no such thing as justice.

I'm in the library wedging a copy of *Flowers in the Attic* between two copies of *Persuasion* when Liz Cooper and Charie Andrews come in. Proof positive a bad day can always get worse. I back into the narrow shelves until I'm out of sight and they pass by, talking low, and end up in the stacks directly behind me. Charie is a total no one, but Liz is this faded-out yellow-haired girl-ghost I've gone to elaborate lengths to avoid because being around her makes my stomach ache. I reach into my pocket and force an antacid between my lips, chewing it in hopes that will make it work faster.

They're talking about me, of course. I'd be shocked if they weren't. I get as close to the books as I can and hope they don't see me spying on them through the shelves. I don't even know why I'm eavesdropping. They won't say anything I want to hear.

"Donnie didn't even show today," Charie is saying.

"He's probably out getting wasted," Liz replies, and she's probably right. For Donnie, sobriety is a fate worse than his inevitable death from liver failure.

"Did you see her looking for somewhere to sit at lunch? It was totally hilarious. I kept hoping she'd come over and ask if she could sit with you."

"Why?"

"So you could tell her no." Charie laughs because it's *totally hilarious*. Liz doesn't laugh, but I almost wish she would. It's always easier when the people you've ruined decide to really hate you—like Michael does—because then your defenses go up and you can't even really feel the bad things you've done.

"She sat with Michael," Liz says.

"He's too nice." Charie's voice is all disappointment. "I caught up with him in history and asked him if she was really upset, but he said she seemed normal. It has to be a front, though, right? She gets kicked out of her clique and they all hate her and Josh dumped her—" I jerk back. I don't remember that part happening. ". . . She'll be slitting her wrists soon enough."

I swallow. I swallow again. I don't know what feels worse: Josh breaking up with me *without breaking up with me*, Charie joking about my suicide, or Liz's gentle admonition of it—"Charie, don't."

"Hey, it could happen," Charie says. "Anyway, I've got to catch Paul. See you."

"See you."

Charie flits by my shelves. I wait while Liz rifles through book after book after book after book. After a while, she settles at a table nearby and opens up a paperback. I lean against the shelf and close my eyes. I'm trapped here until she leaves. Facing her is not an option.

"Regina," she says, and my heart stops. I open my eyes and she's staring in my direction. "I know you're there. You can come out."

I step out slowly. She looks me over, starting at my feet and working her way up to my eyes. I have to force myself to hold her gaze. I don't like looking Liz in the eyes. It's stupid, but I'm afraid I'll see her like the last time I really saw her. Totally broken. I mean, I still see that on her—everyone does. It'll be all over her until she graduates.

But I'm afraid I'll see it now like I saw it then.

"Aren't you going to say anything?" I ask her.

"What would I have to say to you?"

"I just thought you'd enjoy this, is all."

"That still doesn't mean I'd have anything to say to you."

The moment should end here, but I'm rooted to the spot. I stare at the literacy poster tacked on the wall behind her head. "Read or die." I feel like I should be saying something important, but the chance for that has passed. A long time ago.

"The locker was impressive," she says. "What do you think they'll do next?"

"I don't know," I say. "Guess you'll have to tune in to find out."

She closes her book. "Well, I'm here every day. But I don't know, it's kind of boring. I've seen this show before. I totally starred in it once. Remember?"

A familiar, horrible feeling consumes me. I want to tell her it wasn't easy for me, either, watching Anna torture her every day until the light in her eyes went out. I want to tell her, but that would be dumb.

"Got any tips?" I try to keep my voice light.

She laughs a little. It's been ages since I heard her laugh and mean it, and even though it's at my expense, and for a minute it's so familiar it's like we're in her room, giggling about things that don't mean anything, a really happy moment until Anna would call her cell phone, looking for me.

"Good luck, Regina," Liz says. "You'll need it."

tuesday, after school

The night air is thick with heat, awful. Every breath in is stale and gross. I'm starting to think this weather will never break. We'll just choke on it and die.

Josh's house is strange and lonely looking when it's not the backdrop for the crazy parties that have made him legend around the halls of Hallowell High. The front lawn is a broad green brushstroke, and the house itself, a picture out of a magazine—tasteful, but flat. I walk the stone path to the front door and push the doorbell.

He answers in boxers and a T-shirt, his blond hair tousled.

"No," he says, taking me in. "No way. I have nothing to say to you—"

I shove my sandaled foot in the door at the exact same time he closes it, hard. I yelp and jump back, sucking in a breath through my teeth before the pain hits, and then it hits. *Fuck.* He opens the door, his mouth hanging open like a total idiot. Fuck him. I turn and hobble back down the walk.

"*Why* would you put your foot there?" he demands.

"Because I didn't want you to shut the door in my face!"

I sit on the steps leading to the driveway and rub my foot, tears in my eyes. Josh walks over and stares me down, looking every inch the asshole that he's turned out to be. The saddest part is, it's not even that much of a surprise. Josh is stupid-smart. Knowing him, he probably severed all emotional ties to me when I stopped being his girlfriend and started being a social liability.

"Are you okay?" he asks, like it's the last thing he wants to ask.

"I'm *fine*."

"Okay, good. Now get off my property."

I stare at him. "Are you *kidding* me? You're not even going to hear me out?"

His cell vibrates in his pocket. He takes it out, glances at the screen, and sighs. "Lynn Parks wants Adderall for resale because the other girls are too scared to buy from me, even though it'd be cheaper." He shakes his head. "I could get these retards Percocet and they just want Adderall."

That is not the thing he should be saying.

"Fuck you, Josh." I get to my feet. "You totally—"

He shoves his cell back in his pocket. "Okay, okay. Regina, just—wait. I'll hear you out, Jesus. What, did you think I'd be *happy* to see you after you fucked Donnie?"

I didn't sleep with him. The words are stopped by a dead-sick feeling in the middle of my chest. *I didn't sleep with him, he tried to rape me.* I open my mouth and close it again, while Josh stares at me expectantly, waiting for me to speak.

But I can't.

In the washroom with Anna, it made sense to just blurt it out; I didn't have a lot of time. But Josh is, like . . . not Anna. I need to think of a way to say it that doesn't betray the feel of Donnie on me.

"He tried to . . . Donnie tried to . . ."

My tongue gets too thick to talk around. A tear slides down my cheek. I wipe it away. I don't want to cry in front of Josh.

"Tears? Come on."

I recoil. "I can't believe what a total dick you're being. You're going to feel so stupid when I tell you what really happened—"

"Then hurry up and tell me, because I haven't got all night—" A car goes by, interrupting him. He *lets* it interrupt him. That's how little this means to him. And then his cell goes off again and he checks it. "It's Anna."

"Don't answer," I say. "Josh, don't answer—"

"Just wait a second. I have to take this and then we'll—"

I storm down the driveway. He calls after me once, and that's it. By the time I've hit the street, I can hear the faint strains of his conversation with Anna.

I jog down the street, trying to outrun the feeling building inside my stomach, until I can't, and then I pick up antacids at Ford's Convenience Store. They're in the fourth aisle down and seventeen steps in. I make the switch from Generic Brand J to Generic Brand K, superstrength, because I don't think the old ones are really working anymore.

They all stop working after a while.

wednesday

"Come on, Anna—just talk to me, *please*."

I stretch, touching my toes. It's gym. It's too hot out to instruct, so Nelson tells us to do what we want. All the boys are playing basketball on one side of the room, and the girls are on gym mats, occasionally offering the illusion of movement, because we're smarter than the boys. I'm trying to block out the voice behind me. It's uncomfortably close and it belongs to Donnie. He's squatting next to Anna's mat and begging for her time, to get her to hear him out. She's enjoying it, but she's not about to give him anything. It's all in her voice when she says, "Go to hell, Donnie."

Kara giggles beside her. Before he made his way over, they spent the period whispering the words *slut*, *whore*, and *bitch* in my direction. Anna has also decided to torment me with fashion sameness. Today they're all wearing blue. I'm wearing green.

I felt stupid passing them in the hall.

Donnie lowers his voice. "We need to talk—"

"*Don't* touch me."

She says it loud enough that it carries across the gym, and I can't help it. I turn and look. Donnie has his arm on her shoulder, a tight grip. I can see his fingers digging into her shirt. If it hurts, it's not on Anna's face. She's cool, disinterested. All eyes are on the two of them. She doesn't waver, but he's already shrinking. His face turns red, and his gaze shifts to me, and I edge away. I always waver. I spot Kara smirking out of the corner of my eye.

"Problem?" Nelson calls across the gym.

Anna won't speak for him. Donnie lets go of her shoulder and stands, trying to recover the moment. He straightens and walks past, pausing almost imperceptibly when he gets near me. I'm the last person in this school he can intimidate. And I hate that I'm the last person in this school he can intimidate. As soon as he's across the room, I get up and head over to the corner, stretching my hands over my head, trying to look casual, but my fingers are tingling and I can't breathe. Kara and Anna laugh. I can hear them laughing.

I inhale slowly.

When I face the gym, I spot Michael. He's sitting on the bench, hunched over, hands dangling between his legs, fresh off the court and taking a breather. His hair clings to his sweaty forehead, and he pulls the collar of his shirt up and wipes his face. Then he pauses and our eyes meet.

Josh jogs between us, momentarily obscuring our view, and when it's clear again, Michael's watching the game. I'm about to head back to my mat, but I stay back when I see Josh talking to Anna. Their heads are ducked together. Anna glances across the gym and tells him something. He nods and goes back to the game, beckoning to Michael to take center and sending Jack Olson to the side. I head to my mat and try to find the will to pretend like I'm doing something and none of this bothers me.

It takes, like, ten minutes.

"GODDAMMIT, YOU FUCKING *ASSHOLE!*"

The shout cuts through the hustle and bustle, and everyone stops what they're doing and turns their attention halfway across the gym, to where a few guys are huddled around Donnie. Ms. Nelson blows her whistle and hurries over.

Even from here, I can see the blood.

"Wow," Kara says behind me. "Nicely done."

"Thank you," Anna says. She makes her way over to the scene, Kara trailing behind her. Donnie's still screaming, clutching his nose. I wait a second and I go, too.

"Calm *down*, Henderson," Nelson says over Donnie's shouts. She tries pulling his hand away from his face, but he won't budge. "Tell me what happened."

Donnie wrenches away from her, and his hand comes down, revealing a bloody mess. His nose and the area under his right eye is swollen and angry, painful.

"You fucking elbowed me in the fucking face on fucking *purpose*, Josh!" Droplets of blood go flying everywhere. *"Fuck you!"*

"Mouth, Henderson!"

Donnie's hand goes back to his nose. His shoulders heave, and the parts of his face not covered in blood are a matching, apoplectic red. Everyone turns to Josh, who stands outside of it all, looking vaguely annoyed.

"Yes, Donnie, I elbowed you in the face. *On purpose.*" He says it like it's a completely preposterous idea, like people don't elbow people in the face on purpose, in the history of mankind. Ever. A few people chuckle, and he goes in for the kill: "It was an accident, man. You got in the way."

I try to let the blood that's still gushing from Donnie's nose fill me up, but then Nelson blows her whistle again and the moment is over and it's not enough. It's nowhere near enough.

And it just means I'm next.

"Brooks, escort Henderson to the nurse's office. The rest of you, back to what you were doing. There's still twenty minutes of this period left!"

We scatter back to where we're supposed to be. Josh winks at Anna.

I want to punch him in the face.

Getting to the Garbage Table is easier this time.

Anna, Kara, Marta, and Jeanette aren't around. Off-campus lunch. We liked to break out at least once a week, so they'll all be clustered around a McTable in matching outfits without me. I sit across from Michael; I've brought a drink to wash my antacid down, and he's got juice and a salad. The cafeteria noises are all around us, but they don't seem to touch the quiet settling here. I know he hates me, but I can't believe he doesn't have anything to say about what happened in gym. It's a big deal.

I watch him eat while he looks everywhere but at me. I used to be able to eat here. Ninth grade. Did it without a thought. Food, lunch. It didn't mean anything.

And then Liz happened.

"I don't know how you can stand sitting back here," I say. He doesn't respond. Still doesn't look at me. "Every day. Who wants to sit alone at lunch?"

He takes a long swig of his orange juice.

"It's not like I had a choice," he says.

"It's not like you didn't want it."

"I'm not afraid to be alone like you are."

He thinks he insulted me, like I should be above codependence in this wilderness, but here's how it is: Lunch with Michael is the new thing I'll cling to, the only thing keeping me from getting totally eaten alive. Before that, Anna kept me safe from people like him. My life has become the art of putting things between me and the people who hate me. Yes, I'm afraid to be alone.

Who would hold that against you in high school.

He stabs a few leafy greens onto his fork and shoves them into his mouth. I take the opportunity to study him further. His hair is a little damp, and any sweaty vestiges of gym are off him. He hit the shower and he looks good. He glances up and catches me staring at him. For a second, I swear he knows what I'm thinking. I blush and look away.

This is dumb.

"So you knew my mom, huh?" he asks, and it's a relief to have him ask because it means we have to talk to each other, and that's better than him staring at me or not staring at me and chewing food and not saying anything.

I nod. "We were friends."

"You know, I have a really hard time believing that," he says, "so tell me something a friend of hers would know."

"Why is it so hard to believe?"

"Because you're so afraid to be alone. I think you'll say anything to sit with me at lunch."

I think of his mother. I try to think of something that would make him believe we were friends. I trace circles on the table with my finger and picture her face. She had light brown hair—not like him—and light blue eye—like him—and she was my doctor, but she was a person, too, and she liked . . .

"She loved Gary Larson's comic, *The Far Side*. She thought he was—" I try to remember how she put it. "—Twisted. That's how I found out about Gary Larson. Your mom. Because she really liked him."

His face darkens. He hates and loves what I just said. He loves that I said it, but he hates that I'm the one who said it. He picks at the label of his orange juice.

"Yeah, she did," he says.

Chunks of broken concrete. A hint of a car underneath. The person inside is crushed to death. The person inside is Michael's mom. Overpass collapse.

It was all over the news.

"It's not fair," I tell him. "That she died . . ."

"You wouldn't know."

He's right. I wonder what it's like having a dead parent—how he can walk around under the weight of that kind of grief. My parents are useless, but I can't imagine either of them not being here, being useless.

"She did like *The Far Side*, though, you're right." The skepticism in his voice remains. "How did you two meet?"

She liked reading. I take my cue from that: "Library."

He nods slowly, a million miles away, absorbing this. I guess I pass, because he doesn't press it or demand any more specifics. Another tense, awkward silence falls between us. Awkward for me. I wonder how many more times I'll have to sit here before the tension dissipates.

He'd probably have to forget he hates me for that to happen.

I look around the cafeteria. Josh, Henry, and Bruce are laughing obnoxiously together. Josh looks so proud of himself for what he did to Donnie.

I turn back to Michael. His Moleskine catches my eye, triggering a memory. Eager to fill the silence, I start babbling more things I know about his mom, just so I can hear him say something back. I bet if I talked about her enough he'd forget he hates me.

"She was really big on writing things down," I say. I nod at the Moleskine. "Is that why you keep that thing? She always used to say, 'Write it down today, put it away, make sense of it tomorrow.'"

"Yeah, she always used to say that to her patients," he says, nodding. *Oh my God. Oh no. Why did I say that?* It dawns on him slowly, horribly. His eyes widen and he laughs in disbelief. "You have got to be fucking kidding me."

My face turns red.

"You?" he asks. *"You* were one of her patients?"

"I'm sorry," I say quickly. I don't know what else to say, but I really don't want to eat lunch alone tomorrow. "Michael, I'm—"

"Were you one of her patients?"

I can't believe I fucked this up this badly and so quickly.

"Answer me."

I nod feebly.

"I knew it," he says. "I *knew* you were lying. I couldn't figure out how a bitch like you would know my mother, much less be *friends* with her."

I bite my lip and dig my fingers into my jeans and try to channel Anna so he can't see how much that one hurt.

"You were her patient. *Why?"* I shake my head. I'm not giving him anything else to throw in my face. "So when you saw my mom for whatever you saw her for, did you tell her you were spreading vicious rumors all over school about her son? Did that come up during your sessions? I'm sure she would've *loved* it."

I don't say anything.

"And then she died, and you—" He edges his chair back, like he can't stand being this close to me. "And now you're sitting across from me. . . ." He just can't believe it. "I don't know what you needed, but you didn't deserve to get it from her."

"I needed help."

He gives me a disgusted look and gets up from the table. My heart seizes. He can't leave me here. Alone.

"Where are you going?" I ask.

"I don't owe you anything," he tells me. "And forget about sitting here tomorrow. Stay away from me. I'm serious."

He stalks out of the cafeteria. I fight the heat working its way up to my face. I get up fake-casually, grateful Anna and Kara aren't around to see this, and decide to wait out the rest of lunch in history class, which is where I'm due next. I walk the mostly deserted halls to my red locker, yank the door open, and—

My books are gone.

All of them.

There's an envelope taped to the inside of the door. My name is scrawled on the front in loopy, cutesy handwriting. I rip it off and open it up. Written on stationery that's decorated with cartoon stars—Kara's stationery—is the word *pool*.

I wasn't supposed to get this until after lunch, when I'd have to scramble for my books in front of everyone.

Small mercies.

I crumple the note and make my way to the pool. At lunch, nothing happens here. It's off-limits. Two week's detention if you're caught anywhere near it unsupervised, since drowned students don't reflect so well on the administration. My only obstacle should be getting past Sadowsky's office, but he's probably enjoying a nap in the teacher's lounge about now. I push through the doors and find my books drifting across the water. I grab the skimmer and fish them out quickly. My notes are pulp. The damaged textbooks will have to be paid for and replaced.

I gather everything in my arms and get the hell out. Perfect timing; I pass Sadowsky in the halls. The books soak through the front of my shirt and trail water behind me, but all he says is, "Get to class Afton, or do you *want* another detention this week?"

Teachers never go out of their way to notice anything.

Anna, Kara, Jeanette, and Marta spend the day stalking me in yellow.

They're always in the background and they always disappear when I try to get a closer look. The dumb thing is, I used to do this to other girls. I know how it works. No one ever goes in for the kill, but I still can't keep my heart from trying to claw its way up my throat every time I glimpse them.

Between classes is open season. I get stared at. I get muttered insults, spewed insults, shoved, and laughed at.

I am a *bitch whore slut*.

These names attach themselves to me in the halls, flutter away during class, and reattach themselves as soon as the bell rings.

I'm between first and second period, my head ducked, clutching my books and weaving through the hall like an idiot, which is okay as long as I don't have to look anyone in the eyes. I end up crashing into Henry Carlson. He grabs me by the arm and doesn't let go. He's alone. No Josh, no Bruce, no Anna. But Anna's always here, even when she's not.

"Better watch it, Afton," he says, grinning. I jerk my arm away, and he frowns, like I've wounded him. "Ouch. What's the rush?"

"I have a class to get to." I try to step around him, and he blocks my path. I sigh and level a glare at him, like any look I give him could make him submit. "Get out of my way."

"Just give me a minute."

"Henry, I'm warning you—"

He catches sight of something behind me, and before I can turn to look, he grabs me by the shoulders and forces me back, a light push that startles me enough to send me reeling into a wall of flesh. The wall of flesh shoves me back. I drop my books, turn, and find myself face-to-face with Donnie Henderson. He grabs me by the arm and pulls me close enough to say, "You'll pay for talking."

All I can see is his wrecked face. There's nothing else. My vision blurs, like my eyes are totally rejecting him, can't handle it. I wrench away, and as soon as his hand is off me, the hall comes back into focus. People are watching.

They all think I slept with him.

They all think I wanted it.

Donnie stomps away. Henry hangs around to laugh at his handiwork, a picture of lazy triumph. I grab my books and head in the opposite direction and the bell rings, and all I can think is *next, next, next, next class.*

By lunch, I'm a mess. I spend the period in the girls' room with a bag of chips from the vending machine, but I can't eat.

I roll up my sleeves and stare at what's left of my bruises.

I want to run away and I never want to come back.

When the last bell signals freedom, I'm on edge. Spent. I get my stuff from my locker—warped history books and all—and push through a flood of students.

Totally alone.

I'm halfway down the stairs when someone pushes me from behind. I lurch forward and I'm flying, steps blurring past. I land at the bottom of them with a sick *thud.* The pain is immediate. So is the laughter. It comes in from all sides, and I stay on the floor, surrounded by it. It's amazing how one day you wake up and this is your life.

I am not going to cry.

"Way to walk, Regina."

I look up. Kara. Anna. Jeanette. Bruce. Josh. Josh averts his eyes, and Anna grins and she's gone; Kara whisks her away. They low-five. Josh and Bruce follow after them. I am *not* going to cry.

"Oh!" Ms. Arnett, the school's secretary, materializes in the middle of the crowd and hurries over to me, her face full of wrinkly concern. "That was a *nasty* fall you took, Regina! Are you okay?"

"I'm fine," I mutter. She pulls me up by the elbow and looks me over. My left knee aches, and a small patch of blood is soaking through my jeans.

"Oh, but you're bleeding. Come to the office and we'll get—"

I shrug her off me. "I said I'm *fine*."

She stares at me with her watery blue eyes.

"Well . . . ," she says, "if you're sure."

I hobble away from Arnett, everyone, and push through the front doors. The warm air envelops me, and my head is full of the fall and after the fall: the stairs, my palms pressed against the floor, Anna, Kara, Josh. *Way to walk, Regina.* Arnett. As soon as I'm out of the parking lot and onto the street, I stop. I just stop.

I think of the year stretched out before me like a tunnel, and I see myself in it, awake and running.

A car pulls up to the curb and snaps me back to life. I resume my stilted walk home. Ten steps later, I notice the car is keeping pace with me. I have this crazy thought it's Anna and Kara and they're going to egg me or something, but when I look, it's only Michael in the shoddy blue Saturn he drives to school every day. The window is rolled down, and his arm hangs out the side, casual. He taps his fingers along the door, dividing his gaze between the road and me.

"I'll give you a ride home," he says.

"No, you won't."

"Kara pushed you." I ignore him. "Are you sure you don't want a ride?"

It's tempting: It's hot and gross out, and my knee hurts. But I won't. Not after what happened in the cafeteria yesterday. I force my-self to keep going, and he keeps creeping alongside me in the car. I squint up at the sun.

"Do you have air-conditioning?"

"It's one of the few things in this wreck that works."

Michael rolls up his window as I walk around to the passenger's side and get in. It's really weird to think that not that long ago, this would be Josh's car and I'd be sitting in it.

Michael pulls away from the curb. "Where do you live?"

"Keep going down this road, past the phone booth. It's the second left turn, seven houses down. You'll see it. It's the first brick house."

I run my hand over my knee. It's stopped bleeding.

"I was so sure you'd go crawling back to them by now," he comments. "I'm amazed you have any pride."

I don't say anything for a minute.

"I bet you're sure of a lot of things." I eye the Moleskine resting on the dash. "All you do is watch us and write."

"Yeah."

"So what do you see?"

"Everyone's afraid." He looks at me. "But no one more than you."

I point. "That's my house."

He eases the car to a halt and lets it idle while I sit there and try to think of something to say, but I can't. I get out of the car and step back into the heat, stand on the curb, and watch him pull out. As soon as the Saturn is a speck in the distance, I roll up the leg of my jeans and inspect the damage. Superficial wound.

It still really stings, though.

I'm in the girls' washroom when Kara comes in. She's in red.

Today they're wearing red.

She takes her place beside me, and our eyes meet in the mirrors. I rinse the lather from my hands and watch the suds swirl down the drain. I turn the water off and reach for the paper towels resting in a nearby puddle of water. Kara pushes the soap dispenser and lets the electric green liquid gush onto the cheap plastic counter below.

I just want to kill her. I've never felt a more honest urge in my life.

"You look like shit," she says. "It suits you."

"You'll pay for this," I tell her. It's an empty threat. Empty threats and the strong urge to bash her head against the pavement—the only two things I seem to have these days. They're better than nothing.

"No, I won't," Kara says. Her eyes light up. "Hey, I never said thank you, did I?"

"That's so fucked up. Do you even get what Donnie—"

"Yeah, and I should thank him, too. It's like winning the lottery. I couldn't believe you actually thought I'd *want* to help you after everything you've done to me—"

"I was *a lot* nicer to you than I could've been—"

"No," she interrupts. "You weren't."

We stare at each other. There's always this one girl. She's desperate and she's weird and she's jealous, and you're stuck with her, no matter how hard you try to get her off your back. Just throw some really fucked-up self-esteem issues into the mix and you have Kara. She could never keep up with us, and she knew it. And we knew it. And she was fat. Our relationship is as simple as it is complicated. I played messenger for Anna one too many times.

And I guess I enjoyed it more than I should have.

"The best part about all of this" she stops for a second, unable to contain herself. "Is how *awesomely* Anna sold you out. I thought she'd hold back a little, but she told me *everything*. I never had anything on you before—nothing she'd let me get away with using—but now . . . it's going to be a great year, Regina."

"Just wait until she finds out you lied to her."

"It's not going to happen. And what are you going to do about it, anyway? It's not like you can rally the troops. You have no one. Well, except Donnie. Maybe he'll have you."

She leaves. I'm a volcano. Something inside me snaps, and next thing I know, I'm in the hall and Kara's there, meandering, and all I can think about is how much I want her to hurt.

She doesn't see me coming until it's too late. I shove her and she yelps, and I shove her again, into a row of lockers. The sound she makes as she hits them is nice—it's *so* nice—that I shove her again. She tries to shove back, but I'm too quick. Another *bang* against the locker. Her head. A crowd assembles behind us and I know they're thinking *Fight!* even if they never say it. I can feel it coming off them and me; I'm adrenaline.

I'll give them a fight.

But before I can make another move, I'm pulled back.

There are hands on me and they're pulling me back.

"Get off her, Regina! Jesus, what the *fuck* are you doing?!"

The comedown is fast, intense. It's over. I'm suddenly aware of how noisy the halls are, that people are talking loudly, and they're pointing at me.

They all look surprised.

"Crazy bitch," one of them mutters.

The hands that are on me belong to Josh. Kara's pressed up against the locker looking like I've done exactly what I just did. Her face is red and her hair is everywhere. I shove Josh away.

"Don't touch me."

"Kara—oh, my *God,* Kara, are you *okay?*"

Anna pushes through the crowd and starts fussing over Kara, who points at me, panting. Anna doesn't miss a beat and marches over, livid. Josh moves, positioning himself beside her.

"What is your *problem,* Regina?"

I glare past the edges of Anna's red hair, to Kara, because I'm too afraid to look at her, and then she grabs me by the chin and makes me do it. I grab her wrist, get her hand off me. Big mistake. She raises her other hand like she's going to slap me. She doesn't, but the threat is enough to make me flinch, and the whole hall goes quiet.

We stare at each other. I jerk away.

My problem, my problem, what's my problem?

I walk away from all of them, turning corner after corner until I end up in a deserted hallway with doors that offshoot into nowhere rooms. The fight that almost was feels like a memory already, like it didn't even happen, and I'm numb all over except for my stomach, which is just acid, so I take an antacid, even though what I really want to do is scream until I can't scream anymore.

"Regina?"

Michael. He startles me. He must have seen the whole thing.

"What?" I have to fight every part of myself to let that simple word come out of my mouth, because I really, *really* want to scream. "What do you *want,* Michael?"

He blinks, taken aback. "Jesus, just forget it."

I watch him stalk back down the hall. I stand there alone until the urge to scream disappears, and then I decide to follow after him, because he can't just tell me to forget it and walk away.

He has to know I'm trailing him, but he doesn't look back. He keeps walking until he finally forces his way through the front doors and steps outside. Leaving. He's *left*. That's a really good idea. I glance over my shoulder for teachers. None.

I step through the door, and the heat is instantly on me.

Michael's already halfway across the parking lot.

"Michael! Michael, *wait*!" He stops. By the time I reach him, I'm already sticky with sweat. "Where are you going?"

"Home," he says.

Home. I could go home, to my place. No one's there. I glance back at the school. I can actually see the heat coming off of it. And I hate the people inside.

"Can I come with you?" I beg. He looks like he's about to tell me to fuck off, but I cut him off. *"Please?"*

He turns and heads for his car. I follow him.

He lets me.

Michael lives near the outskirts of town.

It's an old house. The painted exterior is flaking away, and the front porch looks tired. The wooden fences that separate it from nicer homes on either side are in desperate need of repair. He didn't always live here. He used to live in a bungalow a few streets over, and then his mom died. I always figured it was one of those situations where he and his dad couldn't stand being where she'd been, but I don't know if that's true.

I thought it once and I've tried not to think about it since.

Michael gets out of the car. I do the same. Now that school is behind us, the whole situation feels less dire and kind of stupid, like I shouldn't have come here. I wipe my palms on my shorts, and Michael gestures for me to follow him. We bypass the front door and edge down a narrow path of dried-out yellow grass between the fence and the house that leads into the backyard.

Where there's a pool.

It's in-ground. A quietly neglected piece of paradise. A few leaves float across the surface of the water. There are two chaise lounges at the side and worn-out wicker furniture taking up space on the patio. A sliding door leads inside.

Michael pushes open the back door. "I'll be right back."

I wonder if he will be. While he's inside, I meander around the pool. I get it. It's like neutral ground. It's as close to inside as I'm getting, and that suits me fine. I entertain a visual of us in his house, on a couch, side by side or something, and it's parental-inspection-on-prom-night shades of weird.

Not that this isn't weird.

I spot a fly floating on the surface of the water, its little legs pumping madly as it fights to keep itself afloat. I know that feeling. I roll up my sleeves, cup it into my hands, and seek out the least-dead patch of grass I can find. I set it down and it stays there, stunned. It's still not moving when Michael returns with three bottles and two glasses. He sets them on the table. Coke, Jack, vodka. He faces me, and I try to ignore how much I understand what he just did. At Josh's parties, I was usually the first to start drinking and the last to stop, and it wasn't because I enjoyed the taste.

It was because I hated the people I was around.

He half turns to me. "So why'd you do it?"

"She deserved it," I say.

Michael mixes two Jack and Cokes and hands me the first. I halve the glass quickly and then I polish it off. I can't tell if he's impressed or not. He takes a generous drink from his own glass, and his expression never changes.

It makes me feel even more awkward than I already do.

"My dad keeps his liquor cabinet locked," I tell him.

He sets his glass on the table and wanders over to the edge of the pool. He rolls up his jeans and sits down, dangling his bare legs in the chlorinated water. He doesn't invite me to join him, and I feel dumb about that, too, so I pour myself a shot of vodka, knock it back, and then I just go for it. I sit next to him, cross-legged, and try not to look as tense as I feel.

"What happened to your arms?" Michael asks.

I look down. What's left of the bruises Donnie gave me are in plain sight. My stomach twists. I roll down my sleeves, until I realize the act of hiding them will inspire more questions.

"Nothing," I mutter.

"Is that why you were seeing my mom?"

I laugh. "Yeah, totally. I punch myself in the arms a lot. It's a real problem."

He doesn't say anything, and I wonder if his mom actually *did* see people who punched themselves in the arms a lot, and then I feel *really* stupid. And then I figure if I feel this stupid, I might as well go double or nothing:

"So can I sit with you at lunch on Monday?"

"No."

He gets to his feet. The way he moves is so light, easy. I'm jealous of how he walks around school with everyone thinking these horrible things about him, like it doesn't mean anything. I can barely maintain eye contact anymore.

He grabs the vodka and takes a long sip from it. When he's finished, he wipes his mouth and contemplates the bottle, and there's something so beautiful and lonely about it that I almost wish I had a camera. I shake the thought away. He sets the bottle down and returns to his spot beside me. Dips his legs back in.

"What'll you give me for it?" he asks.

I stare. "What?"

"To sit with me at lunch on Monday? What will you give me for it?"

I flip him off. He laughs. I guess I could hide in the washroom for the rest of the year, but I don't know. It'd be nice to make Anna think that I had an ally. The illusion of someone being on my side. I reach into my pocket for an antacid and shove it in my mouth.

"What do you want?" I ask him.

He shrugs. "I don't know. Maybe I should stop putting dents in my crappy reputation. It's bad enough being a waster, but it's a thousand times worse being a waster who hangs out with Regina Afton, right?"

I ignore that. "You want to know why I was seeing your mom?"

"Why else do you think I let you come here?"

"Guess. If you guess right, I'll tell you."

He leans back and stares at the sky. "I can't. I have you mostly pegged, but I just can't figure out why you of all people would *need* my mom's help."

"You have me pegged," I repeat.

He nods. "You're Anna Morrison's right hand. That's the lowest form of life on the highest part of the social ladder. There's not much to you." He straightens before I can reply. "Okay, let me try: Your dealer ex-boyfriend got you hooked on Adderall, and shrink visits were part of your recovery process."

I roll my eyes. "Wow, got it in one."

"It's probably something boring like an eating disorder."

My stomach lurches. I don't want to talk about this with him anymore. "Forget it. I'm not telling you even if it means I have to sit alone every day for the rest of the year."

"I'll walk you to your classes," he says, looking at me.

I stare at him. He's serious. He'll let me sit with him and he'll walk me to my classes if I tell him why I was seeing his mom. My fingers tingle—some kind of physical response to let me know this is a deal that's too good to pass up, and before I've even really decided to tell him, I'm telling him, just spewing it out: "I couldn't eat."

"So I was right." He sounds disappointed. "Eating disorder."

"It wasn't an eating disorder," I say. He raises an eyebrow and I flush, trying to figure out a way to explain it. "I wanted to eat and I couldn't."

Everyone thought it was an eating disorder, at first, and that's when Kara *really* started hating me. It drove her crazy every time Anna slid half her lunch to me looking all concerned. When I stopped eating, people cared.

"I went to a bunch of doctors, and they couldn't find anything physically wrong me . . . so I started seeing your mom."

"But you can eat now?"

I think of the pills in my pocket. "Mostly."

"So you just woke up one day and you couldn't eat anymore? Really?"

I nod. "Something like that."

Liz is out. I put my hand in the water and try to ignore that voice in my head. *Liz is out.* I remember waking up that Monday, sitting down at the table for breakfast, and ending up over the sink, puking. I thought it was nerves. I thought it would go away.

"Why?" he asks. "What was the reason?"

"That's between me and your mom," I say, but it's a lie. I never told her why I couldn't eat, even though I knew. I just fed her half-truths because she was so warm and I wanted her to like me more than I wanted her to help me. And she would've never liked me if she'd known. "So can I sit with you or not?"

"No. But thanks."

I stare at him. He stares back, a small smile at the corner of his mouth.

"You're an asshole," I tell him.

"What did you think was going to happen? I hate going to school and you're the reason why. Just think about that for a minute and then tell me if you're still shocked."

"It didn't have to be like that for you," I snap. "You think about *that.*"

"I'm so sorry that I came to Hallowell and forgot to genuflect in front of your best friend," he snaps back. "Not that it makes a difference. Liz Cooper was on her knee for Anna all the time, and it didn't do her any favors in the end, right?"

"Shut up."

"But don't you want to talk about Liz? Don't you want to talk about that time you sabotaged her homework? Broke into her locker? Trashed her things?"

I bite the inside of my cheek. "Michael, stop—"

"Started that rumor campaign about her? Hey, remember you told Duane Storey she was a total dyke when she was *really* into him?"

"Michael—"

"And I've been dying to know . . . was there actually a weekly 'Make Liz Cooper Cry' competition, or did it just turn out that way?"

"Liz was the reason I saw your mother," I snap. It catches Michael off guard. His eyes widen, just a little. "You don't have me pegged." I bite my lip. Hard. "And I *liked* Liz. I didn't get off on watching Anna torture her every fucking day. She was my—"

"Friend?" he finishes in disbelief.

Once upon a time. Once upon a time, I really, really liked Liz. Total girl-crush. Being around her was so easy. And Liz liked me too. A lot. That was the problem.

She's pulling you away . . .

"Okay, wait, so *you* fucked *her* up," Michael says slowly. "And *you* went to my mom because *you* couldn't eat because *you* were fucked up because *you* fucked *Liz* up?"

"Something like that, yeah," I mutter.

Somehow this new piece of information only makes him hate me more. "Always the victim, right? Liz tried to kill herself, and I'm supposed to sit here and feel sorry for *you* because you feel guilty about it?"

"She tried to kill herself?" I whisper.

"Oh, you didn't know?" He nods. "Took a bunch of pills over spring break at her grandparents'. Her grandmother found her." I shake my head slowly. "And she *still* came back to school. That's amazing, isn't it? And that whole time you were ruining my life in the morning and seeing my mom in the afternoons. . . . " I press my hand against my mouth. "What do they say, again? You reap what you sow."

I didn't know she tried to *kill herself*.

"Then this should make you feel good," I say. "Donnie Henderson? I totally didn't have sex with him, but not for lack of him trying *really* hard—" My voice breaks. "I even have the bruises to prove it."

Silence. He gets it, and for a second he almost looks sorry, sick. "Regina—"

"Tell Liz," I say, "the mean girl totally got what she deserved in the end."

This was stupid, coming here. I turn away from him, make my way across the concrete to that small strip of grass that will lead me out. I'm almost there when he calls my name, and then I stop and he says, "Nobody deserves that."

My house is quiet. Empty.

My parents work. They work and work and work. Except there's no work in Hallowell, so they go to the city, even though they're too old for the hours and commute, but that's okay with me because otherwise we might have to talk.

I sit at the kitchen table and press my face against its cold wooden surface. I stopped crying between my house and Michael's, but I could start again, so I just want to stay here and not move. I am not moving. Everything is fine, just so long as nobody moves me. But then the sun goes down and the room gets dark and I haul myself up from the table and shuffle to my room. I turn on the light and sit on the bed. *Nobody deserves that.* I imagine the words coming from Anna's mouth, Kara's, Josh's mouth, and then I do cry. One stupid tear after the other. My stomach doesn't feel so great, so I take an antacid and then I take another one. *Nobody deserves that.*

But I'm starting to wonder.

To: Regina Afton
From: The YourSpace™ Team
Subject: You have been invited to join the IH8RA group on YourSpace™!

Dear Regina,

You have been invited to join a fun new group on YourSpace™!
Click the link to sign into your YourSpace™ account and find
out who wants YOU to be a part of THEIR group!

Regards,
The YourSpace™ Staff

It's probably from some band. No one I know e-mails me anymore.

But it's fun to pretend to be wanted.

I click the link and I'm sent to a page that prompts me for my
username and password. I type them in and wait for the browser to
load.

A few seconds later, this pops up:

You've been invited to join the IH8RA group on YourSpace™. If
you would like to join this group, click ACCEPT. If you do not

want to join this group, click NO, THANKS (the group will not be notified).

My cursor hovers over *ACCEPT.* IH8RA. It's an acronym. I contemplate it, even though I could just click the link and the mystery would be solved. But that's no fun, and I'm smart enough to figure this out and—honestly—I've got nothing better to do with my time. My brain works to put the pieces together.

I H 8 R A. IH8RA. IH8RA. IH8. I H8. I hate. IH8 RA. I hate RA. RA.

Regina Afton.

I Hate Regina Afton.

You have been invited to join the I Hate Regina Afton group on YourSpace™!

I throw up.

I'm hunched over the toilet watching dinner come up, and my mind is doing this the whole time: *It might not have anything to do with you it could mean anything you haven't even seen the page yet how do you know it's about you it could be a promo for some band it might not have anything to do with you how do you know it's about you.*

Knock-knock on the bathroom door.

"Are you sick, Regina?" Mom.

Yes.

I wipe my mouth and flush the toilet.

"I'm okay. It's nothing."

"Let me know if you need anything?"

No.

"Sure."

But for a second, I think I do need her.

"Mom . . ."

She's gone.

I run the tap as cold as it will go and splash my face. The computer hums in the next room, waiting for me, and I don't have what I need to have inside me to go back in there and click the link. Courage.

But that's not going to stop me from doing it anyway.

Psychedelic-colored shapes float across the monitor's face. Screen saver. I jiggle the mouse, and the YourSpace page pops up. I stare at my choices: *ACCEPT. REJECT.* I choose neither. I click the blue link to take me to the group's page to see what it's about, because even though I know what it's about, some small part of me hopes I'm wrong.

The page loads.

I fall back into the chair. The soft sounds of the television in the living room drift in, and then other sounds follow: Dad rocking in his recliner. Mom washing dishes in the kitchen. I can hear the clinking of glass in the sink. A day off. A fan *whirs* next to me, raising warm air. It's all so quiet and so family and it's so perfect, and I have to share it with this—a page as red as my locker.

In the upper right-hand corner of it is a picture of me. I minimize the screen, horrified, before pulling it up again. It's not a nice picture. It wouldn't be. I'm staring at the camera through half lids, caught in midblink. I look stoned. My mouth is lax, and my hair is sticking out at all ends. I'm not stoned. Anna woke me with the camera at a sleepover, and twenty-four hours later she had prints. It's hideous.

The entire world can look at it, and they can see me hideous.

THIS IS A GROUP FOR PEOPLE WHO HATE REGINA AFTON. DO YOU HATE REGINA AFTON? FRIEND US AND LEAVE A COMMENT!!

I scroll down. The group has only one interest listed—hating me. Anna heads up the featured friends, followed by Josh—

And Kara and Marta and Jeanette and—

IH8RA has 300 friends in total. There are only 450 students at Hallowell High. The remaining 150 either don't have a YourSpace account or they haven't checked their e-mail yet. I click through the page slowly, checking out avatars, recognizing faces. So many people. Some I've spoken to, others I've never spoken to. Some I loathe, others I've never spared a second thought. A few I considered acquaintances. They're all here, all tied together by their apparent hatred of me.

I navigate back to the main page, to the comments.

YOU ARE VIEWING THE MOST RECENT OF 202 COMMENTS.

I shouldn't read them.
I have to read them.

I fuckin hate that bitch.

The first—and latest—comment belongs to Jake Martin, some sophomore I've never really given a damn about. I thought he felt the same about me, but I guess not.
I guess he fuckin hates me.

Team Anna! :)

Kara, Jeanette, and Marta leave this comment several times, smiley face and all.
Team Anna.

Thnx for the add.

My less-astute classmates leave this comment. The ones who add anyone and everything and drop a little thank-you note before moving on to the next one, because that's social networking for you. They don't get it.
Or maybe they get it and they just don't care.

slut
whore
tramp
keep trying with those sweaters, regina! they can't hide what a
    slut u r
loose
slut
whore

slut
i fuckin hate that bitch
i fuckin hate that bitch
i fuckin hate that bitch
slut
thnx for the add
Team Anna! :)

The same things over and over again. Each comment taking a cue from the last, each one a sharp jab at me. After a while, I even start feeling bruised. I scroll all the way down to the bottom of the page, and a link catches my eye:

REPORT ABUSE

My cursor hovers over it. *Click it. Click it.* Report abuse. Easy:
Dear YourSpace, I'd like to report abuse.
My friends are abusing me.

REPORT ABUSE

I refresh the page, and the friend count has jumped. 302. So have the comments. 203. I refresh again and the comments jump again. 204. I straighten. People hate me and they're online right now, hating me. I want to know who they are and I want to know what they'll say. I *have* to know, so when I step into school tomorrow I'll have every comment tied to a face, so when I see those faces in the halls—I'll know.

I refresh the page.

The buzz of my alarm clock jolts me awake. My mouth is parched and there's a crick in my neck. It takes me a minute to remember why I'm not in bed. I fell asleep in front of the computer. The last time I looked at the YourSpace page, it was 6:00 A.M.

Now it's a quarter after eight.

Forget coffee; I barely have time to get dressed, brush my teeth and hair. It isn't until I'm racing across the parking lot that I realize how stupid this is: I'm *rushing* to get to *school*. When I reach the front doors, I hit a wall. I can't step inside. I have one hand on the door handle, and it's like I'm paralyzed. My mind tells my hand to open the door, but my hand won't do it. My insides are made up of millions of feral butterflies gnawing at every bit of peace inside of me until there's none. I can't open this door.

"Fucking *move*," someone mutters behind me. When I don't, they shove me out of the way. It's "Thnx for the Add." Nora Green. She glares at me, opens the door, and steps inside. I follow her in before it swings shut in my face.

I'm ten steps in when "Slut," "Whore," and "Loose" walk by. Jeri Waters, Elliott Pike, Mary Schwartz. "I fuckin hate that bitch" is talking to Gary Doyle at Gary's locker. I start to shake. They both look me up and down when I pass.

Donnie is crossing the hall. I don't notice him until it's too late.

We slam into each other and stumble backward. He looks as bad as me, maybe worse. Unshaven, dirty, disgusting, wrecked.

It's only been a week.

He glares at me and then he gets close, so close his mouth is inches from mine. I'm afraid he's going to do something like he did at Josh's party, and I wonder if anyone would do anything about it if he did, because they all hate me.

"Die," he says, and then he walks away. I close my eyes, trying to keep it together, and when I open them, Michael is halfway down the hall, at the water fountain, watching me.

I head for my locker, where my lock refuses me. I try it over and over and over again and nothing happens. So I kick it.

"What's the problem?"

Michael. Behind me. I point at the lock. "I can't get it open." I swallow hard. "It won't open."

I must look really pathetic, because he nudges me aside gently and grabs the lock. I can smell his aftershave. Sort of earthy and clean at the same time. I take a step back because I don't want to be this close to him.

"What's your combination?" he asks.

"Uh . . ." *Never tell anyone your locker combination.* Ninth-grade orientation. It was the first thing they told us, but who follows the rules? "Twelve, twenty, thirty-two, and two . . ."

I watch his thumb spin the dial slowly, each number hitting its mark like I swear to God my thumb did. I rest my head against the locker.

"Maybe you should sit with me at lunch," he says after a minute. "Maybe it's safer that way. . . ."

"I didn't tell you about Donnie so you'd feel sorry for me."

"Your call." He gives the lock a jerk. It breaks free. Miracle. "There you go."

When I raise my head to thank him, he's gone.

"I told them to set up the net," Nelson mutters, surveying the gym. "Where. Is. It?"

I don't know who "they" are, but I'd hate to be them when they run into Nelson later. Red creeps up her neck to her face: She's ready to blow. I overheard someone say her name and the word *hangover* in the same sentence earlier, and I think it might be true, because she hasn't touched her whistle.

"Morrison!" she barks. "Afton! Go get the volleyball net out of the storage room, and the rest of you, get out there and jog until I tell you to stop!"

No one moves. Everyone's holding their breath. It's so quiet I can hear the vein pulsing in Nelson's forehead. *Morrison* as in Anna. *Afton* as in me. The net in storage. *Morrison! Afton! Go get the volleyball net out of storage.* Together.

"What's the matter with you people? Didn't you hear me?" Nelson winces at the sound of her own voice. "*Move!* Morrison, Afton, don't make me tell you twice!"

"Ms. Nelson," Anna whines from her spot beside Kara and Josh, "can't Kara come with me instead?"

I glance at Michael. He's across the gym standing near some guys, not quite a part of their group but definitely a part of the scene. He rolls his eyes, bored.

Muttering. The people around us are muttering. Nelson takes several deep breaths in and out, like Anna's just asked her the stupidest question in the world.

"*Morrison*," she repeats, "and *Afton*. Get. The. Net."

She jerks her thumb at the door. Anna's not dumb enough to tempt fate twice. Josh squeezes her shoulder sympathetically. Anna gives a horsey shake of her head, turns to Kara, mutters something bitchy, and walks across the room like she's on a catwalk, leaving me to chase after her.

"The rest of you, *jog!*" Nelson shouts.

The jogging starts up—a stampede. Noise explosion. As Anna and I exit the gym, Nelson orders everyone to do sit-ups instead.

"Don't talk to me," Anna says, as we march down the hall. "I'm serious. Anything you want to say to me, I don't want to hear."

"I don't have anything to say to you."

"Good," she says.

"Good," I say.

"Fine," she says.

"Fine," I say.

"You—"

She makes an exasperated noise and keeps walking. I start stressing. And then the stress turns to laughter that tries to bubble up my throat and out of my mouth. It's not funny. If I laugh, I'm dead. But I really want to laugh.

That must mean I'm losing it.

My stomach reminds me this is no laughing matter. I find myself stopping in the middle of the hall, searching my pockets for an antacid. Anna doesn't realize I've fallen behind until I'm shoving one in my mouth and forcing it down, and then when she sees me, she rolls her eyes. I'm white hot, like with Kara in the hall, except I don't want to hurt Anna, I just want her to see what a mistake she's made. My hand autopilots back into my pocket for another antacid because I can feel my stomach boiling.

"Pathetic," she says.

I don't blame whoever bailed on Nelson: The volleyball net is wedged at the back of the storage room, unraveled behind a row of gym mats against the wall.

"Forget it," I say.

"You want to be the one to tell Nelson that?"

I sigh and we start shifting mats. They're awkward as hell. The first ten minutes pass in the sounds of us breathing and the shuffle of the mats as we move them. When my arms start to ache and cramp, I notice she's stopped, letting me do the work for both of us, waiting for me to catch on.

"Would you *help*?" I ask. She just stares. I grab the edge of a mat and get back to work. "Fuck you, Anna."

"Fuck *you*," she returns. "I thought I could trust you, but I should've known you'd stab me in the back, especially after Liz. You were never the same after that. I should've known you'd fuck me over."

I don't want to hear Liz's name come out of her mouth.

"Anna, shut the fuck up—"

"Don't tell me to shut the fuck up. He was *my* boyfriend. He was *my* boyfriend for two years, and no matter what you felt about him, whatever you think it was, he was still *my boyfriend*."

I let go of the mat. "*I didn't sleep with him!*"

"Shut up—"

"I didn't sleep with him."

"Regina—"

I'm going to keep saying it until she hears it. "I didn't sleep with Donnie, and Kara is totally setting you up. You look like a fool—"

"*Regina*—"

"Anna, he tried to—"

"Shut up!"

She pushes me. I hit the row of shelves behind us, and the metal edges dig into my skin, and then she's gone and I'm alone. I sit on the floor and close my eyes, and when I open them again, it's not quite three-thirty, but close, so I leave.

tuesday

The air-conditioning lasts the first five minutes of homeroom before dying a spectacular death, and now I'm navigating my way to my next class through too many sweaty bodies, and I want to tell everyone to stop exhaling because they're just making it worse.

"Hey, Afton!" I only stop for a second, until I realize it's Bruce, and then I keep moving. His voice follows me down the hall. "Is it true you like it in the dark?"

I ignore him. So does everyone else. His is one voice among many.

"Because Josh says you liked it in the dark."

I face him. He's annoyingly self-assured, smug. He makes his way over to me, talking the whole time, his voice carrying over the noise, forcing people to listen.

"You know. When you have sex. You like it in the dark."

"Shut up."

An uncomfortable heat works its way up to my face from my toes. Everyone seems to have paused to listen now, and the people walking in on the moment slow down, knowing instinctively that whatever comes out of Bruce's mouth next has to be heard; that it's going to be good. A redhead and a blonde are in my periphery. They're grinning.

"Because you hate the way you look. I mean, that's what he told me." *Go to hell.* I can't say it. My voice is gone. Bruce smiles. "How'd he put it? . . . you 'wish you were a little more filled out.'" A few girls snicker behind me. "He wished that too."

"Stop—"

"And you won't let him go down on you, right? What's up with *that?*"

I force my way down the hall through the crowd that's gathered, but Bruce follows me. I try to tune him out. I can't.

"Is there something about you we should know? Should Josh get tested?"

He keeps talking. Everyone's laughing. He stays on me. I dodge into the girls' room, but he grabs the door and holds it open.

"I'm not done," he says.

I beg him with my eyes to stop. "Why are you doing this to me, Bruce? I have never done anything to you."

He doesn't say anything. He just stands there grinning. It's not like I need an answer. He's working for Anna. He's crushed on her for ages.

"Josh didn't tell me shit," he says. "Anna gave me all my lines. Is it true? Do you really like it in the dark?"

"If you think doing Anna's dirty work is going to get you a free pass into her pants, you're mistaken," I tell him. "I'm pretty sure she thinks you're too small."

His face turns red and he raises his voice. "Josh called you a *good* lay, but not a *great* one—"

I yank the door shut, but he keeps shouting through it. I lock myself in one of the stalls and bite my fist until I gag, and every muscle in my body is tight and my joints are all seized up. I breathe around my fist, sucking in air through the narrow space until Bruce finally stops and goes, and then I thaw. Slowly. The bell rings. I study the teeth marks in my skin, slimy with sweat. Phys ed. I have to show my face in front of a gym full of people who think I like it in the dark. *Is it true? Should Josh get tested?*

When I step out of the stall, Liz is in front of the mirror brushing her hair. My heart flip-flops. Liz isn't surprised to see me. She's never surprised to see me. She runs the brush through her hair, takes an elastic from around her wrist, and pulls her hair into a ponytail. I feel hollow, just like I felt in the days after it became devastatingly clear to her we weren't going to be friends again and I was going to have to make her life miserable. Enough for her . . .

. . . to want to die.

"I'm sor-ry," I say, and my voice cracks, splitting the word *sorry* in two.

She lowers her hand and turns to me slowly, setting the brush on the counter. "What did you say?"

I try to find the word again—*sorry*—but it's gone. I want to tell her she's brave, she's stupid brave for coming into school day after day knowing what is waiting for her, and I want to tell her she was the best thing in my life for one brief moment in time, and I want to tell her that I'm sorry I stood by while she was ruined, *I'm sorry, I'm sorry, I am so sorry.*

She turns back to the mirror, silent.

When Nelson orders us to stand in a line against the wall, I know what's coming next.

She'll select two captains and they'll pick teams.

Since we have an uneven class, the last one left keeps score, because the last one left always keeps score, because alternating is a pain in the ass. I've spent the first half of my life being one of the lucky ones; I've always had a team. Now my lack of a team, the lack of people *wanting* me on their team, is going to satisfy two sets of people—my ex-friends and everyone I've gotten picked over in the past. Picking teams.

How do teachers forget how horrible this is.

We line up. My hand goes for my pocket, but I stop short of getting an antacid. I don't want to give anyone the satisfaction.

"Basketball," Nelson says, blowing her whistle. "Myers and Carey, pick your teammates, and be quick about it."

Kara and Josh amble up to the front. It says something about Nelson that she never gives losers the opportunity to captain. I don't think she's ever picked Kara to captain before, and I wonder if teachers always acquiesce to these shifts in popularity, like everyone seems to, whether they really want to or not.

Josh and Kara do a sweep of the room. Their eyes linger on each of us, sizing us up for a basketball game no one will give a damn about after everyone's picked. When Josh gets to me, I feel like a piece of meat.

He nods at Bruce. "Burton."

Kara grins and points at Anna. The whole ordeal lasts only ten minutes, the deliberations taking longer and longer the less people there are to choose from, until there are only two of us left. Me and Donnie. We stand beside each other, tense.

Last call belongs to Josh.

"*Not* Regina," Anna says really loudly. I try to pretend I don't care, but I do.

It's completely humiliating.

"Whatever," Josh says, nodding at Donnie. Donnie sags with relief and makes his way to Josh's side, weaving slightly. I glance at Nelson. She notices—I can tell by the look on her face—but she doesn't say anything.

I hate this school.

As soon as Donnie is hovering on the outside of Josh's team, this is what the whole scene looks like:

TEAM 1   TEAM 2
ME

Nelson blows her whistle.

"Bench, Afton," she says. "It's your lucky day."

Someone dog-whistles and barks at me, and everyone snickers. I make my way over to the bench. The game starts. I lean my head against the wall and stare at the ceiling. One of the fluorescent lights overhead flickers, and somebody scores and somebody else scores, but no one ever asks me for the tally.

I shift my focus to Anna. Her auburn hair dances around her face, and her skin is shiny with sweat. And then I watch Kara and my fingers get that familiar itch. Instead of curbing this uncomfortable feeling with pills, I decide to stew, to let their betrayal build until I can hear the blood rushing around my head. It sounds like a dam after spring thaw. The ball goes off-court and rolls my way, and I watch Kara chase after it, laughing, and I'm *angry* and I need to do something about it.

Do something.

It's a small voice inside of my head. *Do something.* The ball gets closer. *Do something.* She gets closer. *Do something.*

I stick my foot out.

Don't do that.

But it's too late to take it back. Kara's foot slams into my ankle—it hurts—and she shrieks. Everyone stops what they're doing to watch her fly. It's one of those running falls that seems to last forever, too. She stumbles onto the floor, and the sound she makes when she finally hits it face-first goes straight to my bones in a really good way, and in the heavy pause before she starts wailing and everyone else starts buzzing . . .

I laugh.

I clamp my hand over my mouth, and her audience becomes mine. They're torn about which one to look at—her or me? Another giggle escapes through the crack in my fingers. I clamp my other hand over my mouth.

Stop. This is bad.

When Kara gets to her feet, furious and red-faced, she's a mirror image of me. Both of her hands are pressed against her mouth, and there are tears in her eyes.

Don't laugh.

The room stays quiet. Nelson jogs over to Kara, but Anna manages to get to her first. She tries to draw Kara's hands away from her mouth, and I remember Donnie, Donnie with his hands over his bloody nose and it's great, and then the tears come, tears are streaming down Kara's face and she's hurt. Kara is hurt. *I hurt her.*

"What is it, Myers?" Nelson barks. Kara jerks away, shaking her head. A sob escapes her lips, and she walks away from both of them. "Myers, get back here!"

Kara keeps her back to all of us, crying. Anna ventures over, murmurs something at her, and Kara sobs something back and moves her hands from her mouth, and I remember Donnie and the stairs flying past me and the YourSpace page and the books, and however hurt Kara is, it's not enough. I want her to hurt until there's nothing there for Anna to comfort. I dig my fingernails into my palm and breathe.

I got to hurt her *some*.

That's something.

I just wish she'd turn around and show us all how much.

And then she does.

"You did that on purpose!" It's not obvious—whatever damage I caused. I search her face and can't find it. "You tripped me! I saw you stick your foot out—*owww*—"

She covers her mouth again and cries. Nelson blows her whistle in an attempt to reclaim control of the situation and forces Kara to remove her hand.

"Mouth?" Nelson asks. Kara nods. Nelson tilts Kara's head back and inspects her mouth. I step forward for a better look. So does everyone else.

"Chipped tooth," Nelson mutters, and I finally see it.

Chipped is an understatement. Half of Kara's right front tooth is missing, and I wince in spite of myself, because I know how much they hurt. But I stop feeling sorry for her as soon as the picture really registers, because *she's missing half her front tooth*. That's hilarious. *Don't laugh. Don't laugh. Don't laugh.*

Laugh later.

"Get to the office, call your parents, see if you can get to a dentist today," Nelson says. "You'll need it, Myers."

"Ms. Nelson," Anna breaks in, "Regina tripped Kara. She was laughing—"

Kara nods frantically. "She did it on purpose—"

Her tooth interrupts her. She closes her eyes, clamps her mouth shut, and rides it out. I watch the impression of her tongue bubble

up under her lip as she runs it over the place her tooth isn't anymore. Nelson turns to me, face hard. Her face is always hard.

"Is this true, Afton?"

Everyone stares at me.

"It was an accident," I say innocently. "She got in the way."

Josh's head whips up. Anna's mouth drops open. Kara looks
ready to explode. Nelson orders her to the nurse's office and shouts
us back to the game. There's room for me to be on the team, but no
one wants me, so I go back to keeping score.

Today, it's Regina: 1, Kara: 0.

"Donnie's off the basketball team," Michael tells me at lunch.

He said it was my call, so I made it. I decided to sit with him instead of hiding in the girls' room because I didn't want to run into Liz again. I was nervous crossing the room and making my way over, but he didn't look *un*happy to see me, I guess.

"Basketball was the only thing he loved doing sober," I say.

"I overheard it in the changing rooms," Michael says. "They forced him off by threatening to tell his parents he was cheating on the drug tests. I thought of you when I heard it. I thought you'd want to know."

"Thanks." I want it to feel good, but it doesn't, because it's smaller than what Donnie did to me. So he can't play basketball. So what.

The center table is completely empty. It's like they all took the day off to go with Kara to her emergency dental appointment or something. Everyone's talking about Kara's tooth, and no one is talking about how I like it in the dark. It's so perfect I wish I'd planned it.

"They made this YourSpace hate group about me," I say.

It gets quiet—as quiet as it can get in the cafeteria—and it's unnerving. I don't know Michael well enough to understand his quiet. When Anna's quiet, she's mad or bored. Kara gets quiet when she's thinking of ways to bring everyone's attention back to her. When Jeanette gets quiet, she's spacing, and when Marta's quiet, she's sad.

"I know," he finally says. "I got an invite in my e-mail."

"Did you join?"
"No. It's stupid. They could've been more original."
Probably.
But it still stings.
Michael grabs his tray and stands. I stand.
"Thanks . . ." I say awkwardly, gesturing to the table, ". . . for this."
He nods curtly and leaves without me.

I'm sitting at my desk in my bedroom, where there's a photo of the five of us.

The Fearsome Fivesome.

Me and Anna are laughing about something, and Kara stares at us, smiling, longing to be in on it. She's there, but she never matters. Marta and Jeanette are in their own little world, forever okay with it because they have each other. I set the photo face down. Behind it is a little box. What I'm looking for.

I reach for it and fumble with the lid and find the notes.

Every year of high school is chronicled in scrap pieces of paper in this box. Our secrets. I save the ones Anna didn't get her hands on, because I knew what she wanted to keep them for—insurance, and then, if needed, ammunition. I dump the papers on my desk and run my fingers over them, all folded to perfection. I pick one, unfold it, and squint at the tiny handwriting in the margins of some old math homework.

Are you mad at me? My handwriting.

Would you quit *asking me that?* Anna.

I'm sorry.

I crumple the paper and toss it aside, rifle through the pile and pick another.

Another exchange between Anna and me.

Liz is out.

Are you serious?

I'm serious. She's out.

Rethink this. Please.

<u>*Liz is out.*</u>

Wait. I trace the letters with my index fingers and close my eyes. I'm sitting at my desk, writing. *Please. Please* with all of my heart. I slide the note over to Anna. She unfolds it, scribbles down those three words again and slides it back to me. And that was it. I rifle through the notes until someone else's handwriting catches my eye. It's so girly, it's Kara's, of course. I smooth out the paper and read. An old one:

I'm at my goal weight. Now I'm readjusting the goal!

That's all it says. No reply, nothing. It might not have even been for me. Maybe I just collected it. I separate all the papers that have glimpses of Kara's handwriting on them and push the rest aside. I examine the notes, one after the other.

Can I hang out with you and Anna tonight?

<u>*NO.*</u>

I don't even soften the blow. It's just there, hard lines etched into the graph paper—*NO*—underlined for effect, in case she didn't get the message, because Kara never got the message. On the other side of the page, her writing again. One question, no response:

Please?

I close my eyes briefly and reach for another note. I started this one:

Quit sulking. Me.

I'm not. Kara.

Yes, you are. You have been since lunch. So Bruce called you fat—so what?

From the earlier days.

It was humiliating.

You've been fatter.

I look awful.

So do something about it.

Like what? Have you talked to Josh for me yet?

I remember that next line:

You can buy diet pills over the counter, you know. You don't even need
Josh.

Really?

Yes. I'll go to Ford's and show you. I'll even buy them for you if it stops
you from fucking whining.

I stood next to her at Ford's while she bought the over-the-counter diet pills. And then, from that point on, I watched her melt. It made Anna happy.

Another:

Are you mad at me?

I can't talk now.

Just tell me if you're mad at me.

Yeah, kind of. But I wasn't. I can see it in my handwriting. I wasn't. I was just saying it because I liked gutting her. I got harder on Kara after the Liz thing. I was so angry, and she was there. She let me.

What did I do? Kara's handwriting. *What do I do?*

I crumple it and push the lot of them off my desk, missing one. I don't recognize the handwriting edging out into the corners of the page, and then I do.

And I don't want to look at it but I do:

Regina,

I know this is a shot in the dark, but I really don't think it's that much of a shot in the dark, because we seemed to really click and I think you're cool. I don't care about being Anna's friend. Really, I don't. But I'd like to stay yours. I know she doesn't want you to talk to me, but hear me out: Can you talk to her for me? I can't figure out what I did. So if you could find out and let me know how to fix it, that'd be great. If you could put in a good word for me, that'd be even better. I really want to sort this out before it gets really bad, and I really want to stay friends with you. Let me know.

Liz

I have this memory of Liz. We froze her out, sabotaged her, finished up the rumor campaign, and she had no reputation and no friends, and Anna was bored with it, uninspired, but she wasn't done, because she wanted to make sure I got the message.

So this one day, Anna got Bruce to play keep-away with Liz's books. Everyone stopped to watch. It wasn't a big deal. Nelson intervened really quickly, and the crowd dissipated, but Liz just stood there and looked so lost, like she didn't want to be there anymore. I imagine her sitting on her bed, in her bedroom with a bottle of pills.

I look at the note too long, running my fingers over the old stale dried ink.

wednesday

Josh and Anna flit by my locker. Laughing and talking.

It's weird hearing their voices, animated, playing off each other—a scarily vibrant conversation. At first I think I'm dreaming, but I turn in time to see them walking down the hall side by side. Anna tosses her hair over her shoulder. She's flirting with him and he's flirting back. How could he resist a Siren? How could anyone? Anna doesn't like being single for lengthy periods at a time. She likes being taken and unattainable. Josh was probably in her sights as soon as he dumped me.

They're totally perfect for each other.

But in math class, I start thinking about it, and it's not okay. In ten days, I have not held his hand in the hall. He hasn't waited for me at my locker between classes. He hasn't given me a kiss on the cheek when the bell separates us. I carve myself out of all these memories and put Anna in my place, and my chest aches, not because I'm romantic or sentimental—I hate Josh—but because these were things that belonged to me and now they don't belong to me anymore.

When the bell rings, I'm cemented to my seat by this thought. The room empties, and Brenner looks up from his papers.

"Don't you have a class to be in, Afton?"

I do, but I skip it for the library. I can't wait until my parents see my report card for this term, but I wouldn't trade that moment for this one, in the library, where it's nice and quiet. I move in and out of shelves, trying to act normal, like this isn't me hiding, but it's always, always me hiding. *I really want to sort this out before it gets really bad, and I really want to stay friends with you.* This is the only reason I miss Anna: She used to tell me it was okay, no matter what.

"Don't you have a class to be in?"

That's not Brenner's voice. That's not any teacher. I turn. Michael's at the computer terminal. I hesitate before edging over. If I didn't know any better, I'd think he looked happy to see me.

"Don't *you*?" I ask.

"Free period," he says. He gestures to the computer beside him, and I sit down. He's got a game of solitaire drawn up. I don't know what to do. I watch him shift red cards onto black and black cards onto red before I turn to my monitor, sign in with my username, and connect to the Internet. I type the IH8RA URL into the address bar and watch the page load slowly on the school's crappy connection. The red background comes up first, and next, that horrible picture of me. The members and comment count have both jumped, and I think I'm sitting next to the only person in this school who hasn't joined up.

"Report abuse," Michael says, startling me.

I shake my head. He puts his hand over mine and guides my mouse to the **Report Abuse** link. The cursor hovers over the bold lettering, but I can't bring myself to click it. His index finger presses down on mine slightly, and the weight of his hand against my hand is so strange. He's waiting for me to give him the go-ahead.

"Don't," I breathe, and his hand comes off mine. He stares at me like I'm an idiot. "Anna would love it if I reported it. If I do, they'll just bring out something worse."

He nods at the screen. "Nice picture."

"Yeah, tell me about it."

"Were you stoned?"

I close the browser. "I was half asleep."

He studies me and then turns back to his game. After a few minutes, he's in total solitaire mode. It's just him and these pixelated cards on-screen and nothing else. This must be how he spends all of his free periods. He must sit in front of the computer and play games that only require one player. His face is intent. It's like I'm not here.

I turn back to the computer and then, impulsively, Google his name. The seventh result is an obituary. I click it.

HAYDEN, NATALIE JUNE
Suddenly on September 30th. Natalie Hayden
(nee Adams) of Hallowell, Connecticut,
in her 41st year . . .

It's like looking at porn. I rub the back of my neck and try not to *look* like I'm looking at porn and read through it, learning more about Michael in a few paragraphs than he'd ever tell me himself. His maternal grandparents are dead, which is something we have in common. He has no aunts or uncles. It's just him and his dad. I wonder what his dad is like. When I glean all the information I can, I x out of the page and Google the accident. The overpass collapse. It's morbidly fascinating to find the earliest reports of it—the ones with guesstimated body counts—and click forward from guesses to actual numbers to actual names. Entire families under concrete.

It's hard to think of Dr. Hayden that way. I can feel Michael next to me, really next to me, and I know I should stop before he sees me, but I can't.

"Why are you looking at that?" Michael asks. His voice is flat. I make the browser disappear, but it's too late.

"I don't know. I was just—" And then I say something really stupid: "My grandparents are dead too."

"Let's see what happens when we Google you," he says. He shuts down the game of solitaire, pulls up Google, and types in my name. The first result is some woman on a high-school-reunion site. The second is the YourSpace page. He smiles. "Funny how the last thing we want the world to see is almost the first thing to show."

"At least your future employers aren't going to think you're a slut."

I log off the computer for lack of anything better to do, and Michael does the same, and then we just sit there, staring at the blank screens.

"Do you usually do this with your free period? Come in here and play solitaire?"

"Mostly," Michael says. "Lately, I've been writing."

"That's right. I haven't seen you scribbling in the cafeteria lately."

"Well, there was this hostile alien takeover at my lunch table. . . ."

"I don't know how you can even bring your journal into this school. If I did, it'd be gone in a second."

"Nobody's interested in my secrets," he reminds me. "They're afraid of them."

"Blueprints for murder." I smile. "The next great school shooting. That's what people think of you." Pause. "Because of me."

"Because of you," he agrees.

He looks at me. The moment closes in, and I feel so bad about it that I *laugh*. It's not funny, but the tension is killing me. I stop laughing, and my whole chest is pins and needles, and I really feel like I'm going to cry or throw up, so I get up and I just leave him there, when what I really want to do is tell him I'm sorry and that I mean it, except it wouldn't mean anything to him. I don't know how it could.

thursday

"I think he's into me," Anna says, and then she raises her voice so I can hear. "Josh."

I take the bait. I look up. Postgym. Changing in the changing rooms. I'm sitting on a bench wedged in the corner, glimpsing Anna's pink push-up bra as she changes into a soft, blush-pink sweater. They're all in pink today.

Jeanette catches me staring and nudges Marta.

"Dyke," Jeanette spits in my direction. Anna yanks her shirt down quickly, like I'm sitting here and I really give a damn about her breasts. I zip up my jeans.

"I need to get him like, *alone*-alone, because we only ever talk at school, right? It doesn't matter what you say in a building full of people; what you say when you're alone, *that* matters." She straightens her sweater. "But I don't want to look desperate."

"You're chasing after my castoffs," I say. I shouldn't, but I can't resist. "I think it's already too late."

"Do you hear something?" Anna asks loudly. "Hey guys, listen to this: Did you know Donnie totally tried to rape Regina?"

They laugh. I grip the edges of the bench, riding out a wave of anger that gives me such a head rush, the room momentarily tilts. They're laughing.

They think it's funny.

Kara studies her reflection in the mirror hanging on the wall, a pink sweater clutched in one hand. Spidery, silvery lines snake up the sides of her flat, undefined stomach. Stretch marks.

"We'll do a group thing," she murmurs, and her voice sounds tinny, far away. I am glued to the bench in this rage, torn between getting up and leaving or attacking her. I can't figure out how to move and be this angry. "This weekend, we'll do some group thing and then, at some point, we'll disappear. You'll have him alone."

"Kara, you're a fucking genius," Anna says. "But I can't wait that long." She pauses. "Maybe I'll drive to his place tonight."

There's something quietly amazing about this moment, where I'm looking at Kara and she's acting like she's me. The bell rings. People filter out. Jeanette and Marta beeline for the door, but Anna holds back, waiting for Kara, who is putting on her shirt.

She turns to Anna. "Do I look okay? I look okay, right?"

Before, Anna would've rolled her eyes. *I refuse to feed into your insecurities, Kara. Own it or fuck off.* Now she says, "You look great."

"I'll be there in a second," Kara tells her. Anna leaves.

She leaves the two of us alone together.

"Get the hell out, Regina," Kara says, like the room belongs to her.

She starts fussing with her hair. She's been obsessive about her hair since the photos from sophomore year—the wig. I remember pulling her aside in the hall after they were taken. Anna told me to tell her. *Kara, do something about your . . . hair.*

She's thinking the same thing. She frowns, letting the strands of blond hair slip between her fingers. She turns to me.

"You made me hate myself." She says it in a voice like it's this epiphany she has over and over. "You know that, right?"

"I'm not sitting here and listening to how wronged you feel," I say.

"I just want you to understand what I've done to you this year is *barely* what you deserve. I'm going to make you *so sorry*—"

"But you started out too big," I interrupt. "You went too far, too soon. I can't believe you spent all that time with me and Anna and you never learned anything. I *might* have felt bad, but you pushed it, and now I'll never be sorry."

She stares at me. "Guess I'll have to try harder."

She leaves.

I don't know why, but I start thinking about Liz. And then I think about Donnie. I bring my knees up, curling into myself as much as I can on the narrow bench. I press my forehead against my jeans, and then I start to cry. I don't want to cry. Soon there's a nice wet spot on my left knee because I can't stop.

The lunch bell rings. Some girls will trickle in here to change, so they can spend the time they're meant to be eating working out in the gym. I check myself in the mirror. I look like I've been crying.

I brave-face the cafeteria, entering the bustling room and wandering through a maze of bodies, straight to the Garbage Table. Michael's already there, a tray of food beside him. He's scribbling in his Moleskine, and his face inspires another apology I'll never have the guts to give him. He stops writing when he sees me. He closes the book, sets it aside, pulls the tray of food toward him, and starts eating.

"Didn't think you were coming," he says. I dig into my pocket for an antacid. "Have you been crying?"

It's obvious. I don't know why he has to ask. "Why?"

"Just thought I'd ask on the off chance that you have been."

I stare at the table and my eyes well up. This is totally fantastic. I wipe at my eyes, which only seems to cause more tears, and when I chance a look at Michael I can tell he's trying not to look like this is a big deal or that it's weird.

"You know, you never asked me what I did to Kara to make her hate me," I say. He stays silent and waits for me to tell him. I lean forward and press my hand against my eyes and I start laughing— I don't know why—*and* crying, and I feel like a freak and I can't stop. I lean back in my chair, taking big gulps of stale cafeteria air.

Michael stares at me like I've lost my mind.

"My mom must've had a field day with you," he says.

"The second time I was in your mom's office, she asked me if I wanted a Lifesaver, and I thought she was talking about herself, you know, but it was—"

"The candy," Michael finishes. "She did that sometimes, but only to people who she thought had a sense of humor. She must've thought that about you."

"You look like her," I tell him. "She was so nice."

"She was."

"When I saw her, I really didn't want her to know I was—"

I stop. I don't want to finish that sentence, and Michael is leaning so far over the table it makes me uncomfortable. There's a heartbreaking eagerness about the way he's listening to me. It scares me. I need something to do with my hands. A distraction. I reach for his Moleskine and run my hands along the edges. It's half swollen, half scribbled in. I flip it open to the first page and glimpse his handwriting—*If found, return to Michael Hayden. 555-3409, 11 Hutt Avenue, Hallowell, Connecticut*—before he rips it from my hands.

"If I ever want you to know what's on those pages, I'll show them to you," he says, and he's flushed, like he's angry at himself for letting me hold it for even a second. "They're private."

"I guess I'll never see them, then," I say.

"You're right. You won't."

Time is going by so slow today. I watch the minute hand on the clock snail forward.

"You really didn't want her to know you were *what?*" he asks quietly.

I pull my gaze away from the clock to look at him, and he's staring at the table. He really wants to know, but I can't tell him, and as soon as that becomes apparent, he shakes his head and returns to his lunch, disappointed.

I pick at my fingernails and pretend not to notice.

friday

It's hard to wake up. Even the promise of the weekend can't inspire me to get out of bed so I can get the day over with. The sky is overcast, gray. The weatherman says rain, but I'll believe it when I see it.

I swallow down my antacid and coffee at the breakfast table while my parents get ready to leave for work. Dad's the first out the door, but Mom hangs back.

"The school called," she says, rummaging through her purse. "I know it's senior year and you've got a lot of energy to burn, but if you keep cutting your classes, Regina, you're going to start losing privileges."

"What kind of privileges?" I ask, staring down my coffee mug.

"No more talking to Anna or any of your friends on the phone after school, no Josh on the weekends, no parties, you'll have a curfew, the works."

This is so depressing, I want to laugh. Instead, I chew on my lower lip and try to act, like, you know, wow. Never seeing my friends again. *Ouch.* I think I'll just stop cutting class, like, *immediately.*

"Okay," I say.

"Get it together," she tells me. "And have a good day. I love you."

She leaves. I wait until I hear her car pull out of the driveway and then I ease my way from the table to the sink. I fill my mug and watch as the bit of coffee I left in it turns the water murky before it goes clear. Thunder rumbles in the distance, and I stop dragging my feet. I get my stuff and step outside. It's hot, but the breeze is cool.

It's going to storm.

I've barely thought it when the sky opens up. I do that stupid caught-in-the-rain running jog for all of five seconds before giving up. I'm soaked.

I spot Michael's Saturn in the parking lot when I finally reach Hallowell High. He's in the front seat, waiting for a break in the rain, but I know that's not happening. I make my way over to the car. He rolls down the window.

"You're drenched," he says.

I pull his door open. "You will be too."

"I'm waiting for it to stop."

"Live a little."

I almost reach for his arm to pull him out of the car but think better of it. He rolls the window up, steps out, and is instantly wet. His hair is plastered to his forehead and his shirt hugs his torso, leaving an impression of the muscle underneath. A clap of thunder makes us both jump. I stare at the school. Spending the day there makes less and less sense, the more I think about it.

"We can't go in like this," I tell him.

"We're not getting into my car like this."

"Okay."

I make my exit. I don't really care if he follows me or not. Lightning flashes, momentarily breaking up the gloomy gray and sending the rain down even harder. I'm halfway across the road when I hear Michael's sneakers slapping against the wet pavement as he makes his way over to me.

It's still raining when we push through the door to Val's Diner. The place smells good. Frying-bacon-and-eggs-and-toast-with-butter good, and it's been so long since I had an actual breakfast, my mouth immediately starts watering and my stomach growls.

Today, I could eat.

"I can't believe you've lived here and you've never been *here*," I say, guiding Michael past rows of uncomfortable plastic booths. "I come here, I mean, *came* here once a month with—" *That jerk I used to date.* "Anyway, it's good."

"Checkered floors." He sounds amused.

I slide into a plastic booth near the back. Michael sits across from me. Our clothes squelch against the plastic, and water drips off my clothes, making little puddles at my feet, on my seat. The place is full of rain refugees but no one from school, which is good, because otherwise I wouldn't be able to eat no matter how tempting the smell.

We settle in and the waitress appears. Her nametag says ANGIE.

"Shouldn't the two of you be in school?" she asks, like we're the first teenagers who have ever come here when we should be there.

"No," I say, and then I launch into my order. "I'll have an egg, sunny-side up, with a side of bacon and toast and home fries and orange juice with the pulp, please."

Angie turns to Michael, frowning. He flashes a smile at her and he has a nice smile, but it leaves her totally unmoved. "I'll have the same."

"You two should be in school," she says, and then she goes.

"Food's good, but the waitstaff is self-righteous," I say when she's out of earshot. He laughs, which makes me smile. I pick at the jam packets in the glass bowl beside us. I select one of each flavor and line them up between us.

"I hate apricot," I say, pushing the pale orange packet his way.

"Not a fan of blueberry," he returns, pushing that packet my way. I alternate pushing the other three my way and his, creating an elaborate jam-packet design on the table. I can't wait until the food gets here.

"This is uncomfortable," Michael says.

I gather up all the jam packets and put them back. "I didn't mean—"

"No, not that," he says quickly. He shifts and there's this ridiculous squeak of wet clothes against the plastic. "Wet jeans don't feel that great."

"We'll dry out soon."

Michael stares out the window. It's still pouring.

"And then we'll get soaked all over again," he says.

"It's not the end of the world." I watch some poor woman get totally doused as she crosses the crosswalk. "I think it's going to break the heat."

"I'll eat to that."

We wait for Angie to bring us our food. After ten minutes or so, it comes. I zone out; I shove huge forkfuls into my mouth. Everything tastes amazing. Breakfast—what a concept. I'm halfway through my plate when I notice Michael staring. He's barely made a dent in his meal, and I feel stupid.

"I just realized I've never seen you eat before," he says.

"I can't eat at school," I say. "It's too stress—"

I stop. Awkward.

"Actually, this is the first time I've had breakfast in a while, too."

Michael looks at his plate. "Dad isn't much of a cook. Neither am I. Neither was my mom for the most part, but she made awesome eggs."

"So what do you eat? It's the most important meal of the day."

"Granola bars, cereal," he says, and then he laughs.

"What's so funny?" I ask.

"This is a very involved conversation about food." He leans back in his seat. "Yeah . . . my mom liked the idea of food better than actually making it. We were fast-foodies. It was her dirty little secret."

I shrug. "So she didn't like to cook. She wasn't making a career out of it."

"She liked to listen," Michael says. "She made a career out of *that*. And it was a brilliant one. She was really good at what she did."

"Yeah, she was." I miss her. Just like that. I feel it. I miss her.

"So—when did you hear? I mean, when did you hear about . . . it happening?" he asks.

I can't remember exactly how I heard. My parents. It was one of my parents. It wasn't that long after. I take a sip of juice, buying time, hoping he can't see it on my face. The diner's phone rings, sparking a memory.

"The office called the week it happened," I say. "We sent a card."

"We got lots of cards," Michael says, nodding. "She had this one patient, he had OCD, like, bad. He freaked when she died. He left all these messages at the office. . . ."

He trails off and it gets quiet. A month ago I would have never pictured myself here in Val's Diner with Michael. With no friends. And not feeling like it's not that bad a thing—to be here with him. With no friends.

"I was at school," he says suddenly. He runs the tines of his fork through the leftover egg yolk on the plate, drawing designs in all that sunny yellow. "I don't know if you knew that. I got sent down to Holt's office, and Dad was there. He was crying and I just didn't get it. If you knew my dad, he's really stoic, right? But he was crying and he told me, and I thought it was a joke until I saw it on the news. I

didn't think of her as . . . crushed until I saw the wreckage on TV. It
was bad because I—" he shrugs and sets his fork down. "I thought
I'd get to see her."

"You wanted to?"

"Yeah." His voice cracks. He presses his lips together tightly, and
my gaze travels down to his hands. He's clutching the edges of the
table so hard his knuckles are white. I want more than anything to
reach over and touch his hand, some small gesture that means it's
going to be okay, because that's what I would want, if I was him. I've
almost gathered the courage to do it when he takes a sharp breath in
that startles me and keeps my hands at my side.

"Michael, I can't—"

"No. You can't."

I can't imagine how horrible that would be.

He swallows once, twice, three times, trying to keep it together.
I want to ask him why he even brought it up if he can't talk about it
yet. And then his eyes get bright: He's close to crying. I want to give
him some privacy, but I can't look away. I watch him clench his
jaw, just fighting with himself to keep from letting the tears spill
out. His mom dead in an overpass collapse—that's a waste. That
makes everything Kara and Anna are doing to me nothing. Or it
should.

I don't know what to do.

"The heat's going to break," I say feebly. I already said that. And
then I do something really stupid and I say it again. "The heat's going to—"

"Don't." He uncurls his fingers from their painful death grip on
the table, takes a shaky breath in, and pushes his plate away. I wonder if a moment like this can be salvaged. After a long, long silence,
he takes another shaky breath in and goes, "So what do your parents do?"

"They work at a call center in Colfer." It's a relief to be able to say
something that doesn't sound so stupid this time. "The commute's a
killer. I hardly ever see them, but they're okay."

He nods and looks out the window. The meal is over. I hail Angie, who brings us the bill. We both reach into our pockets at the same time. I hold my hand up.

"I'm paying."

"No," Michael says. "I've got it."

It becomes a race of who can get into their drenched, stiff pocket first. I win. Michael's got a whole wallet to contend with, but I deal in crumpled dollar bills. I hand them to Angie and tell her to take her tip out of the change. It's still raining, not as hard as before but steady. I get to my feet, and Michael follows me out of the diner and back into it. I stretch my hands out and feel the rain against my palm.

"Well, you've been to Val's," I say. "Now you can say you've done everything, unless you haven't done the bowling alley."

"I haven't done the bowling alley," he mutters. His shoulders are hunched and he's got his hands in his pocket. I can tell he feels bad about what happened, and I don't want him to feel bad about what happened, so I keep my voice light.

"What about the pool hall?"

"Nope."

"Arcade?"

"Not even once."

I force a smile. "So what do you do?"

"Nothing. Now ask me why."

I stop. He stops. He's rigid, tense. I get it. He's embarrassed, and everything about him is asking for a distraction. He's chosen a fight. I should give him one as a favor, but there's nothing between me and school without Michael there, and more than that, I don't want to fight him. I just want to tell him how sorry I am.

But I swallow it and it settles in my stomach with the guilt that's always there. We walk in silence after that, leaving the main street for the back roads. The rain turns to spit, and eventually we turn down Hutt Avenue, and I guess that's it. We'll end up at his place, and I don't think he'll be inviting me in.

I want him to invite me in.

I clear my throat. "Michael—"

"I don't want to talk about me," he says abruptly. He slows as we reach his place. The weather, the rain, it makes his house look emptier than it did before. Like, nothing about it looks remotely homey. But people live here. Michael lives here. That's sad.

"I'm so sorry, Michael."

He takes a step back. "What?"

The repeat is always the killer. Everything inside you goes into saying the word once, but *sorry* is the kind of word the person you say it to always wants to hear twice. "For what I did to you. I'm sorry. I just wanted you to—"

"Don't." He takes another step away from me and another, up the path. "I don't want to hear it. You're not sorry; you're guilty. That's why Liz didn't forgive you. Because you just feel sorry for yourself." My mouth drops open and he nods. "Yeah, she told me you apologized. Even she knew it. You don't deserve it."

"I knew she wouldn't forgive me."

He keeps moving away from me, digging into his pockets for his house key. "Then why did you even say it?"

"Because I meant it," I say pathetically. "But I'm not a good person and I'll never be a good person, so who cares if I meant it, right?"

"You finally get it," he says. "If you really cared, then why didn't you tell my mom what you did to Liz? Because you didn't, did you?"

I shake my head. The thunder rolls, distant, the storm moving out or coming back in. I don't know.

"And you didn't tell her about what you did to me," he says. "So what did you tell her about? How could she *possibly* have helped you if you just sat there and lied to her? You wasted her time."

"I told her about Anna."

"Coward," he spits.

My eyes fill with tears. He takes another few steps to the front door. I bet he's going to relish the weekend. There'll be no stupid, crazy, needy, antacid-popping girl hanging off him in a building full of people who didn't give him a chance because of some stupid, crazy, needy, antacid-popping girl.

"I shouldn't have apologized to you," I say.

He stops, but he doesn't come back. "No, you *should* have. A long time ago."

"Michael, I'm—"

"So do you actually think we could be friends, or do you think I'm just tolerating you, or do you think I feel sorry for you? I'm really curious, now that you've bought me breakfast and all."

"You tell me," I say.

"When I think of you, I think of a girl who is so afraid of everything, she would fuck me over in a second if it made her life easier," he says. "That's what I think."

"I won't—"

"But that's what you do, isn't it?" he demands. "You did. You did it to Liz, you did it to me—and you didn't even know me. Who does what you did to people and—"

I finally snap. "Then why did you even let me sit with you in the cafeteria that first day? Why wouldn't you tell me to fuck off if you hate me that—"

"Because I wanted to call you a bitch to your face, and I wanted to make you uncomfortable, and I wanted to see you suffer up close, that's why. God, maybe I'm as bad as—"

He stops. There's this stunned silence. *I'm as bad as you.* I want to dare him to say it. He's as bad as me, and Kara's as bad as me, and I'm as bad as Anna, who killed all the things that were good about me before they got the chance to do any good.

"I ruin lives—I get it," I say. "I don't need to be told over and over and over."

He shakes his head and walks the path to the porch, and I watch him for a minute, and then I make my way home, and it rains the whole way there.

It rains the whole weekend.

. . . Starts off with a bang, a buzz.

Lynn Parks gets caught doing lines of something Josh sold her in the girls' room. Josh spends the morning sweating until word gets around she's not talking. Holt works fast and furiously. A new rule is implemented: Students will have to sign out of class to go to the bathroom, and if they haven't returned within ten minutes, they will be retrieved.

Which is stupid, because I could do, like, a million drugs in ten minutes.

Effective immediately, there will be no more loitering in the washrooms at lunch. No more seeking refuge there during class. The teachers will *make sure* of this. This could not have happened at a worse time, because I'm pretty sure Michael has revoked his invitation for me to sit with him at lunch and I need a place to hide. My brain is having a hard time accepting life in school without a space where I can disappear.

It comes to me—that storage room Anna and I had to get the volleyball net from. Josh and I used to meet there and have impromptu make-out sessions sometimes. I lived for him against me under that forty-watt bulb, against a background of ratty old gym mats and leftover, broken equipment. I make my way through the halls, past people heading to the cafeteria and past Brenner, who is hovering outside the boys' washroom.

Usually, the storage rooms in the school are locked, because the administration values paper and athletics equipment more than its students, but this one is always open. No one steals or would want to steal mats. I step inside and turn the light on. I'll have to use this space only when I really need it, until the memory of Lynn snorting things up her nose fades and the teachers remember how not to care.

My new hiding space secured, I wander the halls, waiting for the bell to ring, a strange nervousness in my gut. This is what being really alone feels like. I take an antacid. And another one.

"Regina?"

I hate myself because his voice gives me hope in the place in my stomach that's most anxious, and then I hate myself even more because when I turn, seeing him makes that feeling worse. Or better. I don't know.

"I was looking all over for you," Michael says, causing another desperate, hopeful twinge in my gut. "I wanted to talk to you. About last Friday."

"Okay," I say.

"I don't think we should hang around each other anymore."

He doesn't try to soften it or anything; he just says it. *I don't think we should hang around each other anymore.* Before I can even try to get a grip on it, he's saying more things I don't really want to hear.

"I wasn't fair to you. I let you sit with me at lunch and I let you do it for the wrong reasons and I should've known better—" He pauses. "—Even if you deserved it."

My mouth goes dry. "Great."

"Regina . . ."

"It's fine."

"I just think it would—"

"It's fine, Michael," I say.

"I can't . . ." He trails off. I don't even understand why he's still talking, because I said it was fine. "And you're really in it, and I just think it's bullshit. It's a waste of time."

"Okay," I say. "Thanks. I'll see you—" I laugh. "Oh, wait. I won't."

"I'm just trying to give you a reason—"

"My life is bullshit. I got that part. And I deserve it. You don't need to say anymore. I got it."

"That's not what I—"

"Kara and Anna—total bullshit. Got it. And Donnie? That was total—"

I press my fingers to my lips before I realize what I'm doing. It's like my body won't accept calling it bullshit because it wasn't. What Donnie did to me is still with me. It doesn't go away. A horrified realization crawls across Michael's face, because he didn't think that far back, which is okay, because I didn't deserve that.

But it hurts.

"Regina—" He sounds stunned, like he can't believe he has to backtrack on his awesome speech about how my life is such bullshit. "Regina, I—"

"It's fine," I repeat, stepping around him. "You don't owe me anything."

And then Kara shoves me.

It happens like this: I'm heading to class, I walk past her, she shoves me. My books go flying, which is the point, because then she kicks them down the hall. And there's nothing spectacular about it, even though everyone around us seems to think otherwise. I get my books—by the time I reach them, they've been trampled—and walk away without looking back, and then that little voice in my head:

Do something.

The bell rings. I circle the hall. I circle it again, thinking. How does Anna weigh the crimes against the punishments? "Sleeping" with Donnie is worth my total destruction, and Anna thought *I* was worth Liz's total destruction, so I look at my books and try to guess how much they're worth. They're bent, battered. And I have to factor in embarrassment, too, because it was mildly embarrassing.

I don't know how long I stand there contemplating it before I realize I'm standing directly in front of Kara's locker. I've *been* standing in front of Kara's locker.

Eleven, twenty-seven, three, ten. Her combination. I've been armed with it since that day she unexpectedly got her period and had to hole herself up in the bathroom while I got her a tampon. Eleven, twenty-seven, three, ten. My hands tremble. I grab the lock.

Eleven, twenty-seven, three, ten.

It comes undone. I open it. Kara's locker is painfully neat. The inside of the door is decorated with photos of her after she lost the weight, but none from before. There are group shots of her with Marta, Jeanette, and Anna, and jagged edges mark the places she ripped me away. My eyes drift past her books—they could go into the pool, maybe—to the personal affects lining the shelves, the things you stick in your locker to help you forget you're in school every time you open it up. I grab everything quickly. This is total suicide, and she'll know it was me. But I don't care.

It takes me three trips to get everything to the garbage two halls over.

When I'm done, I feel empty, but only for a second. Because I get it; I do. I get why Anna was my best friend. Why I couldn't be friends with Liz and why I couldn't save her and why I couldn't eat. Why Kara hates me. Why Michael can't be around me. Kara lost the weight. It didn't matter. Same school, same teachers, same classmates, same friends. No chance. In high school, you don't get to change. You only get to walk variations of the same lines everyone has already drawn for you.

So I should just make the best of it.

tuesday

I'm not even going to bother getting out of bed today.

wednesday

Anna, Kara, and Marta are huddled behind the front doors.

It's the first cold day since the heat broke. I stand in the parking lot, waiting for the bell to ring or Jeanette to show, whichever comes first. When they move out, I'll be able to go in. I wait and wait. My hands are numb and I'm shivering. A blue Saturn and a black convertible pull in at the same time. Anna. Kara. Marta. Michael. Donnie. The moment becomes a contest: Who do I want to avoid more?

Donnie. The others didn't have their hands on me like he did. I take a deep breath and push the door open. Maybe if I keep my gaze level and stare straight ahead, the girls won't engage.

"Regina."

I jerk my head in their direction. Anna and Kara stand shoulder-to-shoulder, Marta slightly behind them. I'm stuffing an antacid into my mouth before I can get my brain to tell my stomach to be stronger than that. Anna's mouth quirks.

"What do you want?"

Kara steps forward. Every time she asserts herself, it's unbelievable: I can't wrap my head around how comfortable she looks. How she can just grow into that skin when she's spent years cowering and being stupid and worthless.

"I know you were the one who fucked up my locker."

"I don't—" my voice breaks, instant giveaway. I hate this. I used to *own* her. "I don't know what you're talking about. . . ."

Kara takes two steps forward. I take two steps back. Anna oversees us, her arms crossed. She loves this. She loves every second of this.

"I know it was you," Kara says.

She takes two more steps forward, forcing me to back up. Everything about her is predatory, from the curve of her mouth to the glint in her eyes. She takes a quick step forward, and I leap back at the same time the door swings open and nails me in the back, knocking the wind out of me. I stumble forward, glimpsing Jeanette. She high-fives Kara, and the entrance congests. Donnie and Michael and a few others are trying to make it through, and they witnessed the whole thing.

There's always an audience.

The worst part is, I have to sit down. Right there. My back hurts and I can't breathe. I move to the corner like a gasping, injured dog and sit on the floor, trying really hard for air. Not getting any.

"I *know* you fucked up my locker," she repeats. "Don't think for a second we're finished."

"I never for a second thought that," I wheeze.

They clomp past me. I close my eyes and imagine myself on Tuesday, in bed, where there was this brief moment between waking up and being totally awake where my mind was completely empty and it was so peaceful.

When I open my eyes, I can breathe again and everyone is gone but Michael.

"Are you okay?" he asks.

"Get away from me, Michael."

"I'm serious. That looked really painful."

"You should be happy. You totally just got to see me suffer up close."

He pales and slinks off, and it's satisfying, but it doesn't last.

It never does.

Brenner calls me up to the board to solve some complicated equation he's spent the last ten minutes chalking out, even though I'm not wearing a skirt or a low-cut top. I don't know the answer, so I have to stand there staring blankly at numbers until he tells me to sit down again. On my way back to my desk, Kara forces her chair out, slamming it into my side.

"Oh, God." She pushes herself to her feet so the hard plastic edges dig into my skin on her way up. "I'm so . . ."

Sorry. She never says it, but Brenner acts like he heard it, and that's the end of it. I rub my side, biting my lower lip. Kara smirks and sits, satisfied.

I want to push her down a flight of stairs.

I actually stake out a staircase between periods so I can do it. It seems so reasonable. It seems so fair. Kara comes this way for her next class and all I have to do is trip her from the side or get her from behind, like she got me, and down she goes. I lean against the wall and wait. By the time the crowded hall thins out, I'm salivating. It looks so good in my head. I have to make it happen. I *need* to make it happen.

So of course she never comes.

The bell rings and I sit down on the stairs, a slowly deflating balloon. When the bloodlust finally fades, I feel stupid. I stay on the steps for a long time, until Liz rounds the corner. Our eyes meet. There must be no other way for her to get to where she wants to go, because she sighs and begins the trudge up. Every time I see her now, I see her suicide and it makes me want to puke. She passes me. I listen to the sound of her heels as they clack down the hall. Then they stop and clack back.

I don't know how to be around her. People have to live with things they don't want to live with all the time, but—how? After Liz, every time I ate, I tasted guilt, and I don't know why. What I did to Kara didn't make me sick. What would Dr. Hayden have told me if I'd been brave enough to tell her the truth about me, that I was just as bad as Anna? Dr. Hayden listened to my select truths and said the right things—*Anna* was the bad one—until I almost believed it wasn't me, and then I discovered antacids, like that was my problem all long, and I could eat again, and it took me the rest of the way. I never thought it would catch up with me before I graduated.

"Michael told me he told you about—" She stops. "—What I did."

I look up at her. Liz is vaguely intimidating from this angle. She looks sort of mad, nose up, even though she's staring me down.

"Yeah," I say.

"I never wanted you to know that."

"I never wanted to know that."

I lean my head against the wall and wait for her to go. She doesn't.

She crosses her arms. "Have you gotten used to it yet?"

"When did *you* get used to it?"

"What made you think I did?"

"I'm sorry we're not friends," I tell her. I don't know why.

"I'm not," she says. "I'm sorry we *were*. I never thought I'd be your claim to fame. From the boring, bitchy, popular girls to the kind that go that extra mile to make people's lives hell. After me, you guys were all set. Anna owes me, when you think about it."

"I wouldn't try cashing out, if I were you," I tell her.

She rolls her eyes and walks away.

By the end of the day, my body is all bruises and scratches. My back, the door. My side, the chair. Jeanette sits behind me in English class and jabs me in the shoulders with the sharp end of her pencil until the period is over, and I just sit there and take it.

Dodgeball.

Nelson splits the class down the middle, and the divide is such that she can't be as stupid as she looks. I think she's just as bored as the rest of us, because Kara, Anna, and Josh are on one team, and I get stuck with Bruce and Donnie and Michael.

Maximum entertainment value.

In elementary school, we had a Safe Ball. It was this soft, foamy thing that didn't hurt at all but still managed to strike fear into your heart when someone caught it and took aim. It felt so personal.

Now we've grown up and graduated to hard rubber.

I'm nervous, but in a good way. I want to move. I want to hurt them. I'm a horrible person; they're horrible people too. We might as well take each other. Anna and Kara whisper to Josh and Bruce, who hangs around until Nelson shouts us into positions, then Bruce wanders to my side of the court, glaring.

Everyone gets into place. We're using one ball today, not six. Organized chaos. Anna's team gets the ball first, and then it goes to Mehmet Erdogan, who whips the ball at Donnie, who doesn't even try to dodge it. Nelson blows her whistle. He's out. Bruce grabs the ball and gives it a hard throw in Josh's direction.

"Hey!" Josh yells.

"In it to win it," Bruce says, and there's an edge to his voice. I bet he's pissed about Josh and Anna. I glance at Josh. He frowns, retrieves the ball, and sends it Bruce's way, hard. Bruce catches it and aims for Josh.

"You guys," Anna says, amused. She knows exactly what's going on. Bruce sends the ball at Baz Jones. It hits her thigh. She shrieks and heads for the side. I'm impatient at this point. One of them has to eventually take a shot at me.

I beat Samantha Mantle to the ball and throw it at Kara before she realizes I'm aiming at her. It whaps her in the chest. She staggers back, startled, and no one can call me on it because that's the game.

But the whole room goes quiet because they know it's more than a game.

Nelson blows her whistle. "Off the court, Myers!"

Kara marches to the sidelines. It's the most exciting thing that happens for a while. I dodge the ball and watch more people get taken out. I'm disappointed when Anna takes an unexpected hit from Megan Gunter. I wanted to do that.

The numbers dwindle slowly. Michael and I stay alive by keeping close to the back of the gym. We have the edge on the other side. Josh is all over, untouchable. He's always good at weaseling away from a hit. Each time I get the ball, I make him my target, until it's so obvious, he backs into the corner of the gym because I can't throw that far.

And then the game gets a whole lot more boring.

"Come on, Josh," I call. "The game's up here."

Josh scowls but he stays in his corner.

"Don't push it," Michael says. He sounds close.

"Why do you care?" But when I turn around, he's already walking away from me. I focus on Josh and shout for him to "man up," because I need to hit something with a ball and he's all that's left.

"Shut up, Regina," Anna snaps. "Seriously."

"Aw," I say exaggeratedly, "so cute, Anna. I'm sure Josh appreciates it."

"Too much talking and not enough playing," Nelson says. "Get up the court, Carey. I don't grade you if you don't play."

Josh's face turns red. He takes a couple steps forward. The ball goes back and forth and nobody's out. Back and forth. Back and forth. Back and forth. Josh edges back to his corner. I make an exasperated noise.

"Come *on*, Josh."

"Leave him alone, Regina," Anna shouts from the side. "Ms. Nelson—"

The toss of the ball interrupts her, and then—Michael's out. Whitney Lodge gets him, and it's one of those blink-almost-missed-its, where the ball *maybe* grazed his ankle, but no one can really say for sure. But with Anna and Kara insisting "It totally hit his ankle we saw it he's out we saw it," Nelson calls it. Bruce retrieves the ball.

"I was having so much fun, too," Michael mutters, making his way off court. I head back to my corner.

And then the room explodes.

I don't see it. It happens around me. Behind me. Noise. Lots of noise. At first I think it's me because it's near me, but it's not me.

Nelson blurs past me to get to—I whirl around—to get to . . . Michael.

I was standing here, Donnie was over there clutching his face, and there was blood. Lots of blood. Now I'm standing here and Michael's there and there's lots of blood and he's clutching his face. But where Donnie was loud, Michael is quiet.

Nelson compensates by blowing her whistle so hard it pops out of her mouth.

"BURTON—OFF COURT! PRINCIPAL'S OFFICE! NOW!"

"Ms. Nelson," he protests, "I didn't—"

She blows her whistle and he shuts his mouth. "You did that *deliberately*, Burton. Get down to the principal's office *now*."

Bruce swears under his breath, earning another blow of the whistle, and pushes through the doors so hard they hit the wall. Nelson goes to Michael, and it really hits me.

He's hurt.

I hurry over while Nelson checks him out. Once you've seen one bloody nose, you've seen them all, but this is different. It's Michael. It doesn't look good on him.

"Is it broken?" I ask.

Michael sniffs. "He didn't hit me that hard."

"Hayden, get to the nurse's office and clean up. Afton, escort your friend down there." Nelson turns to the rest of the gym. "What is wrong with you people lately? This is a gym, not a battleground!"

I follow Michael out of the gym. We walk the hall in silence. He keeps his palm pressed against his nose, switching hands every now and then, trying not to get blood on the floor. I think about what Nelson said. Friend. Hilarious.

"I'll just clean up in the washroom," Michael says. He sounds stuffy.

I push open a familiar blue door. "Here's one."

He stops. "No way. That's the girls' room."

"It's fine."

I push the door open and check every stall twice. The coast is clear. I ignore his protests, grab his hand, and drag him inside. I wedge the garbage can under the doorknob for added security. When I face Michael, he's hunched over the sink, gazing at his reflection in the mirror. I'm not sure why I didn't just let him take care of it himself. Maybe because being around him means not being alone.

"Are you sure it's not broken?"

He runs his hand over his nose. "I don't think so. I think he just hit it the right way. Looks worse than it is."

I grope for something to say, trying to piece together what happened while my back was turned. Bruce hit Michael with the ball. Deliberately. Michael said something. Michael had to have said something to make him do that.

"What did you say to him?"

"What?"

"Bruce. Why did he throw the ball at you?"

"He didn't. He threw it at you," Michael says. "He threw it at you as soon as your back was turned. I intercepted."

"So it's my fault," I say stupidly.

"It's totally your fault."

"I didn't mean to—"

"You did. All through gym class, you were out to kill. They were laughing at you the whole time, and you didn't even notice. It was dumb."

"That's not fair."

He points to his nose. "Neither is this."

He turns on the tap. I make my way over, and we reach for the paper towels at the same time. I push his hand away, rip off a swath, and pat the counter space between the sinks. He hesitates and then hoists himself up, and I wet the towel and hesitate before dabbing at the fresh and drying blood on his face. My hand trembles. I don't even know why I'm doing it. Maybe because I'm glad he stood between me and Bruce and I don't know how to tell him I'm glad he stood between me and Bruce.

He clears his throat. "I probably wasn't fair to you. . . ."

"Hold still." He stills. I keep dabbing at his face. I dab until he stops bleeding and there's no blood and it's all off his face. But he's on to me. He takes my wrist and lowers my hand, and I know talking will ruin this, whatever this is.

"What I said about bullshit . . . wasting time—"

"I know what you meant. Forget it."

"But what Donnie did to you wasn't bullshit. I didn't mean that." He stares up at the ceiling, quiet for a moment. "Look, I don't hang around a lot of people."

"I know." I know everything. "Because of me."

"No. Well, yeah, but what happened at the diner was weird, and that it happened with you was even weirder." He pauses. "And then you capped it off with that apology and it was—it just made me really angry."

"I didn't mean to make you angry," I say. "I'm sorry."

"I know you didn't. . . ." He clears his throat again and looks at me. "And I believe you when you say you're sorry, but it's so much easier for me to think of you as a total bitch, you have no idea."

"You *don't* think I'm a total bitch?"

I wish I could take it back as soon as it's out of my mouth. It's embarrassing. I have to look away from him. But I can't even describe what that feels like—that there was a moment where Michael didn't hate me for what I did to him.

It makes me feel human.

"Maybe," he says quietly. "But I feel like that's what I have to keep doing. . . ."

I can't hold that against him. I get how important the illusion is. If the difference between Michael thinking of me as a total bitch and not thinking of me as a total bitch is him trying his hardest not to cry at a restaurant, hurting over his dead mother—I'd think of me as a bitch, too.

"I didn't want her to know how mean I was," I say.

"What?"

"Your mom." I try to swallow and can't. "Because she was so nice and warm and funny and caring and she listened, and I just wanted her to like me, because everyone here hates me, and the people that didn't, like Anna, made me hate myself. So I . . . just wanted her to think I was good. And I didn't tell her about what I did to you or Liz because I really, really liked her and I didn't want her to hate me too."

He gets the saddest look on his face.

"Regina, she wouldn't have hated you," he says. "Even if she knew, I doubt she would've hated you. She wouldn't have been happy, but she would have helped you. . . ."

His breath catches in his throat, like he just realized it: She wouldn't have hated me and she would've helped me. And I don't know if he hates knowing that or not. He's still holding my wrist, his fingers pulsing against my skin. I stay still because I know if I move it will stop. I don't want it to stop.

What changes a moment like this.

I move forward, tentatively, and his hand stays on my wrist. It's going to be a kiss. Even if he hates it. One of those out-of-nowhere kisses. It has to be.

I want it to be.

He moves closer—

And then he stops.

We stare at each other, and I want to ask him why, but before I can gather the nerve, he slides off the counter and we're closer than ever. He exhales slowly and edges away. He moves the garbage can and leaves the washroom, and I stay there too long, my stomach all twisted up, until I'm caught by Ms. Crager, who's on washroom duty.

Strike one, she tells me.

friday

"I'll drive you to school today."

I choke on my coffee. "What?"

"I'll drive you to school today," Mom says, and I'm all over it, protesting—*no, it's okay, forget it*—when she holds up her hand. "No arguments, Regina."

I get the kind of uneasy feeling that begs for an antacid. This cannot mean anything good. I finish my coffee, get my things, and follow Mom to her car. It's total silence as she pulls out of the driveway, and then when we hit the road she says, "We have a meeting with your principal today. It should be fun."

I close my eyes and lean my head against the seat, and the word *fuck* just repeats itself over and over in my head, because *fuck*.

"So do you want to tell me what's going on before we get there, or do I have to play twenty questions with your principal? Because I don't have the time—"

"It's nothing." I open my eyes. "It's just—"

"Cutting so many classes in such a short amount of time isn't *nothing*, Regina. Your father and I are very concerned. We don't know where you go, what you're up to—"

"Someone spray-painted the word *whore* on my locker, okay?"

"*What?!*"

She actually stops the car. Pulls over and turns it off. She stares at me, looking equal parts disbelieving and devastated.

"Someone spray-painted the word *whore* on your *locker? Who?* Who would do something like that to you? Why didn't you *tell* me? *When? Why didn't you tell me?*"

The last part sounds the worst. Like it really bothers her that I didn't tell her. I'm sure it does, but I feel bad enough as it is, and I need to organize my thoughts enough to lie, because I'm not interested in dealing with the truth and feeling even worse. I just need her to go into Holt's office on my side, feeling sorry enough for me to forgive me if I miss more days after this. And I'm sure I will.

"It was a few weeks ago."

She starts spluttering. I cut her off before she can start demanding answers to questions I haven't prepared answers for. "I didn't . . . tell you because it was embarrassing. I mean, who wants to tell their *mom* something like that?"

I cross my arms and try for a petulant teenage look. Like it doesn't bother me. Like being reminded of it every time I open up my stupid red locker doesn't bother me.

"Who did it?" she demands. "What did the school do?"

"I don't know. Holt had my locker repainted."

Mom sighs and rests her head against the steering wheel, and then I feel really bad. Really, really bad. I look out the window. After she's had her moment, she reaches over and squeezes my shoulder. Like a mom.

"Oh, Regina . . ."

My throat tightens. She sounds really—like she cares. I mean, I know she does, but I haven't heard that in anyone's voice in a long time.

"I just hate being there," I say.

"Well, what about your friends?" Mom asks. "Anna, Kara . . . Josh—Josh must be a help, right? You have your friends. . . ."

God.

The last thing I expect to do—cry. In the car, next to my mom. And it's the best and worst thing I could do. The best because I have her like that, and the worst because my tears have this stranglehold on me. Now that I'm crying, it's all I want to do. I want to scream and really let it out. Instead, I stare out the window with tears streaming down my face. Stop. Stop it. Get a grip, Regina.

"This isn't like . . ." Mom hesitates. "Should we be calling someone—"

"No." I take a deep breath. "I just hate being there sometimes, and sometimes I have to leave. I'm sorry."

She presses her lips together. She starts the car, and then we're back on the road, and she says, "I'm going to take some time. We'll have a day."

Like that would solve *anything*.

"Sure," I say.

I check my face in the mirror. My eyes are red and swollen. Mom parks across the road from the school. We make our way across the school parking lot, and this is as close to invincible as I get: No one's going to touch the girl who brings *her mom to school*. I get so preoccupied with how dumb I must look right now, I follow her into the front corridor, where Anna and Kara are waiting. I'm heart-stopped, frozen, and Mom's warm and smiling, asking them how the semester's been treating them.

"Look at you girls!" She has Anna by the hands, stepping back so she can get a good look. Anna grins at her, and Kara smirks at me, her eyebrow arched. "You're almost out there, huh? Graduating and heading into the real world!"

Anna laughs. "Long time no see, Mrs. A."

But it's the *way* she says it. Mom's face changes as Anna's words sink in, making her a picture of polite puzzlement. She looks at me.

"That's true. Regina, where have you been keeping your friends?"

They're not my friends.

"Oh, it's senior year," Anna says. "You know how it is."

"Vaguely," Mom says, laughing.

Anna and Kara laugh in unison. Pretty-girl-nightmare-robots.

"Mom, we have to see Holt," I say. A flicker of something— panic?—crosses Anna's face. "Come on, let's go."

Mom finally drops Anna's hands and gives her a parting smile. "Right. Well, I'll see you girls again sometime soon, I hope."

Anna's eyes are on me. "That'd be nice, Mrs. A."

Mom turns her back to us and heads up the stairs. Anna grabs my arm and jerks me back, digging her nails into my skin. I wince.

"You tell Holt *anything*, and you're—"

I slap her in the face with my free hand. I'm not even thinking. Pure instinct. *Slap*. And a strange thrill courses through me, because it felt *that good*. Kara gasps, and Anna drops my arm, and I watch her shocked face cycle through every shade of red there is, because *I just slapped her*.

"Regina, are you coming?"

Mom stands at the top of the stairs, waiting. She missed it. I hurry up the stairs after her, my heart in my throat. I'm dead. I am dead. All through the meeting with Holt, I run my index finger over the tingling palm of my right hand, the one that slapped her, and I try to focus, but it's impossible because I am so dead. Mom and Holt talk about me, volleying each other toward some kind of resolution or something. I don't know.

All I know is *I slapped Anna across the face*.

"How does that sound, Regina?" Holt asks, jarring me out of my thoughts. He and Mom stare at me expectantly. I have no idea what anyone just said.

"Good," I say.

They smile. Good. They stand. They shake hands. Good. The meeting is over and it was good. I lead Mom out of the office and past Arnett, who is working diligently at her desk, to the front corridor, where she gives me a long hug and a kiss on the forehead, pushes open the door, and steps outside.

Into the "real world."

The halls are empty. It's lunch.

I've been skulking around corners, hiding in shadows, trying to avoid everyone, because everyone knows I slapped Anna in the face. I'm guessing Kara let it slip, because Anna would never tell anyone that story unless it ended with her kicking my ass. So far, I haven't managed to meet up with them since it happened. That's good. If I can get through the rest of the day without that happening, that would be great.

"Are you *suicidal*?"

I jump out of my skin. The last person I expect to see—Josh. He's alone and he wants to know: Am I suicidal?

"Fuck off, Josh," I say. I remember the day he asked me out. I needed him to help me set up Liz's locker so it wouldn't open with or without the lock, because Anna told me to. That kind of says it all.

"Slapping Anna in the face? You must be," he says. "By the way, I liked that stunt you pulled in the gym the other day. Dodgeball. 'Man up, Josh.'"

I cross my arms. "I really liked it, too."

Josh shifts his book from one arm to the other. "You're just making things difficult for yourself. If you keep it up, Anna's gonna kill you."

I wonder how far he's gotten with her.

"Having fun with your new girlfriend?" I ask.

He smirks. "More than I had with you."

"Asshole."

I'm halfway down the hall when a minicrowd surges out of the cafeteria. I duck into an alcove by the water fountain. It could be Kara, Anna, Marta, Jeanette. Any of them. The crowd passes by and it's none of them, but the group of students spot me as they pass, and I hear a buzz of recognition. "That's the girl who slapped Anna Morrison in the face." I wonder if I even have a name to these people anymore.

When the coast is clear, I continue my way down the hall. More people come out of the cafeteria in little fits, and I keep ducking into corners whenever I can.

I just need to get down this fucking hallway alive. That's it.

"I take it the rumors are true."

I turn around and Michael's behind me. My gaze goes straight to his lips. *We almost kissed.* I actually have to fight those words from coming out of my mouth, and then I have to fight to keep a blush off my cheeks because I actually have to fight to keep those words from coming out of my mouth.

I don't understand what happened between us, but I really, really want to.

I nod and lean against the wall.

"Yeah," I say, and then I laugh. I didn't believe it before, but now I really, *really* don't believe it. "I slapped her, Michael, I just—did. I'm so dead."

He leans beside me. There is no trace of the bloody nose he was sporting yesterday. He's wearing a blue sweater, and it really brings out his eyes. He runs a hand through his hair, pushing the brown strands away before they fall back across his face. He looks good. This is a stupid time to notice something like that, but I'm a dying woman right now and we almost kissed so I guess it's allowed.

"Who came into school with you this morning? Was that your mom?"

"We had a meeting with Holt," I say. "I'm missing too much school."

"But are you really missing it?"

I smile weakly. "I seriously think I need to go into hiding."

"It's Friday. Maybe she'll cool off over the weekend."

"Anna doesn't cool off," I say. "What are you doing out here, anyway? Shouldn't you be in the cafeteria, writing in your Moleskine or something?"

"I heard what happened." He doesn't look at me. "I wanted to make sure you weren't—"

"Dead?" I ask. He nods. "Well, I'm not. But the day is still young. All I have to do is step down a deserted hallway alone, and I'm sure they'll jump me."

"Maybe you shouldn't walk down any deserted hallways alone, then."

Another group forces its way out of the cafeteria. Lunch must be winding up. It makes me nervous, but it's not so bad standing next to Michael. It's safe here, in the hall next to him. I close my eyes and try to enjoy that feeling while I can.

"I could walk you to your classes," he offers. I open my eyes. "And meet you outside of them when you're done . . ."

"I thought you said we shouldn't hang around each other anymore?" I say, and his expression makes it immediately clear that I shouldn't have. "Oh. You still think that."

"You helped me yesterday. . . ." he explains. "The least I can do is help you get through a day."

"Forget it. It's not like it's going to get better," I tell him. "But thanks."

He gives me this look. "Regina, just let me—"

"No."

I walk away before he can say anything else. I feel stupid. Like he'd actually want to hang around me. No. He just doesn't want to owe me anything.

The bell rings. No traces of Anna or Kara. I wish I'd known I was going to do it—slap her. I would've relished it more.

I would have hit her harder.

Reg—
> *This is getting boring. We need to talk. If you want out of this,*
> *meet me in the paper supply closet at lunch.*

—A

There are a lot of ways I expect Monday to go. This is not one of them.

The note is wedged in the slates of my locker. When I open it and see her handwriting, everything stops. The lunch bell rings, and the halls filter out until they're empty, and it's just me and those words and nothing else.

This is getting boring. We need to talk.

I don't believe it.

I want to believe it.

I unfold the note again and study her handwriting. It's definitely hers. The paper supply closet. It's not far from here.

Kara's at the fountain when I turn down the hall to the supply closet. She's bent over, her hair dragging around the drain while she laps up the fluorinated water with her tongue, strongly reminding me of a French poodle. I pass her and hope she won't notice me, but she does. Of course. She straightens and wipes her mouth on the back of her hand.

"You look tired," she says.

The note from Anna circumvents any desire I have to smash my fist into Kara's face while there's no one around to witness it.

"Nice tooth," I tell her. "They *almost* color-matched it."

She rolls her eyes and turns down the hall. I listen as her footsteps get farther away. I reach the supply closet, stand in front of the door, and count to ten. I need to go into this looking right. Anna can see weakness, sense it, and I need to be calm. Calm.

I grab the doorknob and step inside.

It's dark.

"Anna?"

I take two steps forward and grope for the light overhead. My fingers find the bulb when something moves behind me. Anna. I turn. Not Anna. Kara. I rush the door, my shoulder connecting with it painfully, and I grab the doorknob just as she gives it a sharp jerk toward her, and then it's closed. The lock clicks into place.

"Kara, don't—*Kara!*" She's locked me in. I pound on the door. "Kara, I swear to *God*, let me out or I'll—"

"Or you'll what?"

"*Kara.*"

"That's what I thought," she says, laughing.

Set up. Set up by her *again*. I kick the door as hard as I can, choking back a scream until I realize screaming is exactly what I should be doing.

"Somebody let me out! Is there anyone out there? *LET ME OUT!*"

Nothing. Everyone's in the cafeteria. I'll be stuck in here for at least thirty minutes before someone walks by. *If* someone walks by.

I need light.

I go back to fumbling for the chain and give it a yank. The feeble wattage sends a dull glow around the immediate area but leaves most of the room to the shadows. I wait and I wait, and when the lunch bell rings, I yell as loudly as I can, but no one comes.

No one comes, even though I can hear them all just outside the door.

I'm sitting behind shelves of poster board with my back against the wall. It's been an hour. Maybe two. Every time I hear the slightest noise, I tense, preparing to be found. It never happens. I pick at my jeans, waiting. I have to go to the bathroom. I think I'm edging up on hour three when the door finally opens. I scramble to my feet, but the ensuing grunting and scuffling sounds hold me back and keep me from revealing myself.

"Fuck off! Get the—"

"Get his cell phone."

"Get the fuck off me!"

"Easy. Don't make this harder than it has to be."

"Fuck off!"

I peer around the shelves. Bruce gives Donnie a hard shove, sending him to the floor. He eats ground and his eyes are on my feet. I don't know if he's seeing me. I can make out Josh in the doorway. Henry.

"Got his cell phone?" Bruce asks.

Josh holds it up.

"Okay, let's go."

No. Josh and Henry leave. *No.* Donnie tries to grope his way to his feet, but Bruce gives him a sharp kick in the ribs and he stays down. They don't know I'm here. They can't know I'm here. That would be too fucked up, even for us.

I stumble out from behind the shelf.

Bruce isn't surprised to see me.

"Oh, good," he says

Oh my God. My heart sputters and dies. "Don't—Bruce—"

"Have fun, kids."

I lunge for him and trip over Donnie in the process. I sprawl across the floor, my feet all tangled up in him. He swears at me and pushes at my legs, groaning. I get to my feet and crawl to the door just as it closes. *Not this. Not this.* I press my palms against the door, trying to catch my breath—I can't breathe—while Donnie gets to his feet.

Not this.

Bruce, Josh, and Henry laugh themselves down the hall. I curl my fingers against the door. *His hand up my skirt. Mouth on my neck. Not happening. Not happening.*

Not happening not happening not happening.

"Are you ever going to turn around, Afton?"

I need to run. I need to get up. *Get up. Get up.* I grab the doorknob and pull myself to my feet. I need out.

"If you touch me, I'll scream."

"Who would hear you?"

I turn. Donnie hovers at the edge of the light. A shadow falls across his face, adding a disturbing quality to his already grim exterior. Anna must love how badly he wears being an outcast. Or maybe he just looks this bad because he's sober.

I hope.

He moves in my direction. I shudder, feel my throat hitch. *His hand up my skirt.* He was on me. Kara knew what he did to me, *she knew.* I go back to the door, pounding it with my fists until they hurt. A voice inside my head tells me to scream, *scream, scream now, scream loud, louder,* and I keep thinking *I am I'm trying I'm screaming.*

But nothing is coming out of my mouth.

His hand is on my arms. He's behind me. Close. I jerk away and

I do it too easily, which means he let me do it. He let me. He's fucking with me.

"I don't want you to touch me," I say, backing away. I put a shelf between us. His footsteps are terrible and light, and I count them getting closer.

One. Two. Three.

"You never thought I was good enough," he says. Four. Five. Five footsteps. "And you couldn't just let me have Anna. You loved to tell her I wasn't good enough for her either, all the time. Every single day."

I take five steps back, around the same shelf, past the useless locked door. I look around the room for something I can use. Paper. Poster board. I need something heavy.

Something.

"Everyone hates me because of you," he says, quickening his pace. One-two-three. I step back one-two-three. "I'm not on the basketball team because of you. I get my ass kicked and locked in closets because of you—"

I grab a stack of paper. He bursts out laughing when he sees it and takes a quick step forward and back, faking me out. I stumble back, clutching the paper, and then he lunges at me for real and I throw it. Paper blizzard. It distracts him long enough for me to get to the other side of the shelf. All I have to do is keep this shelf between us for as long as we're in here, and we can't be in here together that much longer because these things don't happen twice—where you need help and no one comes.

"Why the *fuck* would you tell Kara?" Donnie kicks at the paper. I flinch and he answers his own question. "Oh, right—it's because *you're a fucking bitch*, that's why."

He shoves his hands between the free spaces in the shelves, reaching for me.

"Stop," I beg. "Please—"

"Why?" He rounds the shelf, grinning. "What have I got to lose?"

I back into the shelf, and its hard metal edge against my spine startles me forward. It's a split-second advantage and it's all Donnie needs. He grabs at me, just missing my arms. His fingers curl around my shirt. I hear the material give, tearing at the seam, up the side. My legs give.

He bends down and breathes on my neck.

"Don't," I whisper.

"Don't," he repeats in my ear. He puts his hand on my shoulder. I cover my mouth. He slips his hand past the collar of my shirt. I choke back a sob and try to crawl away from him, but he pulls me back. Hands on me. Touching me.

I throw up.

"*Jesus,*" Donnie hisses, scrambling back. I scramble around the puddle of vomit, get myself up, and stumble toward the door. *Open. Open. Open open open.*

It opens.

Liz Cooper.

I shove past her before she can get a good look at my face. It's cold in the hall and I'm shaking and I wrap my arms around myself but I can't stop. Shaking.

"What were you two doing in there?" she demands.

"What do you think?" Donnie asks.

Liar. *Liar.* But why bother saying it. No one believed me the first time. I keep moving. Away. I can't see. I try to blink the school into focus, but I can't. I try not to panic. I don't need to see to get out of here. I press my hand against the wall and feel my way down the empty hall. I swallow air until I'm so full of it, I think I'll explode.

I'll explode and I'll be over and I'll be done and that will be okay.

I stop and try to guess where I'm supposed to be. I must have a class, but I don't know what period it is. The bell rings. I find myself elbowed and shouldered down the hall with the type of zeal only reserved for the end of the day. It's the end of the day.

Good. God.

I edge my way out of the herd, into a free space.

Right behind Kara.

Who is giggling with Jeanette.

"I'm going to kill you."

The words fall off my lips, stunned and stupid sounding, but so true. I'll kill her. At some point, I will kill her. All of this has to be leading up to a moment where I wrap my hands around her neck and squeeze.

She registers me slowly. "How did you get out?"

"You're dead."

I want it to sound strong coming out of my mouth. I want her to know it's true; she's dead. But Kara only stares and Jeanette stares and I feel like I'm going to throw up again, so I force myself back into the elbows and shoulders and hope they push me out of here, because I have to get out of here.

An arm yanks me back.

"Who the fuck let you out? Where's Henderson?"

Bruce. I jerk my arm from his grasp and shove him, but his solid frame doesn't budge. He just stares at me, amused, which makes me even angrier. Josh stands beside him, and I know I could shove *him* and he'd feel it, so I do. I press my palms into his chest and push the fuck out of my ex-boyfriend. He staggers back.

Bruce grabs me again. "What's *wrong* with you, Afton?"

"Get off me."

He grins. "Apologize."

"Get the *fuck* off me!"

I shout it loudly enough for everyone to stop what they're doing and look, but no one does anything because it's only me and— Everyone. Hates. Me. Bruce doesn't let me go. I start pushing at him, these small stupid sounds coming out of my mouth, but no words. I'm going to cry and I need to leave before that happens.

"What's going on?"

Bruce drops my hand and focuses on someone behind me. Michael. I rub my wrist and start moving away because I don't want him to see me. I don't want to see him.

"Why do you care?" Bruce asks.

Michael ignores him. "Regina, are you okay?"

I never answer. I'm already past rows and rows of orange lockers, past familiar blond curls and a flash of red, until the front doors are in sight, and I think I hear my name again but it's behind me and I am never going back.

I go home and no one's there.

I suffocate on no one being there. I can still feel Donnie's hands on me. I get vodka from my dad's liquor cabinet, because the lock doesn't mean anything if you really want it, and I want it, I want to drink until I can breathe, but it doesn't really work, so I go to Michael's house because it's after school and he should be there and I don't want to be alone.

I leave with the bottle half empty, and it's empty when I get to his place, and no one's *there* either, and I'm so wasted, I don't think I can actually walk back home. The last time I got this drunk, I was at one of Josh's parties. All of Josh's parties. The night would always end with Anna holding my hair while I puked, and I liked it because after what happened with Liz, it was the only time Anna felt like she was my best friend.

I sneak down the narrow path to the backyard. I curl up on the chaise lounge by the pool and stare up at the sky, and the sky looks so stupid from here.

"—been out here?"

This moment started without me. I can't feel my fingers. I'm static. I blink. I'm still outside, sitting upright on the chaise lounge. I don't remember sitting up. Michael's in front of me, hands on my shoulders. "Regina, how long have you been out here?"

I don't know. Thinking it isn't the same as saying it, though, and I don't have the energy to speak. I close my eyes and push him away. He presses his palm to my cheek, and his hand is so warm, I shiver.

"Cold," he says.

And then another voice. "Is she all right?"

Not that voice. I open my eyes. I force myself to my feet and manage three unsteady steps away from both of them before I fall off the face of the planet. Michael's there, his arm around my waist. I stare up at him. "You told her?"

"She told me she found you," he says, like that's a reason. It's not. I push away from him, but he holds fast until I push at him again. He eases me back down on the chaise. I bury my face in my hands because I don't want Liz to see me like this, even though it's already too late. I can feel her looking at me.

"I bet you love this," I mutter.

"I'm not Anna," she says.

Ouch. I can't believe how bad hearing that feels. And then I have this thought: We probably could've been friends, all three of us— like, real friends. I *hate* that thought.

"I'm sorry," I say stupidly, and then *sorry* is on a loop. I can't keep it from coming out of my mouth. "I'm sorry, Liz, I'm sorry—Michael— I'm so sorry—"

"It's okay," Michael says quickly. "Regina, it's okay—"

I laugh. It's the least funny thing in the world, but I laugh. "It's not okay. It doesn't mean anything. It'll never . . ."

My stomach twists, awful, and I cover my mouth with my hand and lean forward, and there's this horrible moment where I'm sure I'm going to puke, but it doesn't happen. But I'm really tired. I try to curl back into the chair, to sleep, but Michael pulls me forward. "Hey, no, Regina, don't do that—"

"You've got to get her inside," Liz says.

"Yeah."

He hooks my arm around his shoulder and gets me to my feet. I'm still mad at him about *her*, though, so I try to push him away again, but it doesn't work again. He guides me toward the house, and my feet struggle with straight lines. It's not a fun kind of drunk. He swears under his breath while Liz waits for us at the door.

"Why would you—?" He stops, and redirects me for the umpteenth time. I lean into him more than I want to. "Never mind. Forget I asked."

"I was alone," I say, like that's a reason.

He gives me this look I can't decode, like sad but something else. He tightens his grip on me and gets me through the door, telling me when to *step up, be careful*. We bypass his kitchen—I want to look, but only glimpse it—and head for the living room. He pours me onto the couch while Liz hovers behind.

She could've left by now. Should have.

Some small part of her *has* to love this.

"Get her some water," she tells Michael. "Get the phone, too. She's probably not going anywhere tonight. . . . Get her to leave a message

on her answering machine for her parents while she can still sort of
fake sober."

That's an Anna trick. We taught her that.

"Good thinking," Michael says. He leaves. He leaves the room.
He leaves me in the room alone with Liz. We stare at each other. I
wish I could pass out so I could wake up so this nightmare would
be over. Except it's never really over.

"Your shirt's torn. A little," Liz says after a minute. "I didn't want
to say anything in front of Michael. He already freaked when I told
him how I found you." She pauses and she looks concerned, like she
wants to know—make sure I'm okay. But then she says, "I'm not
going to ask you about it."

I swallow. "You had perfect timing, Liz. . . ."

Silence.

"Good," she finally replies, and she sounds like she means it, and
it makes me feel so bad. A tear manages to escape me. I wipe it away
quickly.

"When will you forgive me?" I blurt out. "I got what I deserved. I
know I deserve it, everything, but I need to know if you forgive—"

"Like if you suffer enough I should forgive you?" she asks, totally
unimpressed. I exhale shakily and stare at her feet. "That's not how
it works."

"But I really, really—"

"Look, Regina, you're *really* drunk right now," she says, which is
like *Shut up.* So I shut up and we wait for Michael to come back. I take
in the room. It's tidy but empty. The walls are bare and white, waiting
for color. The furniture is sparse—a couch, a chair in the corner, a
television. It's like they never finished moving in. Like they started
unpacking and stopped halfway and threw all the half-full boxes out.

Michael comes back with the water and the phone. Liz gives him
my number. I can't believe she still remembers it. He dials and holds
the receiver up to my ear. I wait for the answering machine to pick
up, and then I mumble something about being ". . . at Anna's for the
night see you tomorrow love you bye."

I feel like such a loser.

"I'll go," Liz says because there's nothing else here for her to see. She touches Michael's shoulder. "I'll see you."

"Thanks," he says.

Liz turns to me, and for a second I think she's going to say something, but she doesn't. She leaves. After a minute, the sound of the front door closing echoes through the house. I want to die.

Michael holds up the glass of water. He kneels down and presses it into my hands, and it's not that I can't hold it; it's that I don't want to. He anticipates this, cradling the glass in his palm. He sets it on the floor and looks at me.

"Do you forgive me?" I ask. Because Liz is right: I'm really drunk right now, so this is the only time I'll get away with just asking him.

"What?" But he heard me.

"You don't," I say. "Liz doesn't forgive me and you don't—"

Before he can say anything—before I can even finish what I'm saying—I bring my hands to his face and clumsily lean forward. My lips graze his cheek, and he brings his hands to my side, to steady me or to keep me from touching him, I don't know. I bring my mouth to his lips and kiss him because . . . because his lips are nice.

And I'm starved for nice things.

He kisses me back.

"No—" He pulls away and his hand hits the water. It tips, spilling onto the carpet, and some kind of dull embarrassment plants itself in the middle of my brain so I'll feel stupid about this when I sober up. I reach for him, fumble with the buttons of his shirt, and I almost get one undone when he says that dumb word again: "No."

I bring my hands to his face again. I can touch him into this. But he grabs my hands and says, "Regina," and that stops me for the last time.

And then he lets go of my hands.

"I don't feel well," I tell him.

He clears his throat. "Go to sleep. You'll feel better when you wake up."

Right.

tuesday

The house is quiet.

The scene in the closet with Donnie drifts in and out of my head. I let it in and then I force it back out. Repeat.

Rays of sunlight filter in through the minute gaps in the curtain drawn over the glass door leading to the pool. I push them aside and stare at the water. It's still. It's late morning and Michael's not home or he's still sleeping. I'm not sure and I don't want to find out. I think the easiest way to pretend Monday never happened is to get as far away from it as possible.

I unlock the door and step outside. It's cold. I can't believe we were choking on heat not that long ago and now it's cold out. I make my way around the house, down that stupid little path, and end up on the front lawn and—

Michael's there, getting out of his car. He stops when he sees me, stays by the driver's side, like he's not sure how to proceed. My face gets hot. This moment where we cross paths the day after I sloppy-drunk-kiss him isn't supposed to happen.

"Hey," he says. "Hungover?"

"No."

He's impressed. "Lucky."

"Sometimes I get a break."

He stays where he is and I stay where I am. It's a weird sort of face-off. I'm not hungover, but I feel fragmented; lost. Nobody wants me.

"I was alone, right?" I finally ask, pointing back to the house. "Where's your dad? Did he . . . ?"

Michael hesitates. "He works. But he was here. He comes home through the front door, refuels in the kitchen, goes to bed, wakes up, refuels in kitchen, and leaves through the front door. He didn't even know you were here."

"I should go."

"Wait—don't," he says, and then he turns red. "I mean, I want to show you something."

I'm in the passenger side of Michael's car, watching Hallowell fly past, a picture of midmorning quiet. It's overcast and cold, and the sun barely kisses the houses lining the streets. After a while, Hallowell disappears and we pull onto a dirt road that leads out of town. I watch as the wheels kick up dust in the rearview.

Michael is a quiet comfort beside me. I like him beside me. After thirty minutes or so, the road goes smooth and then rough again. Another dirt road. We stay on this one a long time, until a familiar black convertible comes into view.

My chest tightens and my hand goes for the door.

"It's okay," Michael says quickly. "Regina, he's not here."

I stare at the convertible parked on the side of the road. Donnie's not here. It sinks in slowly. What that means. Donnie's not here. But his car is.

And then I feel like I've chased a bunch of speed with twenty cups of coffee.

Michael eases the Saturn to a stop behind the convertible.

"He'll never find it out here." He pulls a different set of keys from his pockets. I recognize the little Swiss Army knife keychain. "Left them in the ignition. Idiot." He tosses them from hand to hand. "No one's going to give him a ride anywhere. He'll have to hoof it for who knows how long. So I was thinking we put the top down, because it's supposed to rain all week, and leave the keys inside for anyone to find. . . ."

Michael hands me the keys. I close my fingers around them. They're warm from his grasp and now they're in mine. Donnie loves that convertible.

It's the only thing he has.

I get out of the car and approach it carefully, slowly. I don't even know where to start, so I get into the driver's side, where Donnie sits every day, and think. And then I put the top down and shove the keys in the ignition. I feel empty. It's not enough.

And then I get an idea.

The coffee-and-speed feeling comes back more intensely than before. I grab the keys again. This is perfect. I get out of the car. So perfect. I fingernail the knife out of the cover. I'm vaguely aware of Michael watching as I drag the tip of the knife down the driver's side of the convertible. I press in hard. It's a beautiful sound.

It's a beautiful scratch.

And then I do it again.

Again. Again.

I step back and admire my handiwork. Four perfect scratches down the length of his classic convertible, but it *still* isn't enough. I could do better.

I need to stop looking at it like a car and more like a canvas.

I drop to my knees. My fingers are wrapped so tightly around the keys they hurt, but it's a good hurt. I move to the farthest side of the car and start making art—a big letter **D**. I follow it with an **O**. **U**. I carve deep, going over the letters as hard as I can. **C**. **H**. **E**. It takes a while. My fingers go numb. I stop at the E and uncurl my fingers. I rub them and wait for the feeling to return. That takes a while, too.

"Nice," Michael says, coming up behind me.

"I'm not done," I say, and then I get to work on the **B**. The letters cross over the original lines I made and this is definitely art. This feels good. I imagine the car is Kara and I imagine the car is Anna. I imagine the metal as their skin, and it feels even better. That's sick. Even I know how sick that is.

It's as sick as locking me in a closet with the guy who tried to rape me.

I drop the knife.

For a minute, all I see is us. Me and Anna. Kara and Jeanette and Mara. No Josh, no Donnie, no Michael. Nothing is complicated. We are the sweet side of thirteen, traipsing down the main street, and we're eating out for lunch, the first time off campus. It's a Big Deal. We have to get permission slips and everything. I see Marta and Jeanette, and they're oblivious, happy. Kara is overweight, dour even when she smiles, and we're not close but we're not there—here—yet. And Anna is this carefree vision that makes my heart ache, because I don't know what happened to her, but she used to be good.

We're sick. We're sick. We're sick girls.

Michael kneels down beside me. "A," he says.

I get back to work: **A**.

G.

Done. I'm drenched in sweat and my bangs are stuck to my forehead. I take a deep breath and press my hands against the ground and just ride it out, and when I'm sure I'm not going to cry, I lean back and stare at the car, and I can feel how close Michael is beside me.

"You did this for me," I say slowly. "But we're not friends."

"Regina," he says, "I . . ."

But he never finishes.

I stare at the ground and all I can think about is Michael's mouth against my mouth and Donnie's keys in my hands and how funny they felt against my palm, like a metal revelation.

It's like the evolution of anger. It doesn't have to be loud all the time.

Now it's just quiet and it's all of me.

I cross the school parking lot and feel like a junkie looking for a fix, but I'm not sure what my next fix is. I just know it's in this building. I pull the front doors open and step into three-quarters of my old crowd. Anna, Kara, and Jeanette stare at me like they can't believe I've done it, and now that I've done it, I can't believe it either. And then I just stand there, paralyzed. I can't move. Something is going to happen.

I'm just not sure what.

"Jesus Christ, Regina, just *go*."

I study each and every one of them, committing their faces to memory. I know what they look like, but I want to make sure I remember them this way, post–locking me in a closet with Donnie. My fingers curl in on themselves, and I bite my tongue so hard, I taste blood. *I hate these girls I hate these girls I hate these girls.*

"Are you fucking deaf?" Kara.

"Forget it," Anna says impatiently. "Marta can find us at my locker."

She moves out and Jeanette follows after her, but Kara stays behind to smirk. All I'd have to do is reach out and choke, she's that close. It'd be so easy and it would feel *so good*. But I can't move.

"*Kara.*" Anna. Her *Here, girl,* voice. I remember that voice.

Kara gives me one last look and hurries after Anna. She's fucked if she thinks I'm done with her. I take a sharp breath in, and my body comes back to me; I can move, but now I have to wait. I lean against the wall and watch people filter in until the bell rings. When it finally does, I head up the stairs and down the hall to her locker, and she's there.

Alone.

She doesn't see me coming until I'm shoving her against the locker. She makes a startled noise, but she rallies quickly and shoves me back, and I shove her again and it's my palms on her shoulders. This beautiful adrenaline rush. I will kill her.

She sees it in me and manages to slip away before I can do it.

I'm not going to chase her. Not yet.

The hall is empty. Class noises ghost in. I lean against Kara's locker and come down, but I don't want to come down. Someone shuffles my way. I turn. Donnie. He looks like shit. There are bags under his eyes and his hair is greasy. It's weird that we're living in two separate but similar hells. That Anna has found a way to make him miserable and I'm not a part of it.

I really would have liked to have been a part of it.

"Where's your car?" I ask.

He stops and looks at me, confused. Not confused about *what* I've asked him, but *that* I've asked him and that I'm not scared. I like the way it feels.

"None of your fucking business," he mutters. And then, "It's getting work done."

"No it's not."

I steel myself. I watch him process it, watch the color of his face start building to a good red.

"What did you do to my car?" he growls.

"Don't worry, Donnie," I say. "It'll turn up. Eventually."

He comes close, so close. At-the-party close. My heart beats crazy in my chest, but I know none of it is on my face, so I just keep going. "What? It still runs."

He brings his fist up and slams his knuckles into the metal beside my head.

"Tell me where it is or you're *dead*, Afton."

He's breathing heavily. He wants to hurt me, but I'm not entirely convinced that he will. We stare at each other, our eyes locked, and I raise my chin.

Do something.

"What's going on?" We turn, startled by this new voice. Brenner stands in the middle of the hall, his arms crossed. Donnie backs off. "Get to class, both of you."

Donnie goes one way and I go the other. *That was stupid. That was stupid. That was stupid. That was really, really stupid.* But I'd do it again in a second, just to have that moment that felt like it was mine.

I walk down the hall. All I can think about is what's next, the next moment that's mine. I'm not going to class. I'm not going to find it in class. I wander the halls seeking it out until the adrenaline fades, and the bell rings again.

It's strange walking with these bodies, all on their way to class. This is their day-to-day. Nothing bothers them, and the things that might bother them are nothing. I roll my shoulders, I flex my fingers. There's something inside me that needs somewhere to go. I feel quiet-reckless-crazy. I feel like . . . I could shove my knuckles into metal and it would never hurt. I feel dead inside.

I round the corner and spot Michael at the end of the hall talking to Liz. I stop. My heart stops. I duck into the spaces between rows of lockers because I'm avoiding him. After the closet with Donnie, the kiss, the car, I see him and I can't breathe. I'm scared of what I felt both times—when my mouth was on his mouth and after he put his hands on my wrists and told me *no*.

I peek around the corner and watch him talk to Liz. I want to see what that looks like—if there's something there when he talks to her that isn't there when he talks to me. It's effortless. They aren't into each other like that, but he's leaning against the locker and she's close the way friends are close. She says something to him and he says something back and smiles and laughs. I'm struck by how amazing it is and how sad that makes me, because I've never seen that. He's not like that around me. The way his mouth quirks and lights up his eyes. He should smile more often. It's so innocent.

I lean back against the wall and chew on my lips, swallowing hard. It hurts being on the outside of something so honest. I want it, but I don't know how I can have it when I'm so angry, and I feel so far from finished.

I spend lunch in my storage room.

I'm sitting on the floor, picking at my fingernails, waiting for the bell to ring. Legs crossed at the ankle. This is boring, but it's okay because nothing is happening, and I'm trying not to think too much, because I think too much and I never think good things. I count the number of mats wedged at the back of the room (four). I find various pieces of broken equipment in a cobwebby cardboard box wedged in the corner and organize them into piles and then put them back.

When the bell rings, I press my ear against the door and wait until all the footsteps fade away, and then I sneak out and drift down the hall.

"Hey, Regina—"

I stiffen. That's Michael's voice. He's somewhere behind me. I duck my shoulders and quicken my pace. He'll get the message; he's not stupid.

"Regina—"

His voice gets lost to hall noises, and I relax because that has to mean he's fallen behind. I don't know what he could possibly want with me. We've come to a natural end. There can't be much left after you steal a car for someone and then stand around and watch while they decimate the paint job.

I slam shoulders with some freshman and slip around them,

narrowly missing someone else. The hall is congested. I push past a few more stationary bodies because my locker's here, and then I . . .

. . . feel it in my bones before my brain processes it.

Everything goes cold.

My red locker door is hanging open, guts splayed out for the whole world to see. The hall is congested because people are pausing so they can point at it and laugh. They make ridiculous faces as they go. I edge wordlessly through the crowd so I can get a good look at what they've done to my locker this time *this time this time again.*

Rancid, raw ground meat. All over everything. My books. My coat. Book bag. The sides of my locker. Everywhere. Everything is ruined. They must have raided the grocery store and bought up all the bargain meat and left it outside for days and days, because the smell is unbelievable. Acrid, sour.

I reach in. My fingers brush over slimy bits of some dead animal.

My heartbeat slows to nothing and then, when I'm sure I'm dead, it thumps once. Twice. Three times. Steady and even. I'm still here. I get to ten beats and then it beats faster—twenty, faster, thirty, faster, forty. Do something do something *do something.*

I slam the door so hard it recoils back.

The crowd murmurs.

"Regina—"

Michael's voice sounds like it's far away, but it's closer than I want it to be. I storm down the hall, away from it. He calls me once more. Part of me wants to detach myself from this anger and go to him, but that part of me is very small. I head for the second floor. Kara's locker. She might be there. Because it was her. Maybe it was Anna's idea, but Kara would've done it.

Anna would never touch that stuff.

I crash into some moron who's decided to go down the up stairs. Books fly. I grab the railing and push myself forward until I hear this: "Thanks a lot, bitch."

And even though she hasn't spoken to me in ages, I haven't forgotten that blonde's breathy voice yet. Jeanette bends down and gathers her books, muttering to herself. Seeing the back of her head gives me a prickly thrill in the pit of my stomach. One of her books has landed beyond her. I grab it. It'd be a dangerous move if it were anyone but Jeanette, but I'm better than her, even when I'm not.

She doesn't catch sight of the book until I wave it in front of her face. *Moron.* She tries to snatch it out of my hands, but I back away and hold it out of her reach.

"Give me my book!"

The venom in her voice surprises me a little. I know she hates me, but I don't think I ever disliked Jeanette. I think I liked her. I didn't respect her, but I liked her.

"Who put the meat in my locker?" I demand. She gets uncomfortable all over, clutching her books like they're a security blanket.

"I'm not allowed to talk to you." She's practically sweating. It's really pathetic. "Give me my book back."

"Tell me who put the meat in my locker and I'll give you your book and I'll leave you alone. If you don't, I'll stand here until Anna shows and sees you with me."

"Bruce and Kara," she blabs. "Now give me my book!"

I keep it out of her reach, because I can and because it feels good. Jeanette stamps her foot, and I can't help but grin.

"Give me my fucking book, Regina!"

I let her rip it from my grasp and watch her storm her way down the up stairs, and then she stops at the bottom of them and turns to me, her face red.

"I'm telling Anna."

"I'm totally shaking, Jeanette." Wait. "Wait. Tell her—tell her you were talking to me and tell Kara to watch her back, but make *sure* you tell them—"

"Fuck you."

She's gone, she's done, but I'm just getting started.

I jog down the steps, past my locker, down the hall. I can't make a Web site about Kara. I turn down another hallway. I already trashed her locker. Can't do that again. I make my way past people going wherever, and I try to block out their voices and the fact that they're pointing and laughing at me *again*. I can't make a Web site about Anna either. Too obvious. There's no one they'd hate to be locked in a closet with. I turn down another hall, a deserted hall, a familiar hall. This is why I got drunk directly after what happened with Donnie. So I didn't have to feel it, but now I feel it, I feel all of it, and it's too much and I—*Do something do something.*

I push through the door to the storage room and slam it behind me because I don't care, and I grab the box of broken things and throw it against the wall. It explodes.

And then it's quiet.

I press my hand against my forehead. My head is throbbing. I'm breathing like I ran a marathon, and my stomach is churning and my throat is tight and I'm hot. I kick one of the old mats and then I kick it again, and then I bite my arm because I'm going to scream; I'm not going to scream and . . . okay.

It's okay.

My chest caves in, deflates; my heart is calm, my heart is pumping calm. No—not calm. Nothing. I should go back. But I kneel down and press my hands against the cold floor and crawl until I'm against the wall instead. I'll go home and talk to Mom and Dad about finishing out the year—not at school. I can't do this anymore.

I bring my knees up and rest my head against them. I close my eyes. I run my hand over the floor, feeling grit and dust, and I have a problem.

Now that I'm down, I don't want to get up.

I guess I can stay here awhile.

I'm just starting to get into that peaceful, falling kind of place between dozing and actual sleep when the door opens slowly, and some vague alarm goes off inside me—*Oh no, you're caught*—but I don't care until the light from the hallway hits my eyelids and rudely jolts me into wakefulness, and then I do. I look up. Michael is standing in the doorway holding a black garbage bag. He flicks on the light and I wince.

"The stuff from your locker," he says, holding the bag up. He sets it inside the door, which he closes quietly behind him, and then he faces the room. I watch him take it all in. The mess I made. ". . . Are you okay?"

"How did you know I was here?" My tongue feels thick.

"I followed you," he says. "I saw you come in here. I thought I'd give you a minute so I cleaned out your locker. It's clean."

"Thanks," I say.

"I can't believe they did that to you," he says. "I mean, I can, but—"

"Yeah."

He crosses the room and sits beside me, close. His shoulder against my shoulder. I tense and then I relax. It's not like he can reject me twice, because I'm not going to make a move. I'm not saying anything. A few minutes pass, and he clears his throat.

"So what *did* you do to Kara?"

I look at him. He looks at me. I laugh a little, because even though it's not funny, it's not anything like what I thought he was going say.

"Uhm . . ." I bite my lower lip. "Kara couldn't keep up. So we—I mean, *I* told her that a lot. It kind of fucked her up. A lot."

And the rest is history.

"So I guess I deserve this," I add absently.

And then my eyes catch sight of the garbage bag against the wall with all of my ruined things inside of it, and my face dissolves. Don't cry. *Don't cry.* It shouldn't matter at this point. Michael's seen me at my worst, but I press my hand against my eyes, taking short pathetic breaths in and out until I'm choking on air, and all I want to do is tell him about how paralyzing it was in that closet with Donnie and how we weren't always like this and how sick it is, but all I can manage are these six, stilted words: "I-just-want-them-to-stop."

"I can take you home," he says. I shake my head and wipe my eyes. "You can't stay here, Regina. Let me take you home."

"No," I say. I sound like a stubborn little kid. *No.* But I don't want to step into the halls again, because I'm tired of being out there and this feels safe. He gets to his feet and holds his hand out, and I push him away. "*Stop.* Michael, stop it—"

"Remember when I told you my mom wouldn't have hated you, even if she'd known what you'd done? She would've tried to help you." He pauses. "That means something to me." I close my eyes and shake my head. "Please let me help you."

I open my eyes. I take his hand. His fingers close around mine and he helps me to my feet. We end up close and it hurts, because I want to be this close to someone who wants to be this close to me. He doesn't want me.

"You hate me."

"I don't hate you," he says.

I look at him and I think he's telling the truth. Before, I could see it—that he hated me. But now it's not there enough for me to see, if it's there at all, and that's the strangest feeling I've had in a long time.

"Regina," he says. "I don't hate you."

He edges closer until there's no space between us and brings his hands to my face so awkwardly, like this isn't what he set out to do, but now that we're here, he's going to do it all the same. This is a test. This is not a test.

He kisses me. Presses his lips against mine gently, hesitantly, and when I kiss back, he kisses harder, deeper. I feel like he wants me. He brings his hand to my neck and kisses me and kisses me again. I bring my hands around to the back of his neck, his hair tickling past my knuckles, and his fingers drift down to my sides. For a minute, I'm dizzy with how good it feels and how amazing it is that I could have this moment that feels so good.

He's so *nice*.

He brings his mouth to my neck. I shiver and close my eyes, my hands still in his hair. He stops for a second and we stand there, his lips just barely there, and he brings his hands up and gently pushes my collar back so there's more of me for him to kiss and my legs feel sort of weak. His mouth comes back to mine. I bring my hand to his chest.

Steady.

The door flies open, puts a space between us so wide it's like we were never on each other at all. I'm breathing heavily and he's breathing heavily. I squint at the figure in the door, waiting for my eyes to focus.

It's Bruce. He bursts out laughing as his stupid tiny brain registers what he's just seen and what it's seeing now, and I feel my face turn red.

"Jesus Christ," he says. "Are you serious?"

"Fuck off," I tell him, crossing my arms. My head still feels fuzzy with the kiss. I shake it a little, to clear it. "What are you doing here?"

He just smiles and he doesn't say anything, and I get this uneasy feeling that he knew—he knew I was here all along. I glance at Michael, and I think he's thinking the same thing, because he clenches his jaw. Even Bruce notices. He backs off and laughs again and then he goes and he laughs himself down the hall.

"Great," I say. "Now they'll know that we—"

"So?" Michael asks, turning to me. "So what?"

We stare at each other. So they know; so what? I wonder if, even after all this, he understands how fragile good things are in my hands and how many times they've been taken away from me. I lean over and give him an impulsive kiss on the cheek, and then I leave the storage room and he leaves after me.

I wake up wired, and I go to school wired, popping antacids like they're candy. It's been one day and I feel sick, excited, nervous.

It was almost easier when he hated me. I'm used to that.

Hallowell High: Everyone's dressed for the weather.

Michael is waiting for me at my locker. The red door hangs open, a useless empty mouth, waiting to be filled with all I could salvage last night. He straightens when he sees me, and I try to ignore the funny feeling in my stomach, but when he smiles, it gets worse in a good way, and it goes straight to my head in a good way.

"Hi," he says, holding out his hand. His fingers are closed around something I can't see. "I have something for you. Open your hand."

I do. He presses something heavy into it. I look down. A new combination lock.

"Thanks," I say.

"The combination is four, fifteen, thirty, and three."

"Thank you," I repeat.

He moves forward, and then he hesitates and moves back. Whatever's between us is that kind of new. He runs a hand through his hair.

"So I'll see you at lunch," he says. I nod.

He studies me for a good minute and then—he kisses me. Like, right here in the hall. In front of everyone. I feel people milling around us, their voices getting louder the closer they get. Breaking news: My mouth is on Michael Hayden's mouth, and he means it.

I glimpse blond hair. Liz. She turns a corner going to the girls' room. Which means she saw this. Michael pulls away and says, "Okay, good."

"Lunch," I repeat. He nods this time and passes me. I watch him go, and then I turn and head for the washroom because I want to see what she makes of it. When I push through the door, she's coming out of the stall. She glances at me and then runs the water, keeping her eyes on her reflection, and I just stand there keeping my eyes on her.

"What do you want me to say, Regina?" she finally asks.

"I don't know," I say.

"I'm not giving you my blessing," she says.

"I didn't ask for it."

"Then why are you here?" I don't know. She turns off the water and I turn back to the door, and she says, "He doesn't know what he's doing."

"But when he hates me, he knows what he's doing?"

"You really fucked him up, so if—" She shakes her head, like this whole turn of events has been pissing her off since the dawn of time. "You probably don't get it, but if he's giving you a chance, that's a big deal."

I grit my teeth. "I get it."

I wish I'd never come in here at all.

"I don't think you do," she says, looking me up and down. I bite the inside of my cheek but I don't say anything. "But whatever, Regina; use him up."

Some people will never give up on their lack of belief in you. I'm used to that feeling, but for the first time ever, it hurts. Maybe because Michael got past it, and now I'm standing here wondering why she can't and if she ever will.

"Thanks," I say.

"I couldn't talk him out of you."

I couldn't talk him out of you. Her voice echoes in my head from class to class, and my stomach aches. When the lunch bell rings, I'm eager to see Michael. I pass Josh in the hall on my way to the cafeteria and keep my eyes straight ahead.

"Are you and Hayden a thing now?" he asks.

I roll my eyes and stop. "What?"

He stops. "Bruce said he caught you two fucking around in a storage room, and now everyone's talking about how you two were making out in the hall earlier. Is it true? Are you with Hayden?"

"It's none of your business."

"If you're making out with him in hallways, it's everyone's business." He looks me over and laughs. "You're not with Hayden. He hates you. Everyone knows he hates you. He feel sorry for you or something? Desperate to get some?"

"Fuck off."

"He must be *really* desperate," he says. "Or maybe you're the desperate one."

"Michael's the best thing that's happened to me."

My cheeks warm instantly. It's one of those insanely stupid-sounding declarations that people laugh at you for, no matter how true it is. But it's true.

Josh laughs at me. "I've noticed a whole lot has changed for you since you decided to hang around with Mr. Mysterious—" I punch him in the shoulder before he can finish, because I can't think of a better or more satisfying way to shut him up. "—Jesus *Christ*, Regina! What is *wrong* with you?"

"What's wrong with *you*? You just stand there and watch every day while Anna makes my life a living hell. Who just sits there and *watches* something like that?"

"*You* did," Josh snaps. "You always did. Her name was Liz, remember? Don't act like you're better than me, Regina. You're not."

"But Michael is," I tell him.

Josh turns red. I know somehow I've hurt him. "Well, maybe your new boyfriend should watch his back."

My stomach lurches and he smirks, satisfied. The threat goes deep. I turn and head for the cafeteria, digging into my pockets for an antacid, trying to understand how I can be this close to fucking everything up already. When I see Michael at the Garbage Table, I'm flooded with relief. He's in one piece.

And he's waiting for me.

I weave around tables and sit across from him. His lunch today— fries and Coke. His Moleskine rests beside him. I just watch him for a minute and I feel like Liz is right. He's really lonely and I fuck things up. Just because he gets to this point where he wants to kiss me doesn't mean I instantly wake up tomorrow brave. I'm afraid of what Josh said.

"What's wrong?" he asks.

I shake my head. "Nothing." Everything.

He doesn't look like he believes me, but then, thankfully, embarrassingly, my stomach makes this awful hungry gurgle and he hears it. He raises an eyebrow.

"Hungry?" he asks.

I wave a hand. "I'll eat when I get home."

"Let me get you something," he says, nodding at the lunch line, and I start telling him how I can't eat in this place, and he interrupts. "I'll get you something small."

Like that would make a difference. But he gets up and goes. I watch him go. My gaze drifts over to the center table, where Josh is leaning over and whispering something in Anna's ear. His mouth moves from her ear, grazing her cheek, and meets her lips; I don't want Michael on their radar.

I turn back to the table. Michael's trusty Moleskine is resting next to his tray.

I want to read it.

He's standing in line and he's not looking my way. I know I shouldn't do this, but I have to do this, and I don't have a lot of time to have an ethical debate about it right now. I grab it and flip it open, flip past page after page, searching for my name. I glimpse words

like *Mom, Dad, hate, yesterday, I, stupid school*, and all of them mean
something, but they're not what I want.

I skip to the end, and then—

Might not last.

I know it's about me. It's dated yesterday. It says I'm not a sure
thing—like I could really fuck this up. I press my index fingers
against the words, as if I could feel what he was feeling when he
wrote it, but it's just ink on paper. I flip ahead, but there's nothing. I
set the Moleskine back where it was and wait for him to come back,
and I guess there's some truth in it. I don't think I can divide myself
so completely between him and Anna.

Someone will get hurt.

Maybe your new boyfriend should watch his back.

I look up at the center table. Anna is watching me, interested in
a way that makes me sick. I spot Michael winding his way back to
the table, a small container of yogurt in his hand, and I am overwhelmed with how much more I like him than I hate my ex-friends.

But I don't know what to do about it. I don't think I'm that brave.

Do something.

After school, I end up at the park.

Small-town entertainment. Kid explosion in the summer. Everyone vies for a shot at the swings and the monkey bars and the playhouse and the slides and the metal merry-go-round thing that some little girl supposedly severed a limb on years ago. Today the place is empty, save for the snack wagon, which doesn't pack up until the first snow flies. I buy some greasy fries from the guy holding the place down, drown them in ketchup, and eat them on top of the monkey bars.

A light breeze pushes the swings back and forth. I finish off the fries and try to enjoy the quiet. It's easy to be out here: I'm not surrounded.

After a long time, two separate cars pull into the parking lot. No one I recognize. Two soccer moms step out of each car, dragging two little girls with them, respectively. Must be a play date.

They stay to the far side of the park, away from the big toys. I watch them and feel a sense of relief when I see the girls don't have much interest in each other. They pick separate spaces of grass and focus on the dolls they've brought with them while their moms talk. I hope they stay away from each other, because odds are good one of them has the making of a total bitch and the other will become that bitch's total bitch.

Because that's how it works. Mostly.

I lean back, hooking my legs over the bars and snaking through the spaces between them until I'm hanging upside down.

"Mommy, look at that!" One of the girls shrieks. "I want to do that!"

"That's dangerous honey," her mom says. "Why don't you go play with Casey? You two can play dolls with each other. . . ."

That's dangerous.

I stay upside down until I feel like my head is going to burst and I ease back up. I lie across the bars and bundle my coat under my head like a pillow. After an hour or so, the women leave with their daughters. The temperature drops and the light shifts.

I stare at the sky and wait for it to come to me.

Truce.

monday

Truce.

I wake up and that word is in my head.

This morning—a pale pink antacid with coffee. Truce. Dad goes through the whole paper, and I'm still debating it. He leaves. Mom is running late, looking for her car keys. I feel guilty watching her. She just wants to be a good mother, and it's weird and sad to me how we're all in some small ways trying to be good.

"I broke up with Josh," I tell her. I don't know why. "A while ago."

Her head snaps up, eyes wide and surprised, and then they glaze over like she finally understands everything that's been going on. She takes this one little piece of the puzzle and puts it into the wrong picture.

"I'm sorry, Regina," she says. "That's too bad."

"Not really." I shrug. "He was useless."

"They sometimes are," she says, amused.

She gives me a kiss on the cheek and leaves. I sit at the table for as long as I can stretch it out and then I grab my book bag and walk to school.

Truce.

I'm not stupid. I know it's dumb and impossible, but it's all I've got. It's dumb and impossible but it's also grown-up and brave. Not the easy thing to do. And maybe Anna will see that and she'll be so shocked and amazed that I asked her—no one's asked for a truce before—that she'll let me have it, and then I'll tell Michael and it will get back to Liz, and Liz will be impressed, and we all untie ourselves from this Regina, and then I get to be the one that's happy and braver and like . . .

Better.

Time passes too quickly when you're getting ready to do something you don't want to do. The morning and afternoon disappear, and I keep trying to figure out how I'm going to do this, but you can't really plan anything when you deal with Anna.

"What's going on?" Michael asks me at lunch. I'm jiggling my knee under the table like a spaz, and my palms are slimy with sweat.

"Nothing," I tell him. I want it to be a surprise. "I'm just . . ." I trail off and offer him a feeble smile. "Monday."

That's all I need to say.

I skip out on my last class and wait for Anna at her Benz. I swallow a couple antacids. I keep wiping my hands on my jeans. Every time I inhale, my whole chest tingles, and by the time the last bell rings, I can't breathe. I can do this. I tense and watch students shove each other out the front door—I duck out of sight as Michael gets into his Saturn and drives away—until, eventually, *they* emerge—the four of them together.

I can almost see myself wedged between Anna and Kara. Kara always kept her distance, slightly removed, because I told her to. I watch Marta and Jeanette break off for Jeanette's car. For a second, I think if I could do it all over again, I'd want to be one of those two, because they don't matter. But I'd never do it all over again.

Kara points me out to Anna. Anna gives me the dirtiest look

when they reach her Benz. I straighten. My fingers curl and a familiar hot feeling spreads through me. I try to bury it.

I need to be beyond that. Now.

"Get," Anna says, pointing across the parking lot, "away from my car."

"I need to—" It comes out sounding like there are hands around my throat. I cough and try again. "I need to talk to you."

Anna crinkles her nose. "How about . . ."

"No?" Kara suggests.

Anna shoves me out of the way and pulls her keys from her purse.

"I need to talk to you about—" Kara rounds the car, rolling her eyes, and I just blurt the words out: "I want you to leave me alone."

Anna and Kara exchange a glance and laugh.

"I mean a truce," I blurt out.

They freeze. Anna's eyes travel from the keys to her hand to the car to Kara, who leans over the hood, shocked. The moment passes quickly. Anna snorts and unlocks her door. She opens it. Kara stays where she is, but I'm not appealing to Kara.

I grab Anna's door and block her path.

"Fuck off, Regina."

This is the closest I've been to her since I slapped her, and she looks as angry as she did then. My heart gets all tangled up in my stomach, and my mouth is a desert. I scrape my tongue along my lips.

"There's no way we're going to be friends with you," Kara says.

"I'm not asking you for your friendship, you idiot. I'm asking you for a truce."

"No," Kara says, at the same time Anna says, "Why?"

At least the suggestion is unprecedented enough to capture Anna's attention, like I thought it might be. I doubt it will be enough to capture her heart. Especially with Kara standing right there. I wish I could push Kara out of this picture and off a cliff.

"I want you off my back," I say. "Why else do you think?"

"No," Kara says. "We're not—"

Anna holds her hand up, silencing Kara. She inclines her head for me to continue.

"We're graduating soon," I say. "I'm tired of this. Truce."

"If you were really tired of this, you wouldn't keep pushing back."

"What am I supposed to do?" I demand. Neither of them says what they're thinking. "Oh, so I'm just supposed to stand there and let you—"

"Yes. After what you did to me," Anna says, "yes."

Anna will never believe what really happened with Donnie. And now I'm the one who has to give. I'm conceding to the girls who locked me in a closet with a guy who tried to rape me.

I didn't think this out. I don't think I can do this.

"Forget it." I raise my hands. "Just—forget it."

"Wait," Anna says. She sizes me up. "If you want a truce, I want something for it."

"No." Her eyes widen. Anna has never heard me say the word to her before. I've never seen her consider a truce, though, either, so I don't want to shoot myself in the foot. I eye her warily. "What do you want, Anna?"

The question stumps her. There's nothing I have that she wants. I get a glimmer of hope in the pit of my gut. If she doesn't think of anything, I could walk away from this intact.

"Give it to me," Kara says. "Anna, give it to me."

"Fuck off, Kara," I say.

Anna's eyes light up, and I hate myself for giving that away. She never takes her eyes off me as she tells Kara, "Okay, K. I'll leave it to you."

Kara doesn't even try to build to it, doesn't want to torture me or list a slew of horrible, degrading things she could force me to do in the name of a truce. Instead, she leans across the car eagerly and says, "Apologize."

She's trembling, she wants it so bad. I guess I can give it to her. For Michael. I open my mouth and wait for the words to come— they don't mean anything—but they stay stuck inside, like being stuck in a closet with Donnie Henderson, like me being stuck in a room with Donnie Henderson. *It wouldn't be so hard to hide the bruises.*

"You're joking."

"Those are my terms."

My mouth moves, but nothing comes out. I want to hurt her. I want to hurt her for having the balls to ask. Kara smiles and says, "Fine. See you tomorrow."

"Wait—"

They're only words. I'll just say them even though she locked me in a fucking closet with Donnie Henderson. *Don't. Don't freak out. Let her have this.*

"I'm"—*not sorry*—"I—Kara—"

I think of all those notes that are still on my desk and try to inspire the same guilt that came over me when I saw the one from Liz, but it's impossible. Kara is my legacy, and I don't regret that because she deserves everything I did to her, and if she didn't *then*, she does now. I *can't* let her have this.

"This is fascinating," Anna says dryly. "But I'd like to go home now."

"I fucking *hate* you Kara." It explodes from my mouth, and now *I'm* the one trembling, because that's how bad I want to tell her. "You're pathetic, you've always been pathetic, and *everything* I said to you came out of Anna's mouth first. It's *hilarious* that you have so little self-respect you'd get me kicked out of our group so you could hang around the bitch that never gave a damn about you in the first place."

"Blah, blah." Kara opens the car door and gets inside. "This is so over."

But Anna stays where she is. She stares at me in amazement. "You don't know when to give up, do you? Even Liz knew—"

"*Don't* say her name."

"Oh, don't act so hurt," Anna says. "You should've thanked me, Regina. I did it for you. You were *that* important to me."

"You're sick," I say.

"But you're the one who sold Liz out so we could stay friends. You let me drive her to the edge. You never once told me to stop. If I'm sick, what does that make you?"

"That's *your* legacy, Anna. What you did to Liz. No matter what you do next, all everyone in this school is going to remember is that you're a horrible fucking person."

"Like I give a damn what these losers think."

"Kara's lying to you. She's making a fool out of you."

She laughs. "That'll be the day. Anyway, see you tomorrow, Regina."

She gets in the car and burns rubber out of the parking lot.

teenylinks.com/28ccyz

:)

—K

I stare at the e-mail for a half hour, trying to figure out what to do. Kara's fed the original link into a URL alias site. If I click it, it could send me anywhere. And since the link is from Kara, I know I won't walk away from whatever it leads to unscathed. A computer virus, maybe. Skeevy porn or worse—it's total bait.

I have to take it. I back up the computer first. That takes longer than I want it to. The e-mail sits in my inbox the whole time, waiting to be read.

I click the link.

When it takes me to the IH8RA page, I feel a sense of relief. I've seen this stupid page. I almost forget it was there. I've like grown beyond it, and it's—

Grown.

THINGS YOU DIDN'T KNOW REGINA THOUGHT ABOUT YOU AND YOU DIDN'T KNOW ABOUT HER . . . (CLICK HERE TO READ ENTRY)
NEW PHOTOS IN THE PHOTO ALBUM!

The comments are bursting, and every one of them has something to say about the new dirt on me. I search for some kind of indication of what I can expect, because I'm too afraid to click the links. I'll have to, though. If most of the school knows what's behind them, I have to, so when I walk through the doors tomorrow—

I'll know.

One comment steals all the air from my lungs.

I hope she fucking dies.

It's from some freshman I don't really know named Katie Langden.

Someone I don't really know wants me to die.

I scroll up the page and start with the photos. Every embarrassing moment Anna managed to capture on camera is on display. I try to make peace with the fact that at least half of the school has now seen me at my worst. It's okay. Everyone at school has been the person who passed out next to the toilet; they just didn't have Anna hovering over them with a Nikon when they were. Bad hair days. Bad fashion choices. This is ugliness, but it's nothing. It's—totally mortifying.

I click away.

Things You Didn't Know . . .

Click. I stare at my handwriting. My notes. All scanned in. A gallery. Anna's ammunition. I couldn't get them all. I tried. I'd always try to end our notes on stupid, innocuous questions, something she had to answer and send back so I could have them, but sometimes I was careless. . . .

I scroll through them, numb. I'd forgotten the time we tore apart all the girls in our English class. Names down one side, physical flaws down the other. It was a group effort, but I was secretary, so now it gets pinned on me. All the fat thighs, big asses, crater faces, lisps. These girls are still at school, and I have to face them tomorrow.

Guys I'd never sleep with and why. The companion list, also in my handwriting. Written on a boring, sweltering hot day in math class. Ernie Sanders heads it up. Quiet and shy, future astronaut, he tutored me in tenth grade, and my handwriting reduces him to the size—or lack of size—of his penis. I called Carter Anders a Cro-Mag.

I thought it was fun at the time.

Some notes are one-sided conversations, little commentaries on people I didn't know enough to like. No one who looks at the scanned pieces of paper will notice the way they're ripped. Anna's replies, which were always usually more scathing, are hacked off the bottom.

And that's not all: My secrets are there. Precious thoughts I committed to paper and trusted her with because I was stupid. Worrying about my first time. Whether or not it would hurt. How useless I think my parents are. Why I like it in the dark.

I wrote it all down.

I stop breathing. My head pounds. The screen starts to gray out. I didn't actually think you could get so mad you could lose the room, but here I am, gripping the edge of my desk and trying to bring myself back enough so that I can click the Report Abuse link and then—

Fuck a truce. Fuck it.

Revenge comes into my head fully formed, so simple and so perfect I don't know why I didn't think of it before. Anna always said to stay above the hate. She's obsessive about it, because she knows everyone hates her. Don't let them know you know. Don't let them see it on your face. Don't be weak. *Never let them know your weaknesses*.

But I've always known her weaknesses.

I haven't even cooled by the time I've created the fake e-mail and the fake YourSpace account. So easy. My fake name is Alison Raft, and Alison Raft wants to join the IH8RA group. Join, join. Don't get mad, get even.

I have to wait for Kara or whoever heads up the group—it has to be Kara—to approve me. That takes an hour, but I've got the time. As soon as it's done, I find the option that lets me send out a mass

message to the inboxes of every member of my anti-fan club. Everyone in school.

I get to work.

**TOMORROW AT LUNCH REGINA AFTON IS GOING TO GET A BIG
SURPRISE, AND WE NEED YOUR HELP TO MAKE IT HAPPEN!**

That will ensure the e-mail gets opened.

And then I just type. I don't even have to think. I write about
Anna's dad leaving the family for someone twenty years younger
and how Anna had to beg for regular visits. I write about the first
time Kara had sex—a vacation in Cancun. He was ten years older.
The diet pills, the purging, the wig. Everyone knows that, but why
not rehash? And the drunken handjob Anna gave Bruce in the ninth
grade. How she thought he was small. The chastity ring Kara's father
gave her after she lost the weight. How Donnie passed out the first
time he had sex with Anna, because he was so wasted. I write down
every doubt and insecurity, the dumb stuff, the mortifying stuff.
Things I guarded with my life and that don't mean anything to me
anymore. I give it all away for free.

It's crude, simple, and effective.

But the most beautiful thing about it is, this is *nothing* compared
to the work they've put into destroying me. Nothing. I don't even
have to break a sweat. Anna's been so untouched for years that she'll
wake up tomorrow and her world will end.

Thank you, Anna. For being so perfect and so ugly.

I sign my name to the e-mail—my real name—and then I send
it to everyone.

tuesday

When I wake up, I head for the computer first.

The YourSpace page is gone.

My first victory. It may be gone, but the e-mail isn't. It's in everyone's inboxes, waiting to be read. If it hasn't been read already. I can be certain of two people who *did* read it, and the thought turns me into a face full of teeth. I can't wait to go to school and see what I've wrought. Damage control will be spectacular. Anna won't have time to think up ways to retaliate, because she'll be too frantic trying to keep herself above this, recovering her reputation. *If* she can recover it.

What a beautiful *if.*

Michael calls and asks if I want a ride. Yes, a million times *yes.* I get dressed for school and sit at the breakfast table with my parents and I *eat.* A piece of toast dripping with butter. It tastes fantastic. I can't believe how great my stomach feels. I can't believe that's all it took. Next thing, maybe I'll get off the antacids.

I can't wait to see Michael. When I spot his Saturn making its way up the street, I can't even play it cool. I run outside before he pulls into the driveway, and then I jerk the door open and practically throw myself inside.

"Hi," I say.

"Hi," Michael says, surprised. I'm too cheerful, but that's how *good* I feel, how happy I am. I should try to get a hold on it, but I don't want to get a hold on it. I just want to *be* it. He pulls out of the driveway. I'm not sure whether I should tell him now or wait. Wait. It'll be a surprise. I lean across the seat and kiss him.

Michael smiles at me and I look away, biting my lip. I feel sick when Hallowell High comes into sight, but it's a five-minutes-before-curtain kind of sick.

We pull into the parking lot. Michael unbuckles his seatbelt, taking his time, but I can't wait for him. I get out of the car and scope out the entrance. They're not there and I want to squeal. *They aren't there*; the doors are clear. People are free to come and go as they please. *I sent them into hiding.* Me. Wow.

I shrug my book bag over my shoulder, and Michael and I walk into school. I'm five feet past the doors when Chelsea Redcliff grabs my arm. I jerk away and edge close to Michael. Chelsea was the crater face in that long list of girls on the YourSpace page. Or the small chest. I can't remember. She's neither of these things now, but if she's angry, I want someone between us.

"Did you send it? That was really you?"

I nod. "Yeah."

"So it's all true?"

I nod again and she stands there, shocked. If I can't see this moment on Anna's face, this is really the next best thing. I watch Chelsea's mouth quirk as she enjoys this victory for . . . everyone. Michael divides his gaze between both of us.

"You're a total bitch," she says in an admiring tone, and then she hurries into school so she can spread the word: *It was Regina, and it's all true.*

"What was that?" Michael asks when she's gone. I can't find the words to answer him, so I duck my head and make my way down the hall. I'm immediately stared at, which is nothing new, but this is different. Even he notices. "What's going on . . . ?"

Bruce slams into Michael then. Hard. Michael manages to stay upright, but his book bag hits the floor and his books go flying. Before I can tell Bruce he's an asshole, he's on me, pointing fingers, red-faced. And I can't help it: I smile.

"You're a fucking *bitch*, Afton."

He kicks Michael's books, sending them into the lockers. A modest crowd witnesses the whole scene, and soon the halls are buzzing, but the buzzing sounds very, very confused.

"Okay, tell me what's going on," Michael says, shoving the books back into his bag. He catches sight of something beyond me. I half-turn and spot Liz. "Don't make me find out secondhand."

"I did something," I tell him. He doesn't even know what I did, but he gets this look on his face, like it can't be good even though it's good, it's great, it's the best. I open my mouth to tell him, but then before I can answer some sophomore I don't know passes us, pointing me out to some freshman I don't know. "*That's* Regina Afton! Last night—"

This is so awesome.

Five minutes before lunch, I detour into the girls' room and try to get it together. It used to be I had to prep myself not to look so miserable when I walked through the halls.

Now I have to try not to look so high.

It's a total high. I stare at my reflection in the mirrors. I haven't seen myself this happy in ages. I run the water really cold and dab at my face and hands. I'm hot.

One of the stall doors opens and startles me. I bite the inside of my cheek hard to keep the smile off my face. I'd love to smug this out all over school, but I can't. Not yet. And it's Liz, so I don't feel like smiling anymore anyway. She stares at me in the mirror and I turn the water off. I dry my hands and head for the door.

"I can't believe you had it in you," she says at my back.

I pause. "Thanks."

"That wasn't a compliment."

"Nothing I do is good enough for you." I face her. "That's okay. But they got what they deserved."

"And what did *you* deserve?" she asks. "Charie called me and said there was this e-mail in her inbox. Well done, I guess."

"Is that what everyone thinks?" I ask.

"Oh, they still hate you," she says. "But they hate Anna more."

I leave her and go to the cafeteria. The center table is devoid of girls. Josh, Henry, and Bruce are there, trying to uphold what's left of their popularity. Without Anna, they're nothing. I find Michael at the back, as usual.

"They've been dogging me all day," he says, nodding at the guys. I take my seat across from him. "Every time I turn around, one of them is there."

I turn, expecting to see some Sinister Group Glare being leveled at us, but the three of them are hunched over their food.

"Have they said anything to you?" I ask. He shakes his head. "They probably just want to tell Anna they weren't totally useless today."

And then I look again. I can't help it. They're just there, and the table is totally dead, and it's amazing because I did that and no one's ever done that before. I turn back to Michael. The bell separated us before I could find out how he felt about it, and the way he's staring at me, I'm not sure I want to find out.

"Smile," he says after a minute.

"What?"

"I can tell you want to do it," he says.

I flush and look away. "You say that like it's a bad thing." When he doesn't immediately reply, it gets my back up. "They deserve it, Michael. You can't tell me they don't."

"You're going to get your ass kicked," he says.

I can feel eyes on me from every direction, but there's something different about it. Like, maybe they hate me, but I'm cool. It feels cool. This is mine.

"No, I'm not," I say, and then I point. "Look at that table, Michael. I have them."

"But why would you want them?" he asks.

It's not an accusation; it's worse. There's discomfort in his voice and . . . disappointment. It hurts in a weird way because I don't know what that means. *They didn't deserve it?* He can't think that. They deserved it. They *deserve* it. I could do it again and again and again and they'd deserve it each time. For what they did to me.

"Why do you want to make me feel bad about this?"

"I don't," he says. "I just don't get why you have to feel so *good* about it."

"Oh, I'm sorry," I say, "Is this too *Anna* for you?"

He leans forward and says very slowly, "I don't want you to get hurt."

I turn back to the table. Josh is gone. I wonder if he's gone to see her. She won't get her reputation back enough to hurt me. She can't. I ate *breakfast* today. That has to be a good omen. I smile at the thought, and when I turn back to Michael again, he's just looking more and more weirded out. Like it *is* too Anna for him.

The day passes in that odd, tense way a day does when you're with someone who is mad at you and you don't fully understand why. It reminds me of Anna, because she used to do that to all of us a lot. Seize up, freeze out. It was always scary.

I'm mad at Michael for reminding me of that.

Still, somehow, we end up in his room.

We end up in his room on his bed.

But not like that.

We are side by side and quiet. He's on his back, staring at the ceiling, and I'm on my side, staring at him. This is the kind of closeness that comes in at you from all sides, the kind that begs you to move and do something before it traps you and you can't do anything at all. Are we mad at each other? Is this a fight? I take a look around the room. It's as sparse as the rest of the house. There's a photograph of his mother on the wall. It's really strange and sad. All I have of her is a memory in a chair in an office. In this photo, she is every inch a mother. No doctor showing on her. She's sitting at a picnic table smiling at a man. Michael's father, maybe. She looks happy.

"I'm sorry," I tell him.

He turns to me. "What?"

"I made things really bad for you."

"My mom died," he says. "Things were already bad."

"I just made them worse."

It's quiet for a long time.

"Yeah."

He reaches over and his hand drifts up my side until it reaches my face, and then his palm is on my chin, but he's hesitant, and I feel bad. I understand it.

But I don't want to understand it.

"Don't be mad at me," I say. "It was the only way it could have happened."

"Really?" he asks, and before I can say anything, he runs his thumb over my lips and I close my eyes. My eyes are still closed when he kisses me. And then he stops, and when I open my eyes, the same close-distance that was between us before is there again.

I sit up and stare out the window, my back to him. Michael's bedroom overlooks the street. His house is a strange quiet. There's no calm in it, just this total emptiness. I watch the wind stir the last of some leaves off a tree across the road.

"Where's your dad?" I ask. "What does he do? He's never home. . . ."

"Lawyer."

"Why didn't you tell your mom about what we did to you?" I turn to him. "You didn't know I was seeing her. You could've told her."

"She listened to people for a living."

"Do you wish you'd told her?"

He shrugs. "I started keeping that journal. It's—"

He doesn't finish, but I know what he's not saying. It makes him feel closer to her. I think of him carrying it everywhere. School. His car. Home. Writing incessantly just to make some kind of connection to a dead woman. His mom.

"I'm sorry," I say again. "But I'm glad I did it to them."

"Okay," he says. It's not enough.

"What do you think?" I ask him. "They deserved it, right?"

"I think . . ." he trails off. "I think some girls are just . . . fucked up."

He eases himself across the bed. He doesn't say he's not—that he's not mad at me or that it's not weird anymore. He might be. It is. So I reach out and push his hair back from his face, and then he kisses me again, and it's like he just lets it go, just for this.

I think.

He kisses my neck and he kisses my mouth. We curl up on his bed together, a tangle of arms and legs. His hand slides up my shirt, and I kiss him and I kiss him again.

I'm not one of those girls.

wednesday

The Formerly Fearsome Foursome is still nowhere to be found for the second day in a row. They're just gone. I'm still dying to see it on their faces, but I'll settle for this not-insignificant change to the landscape. Michael and I separate at the front doors.

"See you at lunch," he tells me, heading down the hall.

When I get to my locker, there's a note tucked in it. I know who it's from instantly. Anna or Kara. Some small part of me is excited to get it, because no matter what it says, they sent it from a place that is now officially beneath me.

I set my bag down, grab the note, and unfold it. But it's not from Anna.

Or Kara.

The handwriting isn't immediately familiar to me. It's a single line on a piece of paper that has a photocopied quality about it.

I hate it here.

Michael.

His name floats into my head for no reason at all.

I turn, expecting to find him behind me. He's not. But—

Oh.

I try to work it out. Why do I have this. Why was it in my locker.

At first, I think it's a gift from him. Something so important and private—he wants me to see it, wants to share it, but he wouldn't, not even now, because that's . . . his mom. I flip the page over and see another line scrawled across the back:

Underneath the water fountain outside of Hartnett's.

The handwriting is deliberately warped.

This isn't bad. Not yet. I crumple the paper and rush for Hartnett's room. I'm halfway down the hall when I realize I've left my book bag sitting in front of my locker, but I don't care. The bell feels like it could go soon, so I leave it.

This is more important.

Ellen Pines is taking the longest drink of her life when I finally reach the fountain, and my head is pounding, swimming. I wait and wait and I'm about to shove her out of the way, when she stands, wipes her mouth, and goes. I run my hand along the porcelain underside until I find the next piece of paper taped to it.

I rip it off and unfold it.

I think I liked being an Unstable Freak better before she died.
I hate everyone in this school, but I want to tell them about her.

I somehow manage to keep the guilt that's invading every space inside of me from turning into tears. This is so private. I flip the paper over and it directs me to the fountain outside of Holt's office. No one's there. I rip the note off and unfold it. I don't want to read it. But I do.

These people all look the same. They walk the same, wear the same type of clothes, talk the same. Nothing that comes out of their mouths is important.
These people are wasters.

It leads me to the fountain on the second floor. It's bad.

I'm the antichrist with the anger-management problem. That's the latest.
Everyone here is afraid. It's sort of amazing in a really dumb way. Liz says it's her fault. I like Liz. She's better than most of what's walking the halls.

I shove my hand into my pocket and find an antacid, and then I shove it into my mouth and chew. The next note sends me back to the fountain on the first floor, right by the entrance. I unfold it.

I hate it here.

Even the poor quality of the photocopy can't hide how hard Michael wrote these words. The ink bleeds out, stressed edges around the final sentence. I can't picture him this way. Hurt and angry and ready to explode—like me. He worked so hard to make sure no one ever saw it. At the fountain beside the lab, the next paper reads this:

I need a reason.

I close my eyes and flip the note over. Open them.

Storage room off the gym

The bell rings. I make a run for it. The storage room off the gym. Michael's journal. They have Michael's journal. They dogged him all day yesterday. Why didn't I pay attention? I should've known. *I should've known.* When I reach the storage room, there's one last note taped to the door. I rip it off. I don't need to read it.

I push the door open.

Anna.

"Where's the notebook?" I demand.

"Close the door, Regina," she says calmly. "We need to talk."

"Give me the fucking notebook *now*, Anna."

"It's already back in Michael's hands. He didn't even know it was gone. Now close the door, Regina, so we can talk."

I close the door. "Give me the photocopies then."

She crosses her arms and looks me up and down slowly. That look. Like I'm not good enough to be acknowledged by her. Even after all this. And then the reality of the situation hits me full on, sinking into my bones, making me step back. I don't understand how she's standing here and looking at me like—

"How—" I can't even finish the question.

"You really didn't think I'd just sit around and stare at my hands, did you? Just let you have it?" Anna raises an eyebrow. "That's more *your* style, Regina."

I shake my head. "No—"

"I would've gotten bored with you by now if you'd backed off. I can spray-paint your locker, lock you in storage rooms, ruin your things, broadcast your secrets all over the Internet, and I can make everyone hate you twice as much as they used to, and you *still* haven't learned." She cocks her head to the side. "Right after your e-mail went out, I started brainstorming. That's the trick: Don't waste time. I

wanted to figure out how to bury you so far into the ground, you'd *finally* get it *and* never bother me again. Except it was harder than I thought it'd be, because the problem with you is you don't seem to care about what happens to you anymore."

I bite the inside of my cheek so hard there's blood. I let the coppery taste reach my tongue and focus on it. Anna has Michael's journal.

She has his journal.

"I was stumped, but then Josh said you'd probably care about what happened to Michael. I guess . . . he's the best thing that's ever happened to you?" She grins, laughing a little as she watches my own words turn my face a ghostly shade of white. "So cute."

"Anna, don't—"

"And *then*," she says over me, "Josh reminded me about Michael's notebook that he always carries around. His journal?"

"Anna—"

"First, I thought we should try to get our hands on it, because maybe there was something in it about *you* we could use. I was skeptical that Hayden had anything interesting to say, but after Bruce got it . . ." She laughs. "And what kind of moron leaves their *journal* in their *car*, by the way? Anyway, after Bruce got it, I was riveted from page one. Michael's very sensitive, did you know?"

"That's a trait you find in people who have souls," I manage.

Her face changes. She's angry, still smarting from what I did to her.

"And how do you think he'd feel if the contents of his *soul* were plastered all over this school? Do you think that would bother him? Given everything he's written, I think it'd bother me, if I were him. He doesn't have much good to say about the people in this school."

"So? Michael doesn't care what people here think of him."

"But would he care if they knew he was so distraught about his dead mother he wanted to die? Like, kill himself? Not that he ever came right out and *said* it, but it's there. It's so obvious."

My brain tries to process Michael that far gone and alone because of—me. And I knew it. It's not like Liz ever told me, but when it's vague, when no one's telling you exactly what you did, it's different. It makes it easier.

"Seriously!" Anna says, relishing the stunned look on my face. "I mean, even *I* didn't think he was *that* depressed! He hid it well, huh? Not like Liz. I always got this vibe from her."

"This is a new low, Anna, even for you."

"Well, I don't *want* to do it, but—"

"I'll tell him. I'll just tell him. No fun for you if I get there first—"

"You tell him and I'll take *this* to Holt." Anna digs into her pocket and hands me another folded piece of paper. I don't want it, but she keeps her hand out until I take it. "*That* was my favorite entry."

My hands are shaking. I don't want her to see them shaking. I have to wait until I feel steady enough to read it.

It's a single line.

I want to kill everyone in this stupid school.

"You don't even need to read between the lines for *that* one," Anna says. "No room for interpretation. It's sort of poetic, isn't it? '*I want to kill everyone in this stupid school.*' Strong sentiment. Dangerous sentiment."

I swallow. "So?"

"The first half of his journal is basically about a crazy, depressed boy with a dead mother who hates everyone in this school so much he wants to *kill* them. In this post-Columbine age, you know the rules, Reg." She nods at the paper. "We're supposed to report any warning signs we see. His journal is officially grounds for expulsion . . . probably a hell of a lot of therapy. They could put him away for this."

"No—he's not—I know Michael and he's not—"

He's not like that anymore.

"*You* know Michael," she points out. "Nobody else here does. In fact, what everyone here *thinks* they know about Michael pretty much supports the kind of picture I'm painting. And whose fault is that, by the way? Oh, right. Yours. Well, and mine. But I'll let you take most of the credit for that one."

"He didn't do anything to you," I choke out.

"Well, at first I thought I might be pushing it," she agrees, "but it turns out Michael's not my biggest fan. It's all in his journal. I'm destined to be a future trophy wife who's catatonic all the time because I'm always on pills to dull the pain of my life."

I go completely numb. My pulse stops spazzing, my heart stills.

I stare at the paper in my hand.

I want to kill everyone in this stupid school.

"What do you want?" I ask slowly.

She sighs. "Definitely not a truce. You don't get away with what you did to me. You get to suffer for it."

"Just tell me."

"We're reconciling!" She claps her hands. "That's what everyone gets to think! Anna and Regina—best friends again! Can you imagine the looks on everyone's faces when we walk into school together tomorrow? Any respect you earned from your YourSpace e-mail stunt will be instantly gone, and everyone will be so distracted by this insane turn of events, they'll forget all about it. They'll think I must be pretty good if I can get *you* back into the fold, and let's face it, I am. And you—" She grins. "You, Regina, will act like you love it."

I'm shaking my head *no*, but she just keeps talking.

"But really, I'll own you, and Michael is dead to you. You will drop him, with no explanations, nothing. He'll have to sit there trying to figure it out until he gives up and hates you all over again."

I'll tell him.

I'll get out of this storage room and I'll tell him.

Anna studies me. It must be all over my face, because she says, "If I think you've tipped him off, I'll plaster his journal all over school and take it to Holt. If you refuse to drop him, I'll do the same."

My heart stills. Expulsion. Those pages all over school. His grief. His secrets. His ruin. I can't let that happen.

"That means whatever happens to Michael is your fault," Anna says, reading my mind. "And even if he *does* find out the truth, do you think he'd forgive you for putting him through this bullshit? He's already forgiven you for a lot. It wasn't easy for him to be with you, you know. He put that in his journal, too."

"He did?" I whisper.

Anna closes her eyes briefly, basking in this moment. This is Anna at her finest. This is the Anna everyone is afraid of. The Anna I'm afraid of.

She opens her eyes. "Didn't you read the entry I taped to the door?"

I clench my hands into fists. "I hate you so much."

"You did it to yourself." She nudges me out of the way to get to the door and hesitates. "He's really sweet, though, isn't he? Anyway, I'll see you tomorrow."

I dig into my pocket for the entry she was talking out. I unfold it and read it.

And then I start to cry.

Weird month. The kind of emotional evolution she'd be proud of.
It's hard, but—I like her. I think it's going to be good.

The bell rings. I leave the storage room and keep walking until I'm pushing my way through the front doors. I can't risk Michael seeing me like this, because he'll ask and I'll be weak and I'll tell him, and then Anna will find out and ruin him again, and I can't do that to him, I can't, I can't, *I can't.* I hit the parking lot, gasping, aching. Stupid, ugly tears, all over my face.

I *almost* had them.

I've never felt a more painful miss in my life.

I go home.

Anna calls nine hours later.

"Skirt and cardigans tomorrow," she says. "Thought you'd want to know."

thursday

Skirts and cardigans.

My throat is all closed up. I try to swallow down my morning coffee and I try to take an antacid but I can't do either, and my parents are just sitting there, and I can't stand it, and I don't know what to do with myself, so I head for school.

My outfit feels stiff and gross, and I can't stop picturing his face when he sees me in it—a fashion clone. The school parking lot is completely empty. I position myself in front of the doors and wait, the familiarity of it suffocating me, until I find myself inside, in the washroom, hunched over a toilet, dry heaving.

Because there's nothing in my stomach to puke up.

I lean against the door and press a shaking hand against my mouth. I could cry, but I'm afraid if I start, I won't stop. I shove an antacid in my mouth and chew it and then try to get it down with a little spit. I can't do this.

I can't do this.

Those four words over and over again in my head while time creeps by and the school fills. School noises leech in through the walls, and it eats me up. I take a deep breath and fumble with the door, but I can't open it.

The bell rings. I miss my grand entrance.

I stay in the stall.

I'm going to stay in this stall. I wedge myself against the door, close my eyes, and I stay still until I'm uncomfortable, and even then I don't move.

If I'm not moving, nothing bad is happening.

Every so often people come in, and then the bell rings again and there's that surge before the next period. I listen to girls talk at the sinks, over stalls, and they peter out, and it's quiet again. It stays quiet for a long time, until the door opens and I hear footsteps cut across the room. A stall door is pushed open and then another and another, until it's the one next to mine, and then it's mine. But I've locked it and it doesn't give.

"Get out." It's Marta. "Now."

"No," I say.

"Okay, let's end this now." Kara. "Anna keeps those pages really close, Regina."

I open the door. Marta and Kara exchange a glance and a smile. I catch sight of my reflection in the mirror. My skin looks waxy, pale.

"Lunch in five," Kara says.

I push past them and head straight for the sink. I run the tap hot and then cold.

"Great," I say.

"I want you to walk behind me," Kara says. "From this point on. Just walk behind me, and don't talk to me unless I address you first."

Marta laughs. "Kara!"

"You heard Anna," Kara says. "We own her. Hurry the fuck up, Regina. We've waited long enough."

I grip the edges of the sink. "Give me a second."

"Now."

I run the water as hard as it will go.

". . . Let her have her second," Kara finally mutters. They leave me at the sink. My second turns into a minute, and then another. The door opens again. Anna.

"You've had your *second*," she spits. I turn off the tap and we leave the washroom. Jeanette's there with the others. As the five of us make our way down the hall together, Anna leans over. "I'm so glad you chickened out this morning, Regina. A lunchtime entrance will be better. *Everyone* will see it."

It isn't until we're at the door to the cafeteria that I begin to register the people around us. They're whispering and pointing, and then I remember our outfits, totally completing this nightmare. I glance at the other girls and it's skirts and cardigans all the way down. I roll my shoulders and try to get the dirty feeling off me, but I can't.

I take a deep breath and enter the cafeteria with them.

It's not like everyone notices at once. There's no awed hush as we make our way to the center table. The room is buzzing the way it usually is, until the realization *Regina Afton is back in* hits the left side, and there's a subtle shift, the frequency changes, and makes its way back across the cafeteria. I feel lightheaded, and my neck is so tense when I turn my head to look at the Garbage Table, I'm afraid it'll snap.

Michael's oblivious. It hasn't reached him yet. I'm comforted by this, like it buys me time—for what, I don't know—

But then he looks up.

His eyes travel over Anna and Kara, and when they get to me, there's this flicker, something torn between recognition—*I know that girl*—and total incomprehension: *What is she doing over there?* Anna jostles me over to the center table, but I can't look away from him, until his mouth drops open and then I have to.

Josh, Henry, and Bruce are already at the table, dutifully waiting for us girls. It's so horribly familiar, I wander to the seat next to Josh, where I used to sit, before Anna pulls me back.

"Best friends should sit together," she says.

She takes my old seat and settles in next to Josh. His lunch tray is fixed up for two. He slides her half over and gives her a kiss on the cheek. Anna points to the seat between her and Bruce, and I sit down. Being this close to Bruce is disgusting and recalls the smell of the supply closet, which sends my gut into a somersault routine. I try to ignore it and take a slow look around the table. Josh's expression is unreadable, or he just doesn't care. Marta is picking at her fingernails, waiting for a cue from a higher-up. Jeanette is giving the straw in her juice box head, hoping Henry will notice. He does. Kara's oddly somber. I thought she'd enjoy this more. A lot more.

Anna unwraps a granola bar and looks at me. "Aren't you eating?"

"No."

"Eat."

"Anna, if you make me eat, I will puke all over you."

"Then at least smile. Let everyone know how happy you are to be here."

I force a smile at her and the right side of my mouth starts twitching. I feel Michael's eyes on me now the most. I really, really don't want to see his face.

"Well." Bruce leans back. "If you're not eating, Regina, I need a drink. I'm sure Kara and Marta could use one, too. Why don't you run up there and get us some Coke?"

"That'd be nice," Marta says. "On Regina."

"I don't have my wallet."

Bruce digs into his pocket and tosses a bill at me. "Get it, girl."

I stare at the money.

"Go," Anna says. "And don't forget to smile."

I grab the bill, push my chair out, and stand. I make the biggest, most painful close-mouthed smile I can muster, and then I'm in a long lineup. Smiling.

"What are you doing?"

My heart goes into overdrive. Michael. Right next to me in this line. I keep my eyes on the menu tacked to the wall, still smiling. I can't look at him or I'll give it away. If I give it away, he is fucked. So the only thing I can think to do is pretend that he's not here. I stare straight ahead.

"It's a joke, right?" The line moves up. "Regina."

"We had a good talk yesterday," I say. The line moves up again. I want it to go faster. I can feel the center table. All their eyes on me. "We're friends again."

"I don't believe you."

"She finally believed me about Donnie," I say distractedly. The line moves up again, and I rub the back of my neck. I blink once, twice, three times. *Don't cry, don't cry, don't cry.* "So it's okay."

"I don't believe you," he repeats. "Not after yesterday." I reach the cash register and ask for three Cokes. He keeps talking. "Why are you doing this? You're wearing the same outfits—"

The lunch lady hands me the drinks. I hand her the bill.

"Go away, Michael," I say.

Anna "rescues" me then. She wraps an arm around me, and I try to act like it's a welcome move by forcing my third smile of the day. At her.

"What's going on?"

"Nothing." I hand her one of the Cokes and shove the change in my pocket. "Come on, let's take these back."

"We're talking," Michael says.

"We're done."

"We're talking."

"No, we're not."

I push past him. Anna is on my heels, her voice in my ear:

"You didn't tell him, did you?"

"Does he look like I told him?"

"No," she says, glancing over her shoulder. "He actually looks pretty devastated."

At the end of the day, I know Michael's going to be waiting for me in his car. He'll trail me home and he'll try to get me to talk. I'm so desperate to avoid it, I ask Anna for a ride home and she laughs in my face, so I have to detour down the main street and then detour into Ford's, where I buy three packs of antacids.

Michael calls. It's the first time he's ever called. I don't answer. And then Anna calls and tells me yellow. Tomorrow we'll be wearing yellow.

I can't eat my dinner.

I skip breakfast and head to school, because I don't want to risk running into Michael. I stake out a spot at the front door and wait for the rest of the group to show, just like old times. It takes about thirty minutes. Kara's first to show. She stands next to me, quiet. I just want to kill her.

"Don't get comfortable," she says.

I turn to her. "What?"

"Don't get comfortable," she repeats slowly. "This was Anna's idea, but I'd rather see you dead after that e-mail than pretend we're friends for the rest of the year, no matter how miserable it makes you. I'm not done with you, so don't get comfortable."

It never stops.

"Don't tempt me, Kara."

"Watch your back, Regina."

"Go fuck yourself, Kara."

Jeanette and Marta bound up to us—to Kara—then. I put a little space between us. Waiting for Anna is hell on my stomach, and I've taken three antacids by the time she arrives, wearing one of the lowest cut tops I've ever seen. Marta whistles.

"I hope you don't plan on bending over today."

"Only in front of Josh," she replies, grinning.

Michael's car pulls into the parking lot before I can roll my eyes at what she's said. My stomach twinges. "Let's go in. Please."

Anna spots him. "No."

I watch him make his way toward the school. It doesn't really hurt yet, seeing him but not being near him. I think I'm still in shock. I hunch my shoulders and edge closer to Anna, like that'll make me invisible, but she notices and steps away from me.

When Michael reaches us, he keeps walking.

"He cannot have gotten over it that fast," Anna says, watching him go. "You didn't tell him, did you? Because if you did—"

"No! I didn't—I haven't talked to him at all. He called me last night and I didn't even pick up. I didn't tell him, Anna, I swear—"

"I know you didn't." She grins. "I just wanted to see you squirm."

"Bitch."

Kara, Marta, and Jeanette gasp.

We're all wearing yellow.

I walk away. Anna calls me back. I keep walking. I'm shoving my hands into my pockets, popping two antacids. I stop on the second floor and lean against a row of lockers. They won't find me here for a couple of minutes. But Liz does. Liz finds me. When she walks into my line of vision, I groan.

"What were they offering?" she asks.

"Liz, go away," I say.

"Michael asked me if I knew anything," she says. "He thinks you have a reason. Like he really thinks that what you're doing right now *doesn't* make sense."

"Anna wanted to be friends again," I say. "I can spend the rest of my year getting locked in closets or I can be friends with *Michael*. And you should be happy. You didn't want me anywhere near him."

"You're a bitch," she says.

"Hey, self-preservation. Don't blame me because you and Michael were too stupid to figure it out and got hurt."

"This is so shocking," she says sarcastically. "But once a coward . . ."

I can't wait until I'm too dead inside to feel this. I leave her there. I make my way to my locker. Josh, Anna, and Henry are there, and all of a sudden I can't see. I can't see, I can't breathe. I turn before they see me. I'm halfway down the hall from them when the bell rings and I realize I need my books for class.

I head back to my locker, and they're still there. I shove Josh aside and fumble with my lock. I don't say a word. They don't say a word to me.

Because I just have to be a part of this scene. Not belong to it.

"Come on," Anna is saying, squeezing Josh's shoulder, nearly falling out of her top. Josh gets all disappointed when she doesn't. "One more party."

"I don't know. It's getting kind of cold out."

"That's what the bonfire's for," Henry says.

Josh punches him in the arm. "You just want to get wasted."

"I don't need an excuse," Henry replies. "But I *do* like getting wasted in a group setting." He belches. "I refuse to accept that last monstrosity of a party as *the* last party of the season."

"Seriously." Anna eyes me. "Come on, Josh. This weekend. You said—"

"Can't," Josh replies. "My dad's here this weekend, and I need to get some of his prescriptions and restock first. I mean, if you want it to be a really *good* party . . ."

The bell rings. They trail down the hall. When they're about twenty steps away from me, Anna notices I'm not trailing after them. She stops. Turns. Snaps her fingers. Points to the empty space beside her.

"Regina," she says. "Here."

My only solace is the weekend.

It comes.

And then it goes.

My YourSpace revenge is dead in the water. Anna's scheme works better than even she anticipated; the re-formation of the Fearsome Five-some distracts everyone for a second and settles too quickly. Every-one in this school has seen me stand beside Anna before.

It's new, but it's old.

Gym.

Nelson is dividing us into teams for basketball when I start feel-ing not right. I take an antacid before I realize it's not my stomach—it's my head. It doesn't feel attached to my neck, and then it does, and then I'm very aware of a slow-building pressure behind my eyes that threatens to become the kind of headache that will make me vomit—or would, if there was anything in my stomach to vomit up.

I raise my hand. Nelson points at me. "What it is, Afton?"

"Can I be excused?" I ask. "I don't feel well."

I wish I could take it back. The whole class hears it. That's Anna, that's Michael, that's Kara, that's Josh, that's Donnie. I don't want them looking at me, and now they are. Nelson studies me, and I must look bad because she doesn't run me through the usual twenty questions reserved for suspected fakers.

"Hayden," she says. Michael looks up. "Escort your friend to the nurse's office."

It's like someone dumped a bucket of ice down my shirt. Michael crosses the gym. My eyes meet Anna's. She gives me a warning look. And a smirk.

"So let's go," he says.

Nelson resumes splitting the class, and Michael and I make our way out. The throbbing in my head gets worse. When we hit the hall, I focus on the quiet and pray it stays, but it doesn't. Of course it doesn't. He wants answers.

"What do they have on you?"

I exhale slowly. I don't know whether to feel really good or bad that he doesn't believe I'd do that to him. It makes it harder, either way.

"They don't have anything on me," I say.

"You look like hell."

"Thanks."

He grabs me by the arm. "You were so happy to be rid of them and now you're *friends* again? Bullshit. What do they have on you?"

"I *said* they don't have anything on me—"

"They have to," he says, desperate. I can see the hurt building, and my stomach isn't having it. "You wouldn't be doing this to me if they didn't have something on you—"

"I—" I focus on the poster tacked to the wall behind his head. A bedraggled kitten is clinging to a tree branch. *Hang in there!* I can't think around my headache. "I told you. Anna found out that it was true about Donnie, that Kara lied, so she's—she felt terrible about it. So—we're friends again."

"You can barely *lie*," he says. I start protesting halfheartedly, because I really don't feel well. It makes it easy for him to talk over me. "If that's the truth, then what about Kara? Anna wouldn't let Kara get away with that."

Goddammit. If he were Jeanette or Marta he would've bought it by now. I'm not making friends with people who are smart, from this point on. Ever again.

"Tell me," he begs.

"I told you. We're friends again. I told Liz—"

"You didn't mean what you said to Liz."

"It doesn't *matter*, Michael," I burst out. "Because whatever it is, even after everything between us, I still weighed it—them or you—and I didn't choose you. I knew how hard it was for you to choose me, and I *still picked them*. I mean, that's basically picking their bullshit over you, right? I didn't choose you, and I totally wasted your time, so even if they *do* have something on me, *it doesn't matter*."

It's a hit. Finally. He flinches like I've slapped him and takes a step back.

"I put myself out there for you," he says slowly. "I can't believe I—"

"I needed someone to put between me and Anna, and you probably never even really liked me." I dig the knife further in, but I'm not sure I need to. "You were really lonely, and I was there after a long time of no one being there."

He takes another step back. "You—"

I wish he would shout at me. He doesn't. This quiet devastation creeps across his face and he fights it, and it reminds me of that day in the diner, and I feel like my heart is breaking. But it's still not as bad as what Anna will do to him if I tell him the truth.

"I should have known," he finally says, and I wince because he was the best thing that ever happened to me. He takes another step back. "Easy way out, every single time. Liz told me—*fuck*—I can't believe I let you do this to me *twice*."

I can't wait for him to go, so I go.

By the time I reach the washroom, my head is killing me, and the disgusting fluorescent lights overhead makes it feel worse. I gag over the sink, but nothing comes out. I lean forward and take deep, even breaths in and out, and then I run the water as cold as it will go, cupping my hands together for a drink. It doesn't help. I wet a paper towel, sit on the floor—gross—and press it against my eyes.

After a while, the paper towel loses its chill, but I can't find the will to get up and wet it again. Michael hates me. He hates me. I start to cry, keeping the paper towel against my eyes and letting it soak up my tears. When the door swings open, I can't inspire myself to care. Getting up and trying to act okay is so beyond me right now.

"Oh, Regina."

Anna's voice is motherly. Awful. I keep the towel against my eyes. She crosses the room and sits beside me. She presses something crumbly and dry into my hands. I look down. An oatmeal cookie. I blink and take in the room. Anna's beside me. Kara's leaning against the door, ensuring no one will come in.

I don't care if Anna sees me cry, but Kara . . .

I wipe at my eyes with my free hand.

"Eat," Anna urges me. I shake my head. She grabs me by the chin and makes me look at her. "Come on. I don't make you *that* sick. Eat or else."

That whole year she thought I was starving myself—after Kara actually *did* starve herself—she used that voice. *Eat.* I take a bite of the cookie and revive a little at the food in my mouth. My stomach doesn't want it. I clamp my hand over my mouth.

It takes forever to swallow.

"Kara, wait outside," Anna says, when I finally do.

"What? No way. I want to see this."

"Wait outside *now.*"

Kara knows better than to argue. She yanks the door open and steps into the hall.

"Talk to Michael?" Anna asks me. I nod. "Did it hurt?"

The last three words set me off. My face crumples and I bring my knees up to my chest, burying my face in them.

"So now you know exactly how I felt when I found out you slept with Donnie."

"Jesus *Christ*, Anna. I didn't fucking sleep with Donnie. He tried to—"

"Don't. *Shut. Up.* Listen to me: All that time I thought you were my best friend," she says. "You were like a sister to me. Now, thanks to Michael's journal, I find out I just made you sick. This will *never* get better for you, okay? I want you to understand what you ruined and how good you had it." She tucks an errant strand of hair behind my ear. I jerk away. "And then . . . I want you to be sorry."

"I'm sorry," I tell her desperately. "Anna, *I'm sorry*."

"No, you're not," she says. "I'll let you know."

tuesday

"Look at this," Anna says as Jeanette, Marta, and Kara cluster around her. We've finished gym. Fresh out of the showers and in the changing rooms. Anna is holding up a thin silver chain with a silver pendant dangling off it. "Just because. That's what he said."

It's like partying all night with people you hate and bypassing home to go straight to your job so you can work all day with more people you hate.

And never stopping.

"Ooh, my God," Jeanette says softly, cupping it in her palm. Anna grins, beside herself with squeally-girl joy. "You know what that means, right? Sex."

And it does, too. I have something similar abandoned in a jewelry box at home. And the five of us talked about what that meant when Josh gave it to me then. This is a special kind of hell—listening to my ex–best friend wax about fucking my ex-boyfriend. I get dressed as slowly as possible so I can avoid walking down the hall with them, but it's a give-and-take. I have to listen to this stupid babbling until they go.

I stare at Anna until she notices and sets the necklace back against her neck. I can't resist: "Doesn't it bother you at all that whatever you do with Josh, I did first?"

"Anything you do, I do better."

"There's a learning curve," I tell her.

"Go to hell."

"Oh, I'm there."

"Speaking of hell," Marta interjects, "has anyone seen Donnie lately? He's lost like, twenty pounds. He looks like a piece of shit."

"He must be good enough for you now, Kara," I say, pulling on my pants. "Maybe he's desperate enough to have you."

"I wouldn't touch your castoffs with a thirty-foot pole," she snaps. "I have some standards."

There's always something amazing about watching people fuck themselves over. We all realize what Kara's said at the exact same moment. Anna's jaw drops, and Kara's face goes from peach to pale in two seconds flat. If I could guarantee she did something this stupid every day, getting up in the morning would be infinitely easier.

"*What* did you say?"

Kara spews apologies. They dribble from her mouth and fall on deaf ears.

"Anna, I'm sorry—I am so, so sorry. I didn't mean it like that. I'm sorry—"

"Because Josh is Regina's castoff, isn't he, so—"

"I'm *sorry*! That was at Regina, it wasn't at you—"

"Fuck off, Kara."

Silence. This is the kind of silence that used to make me so uncomfortable and queasy to be in the middle of and grateful to not be on the receiving end of.

I like it today.

The rest of the girls get dressed quietly and leave when the bell rings. I pull my shirt on and then I leave, too. As soon as I step into the busy halls, I feel weight, pressure. My chest tightens and it's, like—grief. Everywhere.

I pull the collar of my shirt into my mouth and bite and try to get through the moment. I don't know that I *can* get through this moment.

I need to see who I'm doing this for.

I stake out Michael's locker. He's been avoiding me and hanging

out with Liz, which makes sense. I've only glimpsed him in the
halls, and I can't stare at him at lunch too long because Anna gets off
on it when I do, and I'm afraid he'll look back and I will finally
break. After a couple minutes, he shows. He looks as unaffected as
he always does, and I try to talk myself out of this loss, but I can't. I
hope he's angry. I hope he hates me, because then he can have that
and it'll carry him through.

"That's really obvious," a voice says beside me.

I close my eyes briefly. "Go away, Josh."

"Anna told me to tell you." He points down the hall, where Anna's with Bruce and Kara and Marta and Jeanette. She smiles and
waves. "You're being really obvious."

Michael looks up and spots us both. I swallow down the bile
making its way up my throat and turn to Josh. "Nice necklace you
gave Anna. I totally still have mine. That means sex, right?"

Josh scratches the back of his neck. "And I'm totally not comfortable having this conversation with my ex-girlfriend. And why the
hell should you care? At least I waited until *after* we broke up before
I decided to screw other people."

"Fuck you."

"Anyway, the lady beckons." He takes me by the arm and forces
me down the hall, smiling at Anna as we approach. As soon as he's
close enough, he moves away from me, wraps his arm around her,
and gives her a light kiss on the lips. Barf.

"Dad's-out-of-town-Thursday," he says, kissing her between
words. She's putty in his hands. "I've restocked. It's short notice
and I'd rather it be a weekend, but this is our only chance, and the
weather's supposed to be good, so . . . party. My house."

"I like the way you think." She grins.

Josh turns to the hall, projecting his voice and silencing the
idle chatter around us. "Party at my house Thursday. Got that?" He
points to a pair of juniors. "Get the word out. Last one this season."
He turns back to Anna and kisses her on the nose. "You will be there,
of course."

"Of course." She giggles. He smiles and marches down the hall, the boys trailing after him. They stop to tell anyone who's someone about the party.

Anna turns to us, and she has this stupid, stupid look on her face. "Oh, my God, I can't wait." And then it's like, this group squeal that I don't take part of. She notices this and takes offense. "Oh, and Regina? You're coming. Designated driver."

Kara snickers. "Try not to get almost raped this time, okay?"

Die. They laugh. The bell rings. We make our way down the hall, jostling through the crowd until we reach the top of the stairs. *She has to die.*

"Watch it," Kara says, jamming her elbow into my side.

I don't even think about it: My foot slips in front of hers, sending her tumbling down the stairs. A shocked noise passes my lips. I can't believe I did it, but I'm glad I did, until her fall is interrupted by a group of stair-loitering freshman. I stand at the top of the stairs and watch Anna, Marta, and Jeanette rush to her. I read Kara's lips: *I'm fine, I'm fine.* She shrugs them off and looks my way. She knows.

"I hope it's worth it."

I turn. Michael. And the way he says it is so damning, so disgusted.

"It's worth it," I whisper.

It's for him. He shakes his head and walks away. I force myself down the stairs and past Anna and everyone while they're distracted. I don't feel like going straight to an empty house, so I wander around town for a while.

Almost every place in Hallowell is the same kind of unremarkable, except for Josh's place. I stay away from that side of town and turn onto Hainsworth. Jeanette lives here. Donnie. I can see his home from here. It's all gray siding with a weak garden out front, but every little bit of it is immaculately kept.

And his black convertible is in the center of it all.

He found it.

I take a quick look around. The place looks empty. I approach the house, his car, and I take it all in. It should be fantastic. I should love the ugly lines I made down his convertible. I should love that everyone else can see them, too. I should love that there's a crack down the windshield that wasn't there before. I don't.

It makes me miss Michael.

I circle the car, and when I return to the scratches, I reach out. I want to see what that kind of damage feels like. I press my fingers against the metal body.

The front door bursts open.

"Get the fuck away from my car."

"I told you it'd turn up," I say.

Donnie stands there, raging on the steps. I edge over to the front of the car and bring my hand to the windshield. Baiting him should feel good. It doesn't.

"Get away from my car," he repeats. I run my hand over the fresh crack on the windshield. "Stop it."

I trace the line in the glass down to the windshield wipers.

"Stop—"

"Oh, sorry, *you* want *me* to *stop*? Hey, tell Anna. Go and tell Anna that you tried to rape me. Tell her."

His mouth hangs open, like he can't decide to step forward or back into the house, and I hate the silence, so I kick the convertible as hard as I can.

"*Afton*—"

"That's what you get, Donnie." I kick it again. "For what you did to me."

He turns purple-faced and makes his way over to me. A car rolls down the street, slowing as it passes. I take the opportunity to move out, and when I glance back, he's heading back inside his house, slamming the door shut behind him.

I glance at the clock on my nightstand. Eight-thirty. Probably everyone is well on their way to wasted. Designated driver.

Boring.

I used to really hate the last party of the season, even if I drank until I was blind. They were always bigger. Louder. More drinks, dancing, drugs, fucking, more fucking around. Last year, Henry totaled his car while driving home. He broke his collarbone.

I change into a black hoodie and jeans—incognito. Running into Anna is inevitable, but I don't have to make it easy for her to spot me.

"I think it's nice," Mom says as I make my way to the door. I stop and turn to her. She smiles. "That you and Josh can still be friends. Have fun at the party."

"Yeah," I say.

When I reach Josh's house, instant sensory overload. Too many sights, sounds, and smells. It's chilly out, but all the bodies give the illusion of warmth. I pass these crazy girls dancing on the front lawn. They're in the moment, and the moment is them, and the moment is perfect. The party is here and it's perfect. Music. Cars. Friends.

I'm not feeling it.

I step into the heart of the scene, and in a minute flat, a bottle of beer is pressed into my hand by some kid who doesn't know I'm the designated driver. It's tempting, but I leave it unopened. I have a headache. Already. I cross my arms and stay on the lawn, bored. After a while, Anna, Kara, and Jeanette march up.

"Anyone need a ride home?" I ask.

"Party's barely started," Anna says. "We're not over it yet."

"Where's Marta? Is she over it yet?"

"Strip Monopoly," Kara says.

"Hey—" Jeanette stumbles forward and relieves me of my beer. "You can't have this. You're the designated driver." She cracks it open and pounds it. For a second, I envy her. "This is the best party ever."

Anna rips the bottle from her hands. "Jesus, Jeanette. It's too early for you to be this wasted. If Regina has to drive you home before midnight, I'll kick your ass."

"Why?" I ask her. "That's what I'm here for."

"Yeah, but you don't want to be here." Anna takes a sip of the stolen beer. "So I want to keep you here as long as possible."

Jeanette reaches for the bottle. "Give. Get your own."

"Kara, get me a beer out of the cooler," Anna says.

"But it's around the other side of the house," Kara whines.

"I don't care. Get me one."

She goes. It's pathetic how she goes.

"Nailed Josh yet?" I ask Anna.

"Later," she says. "Do you think I should go back there?"

I shrug. "I don't give a damn."

She sighs. "Do you think he'd think I was needy? I didn't call him today or anything. If I went back there, do you think he'd mind? I don't want to be overbearing."

"*You* don't want to be overbearing?" God, I wish I had a drink. "That's funny."

"You should maybe *try* to get on my good side," she snaps. "It doesn't have to be *totally* miserable for you all the time."

"It's never been anything but, Anna." I study her. "So you really like him, huh?"

Of course she likes him. And the question throws her off, like

I want it to. She opens her mouth and flushes, and it's these small things, these gives that Anna works hard to keep off her face that could be her downfall if anyone just looked closely enough.

But I was the only one who did.

"Why?" she asks. "Going to steal him back?"

"Oh, yeah," I say. "Watch out."

She gives me a look like she can't stand being around me, and then she goes, which is totally great. I watch a group of sophomores force a poor frosh to take an impossible sip from a bottle of rye. Jeanette sucks on the beer. After a while, Kara returns with the one Anna sent her for.

"Where the hell did Anna go?" she demands.

I shrug.

"Did she say where she was going?"

"I think she forgot about you."

"Fuck off, Regina."

I cross my arms and stare up at the sky. No stars. Nothing.

"I'm still not sorry, Kara," I tell her.

"And that's exactly why you're there," she says. "And I'm here now."

"Right. Enjoy your moment. Doesn't that bother you? You'll probably go your whole life and it won't be this good again. You've totally peaked."

She stares at me. "What if it's your moment?"

"This isn't my moment," I tell her. "This is my penance."

"For what? For Liz? For Michael?"

I bite the inside of my cheek. "Shut up."

"Isn't it funny how you tried to get back in good with Michael and Liz, and it didn't work? I think that means if this is your penance for anything," she says, "it's your penance for what you did to me, and it will be until you're sorry."

"You think I'd give you that? After all this?"

Her face turns red. "You didn't even have a good reason. You didn't even have one single good reason to treat me the way you did."

"I didn't know I needed one of those."

I leave her there. My stomach aches, aches, aches, and this is stupid. It's stupid because I'm worried what Kara said is true. This is what I get until I pay up, but how can I have gone through everything I've gone through and still not be paid up? *Sorry, sorry, sorry* I never want to apologize to her. Ever. I hate that idea. Hate it. I make my way around the house and find Josh lurking beneath a tree in the backyard away from the party and the bonfire. Anna-less. He's nursing a bottle of Jack Daniels. He takes a swig and I try to pass him unnoticed, but he grabs my arm.

"Regina, wait—"

I pull away from him. "You can't possibly need a ride home."

He doesn't say anything. We stare at each other. It's weird. I move to leave again, but he grabs me by the arm again. His hand stays on me this time.

"What's wrong with you?" I ask.

He takes a long pull from the bottle. The party sounds fill the air. He shakes his head and bites his index finger before speaking. "Regina, I'm sorry I didn't—"

"Shut up." I step back, my heart sinking to my stomach. "Who told you—"

"Anna was laughing about it with Kara," he says. "She said you said he tried to rape you." He looks away from me. "That's what you wanted to tell me that night—"

"Yeah, I know. I was there."

"Fuck. I mean—*fuck.*" He takes another swig of the Jack. "I can't fucking believe this. *Fuck.* I am so—"

"Choke on it, Josh."

He flinches. "Seriously—don't. Like—" He twitches, like he can't stand himself, and I'm glad, that makes me happy because he should know that feeling at least once. "I can't stop thinking about it. It changes everything—it totally—"

"Are you going to tell Anna it's the truth?" I ask. He looks away. No. He's not. "Then it doesn't change anything."

He closes his eyes and leans back against the tree. This is what I wanted this whole time, and it doesn't change anything. No one will ever benefit from knowing this. It's now completely worthless information, designed to make people feel bad.

It still happened and it was horrible. But it's worthless.

I am so empty.

"I'm sorry," he repeats.

"Got any Percocet? Or just Adderall?"

"I've got everything." He takes another swig from the bottle and stares at me. I stare back at him expectantly. "Are you serious?" he says. "You want Percocet?"

"Yes."

"It'll really fuck you up. It's not like you take them every day—"

"One night, Josh. If you're sorry, you'll give it to me."

How can he refuse? He takes another drink, grabs my hand, and leads me around the edge of the house, unseen. We go upstairs, to his room. He digs into his sock drawer, and a second later I have the pills. Plural. He must feel *really* bad.

He must think they'll help.

"On the house," he says. "Unless you want to pay me."

"No."

"Peace offering?"

"Sure." Like hell.

"Regina, I'm really sorry—"

"Shut the fuck up," I say tiredly.

I leave him in his bedroom and head to the bathroom, where I sit on the edge of the tub and stare at the Percocet. Is this what it was like for Liz? Trying to find a decent ending for herself in a bunch of pills? But I don't want to die.

I just don't want to be here. I never wanted to be here.

I'm not sure I've ever been here.

There's something automatic and familiar about the Percocet. I didn't do pills at parties before. I just drank. Because it made it easier to be here, but—

I catch sight of myself in the mirror. There are bags under my eyes and my face is pale and the corners of my mouth are edging down of their own accord. The pills feel heavy in my palm, as heavy as Donnie's keys in my palm. But that was different

I curl my fingers around the pills and close my eyes. I want them. One. That's how I do these things. *Coward.* Liz is right. Coward. I want to be better than that someday. If it's possible. Is it possible. I hope. . . .

I open my hand. I flush them down the toilet.

I stay in the bathroom for an hour and then I decide I'm leaving and I'm not driving anyone home.

I'm making my way out of the house when some sophomore corners me and tells me Bruce is looking for me because he needs a ride. I groan and modify my plans, because I don't want him to get in a car if he's totally plastered. I have to make him someone else's problem. I leave the house and make my way to the backyard, to the bonfire. Henry's lounging in a chair.

"Is Josh here?" I ask him.

Henry shrugs. "He was."

My eyes travel to an empty bottle of vodka lying on the ground.

"Henry," I say.

"He's inside," he says, closing his eyes. And then a warning: "Anna's probably close."

I go back inside and climb up the stairs. Maybe he's in his bedroom, but I hope not. If he's there, Anna's with him. I don't want to see them fucking.

Josh's bedroom door is open. No one's inside. I make my way back down the stairs, and a sliver of light filtering across the floor from inside the den catches my eye.

My last memories of the den aren't good.

But Donnie's not there.

I push the door open. Josh is sprawled on the couch, his right leg dangling off the side, his arm thrown haphazardly across his eyes. I cross the room and stand over him, and his glassy eyes take me in.

As soon as he registers my face, he struggles into a sitting position and pats the space next to him. I sit down.

He rubs his eyes. "Is Anna back?"

"Where did she go?"

"She drove Jeanette home because she couldn't find you. She's very, very mad about that. . . ."

Good. "I'm going home. Tell Anna I went." Josh brings his hand up to my face. I brush it away. "Don't touch me."

His face falls, devastated, like it's some leftover from what happened with Donnie, even though it's more that I still hate Josh. He edges closer to me and says pathetically, "I'm really sorry, Regina."

"Josh, don't—"

It doesn't stop him. He wraps his arms around me, like that's *sorry*. Like it makes everything right, even though it's so far from ever being right again. He tightens his grip on me, like he's trying to get his apology into my bones, but it'll never work. And then he pulls away a little and holds my face in his hand and brings his mouth really close to mine. At first, I think he's going to kiss me, but he doesn't. He keeps his mouth close so he can apologize into mine. I can smell the booze on his breath.

"I'm so sorry," he says, resting his forehead against mine. "I'm so sorry. . . ."

"What's going on?"

Josh lowers his hands. I turn slowly. Kara's voice is soft and interested.

"Nothing," I say. "I'm going home."

She looks me over. "What? Goddammit, you're the fucking *designated driver*, Regina. Who's going to drive Bruce home?"

I shrug. "You look pretty sober to me."

And then she starts spluttering and I go home.

friday

The plan: Get to school before everyone else and hide out in the library, because I'm not looking forward to Anna today. She'll give me hell for bailing.

I leave the house while my parents are still asleep. The air is crisp. Each breath in stings a little, but it's sort of invigorating. A miniscule nice moment in a sea of feeling bad. I try to figure out a way I can hold on to that. I'm holding on to it until Anna's Benz pulls up beside me, and then my moment goes away.

"Kara totally said you'd try to get there before us," Anna says, leaning over Kara, who is in the passenger's side. Marta and Jeanette are in the back. "Get in."

"I'll walk."

"Regina, it's too early in the morning to threaten you with black-mail. Get in."

I sigh. Marta gets out of the car and waits for me to crawl in. As soon as we're all wedged side by side in the back, Anna U-turns. We're headed away from the school.

"Where are we going?" I ask.

"Breakfast. I'm not going in this early."

I pop an antacid and rest my head against the seat, and they get fast food from the local strip. The car fills with that fatty, greasy smell and I try to tune out the chewing and talking, but it's impossible. I keep waiting for Anna to bitch me out for failing my duties last night, but it never happens, so I let myself relax a little and watch the road disappear under the space of windshield visible between her and Kara.

"So good," Jeanette says, popping the last of a greasy breakfast muffin into her mouth. "I'm so fucking hungover. I thought I was going to *die* last night."

"I told you to pace yourself." Anna turns on the radio, settling on a station that will please her and none of us. "That reminds me. Thanks for fucking us over, Regina."

There it is. "You didn't really think I'd stay, did you?"

She doesn't say anything. I reach into my pocket for another antacid. Houses blur past the window. Anna drives aimlessly and turns the car onto a deserted stretch of road. I check the clock. We're going to be late.

"We'll be late if you don't turn around now," I tell her.

"Who cares? It's Friday. Besides, I know you can't stand being around us, so I'm just prolonging your torture," Anna says. "That's worth being late for."

I close my eyes and they start blathering—going over the finer points of the party like they're worth going over—while I focus on the radio. I don't even notice the car roll onto the shoulder until the keys jangle out of the ignition and kill the song that's playing.

We've stopped.

All four doors open. I open my eyes. Jeanette and Marta get out of the car first, followed by Kara and Anna. I'm in the backseat totally alone.

Okay.

"Get out." Kara. "Get out of the car, Regina."

The words come out honey-slow, oozing off her lips and into my ears. All at once, I understand what's happening. Drop and ditch. Bruce planted it into Anna's head when she was brainstorming ways to make Liz miserable, and I somehow managed to convince her it wasn't "cerebral" enough. She really wanted to do it, though.

And now she can.

I leave the car slowly, all too aware of how cold it is now that I know I'm going to be stuck out here. I gauge the distance. Hallowell is a long walk back.

"I didn't see this coming," I admit.

"That was the idea," Anna replies, standing behind Kara and looking strangely second in command. "Give Kara your shoes."

Jeanette and Marta stand behind me like stone walls. Kara grins and holds out her hands, looking like she's got all the time in the world. In the grand scheme of things, this isn't that bad. It's not the WHORE spray-painted on my locker or another YourSpace page, and it's not being locked in a closet with Donnie Henderson. It's not losing Michael again. It's a long walk in sock feet when it's cold outside. It's a long walk in sock feet when it's cold outside without *them*.

So that's practically a vacation.

I crouch down, fumble with my shoes, take them off, and hand them over. My socks are thin and the ground is colder than the air. My toes curl in. Kara throws my shoes into the back of the car, yanks my book bag out, and tosses it onto the road.

"Okay," she says.

Marta and Jeanette grab my arms and force them behind my back. I try to jerk away before I really understand it, but they hold tight.

"What—?"

"You really fucked up this time, Regina," Kara sings.

"Jesus, are you kidding me? Because I decided I didn't want to drive you guys home?"

"No, it's more like because you were all over Josh in the den last night," Anna says. "Kara told me she saw you together."

My jaw drops. Kara grins, daring me to deny it.

"I don't get it, Regina. Did you just give up? A final 'fuck you'? You knew how I felt about—" She crosses her arms. "You knew."

"Yeah," I say, resigned. "I knew."

"Is that all you have to say?"

I nod. Kara nudges Anna, who takes a few uncertain steps forward.

Kara nods at her encouragingly and says, "Just don't forget to tuck your thumb in, okay? In."

Anna nods and brings her arm back.

Oh, wait.

"Anna, Anna, Anna—Anna, don't—"

Her fist connects awkwardly with my jaw, because Anna's never punched anyone before. She doesn't know how. Still, I've been punched. My knees give a little at the shock of it, but Marta and Jeanette keep me upright. It's dead silence and then—

Anna starts to laugh.

"Shit!" she cries, clutching her hand. An achy warmth spreads across my jaw. No, not warmth. *Pain.* "Shit, you guys—that kind of hurt! *Shit.*"

Marta and Jeanette laugh with her. Kara grabs Anna's hand and runs her thumb over it, smiling. Anna keeps giggling, lost to the thrill of punching me in the face.

"You're okay," Kara tells her. "Want to go again?"

Marta and Jeanette tighten their grip on my arms. They want her to. I can feel it. Anna rubs her wrists, chuckling, until she looks at me. My heart stops while she sizes me up. I don't want her to go again. She can only get better at this.

"No," she finally says.

"Oh, come on," Kara says. "We've got her. We can fuck her up. You can't just bring her out this far and punch her *once.*"

"Fuck off, Kara," I say.

Kara turns to me. "What did you say?"

"I said 'Fuck off.'"

She walks over. "You know you have your arms held behind your back, right?"

"You know you'll never have this chance again," I say. "Right?"

She doesn't even prep. She draws her arm back and her fist connects with my stomach, and she hits harder than Anna. I can *see* the hit. It's in front of me—light, everywhere. If Jeanette and Marta weren't holding me up, I'm sure I'd be on my ass. The lights fade and the scene comes back. Before I can get a handle on it, Kara drives her fist into my stomach again and I crumple, my eyes watering. Jeanette and Marta drop me, because even they aren't expecting that second hit.

I can't breathe. I put my hand to the pavement. *Get up. Kara's foot* connects with my abdomen. My insides explode, and then it happens again: She kicks me again. I gag. Anna makes noise somewhere nearby. Jeanette and Marta move away. Kara's foot goes for my shoulder, and my brain sends frantic messages to my body saying *Get up, move*, so I roll onto my side and cover my head, leaving my back exposed, which is exactly where she gets me next. Hard. I roll onto my back, gasping, drowning. Kara kneels over me and covers my face with her hand, presses her palm over my mouth, my nose.

Our eyes meet.

There's nothing between us.

Nothing.

I claw at her arms, digging my nails into the bits of flesh her sweater doesn't cover. She winces and her hand is off my mouth. The air is razor sharp. I've barely tasted it when she grabs me by the shoulders and forces me into the ground. My head hits the road. The ocean is in my ears.

My hands drop.

Kara straightens and gets one last kick in. My side. I go in on myself and the adrenaline leaves me again and again and again, leaves me with this unbearable clarity where I know my feet are cold and my body is screaming and I can't move.

"You were just going to waste it," Kara yells at Anna. "You were just going to fucking waste it! *That's* what we came out here for!"

"Jesus, Kara," Jeanette breathes. "Have you lost your *mind*?"

"No, I'm good." She shakes her hand, glaring at me. "I'm good now."

I listen to the gravel-crunch of footsteps making their way back to the car, car doors opening and closing shut, and then quiet, and I'm alone.

"Get up."

I'm not alone.

"Regina, get up." *No.* Anna's breathing heavily, charged from the electricity of this. "Regina, *get up.*"

I don't say anything.

"I just want to know why," she says.

I roll onto my back and lick my lips. Dirty gray clouds move across the sky, white sunlight filtering in through the breaks. And the sky looks so *great* from here, I start to laugh. It hurts, but I do it anyway.

I laugh so hard I cry.

"Kara got you *again.*"

"She didn't."

"She *did,*" I say, laughing. "She totally did. She got you again—"

"She didn't—"

"*Yes—*"

"*Kara's not that smart.*"

It comes out of her mouth so vehemently, but so sincerely, I finally understand why I never, ever had a chance.

"You're so *stupid,* Anna."

She moves her foot like she's going to kick me like Kara's kicked me, and the laughter dies instantly. I raise my hands and cover my face. Nothing happens. She savors this victory in quiet, until the car starts up and the horn blares.

"Well, it's been really interesting, but I've got to go," she says. "You know. Get destroying your boyfriend underway. Monday's going to be great. Have a nice walk."

Michael. She gets in the car and they head down the road. *Michael.* I curl into the ground until I can feel it's cold everywhere and I know I have to move. I push myself up on my elbows, my knees. *Stand. Stand, Regina. It's easy. Stand.*

You do it every day.

I walk the entire way back to Hallowell on feet so cold I don't even notice when they step through broken glass, until my sock starts sticking to my heel and gravel starts sticking to my sock and I look down and there's blood. I don't know how long it takes me to get into town, but every second settles into my screaming bones. My stomach aches. My back aches. My jaw aches. My feet are numb.

All I can think is *Michael*.

Michael. Michael. Michael. The thought of him drags me to Hallowell, drags me down the back streets, past my empty house, and all the way to the school, because I have to tell him. He has to know what's coming.

I limp across the parking lot and yank the front doors open. I step inside. The place is quiet. Distant class noises float down the hall—the illusion of another ordinary day. The warm air levels me, makes me feel instantly stupid-headed and dull.

My stomach lurches.

I'm going to be sick.

I fumble down the hall, keeping one hand against the wall and the other over my mouth, trying to make my way unobtrusively to the girls' room. I know I can't be seen.

After forever, the pale blue door reveals itself. I pull it open and stumble in.

Charie Andrews is standing at the mirrors, fussing with her hair.

She stops when she sees me. Her eyes go wide as saucers. I lean against the door and close my eyes for a minute.

When I open them, she's looking at my feet. I breathe in and walk stiffly over to the sink. I tell myself there's nothing here to look at. The smell of the soap makes me even more nauseous, and she's barely stepped away from me when I throw up—nothing.

"Jesus," she mutters. I spit and then I rest my palms on the sink and try to get my bearings. I end up with my forehead against the mirror, staring down the drain, vaguely realizing this is not acting like there's nothing to look at.

Get it together, Regina.

I take one deep breath and then another. On the walk back, I could do this. I could see myself doing this, but now I think maybe I need to sit down.

I sit on the floor, my back against the wall, and close my eyes, waiting for every broken part of me to piece itself together enough to tell Michael what's coming, and I feel Charie's eyes on me that whole time, and I don't even have the energy to tell her to go to hell. And then the washroom door swings shut and she's gone.

My toes are thawing, prickling uncomfortably. I open my eyes. I need to wedge the garbage can under the door so no one can come and see me like this. No one else. I press my palms against the floor and try to get to my feet and—

I can't.

I move and every kicked part of me protests, so I wrap my arms around myself and listen to the slow, steady sound of the faucet dripping water into the sink, and it goes deep. For a second, I'm in my bed again. This morning hasn't started.

Everything is . . . fine.

The washroom door flies open. My heart stops and my head jerks up. When my eyes focus on the halo of blond hair set around a pale face, I just—Liz. Always here. No matter what I do, she's always going to be here. This suicide blonde, haunting me for the rest of my life, following me from one awful moment to the next.

"Oh, my God," she says. "Charie said you—"

She stops. We stare at each other, but I can't hold her gaze, and I feel her looking at me long after I look away. I lean my head against the wall and close my eyes.

"*Regina*," Liz says sharply, like I'm dying right in front of her. I open my eyes and laugh a little at that thought. I realize I'm not cold anymore, I'm warm. Hot. My shirt is clinging to every bit of skin there is to cling to. My hair is stuck to my neck and my face.

"Go away," I say. Wait. No. I need her. *Take it back.* "Get Michael for me. I need to tell him something—"

"He doesn't want to talk to you," she says.

"Liz, please—"

"No."

Frustrated tears spring to my eyes. "Fuck you, Liz. You don't even *know*—"

"You got your ass kicked," she says, "*finally*, and you want Michael to come pick up the pieces. I know what they did to you. I was in that stall—" She points. "And Anna and Jeanette came in here giggling about it. I knew you were out on that road."

I stare at the floor. Tears spill out onto my cheeks. I wipe my eyes.

"God, Regina, I don't understand you. This is the *only thing* that could have happened. You think you're making easy choices, and every single time you have a good thing, you ruin it. Because you're a coward. *Don't* expect me to feel sorry for you."

"It's not like you wanted me to have it," I snap. She snorts. I grab the edges of the counter and try to get myself up but I can't. And I can feel how pathetic it is and I know how pathetic it looks. I can't get up and she's just standing there. I slam my palm against the floor. "Why are you even here if you're not going to *help*?"

Her mouth drops open. She looks away from me, ashamed. I've never seen that on her face before, and I don't even know how I managed it, until she says, "I wanted to see it."

It's such a bitch thing to say.

But I get it.

"Okay," I mumble. I don't care anymore. I grab the counter a second time and finally manage to get to my feet. I lean on it. My mouth is dry, parched. I run the water cold and dab it on my face. It makes me painfully, painfully awake. "If you feel like it, tell Michael not to—tell him not to come to school on Monday."

"What? Why?"

"You tell me. You know everything."

I take a hard step on my right foot, the one with the cut, and wince. I just want to get past Liz, out of the washroom, go home, and die. She grabs my arm.

"I'm not telling him anything if you don't tell me why."

I bite my lip. This is not about me and Liz. Michael.

"They have his journal," I tell her.

"*What?* Michael has his journal. I've seen it."

I shake my head. "They stole it. Anna made photocopies and returned it before he knew it was missing. She's going to plaster it over school."

She stares at me. "He has his journal, Regina."

"I saw the pages." My voice cracks. "I'm not telling you what they said. But there was something in there that could get him expelled—"

"I don't believe you."

"I don't care if you believe me."

"You could be lying just to—just to get me to feel sorry for—"

"He wrote that he wanted to *kill everyone in school*," I blurt out. Liz's eyes widen. "They're going to give it to Holt and say it's a death threat. Do you know what that could do to him? *I* don't lose anything if you don't tell him."

I push past her bony frame. The space between the stalls and the sinks is too narrow, and the corner of the counter rams into my kicked side. I make a dying-kitten kind of sound and curl in, one hand on my side, the other on the counter.

"Regina—"

"Just look." I manage. "You wanted to see it." I leave the washroom and make my way down the empty hall. The bell rings at the exact same time I push back through the front door. My toes cringe at the reintroduction to the cold pavement. But this is nothing.

Nothing.

I climb the stairs to my bedroom and study my reflection in the full-length mirror mounted on my closet. My jaw is tender to touch, but I think it's going to be okay, because Anna can't hit. But Kara can. I lift my shirt so I can see the damage. There are already bruises forming, abstract works of art across my abdomen and what I can glimpse of my back.

I raid the mirrored cabinet over the sink in the bathroom. My fingers travel over antacids and prescriptions until I find the Tylenol with Codeine and I take three of those, and then I crawl into bed.

Everything hurts.

I don't want to go to school today.

I get dressed slowly, but I don't want to look at myself. I don't want to see it on me.

Bruises always look the worst when they're healing.

I pull the edges of my sweater down and grab the bottle of Tylenol on my desk. I shake two pills into my palm. I probably don't need them. It doesn't even hurt like it did. Not totally. I take them anyway.

Mom and Dad drink their coffee at the kitchen table. Get ready for work. I stay at the kitchen sink, quiet, staring out the window. It's cold out. It looks cold out.

Anna's probably already taken care of it.

I wonder if it will be big.

I hope he's not there.

I turn away from the window and grab my book bag.

"Be careful in gym," Dad says, nodding at the bruise on my chin. He smiles a little. "Next time *dodge* the ball, huh?"

I nod. Mom looks up from her coffee.

"Going in already?" she asks. I nod again because I can't speak. She gives me a thumbs-up. "That's great. Have a good day, honey."

I count steps on the way to school—283. School is 283 steps from my house.

When Hallowell High comes into view, I feel fourteen again. It's

the first day of school and I'm scared. I'm standing in the middle of
the parking lot. Anna bounds over to me and she's excited. It's the
first day of school and she's a lowly frosh, but she's ready to take
this whole place on. She claimed it as hers before anyone else got the
chance, and we gave it to her because she was the only one who
looked like she knew what she was doing, and I just went along with
it because I didn't know.

I spot her Benz at the front of the school. They're here. I stalk
across the pavement to the front doors. My pulse thrums in my ears,
a prelude to a panic attack. I grip the door handle and pull it open.
It's like my finger on the trigger.

My finger is on the trigger and—

Bang.

The school is quiet. Distant ghost-footsteps reach my ears. I jog
up the stairs to the lockers, and there's nothing. I expect journal
pages taped to the walls, shoved in lockers, everywhere. But the
school looks like it always does.

I don't believe it. It's an illusion of peace. I hurry to my locker
and spin the dial. Here. It has to be here. It's not just his torture; it's
mine. It takes forever to get the right numbers, my hands are shaking so badly, but I finally get it and I pull the lock off and open my
locker and—

Nothing.

But she's here. I saw the Benz. They're here and they're early and
they're ruining lives because that's what they'd do. That's what she
told me she was going to do.

I check the washroom. The empty changing room. The entire
school is mine; it's so early, and I find nothing. How many ways can
they do this?

I'm not clever like Anna. I'm missing something important.

The school begins to fill up. I listen to snatches of conversations,
hoping for some indication, someone else finding it first, but there's
nothing. I wander the halls. It gets busier, busier, busier. The busier it
gets, the more bodies I have to contend with.

I glimpse Michael at his locker and he's okay.

I hide while he opens it up and wait for it—*this is it, this has to be it*—but nothing. Nothing happens. He just stands there, and this is any day. A normal day. He pauses, like he knows he's being watched. He does. He looks around. I back into the alcove and count to ninety, and when I look again, he's gone.

The bell rings. I stay in the alcove while the morning announcements start. If it hasn't happened by now, this is a slow build, a painfully slow build to it. Girl-bombs getting ready to go off and leave us all in pieces. I make my way down the hall and push through the door to the girls' washroom and Anna is there, staring at her reflection in the mirror. Her hands are on her makeup bag, but she's not moving. She's just staring at herself.

I back into the door, the handle jamming into purple-yellow-brown skin all over my back. I wince and turn, pulling the door open so I can leave.

"Come to gloat?" she asks.

I let the door handle slip from my grasp, but I keep my back to her and keep my mouth shut. I stare at the fading blue paint on the door, chipping around the edges.

Come to gloat?

I don't understand what that means.

"What are you talking about?"

She turns her head and takes me in. Checks me, I know, for remnants of what happened last Friday, but there's nothing she can see from where she's standing and nothing I'm willing to show her. Her eyes search mine, and then she laughs, softly.

"You don't know?"

What don't I know. She went straight to Holt. Michael will leave quietly and without a fight. That's not like her. Public humiliation is way more her style. She had a change of heart? I shake my head slowly.

I don't know.

She unzips her makeup bag and rummages through it, but her

usual morning makeup routine seems lost to her. She starts with the lip gloss usually, but now it feels like she's just looking for something to do with her hands.

"I'm done with you. I'm done with Michael. Your little friend, Liz—" She laughs and shakes her head. "She threatened to go to Holt about what *I* did to you. Hilarious."

The words settle in slow, twisting my stomach. I stare at Anna, my mouth trying to form a reply, but nothing comes out. I don't—I don't believe it.

"But the photocopies—"

"Liz has them and I said I'm done with you." She finally finds the gloss. "Go."

"Just because Liz won't go to Holt now doesn't mean I won't," I tell her. "I can still go to Holt. Show him the bruises."

She drops the gloss back in her bag and I notice she's trembling; she's afraid. She knows I could go to Holt and I'd have her. I would have her.

But I want something better.

"You're scared," I tell her. Anna. Scared. She gives me a look that could kill. "You always said none of this matters, and you're scared."

"It *doesn't* matter," she says tightly. "But it's good practice."

I have never hated anyone so much in my life.

I never will again.

I pull the door open and step out into the hall.

I spend lunch outside, sitting on the front steps numb. Relieved. Alone.

Until Michael comes out.

I know it's him without turning around. He shuts the door carefully and hesitates before sitting next to me, his side brushing against mine. I can't look at him at first.

"Liz told me everything," he says.

And then I know that it's okay.

I press my forehead against his shoulder. He exhales slowly.

It's quiet. Postwar quiet.

Later, we'll try to make sense of this. Eventually, the bruises will fade.

But for now, he reaches over and puts his hand on top of my hand, curling his fingers into the spaces between mine, closing them around my palm until they're laced tightly, locked together, school behind us, and I realize Anna is right.

A whole world exists outside of that hellhole.

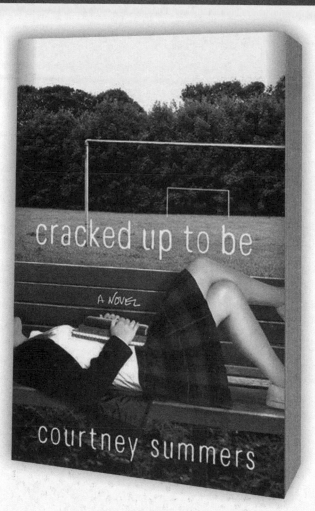